MICHAEL, MICHAEL

Wendy Perriam

HarperCollins*Publishers*

HarperCollins*Publishers*
77–85 Fulham Palace Road,
Hammersmith, London W6 8JB

Published by HarperCollins*Publishers* 1993

1 3 5 7 9 8 6 4 2

Copyright © Wendy Perriam 1993

The Author asserts the moral right to
be identified as the author of this work

A catalogue record for this book
is available from the British Library

ISBN 0 00 224037 8

Set in Baskerville by
Hewer Text Composition Services, Edinburgh

Printed in Great Britain by
HarperCollinsManufacturing Glasgow

For Mary Edwardes Nefdt
who gave me both her Michaels
– and so much else

Si, dans ces tristes lieux, par l'amour amenés,
Quelques amants, un jour, y visitent nos cendres,
Courbés sur notre marbre et les fronts inclinés,
Ah! diront-ils, baignés des larmes les plus tendres,
Puissions-nous, en aimant, être plus fortunés!

From lines inscribed on the tomb of
Heloïse and Abelard

I

'SSH,' SAID TESSA. 'They're starting!'

'No, they're not. Still two minutes to go.'

'My watch says six already.'

'It's wrong, then. Anyway, the clock strikes first, and makes such a frightful racket, we can hardly fail to hear it.'

Tessa shivered, had lost her coat somewhere between midnight and six AM. Though the jostling throng of students should help to keep her warm – some in crumpled evening dress: ball-gowns muddy round the hems, dinner-jackets worn back to front, or white shirts splashed with wine; hordes of others scruffy in old jeans, fighting camera-laden TV crews for a foot or two of pavement space. If noise were heat, she'd be on fire. The crowd's communal mouth had been emitting a continual roar since half past five, or earlier, and the drunken shouts and laughter had now reached fortissimo. She shivered again, though this time from excitement. You'd have to be made of blockish wood not to sense the exhilaration churning the cold air, pulsing through those packed and seething bodies. The bridge itself seemed charged, reeling from the weight of human flesh; Magdalen Tower vibrating in anticipation as the clock-hands crept to six.

'Half a minute to,' crowed Rob.

'Thank God! I'm bloody freezing.' Vicky slipped her hands beneath her armpits, hunched herself around them.

Tessa stared up at the tower, the warm honey of its limestone rebuking the chill greyness of the morning. She could glimpse shadowy figures through the openings of the parapet, moving at the top: the choristers in white and red. She looked still further up, to the eight slender sculpted pinnacles, sharp against the dull haze of the sky; then down again to the Cherwell's sludgy green, a dirty sleepy river bemused by its own ripples and reflections. The month of May seemed reluctant to be born – no glint on shining water, nor glimmer in the clouds – yet the long green hair of willows and the lushness of horse chestnuts were proof enough that winter had retired. She could feel the seasons fighting – a bleak November wind ripping April blossom off the trees; a row of pale spring ducklings chugging in a dogged line over dark and wintry water. Then, a frantic scream and splash, as a man in kilt and dress-shirt toppled into the water from the bank, scattering the ducklings, clutching at his tartan in a vain attempt at modesty. His friends all jeered and catcalled, and a second kilted Scot pelted him with beer-cans; the mother-duck fighting back with pathetic anguished squawkings. Then suddenly the clock began to strike – six booming chimes, silencing the antics of the crowd, demanding their attention, turning all eyes upwards from the river to the tower.

The last stroke died away; the silence so expectant now you could feel it hanging in the air like another sort of cloud – swollen, almost bursting. Tessa thrust her arm through Rob's; grabbed Vicky by the hand; glad when Liz and John and Richard also huddled closer. They must be joined, united, while they listened to the singing – boys' high voices soaring from on high. She couldn't understand the words, though she recognized the Latin; felt gooseflesh prickling the back of her neck as the pure unearthly sound echoed from the tower. She had always found it hard to believe in God or heaven, but this came pretty close – a near-angelic choir, their music floating out across the vastness of the sky. She was almost relieved when they changed to jaunty English: 'Summer is icumen in'. It was now official summer – the song itself had made it so – season of warmth and growth and flowers. *'Groweth seed and bloweth mead, and springeth wood anew.'* Already she felt less cold, as if the music were mulled wine pouring down her throat, thawing her stiff limbs.

She kept gazing at the tower, trying to imprint the scene for ever on her memory – the smoothly solid stone, gold against the leaden clouds; the blurred and white-gowned choristers like ghosts behind the parapet; the sheen and throb of newly hatching leaves. She didn't need a camera, like those scores of flustered tourists so busy with their light-meters and their recording for posterity that they'd missed the here-yes-now. She dodged away from a determined Japanese who was trying to sever her from Rob and squeeze between their group, using his Nikon as a battering-ram. She smiled and let him pass, too happy

2

to be cross. The first time she'd come to Oxford, she too had been a tourist – a gawper and outsider, glued to maps and guidebooks, obeying all those notices which said 'Private', 'College closed'. Now she had free entry, as someone who belonged.

She glanced intently at her friends, wanting to store them in her mind, along with all the other details, preserve them like snapshots in an album: Vicky with her freckles and her lumpy ginger pigtail; Liz in her blue beret; Richard with his almost-beard; lanky Rob; tall John.

'Why are you staring?' Vicky whispered. 'Have I got a dirty mark on my face?' She rubbed her cheek, frowned at her clean fingers.

Tessa shook her head, reluctant to speak, or interrupt the singing, capsize her high-flown mood.

'They're out of tune,' joked Richard, cocking his blond head to listen, then wrinkling his nose in mock-disgust.

Don't spoil it, Tessa prayed. It's beautiful, inspiring, so please don't send it up. But she dared not say a word, especially not to Richard. His free-and-easy confidence always made her shy. He'd probably inherited it from his father – an international banker who drove a customized Mercedes with a built-in fax and television. Actually, she wouldn't reveal her feelings to any of her crowd. That explosive mix of pride and exhilaration would probably sound plain daft. And it wasn't done to enthuse, indulge in moony raptures or superlatives. She'd learned that on Day One; had arrived at Balliol so caught between terror and euphoria, she must have seemed a total prat: far too bubbly and naive, and completely overwhelmed by all the venerable buildings and traditions, the eccentric tutors and strange unfathomable jargon. Even now, after two whole terms, she had to make an effort to appear laid back and cool; to conceal the awe she felt at sitting in a library which had been founded in the sixteenth century and whose ceiling was adorned with hand-painted heraldic shields, rather than slumped in the reading room of her local public library (circa 1961) whose ceiling boasted stained acoustic tiles.

The others in her year were so nonchalant, so blasé, seemed blind to their surroundings, and apparently accepted it as their natural and inalienable right to join the Oxford roll-call, add their names to all those dazzling earlier ones – Shelley and John Donne, Hobbes and Locke and Ruskin, Oscar Wilde and Tolkien, T.S. Eliot. Or were they just pretending, too, faking their sang-froid? She'd probably never know. If they needed to wear masks, or put on a show of being self-possessed, they were hardly going to admit it, least of all to her.

She stole another look at them – Richard yawning openly; Liz fiddling with her hair. Weren't they moved, as she was, all hyped up to be taking part in this centuries-old ritual of greeting dawn and summer from Magdalen College tower? One of the tutors had told her that it had started as a lark, a salute to the goddess Flora, and had now become encrusted with tradition. She loved the thought that they were enacting ancient rites, and that while life rolled on as normal in boring Leeds or London, Oxford celebrated the end of dark and winter by harking back to pagan nature-cults.

The last note of the final song was just dying on the air; pagan still for all she knew, since she couldn't decipher the words. A huge cheer went up from the clapping stomping crowd, as if the students were now making up for their spell of pin-drop silence – or for their coolness all the year. She abandoned her own self-restraint, let her voice ring out. Okay to be effusive when her shout was safely swallowed up in the general roar and bray, and anyway the place deserved a cheer. Oxford had once been the capital of England (though admittedly only for a few short years in the seventeenth century), but now it was *her* capital, the centre of her world, so why shouldn't she applaud it? She took the foaming can of beer John was passing over, drank it with her eyes shut, so that she could transform it to champagne. Secretly and privately, she had never quite stopped marvelling that she'd made it here at all, when her school had been discouraging, and her mother had thought Balliol was the name of a new lager.

She heard a popping cork beside her – real champagne swilled down by a Hooray Henry in a stiff wing collar and a brocaded turquoise waistcoat; his girlfriend looped with streamers and a red rose in her hair. They must have been at an all-night ball, whereas she and Rob and John and co had spent the evening in Queen's College rowdy beer cellar, then ambled back to Richard's room for more drinks and talk and music. At five AM, they'd sallied out once more, linking arms and tripping down to Magdalen Bridge, enlivened by the band already playing in the streets, its oompah, oompah, oompah pounding away their tiredness.

And if there was any torpor left, Magdalen's bells were now pealing it away in waves of jubilation; great golden waves swelling through the sky, defying its persistent stubborn grey. The whole city must be stirring – woken by the bells, drenched and spattered by their

4

foaming crests of sound, which were sweeping the vast crowd along, up the grey strand of the High Street.

Tessa surrendered to the tide; Vicky one side, Rob the other; the morris dancers way in front, leading the procession with their accordions and fiddles. No need to make her feet work; she was simply churned along like a piece of bobbing flotsam. Richard stopped a moment, to buy a doughnut from a stall, but he too was floated back, rolled on by the bells. Tessa could almost taste the doughnut sweet and greasy on her tongue, curdling with the kick of beer; the waft of fresh-ground coffee teasing from the stall. She was starving hungry, but didn't want to stop, be left behind while the huge mob roistered on. It was enough merely to admire the stalls – girls in butchers' aprons doling out hot chocolate; permed and blue-rinsed matrons from the Save the Children shop offering posies of spring flowers in return for a donation; two enterprising students selling cheese-and-pickle sandwiches from an improvised cardboard tray, hung with pink balloons. One of the balloons had drifted free. Tessa grabbed its string, looped it round her wrist, followed as the crowd surged into Catte Street and along to Radcliffe Square. The morris men had already started performing on the stretch of cobbled paving; their straw hats wreathed with flowers, the brilliant coloured braiding criss-crossing their chests contrasting with the milk-white of their shirts.

She squeezed her way to the front, to watch the dancing. There were twelve men in the set, each grasping a long wooden stick, which they beat one against the other. She could almost imagine that she was back in medieval England – no cars around, no shops in sight, nothing but the majestic spires rearing up above her; the same lively crush of revellers celebrating the first of May as the highlight of the year.

'Why do they bang those sticks like that?' she asked a morris man, who was standing on the sidelines with his troupe of white-breeched dancers, awaiting their own turn.

'To ward off evil spirits, my dear. May's not a lucky month, you know, and the first of May is especially bad for witches.'

'You're joking.'

'No, he's not,' his wife chimed in, a plump woman in a matching hat, both brims submerged in sprays of purple lilac. 'May's not good for anything, and especially not for weddings. Haven't you heard the old saying, "Marry in May, rue for aye"? My sister wed last May and she's left the lad already. And May babies never thrive well – nor kittens, for that matter.'

'I was born in May,' said Vicky, who had pushed in after Tessa and was now fumbling for a cigarette. 'And I've had jolly *good* luck.'

'So far,' shrugged the woman. She turned back to the dancers, who'd been joined by a shambling giant of a figure, clothed entirely in green leaves. The leaves were fixed to a stout wire cage which encased his head and body, so he could barely see at all.

Tessa recognized him as the Green Man; laughed at his ungainly steps, and the way he was losing half his foliage, as a shameless child plucked it from the frame. Why dwell on bad luck, when there were all these joyous symbols of fertility and spring, and when the rhythm of the music was so catchy and infectious? One old boy was shiny-bald and another of his fellow dancers looked at least a hundred, with his gnarled and crinkled face and the long white straggly ponytail bouncing on his back. Yet they were all leaping in the air, as fiery as the dragons embroidered on their waistcoats. The dancing made them younger; seemed to rejuvenate the ancient square, as well.

'Look!' said Vicky. 'Food.'

A morris man in a black felt hat was handing round small cubes of what looked like home-made bread – a springy golden loaf which he was serving from the tin. The tin was quite a sight, a circular one in battered fluted silver, with a gleaming sword plunged right through its centre.

'Two bits, please,' coaxed Vicky, holding out her hand.

'Be careful, lass,' he warned. 'It's not just any old cake, you know. If you eat a piece of this, you'll fall pregnant within the year. So a double portion could mean twins!'

Vicky almost spat her mouthful out, looked round for John to share the joke, but the boys had disappeared, along with Liz. She passed the second piece to Tessa, who chewed it greedily. Babies were the least of her concerns. She'd just broken up with Rob, and though things were pretty tense between them, she'd no intention of starting a new relationship. It made life too complicated, demanded too much of her time, when she already had her acting and her writing, not to mention her exams, which although seven weeks away, would still require hard slog. She sucked a cake crumb off her tooth, savouring its spicy taste, wished it were a whole fat loaf instead of just a morsel. She had eaten almost nothing since last night's meagre dinner of lasagne and tinned pears, now felt hollow and suddenly dispirited, as if her engine had run down. Perhaps it was simply hunger – her body complaining about an excess of beer and wine, and demanding something solid to mop up all the froth. 'Shall we go and get breakfast?' she suggested.

'No,' said Vicky. 'We've already lost the others, and if we move they'll never find us. Tell you what, you go and buy some croissants from that stall we passed, and we can eat them here, on the steps of the church.'

'Okay,' said Tessa flatly, accepting Vicky's three pound-coins. She was going to have to squeeze and shove, to fight her way back through the crowds, then maybe queue for ages to be served, but how could she refuse, when Vicky gave the orders, Vicky had the dosh?

Tessa sat shivering on the steps, the bag of croissants clutched against her chest. Her balloon had burst – its pathetic rubber corpse drooping from the string tied round her wrist. She unfastened it, tossed it in the litter-bin, then slumped down again on the wet and chilly stone. There was still no sign of Vicky, nor any of the others. Radcliffe Square was empty, save for a drunken man puking on the grass. Usually she loved it here – the peaceful heart of Oxford, with no throb of buses or roar of Kawasakis; colleges and libraries clustered all around her, dwarfed by the thrusting tower of the university church, which gazed down at the garden blooming at its feet – an attractive sheltered garden where tramps and pigeons fought for scraps, and rambler roses relieved the sombre evergreens. But today it seemed a wasteland, the first brave roses battered, the one lone bird bedraggled. She kicked her shoes off, rubbed her squelching feet. She had trailed to the Turf Tavern, to see if they were there, but the bouncer on the door had ordered her to scat; said they were serving champagne breakfast to ticket-holders only. So she'd jogged back to Rosie Lee's, braving the torrential rain, found it full of giggly Sloanes, out of bounds again to all but the champagne crowd.

Maybe Vicky had decamped on purpose, the whole group glad to shrug her off. Although she hung around with them, they weren't exactly soul-mates. It hadn't been that easy to find a kindred spirit at Oxford, either male or female. She had arrived with high ideals, expecting a Shelley lookalike to sweep her off her feet, or a T.S. Eliot clone to declaim the 'Four Quartets' to her while she lolled back in a punt. Rob declaimed cricket scores, and called Shelley self-indulgent, and though Vicky was amusing, there was so much they couldn't share. Victoria Amanda Shaw had been to private school and lived in a five-bedroomed house with the sort of conventionally wealthy parents who bought hardback books, and claret by the case, then mopped up any spare cash by saving seals or rain forests.

Parents weren't supposed to matter, especially not at Balliol, which was renowned for being non-elitist, and bragged in its literature about wooing state-school entrants with open arms and special grants. True there were few snobs, and even the Old Etonians played at being lefties, but that was half the trouble. Easy to slate privilege when you'd imbibed it with your mother's milk, or to boycott meals in Hall because you'd eaten every day at school in imposing panelled refectories, and found it an amusing change to queue for beans on toast.

The thought of beans on toast sparked her hunger once again. She hadn't touched the croissants, had been waiting for the others – much more fun to share them, enjoy a crazy picnic to the music of a band, or watching Scottish dancers leap across their swords. The dancers had packed up now, discouraged by the weather, the sudden vicious downpour which had lashed the streaming pavements for half an hour or more, and was threatening to begin again. She glanced up at the sky: domes and spires and pinnacles fighting for their share of it; majestic still, despite the lowering clouds. Extraordinary how Oxford could make you feel inadequate – not just in terms of brain or class, but if you didn't match its mood. It seemed wrong to be dejected while living in this perfect place, with its aura, its mystique, its rich icing of tradition. Yet at times it felt unreal, too exalted and superior for the messy lives within it – the awkward clumsy love affairs, or wary not-quite friendships. What she really longed for was someone to confide in, someone she could trust enough to admit that she was lonely; that things hadn't quite lived up to her initial expectations. But lonely was a word to be avoided like the plague, with all its connotations of self-pity, social failure. Nobody was lonely – not in the dream city.

She reached out for her shoes, rammed them roughly on again, grimacing, as always, at her large inelegant feet. She sometimes wished she was smaller altogether: slender and petite like Liz, rather than a strapping five-foot-eight. Big meant bold and brave – except it didn't, in her own case – and being tall and female caused problems with a lot of men. And the strange thing was she often felt quite small inside – not the overgrown brunette reflected in her bedroom mirror, but more a fragile sylph.

The first relentless drops of rain were stinging on her face, dispelling thoughts of sylphs. She struggled to her feet, stood cold and indecisive, torn between heading back to college and making one last effort to find her missing friends. She could maybe try the Queen's Lane Coffee House, if only because Richard fancied a French waitress there, and sought any chance to practise his bad French.

She arrived dripping wet and limping – no Richard, no French waitress – immediately tramped off again, this time back to college. She could do with a complete change of clothes and a mug of steaming tea. She also had some work to do for her tutorial at two. Her essay on Heloïse and Abelard was finished, more or less, but there were still a few references she ought to double-check. Only her pernickety female tutor would arrange a session for two o'clock on May Day, when most students would be hung-over, or catching up on sleep. She shrugged and jumped a puddle, carried on, head down against the rain, turning into New College Lane, which was so narrow, dark and winding, she seemed to be back in medieval Oxford once again. She dived across the road, lost her footing as she tripped on a discarded bottle; heard a car approaching the blind corner. She panicked for a second, shaken by her fall. Was she imagining those crashing gears? Cars weren't meant to come down here, only cyclists and pedestrians. But suddenly the noise crescendoed and a red MG came hurtling round the corner, stopping with a screech of brakes, missing her by inches.

'What the bloody fucking hell do you think you're doing?'

She opened her eyes, paralysed by fear, saw a pair of battered moccasins, contradicted by an expensive sheepskin coat. The driver of the car was standing over her, emitting oaths like petrol fumes. He checked on her perfunctorily, making sure she was in one piece, though he seemed more concerned with justifying himself than offering any sympathy or help.

'How in God's name d'you expect me to stop in time, when you're weaving down the middle of the road?'

She all but choked, fighting tears and fury, trying to control her voice, so it wouldn't sound hysterical. 'Oh, so it's *my* fault?' she retorted, rubbing her raw knees. Only minor grazes, but she could well have broken half her bones, landed up in hospital. 'Christ! You've got a nerve! This lane is closed to traffic, yet you still manage to blame me. You've no right to be here at all, let alone careering along at seventy.'

'I was doing twenty-five. And when I want advice on driving, I won't ask a drunken jaywalker.'

'I'm not drunk! Speak for yourself. You could have killed me, and all you do is shout. You might at least apologize.'

'Apologize? You're the one who should bloody say you're sorry. How's anyone supposed to drive, for crying out loud, with maniacs like you constantly hurling themselves in the road?'

Tessa ignored him, scrabbled for her bag and started gathering up its scattered contents. The croissants were a write-off, completely waterlogged; had split their paper carrier and landed in a puddle. She picked one up, held it out accusingly. 'Look at what you've done to these! They were meant to be my breakfast, and you couldn't give a damn. I haven't eaten anything since seven o'clock last night.'

'And I haven't eaten anything since a sub-standard tuna sandwich at lunch-time yesterday.' He laughed – a disconcerting laugh which seemed to change his mood entirely, dissipate his anger, and transform him from a savage to a Good Samaritan. He crouched down beside her on the pavement, dabbed her oozing knees with an unironed handkerchief; then squeezed her arm – a belated wordless 'sorry'.

For the first time, she looked up at him, took in more than just his shoes and coat; experiencing a shock of recognition. She had never met the guy before, but he could have been her elder brother, the non-existent sibling she'd sometimes pictured in her mind. He was built on the same generous scale – not just tall, but chunky. Unlike her slimmer friends, she had always refused to diet; accepting her large breasts and curvy hips as something she could no more change than her broad shoulders and big bones. But now she felt positively dainty, compared with his six-foot and more, his opera singer's chest – almost the genuine fragile sylph, in fact. Both of them were dark, with the same thick wavy hair, the colour of ground coffee; self-opinionated hair which defied lacquer, combs and barbers. His eyes were darker than hers – Latin eyes with extravagant black brows and almost girlish lashes. A striking man, good-looking – in his middle twenties, as far as she could judge – and dressed conventionally, though the posh coat was missing buttons, and he clearly hadn't shaved: stubble dirtying his jaw, smudging his strong chin. She was suddenly aware of how scruffy she herself must look: hair tousled and still wet, skirt crumpled, flecked with mud. She turned away, embarrassed, mumbled a goodbye.

'What the hell d'you mean – goodbye? We're having breakfast, aren't we?'

'Breakfast?'

'You just accused me of destroying yours.' He pointed at the croissants, floating in the gutter. 'The least I can do is offer you a substitute.' He opened the door on the passenger's side, tried to wave away her protests, but she resisted, stood her ground. Half a dozen cyclists had come swarming up behind them, and were trying to squeeze by, one jangling his bell; another breaking into a boozy off-key version of 'Why are we waiting?'

'Look, for Christ's sake, girl, get in, before those morons scratch my paintwork. We'll argue about it later.' He pushed her in, slammed her door, slammed his own, then accelerated up the lane, swinging right, then left, driving with impatience, as if he resented every lumbering coach or dithering pedestrian.

'Let's get out of Oxford,' he muttered, following the sign for 'Stratford and all traffic north'. 'I've had enough of this damned town.'

'Look here,' said Tessa angrily. 'I don't know who you are or where the hell you're taking me, but if it's all the same to you, I'd prefer to have my breakfast back in college.'

'Oh, a student,' he drawled, raising the black brows and slowing for a second to appraise her. 'You surprise me. You look too stylish for a student.'

'There's no need to be sarcastic.'

'It was actually a compliment. I rather like that ruffled thing you're wearing.'

'That ruffled thing is an Edwardian skirt. I bought it in the Portobello Road.'

'Really?'

'Yes, really. Now d'you mind if I get out?'

'I'm afraid I do mind, yes. We're on our way to Woodstock, to a slap-up six-course breakfast. Not at the Bear, I hasten to add. I consider it absurdly overrated, and it's bound to be awash with tourists anyway. I know another place there, with just as much atmosphere, and an absolutely first-rate chef. Mind you, I doubt if he'll be on at eight o'clock in the morning, or deign to grill our kippers.'

'Eight?' said Tessa, startled. 'It must be later, surely.'

'Eleven minutes past. I'm glad you've got some time in hand. Maybe you won't be quite so keen to rush away.'

'It's not a question of time. I don't know you from Adam. You could be a rapist or a murderer or . . .'

'I'm a doctor, actually.'

She glanced up at his face, to see if he was joking. Did doctors break the speed limit, mow down pedestrians without the slightest concern? And didn't they normally shave, and have clean hands and well-scrubbed nails? His were stained with paint. 'A GP?' she asked, comparing their own well-groomed Dr Cunningham, who drove a tame grey Volvo estate, not a panting red-hot sports car.

'No fear!' he said. 'A cardio-thoracic surgeon. Well, that's the general idea. It may take a year or two – or ten.'

Tessa fiddled with the zipper of her bag. She was so used to meeting fellow undergraduates, it was difficult to change gear to a surgeon, especially when she wasn't sure what cardio-thoracic meant. Cardio was heart, but what about thoracic? She didn't like to ask, and all the other standard questions – 'What are you reading?' 'Which college are you at?' – were clearly inappropriate. 'What's your name?' she asked instead, recalling childhood warnings about accepting lifts from strangers. If she knew his name, it would make him less a stranger, though she still felt apprehensive. He could be an impostor, pretending to be a doctor when he really had diplomas in thuggery or homicide.

'Michael,' he said briefly, as if reluctant to reveal too much, or entrust her with his surname. 'And yours?'

'Tessa.'

'Short for Teresa?'

'No. Tessa plain and simple.'

'I like plain and simple names. The two guys I share my house with are called Joshua and Tristram, though they look more like Keiths or Brians, to tell the truth. Names are damned important. My Ma named me after an archangel, the conqueror of Satan, so I suppose I've always felt I couldn't let her down.'

'And have you?' Tessa asked.

He laughed. 'In my mother's eyes, I can't do any wrong.'

'And in other people's eyes?'

He dodged the question, asked her one himself. 'Which college are you at?'

'Balliol,' she said.

'Oh, a clever girl, then.'

She bridled at his patronizing tone, reflecting for the umpteenth time on the whole matter of intelligence and how relative it was. She'd been the bee's knees at school – A-plus for all her essays, prizes every year, even her photo in the local press, towering over a smirking Miss MacDonald. But at Balliol she was reduced to merely average, overshadowed by all those other students whose brilliance seemed quite effortless; the sort who got Firsts almost on the side, while spending the bulk of their time rehearsing their future roles as prime minister of England or director general of the BBC.

'I was at Christ Church,' Michael volunteered.

You would be, Tessa thought – the cream of the Oxford colleges, with its own private art collection worth a hundred million pounds. She'd been there once, to formal Hall – invited by a friend of Rob's – and though the dinner had been mere spaghetti bolognese, the spaghetti had been served in silver dishes by obsequious white-coated men who looked as ancient as the panelled walls. Rob's plummy friend and Michael had certain things in common: the same Veuve Clicquot accent, the same breezy arrogance. She was becoming uncomfortably aware of her own voice; knew Michael would be judging it as flat suburban London – what he'd call a 'Keith and Brian' voice. She tried to spruce it up a little, frowning with the effort. 'You mean you did your first degree there?'

'Yes – physiology. Then I went on to the John Radcliffe to do my three years' clinical. And I've been working as a houseman there since February. Overworking, you might say. It's only Wednesday, and I've clocked up fifty hours this week already. It'll be nearer a hundred and fifty by the time I've struggled through to Monday morning. I'm on again tonight and all weekend.'

Which might account for your foul temper in the street, Tessa stopped herself from saying. Probably better not to speak at all, since anything she said would either sound sarcastic, or expose her total ignorance of matters medical – including the term 'houseman', which had left her mystified. She'd never been to hospital in her eighteen-and-three-quarter years, and had only consulted Dr Cunningham for the odd sore throat or tummy bug. Her mother watched 'Casualty', if she wasn't working Saturday night, but she herself always decamped to her bedroom once she heard the theme-music. Ambulances and scalpels failed to turn her on.

She peered through the window, which was misted up with rain, though the downpour had abated to a half-hearted lazy drizzle, and even that was easing. They had left the town behind, and the road had opened out; fields stretching either side beneath trees of flaunting green – green so fierce it hurt. Last night, they'd been discussing whether spring or autumn featured more in literature, and though she'd favoured spring, her thoughts had crept back to October – her first confusing week in Oxford, when the trees had been a Joseph's coat of bronze and gold and yellow. Yet for all its gaudy finery, October was a phoney month, dying more each day; its blazing colour concealing flimsy funeral clothes, tattered underneath. Whereas leaf and life were new in May – nothing stale or jaded, nothing smeared with death. Even the sun was trying to break through now, dappling the wan sky, transforming it to watered silk. She breathed in very deeply, as if to gulp down the whole landscape. Much as she loved Oxford, it was a confining crowded city, which choked its sky with spires. One so rarely had the chance of driving out, escaping its stone clutches. Almost nobody had cars – or not in her year, anyway.

She watched the speedometer creeping slowly up, as they streaked past field and farm; felt her spirits leap to match; exulting in this jaunt with a man she didn't know, wasn't sure she even liked.

'I'm starving,' she said suddenly, turning round to smile at him. Perhaps he didn't like her either. She hadn't been exactly gracious; hadn't given him a chance yet. And, anyway, a six-course breakfast in a pretty country town was undoubtedly a better bet than stale cornflakes in her room.

'Good!' he said, veering left and jolting down a narrow road, fringed with spindly poplars. 'Because in just two ticks we'll be pulling up our chairs.'

2

'HAPPY MAY DAY, Tessa.' Michael touched his glass to hers. It was the first time he'd used her name, the first time he'd really looked at her, leaning forward to gaze into her eyes. It wasn't a romantic gesture, Tessa realized, shrinking back. His own eyes were slightly mocking, and he was clearly sizing her up, probably noting her thick eyebrows, or the fact that her hair was wet. Though who was he to carp? He hadn't bothered to comb his hair at all, whereas she'd spent frantic minutes in the ladies' room, battling with the tangles and sponging mudstains off her skirt; trying to make herself more worthy of this elegant hotel. She still felt a shade uncomfortable sitting with a stubbly man who had flung aside his tie as he strode into the restaurant, declaring in a ringing tone that it was bloody hot and could they turn the heating down. The other guests had shot him angry looks, and the head waiter been quite sniffy – at least, until he'd ordered a bottle of the best champagne.

She sipped it from the tall-stemmed glass, relishing the fact that she was now part of the champagne crowd, celebrating May Day in the approved traditional fashion – even if her escort was continuing to attract distinctly hostile glances by scooping ice-cubes from the ice-bucket and crunching them between his teeth.

'What d'you fancy to eat?' he asked, flicking through the menu.

'Oh, eggs and bacon – toast.'

'But you just said you were starving. Why don't we start with fillet steak, and have the eggs and bacon afterwards? Supper before breakfast, since I haven't had mine yet.'

'Okay,' she grinned. 'Why not?'

'And strawberries first. I can't stand prunes, can you? Can't stand any health foods. The word's a con, in fact. In ten years' time, they'll be begging us to eat cream cakes and butter, and chuck away our wholemeal bread and lousy low-fat spread.'

Tessa didn't answer, still couldn't quite believe that Michael was a doctor. Weren't doctors the ones who advocated health foods, deplored the double cream he was now ordering with their strawberries? She glanced at him again. Whatever his diet, it had glossed him with good health – his complexion glowing, his eyes so bright and vibrant they looked as if they'd been taken out and polished.

'What made you take up medicine?' she asked.

He paused a moment, the dark brows drawing down. 'Well, I could give you the usual spiel about doing good, healing people, all that sort of guff, but if I'm honest with myself, there's probably something of an ego-trip mixed up in it as well, maybe even a need to be top dog. I suspect many doctors feel the same, except they'd prefer not to admit it, would regard it as bad form. But a surgeon's got the power of life and death, and that's very close to playing God. Funnily enough, it connects back to my name. As my Ma enjoys reminding me, Michael means "Godlike" in Hebrew.' He took a gulp of his champagne, held his glass between both hands, staring at the bubbles. 'When you cut into a body, it's as if it's dead, in one sense, unable to resist you. And you've got the skills and tools to resurrect it, yank it back to life, cheat nature, if you like. That's pretty heady stuff, you know.'

Tessa shifted on her chair, aware that she was vaguely shocked. And yet wasn't power the motive in so many walks of life? Just two terms of her Oxford course had taught her that already.

Michael was still talking, his voice intense, aggressive. 'Physicians are such ditherers. They sit around discussing what to do, while surgeons get on and do it.' He tossed an ice-cube into his glass, used another to cool his sweaty forehead. 'And cardiac surgery is like a sort of Star Wars at the moment – so many new developments you get dizzy keeping up with them. In twenty years or less, heart transplants may be history. We'll just give the heart a rebore, like a car engine, or bung in an artificial heart, once we've solved a few odd hiccups with pump technology. But then we'll have to wrestle with all sorts of new ethical problems. How much d'you spend to keep a bod alive, and how long d'you keep him going? And does it make a difference if he can fork out the cash himself?'

'I envy you,' said Tessa. 'I mean, a degree in history seems pretty marginal compared with those big issues. And I've never . . .'

'So you're reading history?' Michael interrupted. 'I was about to guess English, or maybe modern languages.'

'I wanted to do English, but there was this teacher at my school – Miss MacDonald – who kept pushing her own subject, and since she was the only one who believed in me, I changed to history, so I'd have her on my side. You see, no one went to Oxbridge, no one even applied – not from Emberfield.' She broke off, embarrassed, hadn't meant to talk about her school. It seemed so long ago now – tubby Miss MacDonald dwindling with the ugly concrete buildings and their Portakabin overflow. Yet she could suddenly smell the Emberfield bouquet: sweaty feet and bubblegum, and the whiff of Pat and Debbie's fags as they lit up in the toilets (which themselves smelt pretty foul – farts and disinfectant mixed). Pat had failed her A-levels and was now working as a dogsbody in an insurance office, and Debbie was married with a new-born baby son. She'd known Debbie seven years, shared everything from confidences to lipsticks, but her once-best-friend had moved away to Sheffield, and was submerged in feeds and nappies, too tired to keep in touch.

'Ah!' said Michael. 'The strawberries.'

Tessa eyed them greedily, glad of a distraction from nostalgia and school smells. She wolfed the biggest down, first piling on white sugar and whipped cream.

'Good to see a girl who eats,' Michael said approvingly. 'There's nothing worse in my opinion than a female on a diet. I went out with this nurse once, who always pushed away her own food, then looked enviously at mine; watched my every mouthful like a hungry slavering dog. And she kept banging on about calories, totting them all up, until, in the end, I wasn't eating steak or pork, but just a plate of lethal numbers.'

Tessa laughed. 'I'm afraid I'm quite a pig.'

'Thank God for that! But do use the right vocabulary. You're not a pig, you're an epicurean, like me. The Romans got it right – endless creative feasting and not a whiff of guilt.' He picked up a fat strawberry with his fingers, raised it slowly to his mouth, sharp white teeth impaling soft pink flesh. 'The most crucial decision in life, Tessa, is whether one's a puritan or a voluptuary. And to put it frankly, puritans should be shot. All they do is ban things – like Cromwell's little lot, who cracked down on everything, including all the traditional May Day celebrations. If the Lord Protector had had his tight-arsed way, we wouldn't be sitting here at all. And the

Calvinists were worse. They forbade the use of spices – even sugar would you believe – called it Satan's helper, just because it adds a bit of zest.' He showered sugar on his last remaining berry, as if deliberately defying all such strictures. 'Ready for your steak yet?'

She nodded, glancing at the waiter as he brought their juice and coffee, removed their empty bowls. He looked a bit of a puritan himself, with his thin-lipped mouth, his expression of disdain, as he mopped iced water mixed with strawberry juice from the once pristine tablecloth. Was he condemning them as gluttons as he returned with two huge steaks, the fried potatoes piled so high they were overflowing the plates? She waited till he'd gone; relieved to turn her attention back to Michael, who was larding his steak with both French and English mustard, then letting rip with the pepper-mill, obviously determined to rile the anti-spice brigade.

They both cut into a mushroom at exactly the same moment, caught each other's eye, started chewing swiftly, as if they'd entered an unspoken competition as to which of them could eat it faster. They repeated the performance, throwing mushrooms down their throats, and then the grilled tomatoes, copying one another, barely bothering to chew now. Tessa sliced a chunk of meat off, gulped it down – one bite. Michael followed suit. It seemed a waste of steak, in one way, especially such expensive steak, which she hadn't had for months, yet there was some provocative excitement in challenging him, competing, eating at this crazy rate. And she was aware that he was watching her, admiringly, delightedly, as she walloped down the food, demolishing the pile of fried potatoes, leaving nothing on her plate but a strip of fat and a parsley sprig, beating him by seconds.

He parked his knife and fork, made a flurry with his napkin. 'Right – that's supper over. Still got room for breakfast?'

''Course.'

'Shall we pause for coffee first?'

She poured it for them both, met the disapproving glance of a man at the next table; was suddenly aware of the silence in the room. Hardly anyone else was talking – several people communing with their newspapers; a grey-haired couple too busy boning kippers to spare time for conversation; another oldish couple glumly munching toast. She and Michael were by far the youngest there. She wished she dared to ask his age. He seemed a different generation from slender boyish Rob, though the whole atmosphere and setting helped emphasize the gap. Rob had never taken her to a four-star country restaurant, only to Pizzaland and the Chinese takeaway, and they'd gone by bike, not sports car.

She passed Michael his cup. 'I suppose I shouldn't ask if you take sugar.'

'Three spoonfuls, please, and cream, not milk.'

They laughed together, the sound stunning the hushed room; tried to stifle another laugh when the waiter brought their eggs. His face was pained, lugubrious, as he set down two more loaded plates – second mammoth helpings of mushrooms and potatoes, as if the ones they'd only just consumed had somehow sprung to life again.

'Bet you can't eat that lot,' Michael taunted.

'Bet I can!'

It seemed vitally important that she did. It wasn't just a matter of a wager, or sheer greed, but some mysterious trial of strength, in which he'd laid down the gauntlet and challenged her to prove herself as a fellow epicurean in their own private May Day ritual. She seized her knife and fork, prepared a daunting mouthful of potato, sausage, bacon, mushroom, egg; forked it deftly in. He copied her exactly, making it a game; both of them speeding up as they checked each other's plates. All the different flavours were fighting in her stomach – the sweetness of the strawberries recoiling from the sting of mustard; the greasy sausage hiccuping as it hit the champagne fizz. Yet she felt wonderfully alive – not over-stuffed or queasy, and with no twinge of indigestion. Each different food seemed to pep her up, recharge her, inflame her appetite, so that she was reaching out for toast now, smothering it with butter.

'No, wait! We must have croissants. You claimed I ruined yours, so I owe you a replacement.'

'The waiter'll die of shock.'

'He's died already, judging by his face.'

They laughed like silly kids, then Michael changed his voice to churchy, to match the waiter's pompous monotone, and ordered croissants – hot.

'D'you know how croissants originated?' he asked, turning back to Tessa.

She shook her head, couldn't speak; her mouth engaged with toast and egg.

'It's one of those bits of useless information that Tristram's always spewing out. He ought to enter "Mastermind". Apparently, Austria won a victory over the invading Ottoman Turks. Don't ask me the date – I'm lousy when it comes to dates and they're your department anyway – and to celebrate the thrashing, the bakers made some pastries in the shape of the crescent on the Turkish flag, so that the Viennese could gobble down their enemies at table, as well as defeat them on the battlefield.'

Tessa swallowed, wiped her mouth. 'I never quite believe those stories. They always seem too pat.'

'Are you calling me a liar?' The jokey tone had vanished; his voice was harsh, defensive.

'No, of course I'm not. It's just a problem for me generally, especially on my history course. I mean, our tutors are always warning us not to take things at face value, and to challenge all the data, but they still continually bombard us with so-called objective facts. I'm always wondering about them – how many were reported wrong, like that game of Chinese Whispers, or were changed by the chroniclers into their own subjective version, or even wish fulfilment, and whether history should be facts at all, or more imagination, or . . . I'm sorry, Michael, I'm not putting this too well. The point I'm trying to make is . . .' The black bulk of the waiter was blocking out the light again. He had glided up on castors, with yet another loaded plate. 'Oh, the croissants,' she said lamely.

'Already? That was quick. Well, let's devour our enemies, since I rather like the story, and refuse to let you doubt it.'

'Okay, I'll believe you. But I haven't any enemies.'

'Now *I'm* the one who's doubting. Everyone has enemies.'

Tessa searched for candidates. Mr Blakenham, perhaps, the lefty Head of Sixth Form? He had certainly opposed her when she'd suggested trying for Oxford – but then he'd really had her good in mind, feared she might not make the grade, and would settle down more happily at East Anglia or Bristol. Or how about her father, Dave, because he hadn't married her mother and now lived with a younger wife? Except her mother wasn't bothered, and she herself had always thought it normal to have a Dad ten miles away, with his own separate house and daughters. The word 'enemy' seemed too extreme, not just for easy-going Dave, but for any person in her life.

She watched Michael bite the neck off a hot croissant. 'So who are your great enemies?' she asked him.

'D'you mind if I postpone that subject? I don't want to spoil my breakfast.'

'I think it must be tea by now, since we're eating bread and jam.' Tessa dolloped apricot preserve on her own thickly buttered croissant.

'I'm still eating marmalade, though it's pretty tasteless stuff – that jelly sort, with no bite to it, or body, whereas I like it full of peel.'

'You mean Oxford marmalade?'

'Yes, I suppose I do. Though I wonder why it's called that?'

'Perhaps because it's sweet and bitter, both at the same time, like life is up at Oxford.'

'You're really quite poetic, Tessa.'

She flushed, unsure if he was mocking her, or had meant it as a compliment. 'I wanted to be a poet. When other girls were dressing up in nurses' uniforms at the age of nine or ten, I told my mother I'd decided to be the Poet Laureate.'

'And what did she say?'

'"Less gab and more grub. Cut the cackle, Pipsqueak, and eat your egg and chips."'

He laughed, and sucked the jam spoon. 'There are quite a lot of Oxford words, when you come to think about it – not just Oxford marmalade, but also Oxford sausages, though God knows what they are. Maybe made from piggish tutors or ground-up grouchy dons.'

'And Oxford accents,' Tessa said, still nervous of his own.

'And Oxford bags.'

'What are they?'

'Trousers – very voluminous ones. And there's Oxford shirting, too, which I suppose you wear with the bags.'

'And Oxford blue.'

'And Morris Oxford cars – though they're a bit before our time.'

'And Oxfam,' put in Tessa, thinking of her local branch where she often found good bargains – old clothes which she could renovate, transform from tat to treasure.

'And Oxford frames.'

'I've never heard of those. I'm sure you're cheating.'

'I'm not! They're the ones with cross-shaped corners. And how about Oxford brogues? You can't call those a cheat. And there's even an Oxford vaporizer. I saw it in a catalogue.'

'Okay, you win,' said Tessa, only now aware that it was another competition. She had won the breakfast marathon herself, since he'd left a sausage on his plate, and at least half his second croissant. One all.

Michael pushed his chair back, tried to catch the waiter's eye. 'All this talk of Oxford makes me feel we should stay out of it. How are you placed for time? We could drive on to the Cotswolds, do a spot of walking, work up a decent appetite for lunch.'

She groaned.

'You don't like walking?'

'I love it. But I think I'll skip the lunch.'

'You disappoint me, Tessa.'

'Do I?'

He suddenly knifed up to his feet, took a pace towards her, leaned down and kissed her mouth – a fierce kiss, long, determined. He pulled away, at last, rubbing his own lips as if the kiss had stunned or bruised them.

'No,' he said. 'Actually, you don't.'

3

TESSA STOOD AT the entrance to her college, waving Michael off as he hurtled round the corner, the crimson of his car still throbbing in her head. Long after he had disappeared, she stayed there, motionless, watching other, less remarkable cars lumbering down the road. Her eyes kept returning to the corner, as if hoping he might reappear, electrify the street.

'Excuse me,' said an impatient voice. 'We want to get in here, please, and you're blocking the whole entrance.'

She moved her gaze reluctantly from the tingling ghost of Michael to the clutch of frazzled tourists encroaching on the doorway with their armoury of shopping bags, damp and crumpled raincoats, and an unwieldy double pushchair. She stepped back to let them through, then followed the long cavalcade, several of them now scrabbling for their guidebooks. They'd be reading in those condescending pages how disappointing the architecture was – substandard nineteenth-century, on the whole, with the older parts pulled down, or so heavily restored they'd lost all their original character; how the front quad was lopsided, and the garden quad not strictly a quad at all. They maddened her, those books. The buildings were fantastic, and today she was more worthy of them. Michael had upgraded her, made her eminent, distinguished – all the things the college was itself.

She was still following the party, unable to overtake, since the pushchair blocked the path. 'It's one of the oldest of the colleges,' a bespectacled northcountryman observed, stopping for a moment to read the entry in his guide. '"Founded in 1263 by Sir John de Balliol" – whoever *he* might be.'

'Funny name,' his friend remarked, adjusting his binoculars so he could peer up at a carved stone shield.

Never mind the name, Tessa longed to interrupt. It *is* the oldest college. Don't believe Merton, which insists it's one year older, or University College, which lies through its teeth and claims it was founded by Alfred the Great. That's myth, pure and simple, like those notorious burnt cakes. And if you go and see the library, just over on the left there, it's still mainly fifteenth-century, and has a hundred thousand books.

A hundred thousand! The number thrilled her, even now, however much she tried to feign indifference. Her mother owned a dozen at the most, and those included cookery books, *Your Fortune in the Stars*, *The Complete Home Doctor* (minus half its cover), and the abridged novels of Daphne du Maurier, which had been marked down at a church bazaar – not that her mother ever went to church, or read anyone as demanding as du Maurier.

She checked her watch. She should be sitting in that library, consulting at least one or two of its hundred thousand volumes, but there simply wasn't time now. Better to read swiftly through her essay, so she'd be well prepared to defend her arguments if her tutor, Ruth Sylvester, decided to swoop down with sharp claws and sharper mind. And then she really must spruce up, scour the Cotswolds off, remove that wash of crimson which she could feel clinging to her clothes, coating her whole body – Michael's colour, dangerous and wild.

The tourists had veered right, to investigate the chapel, while she continued past the library to the garden quad. The guidebooks might complain that it was too large and too irregular, with no real feeling of harmonious enclosure, but she'd like to send their supercilious compilers straight off to her school, and see what they could make of a dreary tarmac playground whose only splash of green was a row of plastic wheelie-bins. Here, green exploded everywhere – the suave green of the well-groomed lawns, the dogged green of creepers festooning the stone walls, the punchy green of conker trees, still full of zest and sap, despite the fact that they'd been fighting storms (and students) for a hundred and sixty years. Green and crimson were both singing in her head – exuberant colours which had enamelled the whole morning, made it special, made *her* special, merely because she'd been strolling through damp and muddy fields with a self-opinionated doctor who talked too much and drove too fast.

She galloped up the staircase to her room – two small rooms, in fact, a sitting-room and a tiny poky bedroom, which looked out on the graveyard of St Mary Magdalen's church. The rooms were always gloomy because of the huge horse chestnut which stood majestic in the graveyard and blocked out half the light, and also rather spooky because the gravestones seemed so near; only a narrow (very noisy) road between the church wall and her own wall. The other first-years envied her. They had only one room each, and lived close to one another, in the newer, less attractive block. Yet she envied them in turn, sometimes felt cut off, away from the main action, so to speak, and having to be quiet because there were third-years directly below her, working for their finals.

She fumbled for her keys, dived into the bedroom and straight to the mirror, which was so worn and mottled it seemed as old as the room itself. She looked nothing like she'd feared – dishevelled, messy, fat – but very nearly beautiful. She disliked her heavy eyebrows, but Michael had just praised them as distinctive and dramatic, and also said he loved her mouth. She'd always judged it over-large (like so many other bits of her), but Michael was the expert. Doctors studied anatomy, and that included mouths and brows. She was glad she'd worn her ruffled skirt, since he seemed so taken with it. What she hadn't told him was that she'd bought it at a knock-down price because it had been badly ripped and filthy. She had washed it, twice, by hand, then spent an age repairing it, and finally covered up the mend with trimming from another skirt. She'd always had a flair for clothes; had withstood taunts at school when she'd refused to wear the 'uniform' of black leggings and black microskirts, as she now ignored her college friends if they labelled her Bohemian. The uniform at Balliol was patched jeans, baggy sweatshirts, or miniskirts again, and any idea of elegance seemed to be anathema. She was too broad-beamed to wear jeans, or skirts which barely hid her crotch, and anyway she liked her arty clothes; had been collecting them for the last three years, rummaging through market stalls or junk shops.

She really ought to change, though – she'd been wearing that same outfit at least twenty hours non-stop, and it must be getting sweaty. But it was half past one already, so she merely dragged a comb through her hair and splashed her face with water, then charged into the other room. She appraised the room a moment, as if seeing it with Michael's eyes. She had tried to make it original, without splurging any cash – hangings on the walls, to conceal the peeling paint; the shabby sofa glamorized with an ancient velvet curtain in a subtle shade of plum. The fabrics had come free, thrown out by her

25

mother's boss when she was refurbishing her house. The furniture was 1960s tat, and couldn't be disguised, but she'd changed the lighting, made it softer, more diffused, so that at least in the evenings the bulky wardrobe and battered chest of drawers were less loomingly obtrusive. Vicky was forever harping on about the neatness of the room: how in heaven's name did she keep it so immaculate, avoid the usual tide of dirty clothes, the overflowing ashtrays, or unwashed cups and glasses sprouting luxuriant mould?

She picked up a hairpin, placed it on the desk. Was she the fusspot Vicky seemed to be implying, or merely glad to have the chance to escape the mess and muddle of her home? She found it somehow threatening – all that mess – her mother's clutter spreading like convolvulus, overrunning the house, even sending tentacles under the door of her own room. Here, she could keep it safely out, do things her own way, pretend she owned this empire of two rooms, instead of being just a lodger, like her mother's string of paying guests – or 'uncles' as she'd called them years ago. She wondered now about those jolly (shady) men. Had they paid her mother only in hard cash, or in some other currency, which had turned them into intimate relations?

She sat down at her desk, tried to boot the 'uncles' out, concentrate instead on a much more famous lodger – Peter Abelard, who'd taken rooms in 1117 with Canon Fulbert of Notre Dame, then seduced his teenage niece while she was studying as his pupil. She removed her essay from the drawer: *'Abelard and Heloïse typified the spirit of the twelfth-century Renaissance. Discuss.'* Six months ago, she hadn't even known of their existence, nor those of all the other dramatis personae whom Ruth Sylvester talked about with as much casual familiarity as if they were guests on 'Wogan', rather than twelfth-century monks and scholars who wrote abstruse Latin treatises about such burning issues as the nature of the Trinity and the question of Universals. Now she, too, was acquainted with the passionate prejudices of Guibert of Nogent, the intense and mystic sentiments of Suger of St Denis, the often caustic letters of Bernard of Clairvaux. Yet it was Abelard and Heloïse who kept tugging at her mind – their brilliance and their obstinacy, their passion and their suffering. So that even at the oddest moments – in the bath, or cycling through a rainstorm – she'd find herself preoccupied with their doomed, dramatic love-story.

Her tutorial partner, Charlotte, was far more cynical, seemed to have it in for Abelard, whom she described as pathological, a warped and devious man with a persecution complex; unscrupulous, unprincipled, yet swollen with his own conceit. But then Charlotte favoured servile men; would probably censure Michael as mercilessly as Abelard; dismiss him as a chauvinist. Tessa's thoughts crept back again to their morning in the Cotswolds – the way Michael had overruled her when she'd begged to see the church at Chipping Norton; insisted that they went to Minster Lovell.

He did resemble Abelard in some respects – arrogant, high-handed, an intellectual snob, the sort of charismatic man who got under your skin, set up a maddening itch. Yet the two were also miles apart. She had always pictured Abelard as a small and slender type, and he was certainly ascetic, not likely to be pigging eggs and bacon on top of fillet steak. But both of them were cultured, born with silver spoons in their mouths – if not sterling silver, then pricey silver-plate. And both were musical. Michael had regaled her with stories of his dazzling career as trumpeter in some fantastic college jazz-band, when he was still a fledgeling first-year. He also claimed to have written songs – words as well as music – as Abelard himself had done. And Abelard was probably dark, like Michael, since his mother came from Brittany. She could imagine him with the same unruly hair, refusing to lie flat; the same fierce brows drawing down in anger if someone dared to challenge him, the same black-molasses eyes.

She shook back her own hair, impatient with herself. She was turning Abelard and Michael into Mills and Boon stereotypes, indulging in romantic slush, when she had only five more minutes to check a serious essay, prepare herself for the battle of wits with Charlotte and Sylvester. The thing about Charlotte was that she could always back her case up; might criticize Abelard, but did it with authority, quoting chapter and verse; knew the texts backwards, and had read some of them in Latin. She'd learned both Greek and Latin at her exclusive all-girls boarding school (along with social graces, archery and horse-riding), then transferred to Marlborough, which was famed for its strong classical tradition and employed seven Latin teachers. Emberfield, in contrast, offered nothing more than a few hours on 'The Classical World' (part of the General Studies course), which skipped from Aristotle to Aeschylus at a helter-skelter pace, then ended – breathless – with a slide-show of the Forum. But then Emberfield had no hope of attracting staff as bright as Ruth Sylvester, who knew a dozen different languages, including several dead ones. Naturally, she favoured Charlotte, and made that pretty clear; gave her the lion's share of attention, let her interrupt. Well, this time, she'd surprise them – both tutor and star pupil. Instead of subsiding with a whimper when upstaged or even snubbed, she'd do a Michael, fight back – and fight to win.

'Well, you were teacher's pet today,' Charlotte bantered half-resentfully, spooning coffee into unwashed mugs. 'Sylvester almost *smiled*, for heaven's sake.' She went to fetch the kettle, which had reached a furious boil and was now spluttering on the threadbare once-blue carpet. 'Do you take sugar, by the way? I can never seem to remember.'

Three spoonfuls, please, and cream instead of milk. Tessa didn't say it, just remembered Michael's voice. She was longing to share her morning, bring up Michael's name, make him real and solid, instead of an empty May Day myth which might vanish by tomorrow. Dr Michael Edwards. The name didn't seem quite right – too English and too ordinary, when he was exotic and exceptional. And yet he'd told her that his parents were . . .

'Tessa!'
'What?'
'I asked if you take sugar.'
'Yes, please. Three.'
'You'll get fat.'

They grinned at one another. Charlotte was petite – five-foot-nothing, and as skinny as a drinking-straw – the fragile sylph *par excellence*. They'd had all the usual gibes – Little and Large, David and Goliath – but then you didn't choose your tutorial partner. She'd probably scarcely have spoken to Charlotte if they hadn't been the only two doing Early Gothic France. In the summer term, you chose an optional subject from a list of seventeen; moved from English History and General History, to concentrate on original texts in much more depth and detail. Rob and Vicky had both plumped for later periods, feeling more at home in the solid nineteenth century than in the unfamiliar twelfth. All that she and Charlotte had in common were a bunch of medieval scholars, an interest in church history, and a love of Gothic architecture. Otherwise, they were chalk and cheese – Charlotte fair, she dark; Charlotte with her country house in Sussex, which would have swallowed up her own suburban semi. If she felt cut off from Vicky, then she felt doubly so from Charlotte, who had never used a washing machine, had problems opening an ironing board, and had never cooked a meal or worked for money, unless you could count a little fashion modelling for some snotty charity ball.

She glanced at the large pinboard where Charlotte had her photographs tacked up on display – her Jaeger-suited mother smiling from the landscaped Sussex garden; her haughty brother in his panelled Cambridge rooms; last year's skiing trip to Klosters, with her well-bronzed jet-set friends, sipping Glühwein after their exertions on the pistes. Her own snapshots couldn't quite compare – her mother in a C & A bikini, sprawling on their scrap of balding lawn; the caravan at Margate they'd hired out of season (cheap), where they'd sat gulping their hot Bovril to counteract the venom of the wind. She kept the photos hidden in a drawer; maintained an edgy silence when Charlotte mentioned Marlborough, or that clutch of clever school-chums who'd come up to Oxford with her, and who gave her instant access to a score of other colleges and an impressive social circle.

Tessa stirred her coffee, tried to imagine Pat at Christ Church, instead of her insurance office, or Debbie speaking at a Union debate rather than burping baby Ben. It wasn't easy. In fact, she realized with a pang that she had grown away from her old friends, transferred to a new world, evolved into a new and different species. Even if the pair of them dropped in on her at Balliol, they'd find her so completely changed, they'd no longer have anything in common, and the conversation might well be very strained. The sort of friend she yearned for now was someone more like Heloïse – a spirited but sensitive type who'd never take the mick, and would understand her feelings even before she'd put them into words. Sometimes, when she read the texts, she had the sense of Heloïse being actually alive still. There was an eagerness about her, a sense of her having lived and loved with such passion and intensity that neither she nor the love could die. Her voice in the *Letters* came over with such force, it seemed to be resounding through the centuries, demanding to be heard.

'You're very quiet,' said Charlotte, splashing milk into both mugs.

'Sorry – I was thinking.'

'What about?'

'Oh, nothing. By the way, can I borrow your last essay – the one on St Denis?'

''Course.'

Tessa smiled her thanks. She was trying to learn from Charlotte:

29

copy her techniques, overlay drab Emberfield with a few Marlborough frills and skills. Charlotte's style was more subtle and sophisticated, less 'schooly' altogether. She was also a proficient skim-reader, who never ploughed laboriously through each page of every book, or let herself be daunted by the reading-list.

She watched her now, lighting a cigarette – even doing that with grace – then settling back with her coffee and an ashtray, musing in her drawly voice.

'D'you know, I'm beginning to suspect that Sylvester's half in love with Abelard. She's worse than you are, Tessa, the way she always defends him. And it's only because the bloody man was talented. She'd forgive Jack the Ripper if he had a good grasp of dialectic and a decent Latin prose-style.'

'I think you're much too hard on him. His life was such a struggle and . . .'

'He brought that on himself.'

'Not necessarily. If you're born with a certain temperament, things are harder anyway. It's simple for a yes-man, or someone far less complex. Even his faith seemed a constant inner battle for him. I mean, remember that thing Sylvester told us about Saint Anselm – or Saint Augustine, was it? – I always get them muddled. Anyway, whichever it was said he believed in order to understand, and not the other way round. But poor Abelard busted a gut trying to understand in order to believe. And when you think that . . .'

'Coo-ee, Tessa! Are you there, pet? I met this little friend of yours, who said I'd find you in the . . .'

Tessa froze in disbelief at the sound of her mother's voice; couldn't quite believe that she was hearing it. How could April be in Oxford on a Wednesday afternoon, instead of in the Horse and Groom, microwaving shepherd's pies? She was on her feet in an instant, but couldn't reach the door in time to forestall her mother's entrance. Flushing with embarrassment, she watched her saunter in – followed by an unknown man – the pair of them dressed up like dogs' dinners. She tried desperately to stop them in their tracks; invent some pressing reason why they must leave at once, go back the way they'd come. Too late. April was already homing in on Charlotte, putting down her cluster of bulging carrier bags, then proffering a plump pink hand studded with three rings. 'Hello! You must be Vicky. Tessa's told me such a lot about you. I'm so glad she's made a friend.'

'I'm Charlotte, actually.'

'Oh, Charlotte. Lovely name! It always reminds me of the pudding. I'm April, by the way. Which means I'm past my sell-by-date, seeing as it's the first of May today. And this is Ken.' She clutched him by the sleeve, drew him further in. 'Ken – my daughter, Tessa, and Charlotte – Charlotte Russe. Ha ha! Just my little joke. You do look awfully thin, my love,' she said, wheeling back to Charlotte. 'Are you sure you're eating properly? I was reading just today about this anorexic business – a whole page in the *Daily Mail*, with photographs and all – and it said students were the worst. One in five are starving themselves. Or was it one in ten? Anyway, according to the article, it's boys as well as girls now, and in America it's kids as young as six. It's a pity the poor things aren't here, because we've brought food enough for the entire United States, and probably Canada as well.'

She started unloading all the carriers, unpacking tins and cartons, covering Charlotte's desk with them. 'There was a big do at the pub last night, and Connie overcatered. You know what she's like – ordering double everything, then blaming me for waste. Don't look so worried, Tessa dear. There's plenty to go round, and your little friend looks as if she could do with some. Now, which of you wants what? There's ham and mushroom volley-vongs in that big square patterned doodah, and prawn tartlets in the Tupperware. Though I'm not so sure about those prawns, come to think of it. Here, take this quiche instead, Charlotte. We don't want you getting food-poisoning on top of anorexia.'

'Mum, listen, Charlotte's busy. She's . . . We . . .'

'Oh, you're busy, dear. I'm sorry. I hope you're not like Tessa – always overworking. She's been the same since nursery school; never could do nothing and just watch the world go by, not even in her pram. Well, that's the trouble with being bright – that and dodgy nerves. And you look the brainy sort as well, so we'd best get out of your hair and leave you to your swotting. Nice room, though, isn't it? At least you get the sun in here, and a decent bit of garden to look out at, instead of dreadful creepy gravestones. Golly! Look at all these photos.' She plunged towards the board; greasy fingers stabbing at the prints. 'That must be your Mum. You're the image of her, aren't you? – same eyes, same skinny figure. Mind you, you can overdo the slimming lark, you know, and I reckon half these diets gum up the works inside. And what about your boyfriend? Does *he* like you quite so thin? Ken always says he prefers a bit of something to get hold of. That's right, isn't it, Ken?'

31

'Well, er . . .'

'Mum, Charlotte isn't slimming,' Tessa interrupted. 'She's just naturally a slim type. And she's also trying to finish an important piece of work.'

'I won't say another word. Work comes first – I know that.' She turned to Charlotte, took her arm confidingly. 'I spent whole evenings creeping round on tiptoe when Tess was doing her A-levels, or watching telly with the sound off, so's I wouldn't make any noise. I'm sure your mother did the same. I'd like to meet her sometime, if I ever get the chance. We mums must stick together. And it was a real pleasure meeting *you*, dear. Heat the quiche, if you can. They're always nicer hot. And don't forget . . .'

'*Mum!*'

'Okay, okay, I'm coming! Keep your hair on!' April collected up her parcels, leaving an onion quiche for Charlotte, and a box of mini-pizzas, then teetered down the stairs, with Ken trundling along behind her. The noise of her high heels (and Ken's white-fringed navy loafers) seemed to echo through the college, disturbing all the people trying to catch up on lost sleep. Tessa's face was flaming, both on her account and Charlotte's. It was shitty to be ashamed of your own mother, yet she could just imagine Charlotte wincing at that dire fake-satin dress – April's current favourite – which had polka dots all over it, and a matching bow to clip on her bleached hair. And what in God's name would she think of Ken, in that quite unspeakable blazer with its pseudo polo badge, when the nearest he'd ever got to a horse was probably losing all his money on it?

Now who was the snob? And snobbery was frowned upon at Balliol. None the less, she still felt mortified. She knew Charlotte wouldn't say a thing, but the memory would grate, remain festering between them like another hopeless barrier. Even her mother's name would be the subject of raised eyebrows. No one was called April – or not in Charlotte's set. Charlotte's mother was bound to be a Sarah, or an Elizabeth, or Margaret – something low-key and traditional – and she'd appear at college with her legal wedded husband, not some pick-up with a gold chain round his neck.

'Slow down, Tess, for heaven's sake, or we'll break our blooming necks. Ken's got this funny tendon, so he can't go haring off like that. How you doing, Ken, love?' She waited till he'd caught her up, then blew him a fond kiss. 'We've been on our pins since half past ten this morning – set off from home at sparrow's fart, and stopped in Henley for a coffee and a wee. Connie gave me the day off because I slogged my guts out yesterday. We didn't get to bed till two, and even then I couldn't sleep. I was that uptight, you see, ticking worse than the alarm-clock, trying to remember whether I'd put the chicken nuggets in the fridge, or left them out to give everyone wisteria. Anyway, here we are – though more thanks to Ken than me. I said to him, "Now listen, Ken, no way are we going to barge in on Tess until five o'clock at the earliest." I do understand you're busy with all these essays and what-have-you. We respect that, don't we Ken?'

She turned to Ken for confirmation, but he was staring at the floor. 'Ken's got two daughters of his own, though they're still at the Blue Peter stage. He's a bit of a late starter, in more ways than one.' She laughed and flicked her fringe back, squeezed his hand a moment. 'I know it's only five to four, but I hoped you might be finished, Toots, and could come out for a cuppa with us. We've found this lovely little place with warming-pans and whatsits on the walls. Cream teas, it said, and home-made cakes, though home-made means nothing nowadays.' She paused for breath at the bottom of the stairs, then called to Ken, who was limping down the passage. 'Whoa, there, Kenny boy, I don't think we're meant to go through there. It beats me how you ever find your way, Toots, what with all these different staircases and buildings. I can't make head or tail of them. It's left here, isn't it?'

'No, right.' Tessa took her mother's arm, tried to chivvy her along. They had now emerged into the garden quad, and would be seen by half the college if they didn't get a move on. Several of her friends were sprawling on the grass, and would be alerted by her mother's voice if she kept exclaiming over everything with such whooshes of delight.

'Ooh, look! They're playing croquet on the lawn. There's posh for you! Do you play, Tessa, love?'

'No, I don't. Come *on*, Mum.'

'I can't understand why you keep rushing about like a steam engine. Where are we off to anyway?'

'Just in here,' said Tessa, stopping at the door at the bottom of her staircase. 'I'm not that keen on going out, so I'll make you tea in my room.'

'But you haven't got the home-made cakes.'

'I've got some Lyons swiss roll.'

'I can't eat Lyons swiss roll with a row of corpses watching me.

You ought to complain about that graveyard, Toots. It's not healthy, living . . .'

'I like the room.'

'And I suppose you like shop cakes?'

'Yes, I do. And will you please not call me Toots. And also please shut up. There are people trying to work here.'

Tessa wrestled with a surge of guilt as she watched her mother subside. The beaming face and dazzling bouffant hairstyle seemed to shrivel and collapse. Even the satin bow had flopped, and the jaunty jade-green polka dots had lost their bloom and shine. Tessa knew that she'd dressed up in honour of her 'brilliant' daughter and to be worthy of a city she regarded with the deepest awe. She could also see from April's plastic carriers that she'd soon be showered with gifts – not just ham and mushroom vol-au-vents, but clothes and scent and souvenirs, books and sweets and chocolates. Her mother had always spoiled her; would spend her dismal week slaving for a pittance in hairdressers or dress-shops (or more recently a third-rate pub), then blue the lot on her ungrateful snobbish child. And it wasn't only presents she'd received. April spread good cheer on everything, like jam, never bellyached or grizzled, or lamented her hard lot as single parent; wasn't even jealous of Dave's new wife and daughters; bought gifts for them as well. It could have been so different – a resentful bitter mother spitting at her ex; instilling in her daughter a vengeful hatred of men. Instead, her first shy boyfriends had all been warmly welcomed, made to feel at home; April sometimes even flirting with them herself. She was only thirty-eight; looked a good two decades younger than Charlotte's grey-haired mother, with her classic clothes and staid conventional hairstyle.

'Mum . . .'

'What, dear?'

'I'm sorry if I snapped. I'm just feeling a bit scratchy.'

'That's all right. I'm sorry too. I mean, I know you said we shouldn't come without giving you any warning, but that's Connie, isn't it? We get days off when it suits her, never mind what *we* want. She's always dreaming up these marvellous schemes – rotas and what-have-you – then chopping and changing right at the last minute, buggering us about. And anyway, it's a problem getting hold of you when you haven't got a phone. Actually, I did phone – left a message with this man . . .'

'What man? You mean the porter?'

34

'Yes. Though I can't think why they're called that. They don't carry cases, do they?' She gave a sudden laugh, as if her good spirits had come whooping back, rarely cowed for long. 'I could do with a couple of porters, to help me lug this stuff around. Ken, watch out – more stairs! Tessa's right up at the top.'

'Look, give the bags to me, Mum.'

'No, not with your bad back.'

'What d'you mean? There's nothing wrong with my back.'

'I thought you said you'd pulled a muscle?'

'No, that was Rob. He hurt it playing cricket.'

'Ah, Rob, your famous mystery man! I can see you're hiding him again. We missed him last time, didn't we? He sounds a really nice type – the quiet sort, quiet and deep. You could invite him round for tea with us, if he doesn't mind swiss roll. I'm sure we'd get on like a house on fire.'

'He's . . . out.'

'Well, that's a shame. I'd love to see him in his whites. And talking of whites, there's a lot of dreadful scruffs around, with dirty hair and their knees out of their jeans. We saw one boy with a ponytail and stubble, stretched out on the grass like those tramps on Clapham Common. It beats me why they don't try and smarten up a bit. I mean, they're all nobs from toffee-nosed schools, aren't they? – and they look more like refugees. I hope your Rob's not got a ponytail?'

'No. Shortish back and sides.'

'Thank heavens for that! Any chance of seeing him before we have to leave? Ken'd like to meet a fellow cricketer, wouldn't you Ken?'

'Yes,' said Ken uncertainly, the first word he'd uttered yet beyond 'Hello' and 'Pleased to meet you' and 'Well, er . . .' He seemed bemused by his surroundings, bothered by the stairs, their steep and narrow treads accentuating his limp.

Tessa ran ahead, unlocked her room, then ushered them both in, feeling a sense of some relief that they were now corralled and contained, couldn't nab a porter, or ask to be included in the croquet.

'Cigarette?' Ken offered, fumbling for his JPS, having dutifully agreed with April that the gravestones were a horror, and the room so dark it was like looking for a black cat in a coal hole.

'No thanks, I don't smoke.'

'She's always on at me, Ken – bombarding me with gruesome facts about bronchitis and lung cancer. Oh, I know you're probably right,

Tess, but it's a funny thing, you know, I find smoking actually helps. The coughing seems to clear my chest.'

'Mum, that's just plain stupid.' Tessa banged the cups down, angry with herself as much as with her mother. Ken must see her as a bad-tempered little prig. Nearly all her college friends smoked, *and* drank much more than she did, and stayed in bed till lunch-time instead of getting up for lectures. A lot of them smoked dope as well – another thing she funked, although she'd frequently been tempted at a party. It made her feel so out of things to refuse a joint as it passed from hand to hand – naive and unsophisticated, and also something of a spoilsport. But she dared not take the risk, feared it might affect her work. She lacked the others' easy self-assurance; was still terrified of being booted out of college. One hangover too many, and she might be banished to the suburban wastes she'd sprung from – a pathetic failure prowling round the Job Centre, or sitting on her own poring over the 'situations vacant'. And yet her tutors were all pleased with her, and even the undemonstrative Sylvester had deigned to praise her work today.

'Hey, listen, Mum, we've got this new tutor, Ruth Sylvester. She's a medievalist, a walking encyclopaedia, but not exactly generous with her praises. The most she'll ever say about an essay is "not bad", or "tolerable", but she just told me half an hour ago that mine was excellent.'

'Of course it was! You were always head and shoulders above the others in your class.' April turned to Ken, blowing out a curl of lazy smoke. 'She gets that from her father. He's another brain-box, and always on the tin-tan. I'm not sure what the poor kid got from me.'

'My size,' quipped Tessa, observing the way her mother's shiny skirt was straining over her ample hips and thighs. Though, apart from her large build, she was nothing like her mother. April had blue eyes – bulgy eyes which looked as restless as their owner, as if they were about to pop out of their sockets and find an urgent job to do. And her hair, beneath the peroxide, was somewhere between fieldmouse and wild rabbit, though it had been blonded for so long now, it had lost all its natural gloss. Her mother's real attraction was in her flash-bulb smile, her exuberance and energy, her willingness to take on Fate and anything it hurled at her, and make her bouncy best of it. Tessa had sometimes watched her in the pub, swabbing fresh puke from the gents' and humming 'Oh, what a beautiful morning' as

36

she wrung out the stinking mop, or answering a customer's rebuff with a cheery joke, a fondle of his arm. April didn't believe in an eye for an eye or a tooth for a tooth, but would sacrifice her own eyes for anyone she loved; pluck out any vital organ a dear friend might require, and present it gift-wrapped with a silver bow on top. Even now, she was unpacking all the tins and bags, suggesting they had vol-au-vents as well as the swiss roll; fretting that the blouse she'd bought might not fit her daughter; explaining that the chocolates were the expensive sort with cream in, and that the book was 'English Literature' and full of lovely pictures.

'It's great, Mum, honestly. And the blouse is really pretty. You shouldn't spend all your hard-earned money on me.'

'I enjoy it, Toots. You know that.'

Tessa glanced anxiously at the clutter on the floor. Her tidy room had been totally transformed – tins and greaseproof paper, clothes and books and bags, littering the carpet or piled up on the chairs; her mother's shoes kicked off, her lipstick on the cup, her fag-end in the saucer, her cheap scent hanging pungent in the air. Crazy to feel threatened. She could restore her usual order once they'd safely disappeared, and the food would be perfect to take to the rehearsal. She picked up the prawn tartlets, placed them on the desk. They'd keep cooler by the window.

'Did I tell you, Mum, I'm acting in this play? It's only a very minor part, but I'm really lucky to have it. Loads of other people turned up for the audition, even a girl who's been to stage-school and has a mother who's an actress – a real star in the West End.'

'*Your* mother's a star, dear – star of the Horse and Groom.' April laughed and coughed at once, gulped tea as medication. 'So when's the opening night? We'll make sure we're there, won't we, Ken, in our tiaras and our penguin suits, and we'll present you with a big bouquet when you take your curtain call.'

Tessa didn't answer. There wouldn't be curtains, let alone a curtain call, and the standard dress for the audience would be sweatshirts and torn jeans. They were performing in a basement to a small and lukewarm audience of fellow undergraduates – those who could be prised away from parties, punts, or pub – and parents were most definitely taboo. She changed the subject quickly, replenished both their cups, watched a still self-conscious Ken uncurling his swiss roll, scraping off the filling, then attacking the dry sponge. She felt sorry for him somehow – obviously a shy man, with no gift for conversation, yet who was trying his stiff best to look at home.

'How old are your two daughters, Ken?' she asked. It was time she made an effort to include him, talked about his own life, instead of always hers.

'Eight and nine.' His accent was south London, flat and unexceptional.

'Oh, nice. And where d'you live?'

'Ashford.'

'Ashford in Middlesex?'

'No, Kent.'

'D'you work in Kent as well?'

'No, London. City Road.'

Straight answers to straight questions. Though there were other questions curdling in the room, ones she dared not raise. Where's your wife? And are the girls with her? And what exactly are you doing with my mother?

There was a sudden awkward silence, as if her private thoughts had been flashed up on a screen, leaving Ken and April defensive and on edge. Her mother's feet looked swollen from her tight ill-fitting shoes, and Ken had smeared butter-cream on his dapper royal-blue blazer. She suddenly longed to hug them both, ply them with champagne, pin medals on their chests or loop garlands round their necks, in return for their own generous cornucopia, their praise of her, their homage. And all she'd done instead was hustle them out of sight, pour them tea in cups which didn't match, and serve them stale shop cake.

She jumped up from the floor, almost capsizing her own cup. 'Listen, I've got a great idea! Why don't we go punting? The rain's stopped now and we could buy some wine, and I'll punt you down the Cherwell in traditional Oxford style.'

She watched her mother resurrect like a Heineken advertisement; her curves and hair and smile and breasts all perking up and plumping out, in instant magic fashion; words and cake-crumbs overflowing as she burbled with excitement.

'And Ken would love it, wouldn't you, Ken? He's got this yen for water. Hey, that's a poem, almost – Ken and yen. Your Mum's a poet now, Tessa, as well as a big star. And Ken's a water-baby. Remember that little spaniel Uncle Norman had – Sally, was it, or Sukie? – I always got their names mixed up. Anyway, take her near a river or some filthy muddy pond, and in she went – splash, wallop!

Well, Ken's very much the same, except he prefers to keep his fur dry. But any sort of boat and he's slavering at the chops. In fact, that reminds me, Tessa – his brother's got this cabin cruiser, just bought it on the cheap, and they're christening it on Saturday week – a big thrash on the Thames. We were hoping you could come. Could you get away, d'you think, just for that one evening?'

Tessa hovered by her desk, pretending to consult her college diary, though she knew perfectly well that Saturday week was blank. Blank and coloured crimson, blank and fizzing like champagne. She hadn't had a chance to fill it in yet, and had actually forgotten it for the last half hour or more, incredible as that seemed.

'No, I'm terribly sorry, I can't. We're . . . er . . . rehearsing all that day.'

'But they won't miss you, will they, Toots, if you've only got a tiddly part?'

'Yes . . . I mean . . . I'm afraid I really can't get out of it. We're so short of rehearsal time, they're fanatic about people showing up. This is the busiest term of all, you see. There are so many other distractions and . . .' She broke off, started clearing up the plates. Distractions like Dr Michael Edwards, who had invited her out on the triumphant eleventh of May, not for a mere morning, but for the whole glorious endless day. She turned towards the window to hide her stupid grin, longed to tell someone, if only the stained and flaking gravestones: 'I'm going out with this fantastic maddening guy who's named after an archangel.'

4

TESSA LAY BACK on the picnic rug, hitching up her skirt so that the sun would tan her legs. There was strength and passion in that sun, a sun more suited to mid-August than the second week in May. She was glad it wasn't August yet. She didn't want the term to end, or Michael to leave the Radcliffe and take up his next job, which might be miles and miles away. She glanced at him, as if afraid he might have gone already, crept away unnoticed while she'd been lying with her eyes shut. But he was still there, warm and heavy, his body nudging hers, a straw hat tipped across his face to protect it from the glare. One arm was bent across his chest, the sleeve rolled up, revealing dark and tangled hairs which clustered round the metal of his watch-strap, continued down his chunky squarish hands. She had slipped her own watch off, wanted time to stop – here, now, at this very moment, with the countryside so lush and fresh, everything was overflowing as spring and summer clashed. They had driven past tall hedgerows which appeared to be sprouting as she watched; brambles reaching out with clawing tendrils; ditches glossed with celandines; sap forcing leaves from buds. Two weeks ago, the chief colour had been yellow – daffodils and primroses, the yellow smoke of catkins puffing from dark boughs. Now blue had taken over – mists of bluebells, hairy stalks of borage – and all the endless greens between, beyond, beneath; still virginal transparent greens, not yet overripe.

'So when's it time for grub, then?' Michael's voice was muffled underneath the hat.

'You can't be hungry already.'

'Try me!'

'Okay, but shall we move into the shade? Everything's melting, as it is. Thanks for laying on a heatwave, by the way.'

'I told you, I like playing God. I'll make sure it rains on Monday, when I'm back slaving on the wards and you're cooped up in some library, reading about that rotter Abelard.'

'You sound worse than Charlotte. Anyway, I've moved from him to Guibert.'

'Who the hell's Guibert?'

'A neurotic mixed-up monk who became abbot of a monastery in Nogent, which is north of Paris, between Laon and Noyon. I've just been reading his memoirs. They're incredibly frank, especially for the time, and psychiatrists have had a field day with him, because he was so preoccupied with sex and violence, and had this very dominant mother who was . . .' She broke off. The word 'sex' had somehow stalled her, was still hanging in the air, reverberating between them, making her uneasy. 'But let's not talk about work,' she shrugged. 'Or Monday. I'll play God myself and make it Saturday for ever – a day which lasts a million years.'

'I'd love to live that long. Think of all the things you could do, and all the power you'd have.'

'I suspect you might get bored,' she said, noting his emphasis on power – another awkward word, and one he used quite frequently, along with 'I' and 'hungry'.

'Bored? Of course I wouldn't! I'd have a thousand different careers, live in all the countries of the world – not to mention Mars and Jupiter and any other planets they may have opened up by then. I'd marry several hundred times, produce whole tribes of children, and several important works of art, and also eat at least a billion trillion meals.'

Tessa knelt up on the rug. 'Well, shall we have our second for today? If we move just over there, into that wooded shady bit, we might stop your runny cheeses from running right away.'

'You got the German Brie?'

'Yes, all the things you wanted.'

'A really ripe gooey one?'

'Yes. We'll probably have to eat it with a spoon.'

'And the mangoes?'

'Whoppers!'

'And how about the challah?'

'I had to try four shops for that, but I found some in the end. You're not Jewish, are you, Michael?'

'No – I just like Jewish bread.'

'I've never had it.' She didn't add that she'd never bought a mango till today, had no idea that German Brie existed, and was shocked by the prices of all the picnic foods he'd ordered. She could hardly expect him to reimburse her, when he'd already paid for brunch, promised her dinner at the Blue Coyote, and also brought along a bottle of what looked like expensive wine.

He hunted for the corkscrew as they settled down in their more secluded spot; a tent of trees above them, mossy grass below. The sun was fidgeting on the silvered bark of beeches, striping them with shadow; filtering between the leaves, spangling their transparent green. Birds rustled overhead, fighting over sites and twigs, or flapping up from branches. She smoothed the rug, then unpacked bread and cheeses, butter, pâté, olives, and a crab mousse thing he'd told her was his favourite, and must be bought at one particular shop it had taken hours to find.

'The bread's so fresh, it's warm,' she said. 'It's a good thing Abelard's not here. He wrote these Letters of Direction to Heloïse's convent, telling them on no account must the nuns eat hot new bread, but wait at least a day until it had staled a bit.'

Michael tore a chunk off, crammed it in his mouth. 'He sounds a perfect hypocrite to me – tucking in to Heloïse when *she* was fresh and hot, then shutting her away for the rest of her long life, so no one else could have her.'

'It wasn't like that, Michael. You don't understand the . . .'

'I do understand – only too well. I loathe that whole ascetic thing – mortify the flesh, instead of glorying in it; call everything a sin which gives life a bit of zest. The Christian Church has always been so life-denying – anti-food, anti-sex; the here-and-now worth nothing, compared with some non-existent afterlife.'

Tessa scooped runny Brie on to a sponge of soft white bread. The word 'sex' again, throbbing and vibrating, as if it contained a tiny firework which exploded into the air every time they mentioned it; sent out a shower of sparks. She busied herself with eating, deliberately ignoring Michael's challenge. They'd had much the same argument earlier on, when she'd been telling him about Abelard's castration, and how, after the first hideous shock, he had eventually come to see it as a blessing in disguise, a just punishment for sin and a means of spiritual growth. Michael had been horrified, denounced Abelard's reaction as 'totally and utterly sick'; refused to listen when she'd tried to explain how very different things had been in a monastic age

42

which regarded celibacy as admirable, and sexual love – whatever its attractions – as an impediment to God's love.

She was determined not to climb back on her hobbyhorse – didn't want to be drawn into a quarrel. Anyway, castration was hardly an appropriate subject for a relaxed and happy picnic in the sun. She was already feeling edgy because he hadn't kissed her yet today, and she was coiled up like a spring inside, nervous and expectant both at once. She had transferred his first May-morning kiss to the museum of her head; constructed a glass case for it, labelled it astounding, dangerous, unexpected, and embarrassingly public. She should have resisted, with all those people watching in the restaurant. She *had* resisted, even tried to pull away, but Michael had overruled her, and in the end her mouth had been so staggered by the skills and depths of his, that she'd blanked out everything save the vehemence of the kiss itself.

She'd been worrying since then. Such an advanced professional kisser made her feel inadequate. How could she measure up, not prove a disappointment if they took things any further? She wasn't exactly inexperienced, but she'd never had an orgasm – at least she didn't think she had. It was difficult to tell, despite the fact that she'd slept with three boys altogether, two at Emberfield. The first one hardly counted – it had been too short and rushed. But the second boyfriend had lasted for eight months, and in all that time, she still wasn't sure if she'd achieved that longed-for climax. Even with Rob, who was slower, more considerate, often asked her anxiously, 'Did you come as well?', she could never really answer with any sense of certainty. Were those rippling restless feelings a real 'official' come, or just one stage on the way to it? And however could you ask, when she and most of her girlfriends were trying to pretend they knew more than they did, or had gone further than they had. Even the sex-books didn't help – in fact made things more confusing, or left you feeling totally inferior because they were written for sexual PhDs, when you were still struggling with GCSE.

She could somehow never discuss it with her mother, despite April's liberality – or perhaps because of it. April had always regarded sex as something healthy, natural and 'good for you', like wholemeal bread or aerobics. She had never shrouded it in secrecy or guilt, but had given her daughter the go-ahead to enjoy an angst-free sex life, so long as she was responsible about things like contraception or avoiding the risks of AIDS. But health-food sex left a lot to be desired. What it gained in openness it lost in mystery and taboo. She found herself yearning for the sort of passion and romance you found in literature – Romeo and Juliet, Tristan and Isolde – not the tragic endings, but the intensity and poetry. The spotty boys at Emberfield fell far short of that ideal, and even the males at Balliol had been a distinct disappointment, many of them plain or gauche, and a few ignoring *her* because she had no natural entrance-ticket to their charmed and well-bred circle.

'Sling that knife over, Tessa. I think I'll try a mango with my cheese.'

'But they're for pudding. I brought some cream and sugar.'

'Okay, half with cheese and half with cream. They're so huge they need dividing.' He reached out for the knife, began to peel the heavy fruit, revealing a moist and glistening flesh inside. She was surprised by its bright colour – peach and orange mixed – which contrasted with its mottled greenish skin. Juice was dripping down his fingers, splashing on his trousers. The fruit was slippery and wilful, seemed to be resisting him, rebelling against the knife. 'Here comes the tricky bit,' he said. 'The stones are perfect brutes. They don't pop out like avocado stones, but fight you all the way.'

She watched the surgeon make his deft incision, slice around the stone; his hands controlled and steady, despite the squishiness of the fruit. She almost wished he'd cut himself, so she could see his blood mingling with the juice. She imagined he'd have hotter blood than most average boring people – a steaming spiced elixir, distilled from chillies and hot peppers, paprika, dynamite. He'd told her he'd snatched four hours' sleep last night, yet he'd bulldozed the whole morning – brightened up the weather, cleared traffic from the roads, ordered all the birds to sing, even hung new leaves on an ancient elm tree stricken with disease, which should have been a barren blackened corpse.

With a final twist, he prised the stubborn stone free, then chopped a wedge of fruit off, coating it with cheese. 'Try that,' he urged, moving it towards her lips. 'The textures are fantastic – one pulpy-wet, one smooth and velvety.'

She took a bite and swallowed; the scented taste of mango clashing with the goat-sour tang of Brie. 'I think I'd prefer it with cream,' she grimaced, mopping juice from her frilled blouse.

'You're not very adventurous.' Michael demolished the remainder, hacked off a second chunk.

'Yes, I am. I'll eat it with the crab, if you like, just to prove I'm game for anything.'

'Don't bother. Where's the cream?'

'Here.' She groped behind her. 'I brought an aerosol, thought it might keep cooler.'

'Great!' He pressed the nozzle, smothering the mango with a whoosh of frothy cream, which rose higher, higher, higher, like a miniature Mont Blanc.

'Hey, Michael, stop! That's far too much.'

'It *won't* stop! It's got a mind of its own.' The cream was still cascading out, spurting over his hands now, spewing on the rug. 'Quick! Help me mop it up.' He tongued a gobbet from his hands, then thrust his fingers into her mouth. She licked them. The cream was sweet and soft, his fingers hard and salty. She kept swallowing and swallowing, as if to prove herself again; gulping cream to show she was adventurous, not a puritan or prude.

Michael laughed. 'You've got a white moustache now. Here, let me lick it off.'

'No,' she said suddenly, pushing him away. His fingers in her mouth were disturbing and unsettling; had affected her whole body, put her on her guard. She was aware that she was sweating, despite the trees' green cool; her skin damp and flushed, sticking to her clothes. She hardly knew this man yet, mustn't let him think he could grab her when he fancied, then discard her as an easy lay, a slut.

He had turned for consolation to the cream, retrieving it from the rug, piling it on bread, on cheese, on mango. 'It's delicious, isn't it? Much lighter than the normal stuff.'

'I expect it's three-quarters air.' Her voice felt strange, strained and slightly breathless, as if she, too, had swallowed air.

'Just as well, since I can't stop eating it.' He sprayed the nozzle directly into his mouth, the cream filling it, and foaming out, gushing down his chin. He used his tongue to scoop it back, and she watched in fascination – the tongue so pink and quick, flicking, lapping, alive in its own right. He squirted in another dose, which overflowed like cumulus, so that he needed hands as well as tongue to cram it in and down. Surely the aerosol was empty now? How could such a tiny can contain that tidal wave of cream, and how could Michael consume it all and not feel sick or sated?

'Ah! That was good,' he said at last, leaning back against a tree-trunk and reaching for his glass. 'I think I need a rest now. Top my wine up, will you?'

Some rest, she thought ironically, as he began to pour out words instead of cream, launching into the subject of his future – and that of cardiac surgery – as he swigged from his replenished glass. She couldn't follow all of it; was stymied by the technical terms, but still marvelled at his enthusiasm for all the new techniques. He was talking like a man in love; his whole face animated, his arms flung out and gesturing; one foot jabbing, as if a current of surplus energy was streaming from his leg into the ground. Her eyes were drawn towards that leg: the battered shoes, the once-smart trousers fraying at the hems, the scruffy-looking socks. He'd probably grabbed the first clothes he could find, whereas she had spent a good two hours sorting through her wardrobe to find the perfect outfit. She tried to imagine him with his patients in an immaculate white coat and shirt, shoes polished, hands well-scrubbed; giving them his full attention as they confided all their symptoms. Surely doctors should be sympathetic listeners, yet Michael obviously insisted on being centre-stage himself, and was still continuing to hold forth, lambasting the authorities now for their chronic lack of vision.

She nibbled on a piece of mango, took a sip of wine. She needed to cool down. He was like another sun, one which couldn't be shut out or blocked by hats and trees, but which scorched her and inflamed her, made her liquefy. She cursed the heavy skirt she'd chosen, longed to take it off. Yet she'd decided to play safe, take things very slowly – allow a kiss, but nothing more. She'd no intention of becoming his puppet, obeying when he pulled her strings, opening mouth or legs at his command. He'd already bossed her about on the matter of the food, expecting her to buy exactly what he specified, without the slightest regard for her own preferences or tastes.

'Ouch!' he yelled, breaking off his tirade about National Health muddle and red tape. 'Some monster's bitten me.'

'Monster?'

'Well, a midge. Or maybe a mosquito. It's come up like a tennis ball! I'm very susceptible to bites.'

She laughed at the idea that a giant of six-foot-three, weighing thirteen stone at least, could be vanquished by a midge.

He slapped his arm furiously. 'Thanks for all the sympathy. Any decent girl would see if she could help, not sit there roaring her head off.'

46

She was astonished by his anger, which immediately fuelled her own. 'Come off it, Michael,' she snapped. 'You're not a stretcher-case. It doesn't even look that bad.'

'Oh doesn't it? If you're an authority on bites, perhaps you've got some anti-histamine, or something I can rub on it.'

'No – sorry, I'm not a nurse, though maybe you're so used to them, you expect every available female to be rushing round with cold compresses and aspirin the minute you get tickled by a gnat.' He'd mentioned nurses twice already, once at brunch, and once en route to Foxlow Woods – not nurses in the abstract, but individual girls with names and foibles. Prue loved cats; Jennifer had problems with her parents. She could see them in her head – Prue petite and dainty, with tiny hands and feet; Jennifer a flirt, flattering and fluttering in her affected Sloaney voice. Okay, so she was jealous, but she'd have suppressed her petty feelings if he wasn't being so insufferable himself.

'Actually, a cold compress might well help. Pass the Perrier, will you?'

'Get it yourself.'

'What in God's name's got into you? I've never known such a bad-tempered little bitch.'

'I'm not a bitch. I just don't like you giving me orders.'

'Look here, Tessa. We've done exactly what you've wanted all damned day.'

'Oh, really? I hadn't noticed. I distinctly remember saying I wanted to go to Blenheim.'

'I'm sick to bloody death of Blenheim. I took my foreign cousin there three months ago.'

'Another nurse, I suppose? I hope she liked it.'

'He's a computer programmer, and no, he didn't like it, and nor the fuck do I.'

'I hate you swearing, Michael.'

'Tough shit! I'll do what I fucking like.'

She jumped up to her feet, stalked off through the trees, tripping on a root, almost crying with frustration. How could he ruin such a perfect day? – or maybe it was her fault. Had she really been a bitch, foul-tempered and unfair, or was he just a moody type forever throwing tantrums? She should have stayed with Rob – straightforward stodgy Rob, who always made her feel she was in control of the relationship.

47

She heard footsteps crashing after her, quickened her pace, running blindly over the rough uneven ground. It was a race again, a battle: Michael determined to catch her; she determined to evade him. He was so close now she could hear his gasping breathing, then a sudden muttered curse as he, too, stumbled, broke the pounding rhythm of his feet. She made one last violent effort, heart thumping in her chest, breasts bouncing and uncomfortable; clothes hampering her, confining; silly shoes slipping at the heel.

He clutched out at her skirt, forced her to the ground, used his mouth to hold her down, his lips a padlock, clamped around her own; his weight and bulk preventing her from moving, though she tried desperately to knee him off, while he kissed her through the protests. No – kiss was the wrong word. It was more of an invasion, as he forced her mouth to open wider, lashed her tongue with his. Her own mouth was fighting back, yelling out abuse; abuse without the words. It was impossible to speak, since her tongue was grappling with his, and he was snicking it with sharp and dangerous teeth. *She* could bite as well – scored his lips, nipped his tongue, heard him yelp with pain. She was astonished at herself. She had never known a kiss could be so savage, and now it *was* a kiss, terrifying, violent, as he probed still deeper, explored the widening cavern of her mouth. She ought to stop him, not cravenly submit, but if she unlatched her mouth from his, it would become small again and innocent, the sort of naive and childish mouth which Rob had pecked so tamely.

She could feel herself actually changing as he kissed her, becoming wilder, messy, wet; a stickiness between her legs; large damp patches seeping from her underarms, staining her chic blouse. Her whole body was too hot – with excitement and with anger – anger at Michael's bullying, the way he'd overpowered her. Her face was stinging, slimy, her saliva drooling out with his, so that she was losing any sense of what belonged to her and what to him. His leg was hooked around her leg, her hair trapped beneath his arm; his heavy, urgent breathing meshed with hers, so that they were breathing with one pair of lungs, together and in time. Even her anger was now shared, fusing with his to become a feverish impatience.

His hot hand moved towards her chest, started fumbling with the buttons of her blouse, seemed frustrated by them, baffled, until it simply slipped inside and found bare flesh. She tensed. The thumb was circling her nipple; feathering it so stealthily she could hardly bear its gentle teasing pressure; feared she would explode from the maddening contrast between languid hand and frantic mouth.

'Wait!' She dragged the blouse off, not bothering with the fastenings, but yanking it over her head. Immediately, his mouth was on her breast, his tongue licking a slow path from her nipple to her throat, then dawdling back and down again, sucking, grazing with his teeth, but still leisurely, unhurried. He was spinning out his pleasure with the lazy afternoon, turning anger into indolence. Extraordinary the way he knew what nipples liked: the gentle steady tugging, the tongue-tip flicking back and forth. The nipple swelled and stiffened; her own mouth opening wider, demanding him again. If only he had two mouths – one to kiss her, one to suck her breasts; or one to kiss her while he used his second pair of lips to nuzzle down her belly. His tongue had reached her navel, was gliding slowly past it, then prowling lower still.

'No,' she whispered suddenly, struggling to sit up.

'What's wrong?'

'I . . . think we ought to stop.'

'But we've only just begun.'

'I know, but . . .' She glanced around her. At least the place was private. They hadn't seen a soul since they arrived, and the trees were like their private guard, arms spread to keep intruders out.

'If you're worried about contraception . . .'

'I'm not. I'm on the pill. But . . .'

Michael was tugging off his shirt, unbuckling his stiff belt. 'Look, you want it, Tessa, I know you do. I adore your greed, the way you're really dying for it. You're a great rutting wide-thighed whore, and you can hardly wait for me to get it in and fuck the daylights out of you.'

'I'm not! I don't. I . . .'

'Liar!'

She couldn't answer back. His mouth had stoppered hers again, and his naked body was glued against her own, a sweaty body whorled with dark coarse hair. The hair felt rough against her breasts, echoed by the roughness of his chin, and the scratchy tickling bracken they were lying on. He was too big to be resisted – big in bulk, big in sheer crude dominance; pressing on her, crushing her, yet kissing so phenomenally, she had to open her mouth, let him eat and drink from it. They were devouring one another, tasting all the foods again – garlic wine and crab-tinged Brie, as they guzzled from each other's tongues. She was only half aware of what his hands were doing – easing down her zip, pulling at her skirt – knew she ought to stop him, groped down with her own hand.

'Don't fight me, Tessa. Right?'

'No, it's not right. I still don't really know you. I'd rather . . .'

'If you want to get to know me, this is the perfect way, okay? Just relax.'

'No, stop, I . . .'

He had somehow peeled her skirt off, and was now clawing at her pants, and as she jerked up to object, he moved faster still, thrust his head between her legs, used mouth and lips and teeth and tongue to distract her, overwhelm her. She chewed her fingers to stop herself from crying out. The bristles which had pricked her face were like tiny needles lower down, piercing her and stabbing, stabbing, with an exquisite white-hot pain.

She was still trying to protest, one part of her alarmed that they were going far too far too fast, doing something wildly private in a stretch of common woodland, but her fears were swamped by the incredible sensations – the barbed-wire chin, the swooping probing tongue. She was aware of his whole head, huge between her legs, burrowing between them; two voracious mouths in contact with each other. And Michael's mouth had tentacles and pincers; kept changing as she bucked and threshed below it; now a clamp, now a scoop, now the lightest of antennae. She was no longer saying no, but whimpering and clamouring, as if her restraining mind had disappeared, and her body ruled her voice-box. She shut her eyes, so that she could focus on his tongue – its deep insistent circling forcing her to move in time, arch her spine, pivot with her hips.

When she opened them again, his wet face was right above her; lips moving down to kiss her as he slid slowly slowly in – pausing, teasing, pretending to withdraw, before thrusting back, then stalling; continually altering his rhythm. She was suddenly annoyed that he wouldn't keep it steady, attune it to her own rhythm, which was building up, building up, becoming faster and more urgent. Her mouth was joining in, repeating the frenzy of her body, trying to tell him in great shuddering gasps that he was miraculous, amazing, and that this was the first time she'd made love, the only time that mattered, and that if he went on any longer, she'd scream, she'd die, she'd overflow, and she was furious with him,

50

furious, for compelling her and bossing her – furious and worshipping, furious and ecstatic . . .

'Ssh, Tessa! Someone's coming.'

'No, no! Don't stop – not now.'

'Tessa, you'll get us both locked up!' He gagged her with his hand, but she bit the hand, kept crying out, even through the muzzle.

'For Christ's sake, woman, hush!'

She tried to stifle her cries, heard crunching bracken, snapping twigs, a sudden gasping 'Sorry!' as two figures loomed above her, two appalled embarrassed faces staring into hers.

She shut her eyes, didn't care. They were only stupid trespassers in Michael Edwards' wood. He owned it, owned her body, and there was no way she could stop. She could feel him slowing, feel his bursting tension as he fought to hold it back, the slamming rhythm now wavering and limp. She ground herself against him, desperate to continue; more aroused than ever by the thought of people watching; strangers' eyes on Michael's unsheathed prick; on her own pale breasts, dark thatch. '*Please* go on,' she begged him. 'Go on, go on, go *on*!'

And suddenly he did go on, stiffening now inside her, until he was fiercer than before; not kissing her, but shouting, 'You randy little bitch – you great brazen shameless hussy,' and the words weren't insults any more, but an electrifying challenge which was working on her, freeing her, and she realized she was coming, and she didn't give a damn whether the whole of Oxford was standing gawping as she heaved and thrust against him, and when she screamed, 'Oh, Michael, Michael, Michael!' she could hear scandalized but wild applause thundering through the startled reeling wood.

'That might have been my *boss*, Tessa – Sir Thomas Thornton, Professor of Surgery, strolling in the woods with his prudish lady-wife.'

'Yes, I expect it was.' She was smiling to herself. Gavin wouldn't recognize her – the modest schoolgirl who'd done it with her skirt still on, in the alley by the boilerhouse. But she mustn't think of Gavin. She had left her school behind now, her cramped suburban home and confining childish standards, and become her adult self – shameless greedy Tessa, whom Michael Edwards loved.

'I love you,' he'd yelled out, when he'd come himself, just afterwards – a great roaring gutsy cataclysm, in which he'd poured out everything: his sperm, his sweat, his desire – a million miles from Gavin's feeble twitch. It had been her matriculation – not the formal ceremony she'd endured in her first term, which had made her an official member of Oxford University – but a more vital rite of passage, which had transformed her into a mature official woman, a woman who had orgasms, stupendous shattering comes. Even Michael was astonished by them, astonished and admiring. He no longer seemed seven whole years older. She had caught up with him at last – his partner, his beloved.

She reached out to pick a crozier of new green sappy fern, stroked it down his chest. Both of them were only partly dressed – he with just his trousers on, she naked beneath her skirt; blouse draped across her breasts, sweaty hair in tangles. She was too bushed to find a comb or fasten buttons, too contented to get up. She lay, unmoving, watching the thin clouds wisp and fray above; the twitch of birds in branches. All her senses seemed sharper, more acute. She could hear the sigh of leaf on leaf; feel each separate bracken frond tingling underneath her back, still taste Michael's mouth. An insect was crawling up her leg. She didn't brush it off, wanted every smallest creature to express itself, enjoy itself, with no hindrance or restrictions. All the usual barriers between her own skin and the world's had somehow disappeared, so that she was now the sky, the tree, the cloud – living their huge lives, yet also sharing the perspective of that tiny humble insect, gaping at each pore and freckle as it clambered up the mountain of her thigh.

She was sore between the legs from the chafe of Michael's bristles, relished the sensation, wore it as a trophy. Her body was still sweltering, yet the fine hairs on her arms were standing up on end, as if they, too, were intoxicated, unable to return to boring flat normality.

Michael had dozed off. She wondered how he could, with the birds so brash and raucous; one boaster in particular stabbing out its mating-song, repeating and repeating it, like a record which had jammed. She envied it its voice, longed to flute and whistle back, have wings to swoop and soar. She was already composing poetry in her head, love-poetry, like Abelard's, which – tragically – had all been lost. Maybe hers would last for ever, Michael's name immortalized in the songs she'd write for him to play. She nudged him gently in the ribs. 'Hey, Michael . . .'

'What?'

'I love you.'

''Course you don't.' He yawned and scratched his belly, peered down at his watch. 'Good God! It's ten to five – way past tea-time.'

5

'*I VERY MUCH fear that I may become a nuisance by daring to besiege your already distracted ears with my repeated petitions. But what else can I do? If I fear to offend you with my many letters, how much more ought I not to fear . . .*'

Tessa laid the book down. She couldn't concentrate. And every line she read, despite the fact that it had been written by Saint Bernard in 1126, seemed to have relevance to Michael, who tyrannized her mind as much as Bernard had dominated Europe through most of the twelfth century with his charismatic force. She, too, had written endless letters, but, unlike braver Bernard, had torn them into shreds, continually trying to convince herself that there was no need to pester Michael or remind him she existed. She would hear from him eventually, mustn't be a drag, the sort of girl who couldn't wait a week or two. Or three. It was Saturday tomorrow – three weeks to the day since they'd last met. Okay, so he was busy – overworked, exploited – all the words he'd used himself, but he still had evenings free, enough time off to phone her college and leave a message with the porter. She'd made every possible excuse for him: he was ill, he'd had a crisis – some emergency at home, or problems at the hospital; he was attending important interviews to fix up his next job – but none of those contingencies would actually have prevented him from sending a brief note or picking up the phone.

She stared down at her hands, the fingers stained with biro, an M scrawled on the palm. It was time she faced the brutal fact that he must have simply dropped her – one fantastic screw, and scat. Except 'screw' was the wrong word. She needed a new word to describe how she and Michael had amazed each other's bodies. All the sexual terms she knew seemed so crude or twee – leg-over and bunk-up, nookie, cherry-pop. She'd even hunted through the dictionaries to try to come up with some foreign phrase, which might express the poetry as well as the gymnastics. She'd found *swyve* in Anglo-Saxon, which was at least a little better; could be spun out on the tongue, as she'd been spinning out the fantasies of her and Michael *swyving* – in rain-forests or deserts, on windswept beetling clifftops, sun-warmed sand, cool moss. Abelard and Heloïse had once made love in a convent refectory, so overcome by what Abelard called 'the violent intensity of lust', they couldn't, didn't wait. She had flicked back to the texts, re-reading all the relevant chunks of the *Historia Calamitatum* with new understanding, insight. *'The newness of these joys served only to make us prolong them ecstatically . . . We gave ourselves unreservedly to love . . . In our eagerness, we went through all the phases of love; we exhausted every refinement that passion can devise.'*

But as the days went by and she had heard no word from Michael, she began to worry that the 'ecstatic joys' had been mainly on her side. Perhaps he hadn't felt a passion close to Abelard's, but had found her selfish, greedy – grabbing all her own thrills without giving any back. Or did he see her as a slag – too easy, too available? Vicky would merely shrug and say you couldn't win with men. If you played hard to get, they labelled you a prick-teaser, and if you pleased their pricks instead of cruelly teasing them, then they pushed off in disgust. But that was too simplistic. Michael had actually told her that he loved her – not once, but twice – the second time at the Blue Coyote, when they'd been sharing a *bombe surprise*: one dish, two spoons, and three brandy-based liqueurs poured over the ice-cream. Had the love been brandy-based, as well, fuelled only by the booze?

She forced her attention back to Saint Bernard's letter, cursed the tiny print and greyish paper, which made it hard to read. *'Deceitfully and not sincerely does he love you; falsely and not faithfully does he counsel you . . .'* She closed the book, sagged back in her chair. Michael had been false, hadn't he, making all those empty promises about how he'd show her round his hospital, introduce her to his friends, even take her to his parents' home for a weekend in the country. She'd already wasted half the term, pining for him, waiting for his call, rebuffing other overtures from three separate boys in college. Tomorrow was the first of June and she'd hardly had a May yet. It had been grey and drizzly almost all the time. Only for their picnic had the sun shone. Michael had been right when he told her he played God, providing cloudless skies when they'd stripped off in the woods, then ordering heavy rain when she was cooped up in the library. She was sick of this damned library, especially loathed its name – the Radcliffe Camera – which jarred her back to Michael once again. She glanced up from her desk at the statue of its founder, Dr John Radcliffe, preening in his niche. She had been to the John Radcliffe – Michael's hospital – panted up Headington Hill on her complaining ancient bike, cursing herself for being such a fool. And the minute she'd arrived there, she'd turned round and cycled back again, terrified of meeting him, arm in arm with some voluptuous nurse. And if he did sleep with half the nurses' home, then she was an utter fool to have had sex with him herself without the protection of a condom. In the excitement of the moment she hadn't given it a thought, but as each long day limped on, all those direful warnings about AIDS and HIV echoed louder, louder in her head.

Or perhaps she'd infected *him*; picked up some ghastly bug from Rob and passed it on unwittingly. Would that explain his silence, and why he'd missed her play? He'd promised her he'd come, noted the dates in his diary, assured her he could manage at least one of them. It had been a great success, in fact, but she'd had to continue acting at the raucous last-night party, concealing her despair behind a mask of bonhomie. Similarly, during Eights Week, she'd rollicked down to the boathouse with a group of carefree friends, downed her Pimm's, cheered the college eights, even bought a crazy hat with ribbons on and flowers, but the flowers were artificial, like her smile. All the things which made the term exciting had turned out like damp squibs, because Dr Michael Edwards wasn't there.

She picked up her pen, tried to make some notes on Saint Bernard's views on justice, his strictures to Count Theobald. It was less than three weeks now to Mods. She'd run the risk of failing her first crucial public exams if she let some macho doctor rule her life. She must accept the fact that she'd lost him – and for good. After Mods she was moving out of college into a house in Juxon Street, and he was moving hospital, so their paths were unlikely to cross. And yet never in her life before had she felt so fused with someone else, as if, after her astounding come, she'd actually slipped inside his skin, seen the dappled beeches with his eyes; used his large and brawny hands to put her clothes back on; breathed purer fiercer air because she'd gulped it through his lungs.

She glared at Radcliffe's statue – hated it, resented it – that disdainful face and foppish wig, that air of snooty arrogance. How could she have ever found this place exciting? Yet she remembered writing to her mother in the first week of her first term, saying she was sitting in a library with a fantastic soaring dome and great arches and pilasters, and a balcony and marble busts, and an amazing sculpted frieze, and couldn't concentrate on work because her eyes were everywhere. She'd even enclosed a postcard of the building, so that April could see it for herself, and her mother had scribbled her a letter back, declaring she'd never known a library could be circular, and it looked more like a wedding cake complete with decorations, and why was it so dirty? Today it seemed polluted, inside as well as out, a grey pall on all the bookshelves, the desks, the walls, the windows; even its human occupants made of stained and dingy stone. The dreary spod beside her had barely moved at all, his nose embedded in his book, while she'd fidgeted and shifted, doodled on her pad. She could have murdered him in cold blood, for no other reason than the fact that he wasn't Michael, and could get on with his work, and because, as a male, he had all the power, power to initiate a date – or sex. Things were meant to be so different in the nineties – women liberated, equal, all the sexist barriers swept aside – but whatever the theoretical advances, she still felt quite incapable of phoning Dr Michael Edwards to suggest they should *swyve* again.

She swept her books off the desk, stuffed them into her bag. No point kidding herself that her mind was on Saint Bernard, when all she could see was naked bodies, picnic rugs. Better to go back to college, tidy up her tidy room, or kill an hour having tea with Vicky, sharing aimless college gossip. Thank God she hadn't mentioned Michael – not to any of her friends. At least they couldn't sympathize, or shrug.

She walked slowly down the stairs, her steps faltering to a halt as she realized that Vicky would probably be with Liz. The two had become much closer, and she felt increasingly left out; especially feared next year, when she and Liz and Vicky, and another girl she hardly knew, would be sharing the small terraced house in Juxon Street. There wasn't enough room in college for all students to live in, and it was usually the second-years who were ejected from the nest. It had been hard to find a house at all; still harder to find flatmates who were congenial, uncomplicated. One girl they'd considered was into heavy drugs; another had bulimia; so, in the end, cutesy Liz and grouchy Alexandra had seemed the best of a bad lot. But if Liz and Vicky were becoming thick as thieves, that left *her* with Alexandra – and her sulks.

She ploughed on to the bottom of the stairs, distracted from her thoughts by a voice she recognized.

'Tessa, hi! Great to see you.'

'Hi,' she replied mechanically, noting with dismay that it must be pissing down outside again, since Colin Linton's hair was dripping wet, his thin blue nylon anorak stained almost black with rain.

'Finished your stint for today?'

She nodded.

'I'm just starting mine. Though I can't say I'm that keen. Fancy a coffee or a beer or something, before I get down to "Morte d'Arthur"? We've got this lousy essay on Tennyson – "Was he a poet of both doubt and faith? Discuss"!'

She hesitated. She could pretend she had a tutorial, or an appointment at the dentist, or was meeting someone else. She'd become proficient at excuses in these last three endless weeks. On the other hand, Colin wasn't bad – a first-year English student, who had been roped in to the play right at the last minute, when one of the cast collapsed with hepatitis. They'd talked a lot at the party and he had suggested midnight coffee in his room, but she'd invented a bad headache, because that had been two weeks ago, when no other man existed except Michael Peter Edwards.

'Okay,' she said now, feeling ashamed of her lie.

'We'll have to make a dash for it.' Colin pulled his hood up as they emerged into the open, grimaced at the puddles. 'King's Arms or Queen's Lane Coffee House?' he asked. 'The pub's a good bit nearer.'

'The pub then,' Tessa said, peering up at the spiteful sheeting rain. So God-Michael hadn't relented yet.

'*What's* it called?' asked Tessa, sipping her second lager and scanning the photograph on the wall of Oxford in the rain – a downpour both inside and out.

'The Naked Lunch Society.'

'Never heard of it – unless it's something to do with Burroughs. It sounds obscene to me.'

'It's not,' said Colin, laughing. 'No one takes their clothes off, or actually has lunch, but they do have brilliant parties. It's very new, only been going for a term. Some wacky girl at Merton dreamed it up, mainly for people in the arts. In fact, there's a do on there this evening – two Irish poets performing with a synthesizer. Which is probably a convenient excuse for getting gently pissed. Why don't you come along?'

Tessa didn't answer, still found it difficult to switch her thoughts from Michael. Every subject led her back to their stupendous Saturday, including 'Naked Lunch' – a perfect title for their picnic in the woods. She'd been hoping for a naked dinner, too; kept all her evenings free since then – which was why they had been so barren: lonely hours of introspection, bitterness and self-reproach. A party might be fun, at least provide distraction. And she and Colin seemed to have hit it off quite well. A shame he wasn't taller, and she'd never liked red hair on men, but apart from his height and ginger frizz, he did have some things in his favour – attractive slate-blue eyes, for instance, and an open, friendly manner. And they appeared to have a surprising amount in common, including the lack of any normal paid-up father and a love of Gerard Manley Hopkins, who had been at Balliol himself.

Colin drained his beer, uncrossed his blue-jeaned legs. 'We could go back to college first, grab a pizza in the JCR, and then make tracks to the river. They've hired a barge for the gig tonight.'

'Oh, great!'

'Does that mean you're going to come?'

'But what about your work?' she asked, still trying to play for time. 'I thought you said you had to get down to "Morte d'Arthur"?'

'It can wait.'

She grinned, enjoying taking precedence over Alfred, Lord Tennyson. If she'd been going out with Michael, his hospital would always come first. He had already told her he worked one weekend in three, was on call at least two nights a week, and was frequently kept late. Perhaps it was just as well he'd dropped her. Did she really want to hang around for hours, have dates and dinners cancelled right at the last moment, or suffer pangs of guilt because she felt selfishly resentful of some patient having a bypass who needed Michael more than she did?

Colin pushed his chair back. 'Tessa, I'm on tenterhooks! Is it yes or no?'

'Yes! It sounds good fun. But we'd better get a move on. And I'll have to change before we go. I'm still soaked to the skin.'

'Same here. Though the rain's easing off a bit now. That's a blessing, or the Irish poets might be drowned by more than just the synthesizer.'

'Have you read the new biography of Hopkins?' she asked him, as they crossed the road into the Broad.

'Yes. Disappointing, wasn't it? It seemed to be bulging with factual stuff, yet somehow managed to miss the man.'

'It was quite helpful on the poems, though. I went back and read a good half of them again, which I'd never have done otherwise.'

She had mentioned Hopkins to Michael, and been shocked by his brusque '*Who?*' Yet why should she expect him to be familiar with poetry when she herself knew nothing about anatomy or surgery? He'd talked for hours about his work while they had been sitting in the Blue Coyote, waiting for their crab-cakes. She'd been confused by all the names – senior registrars and consultants, who appeared to rule his life, and was especially baffled by the initials, which seemed worse than those at Balliol. JR was easy – simply meant the John Radcliffe Hospital – and TT was his boss, but she still hadn't figured out SHO, NDS, RI or NOC. It was better in so many ways to stick with fellow undergraduates in one's own familiar world. If things worked out with Colin it might also help her cope with Rob, who had found a new girlfriend and appeared to be flaunting her deliberately. He seemed to be saying: 'Okay, you chucked me, Tessa, but now I'm free for Kathy, so yah-boo.' She couldn't get away from them – Rob and Kathy nose to nose at breakfast, knee to knee at lunch. If she hadn't been so wretched over Michael, she probably wouldn't have cared; but maybe Colin could provide a bracing antidote to both gloating Rob and heartless, busy Michael.

Rob and Michael were often in her thoughts at once – the two of them stark naked. She somehow couldn't stop comparing them: Rob slender, skinny, hairless, with a slender skinny prick to match; Michael brawny and hirsute, his cock thicker and more squat. She could hardly believe two men could be so different – Rob a timid moped, puttering safely through the side-streets; Michael a brute black Harley-Davidson roaring up the fast lane of the motorway. Rob had never kissed what Michael called her fuzz-pie, and even when he kissed her breasts he did it very tentatively – as if he had been presented with some foreign dish which must be briefly sampled (if only from good manners), before he moved on to the main course. Michael, on the other hand, relished every course; approached each treat and delicacy with a connoisseur's delight, and had transformed a simple country picnic into an epicurean feast.

She turned in at the college entrance, her mind shifting from marshmallow-breast and fuzz-pie to mortarboards and gowns; suddenly aware of all the big shots who had stepped through this same door, from John Wyclif to John Schlesinger. The first time she'd come to Balliol, she'd felt their presence as an inspiration, a challenge, but today she was depressed by it, as if they were lions and unicorns, she a puny goat. The fact that Michael had ditched her – tucked into her just once, then spat her out like gristle – made it still more obvious that she would never fulfil his expectations. She was not in the same league, not a natural goddess who could play consort to his god. Her minor part in the college play should have taught her where she stood. She and Colin had each had a scant dozen lines, which had forged something of a bond between them like their modest (crummy) homes and working mothers.

She touched his arm a moment, wanting to express that bond, make it real and tangible. 'Listen, Colin, if you like, I could rustle up some supper in my room. I'm afraid it'll be something pretty basic, but at least we won't have to queue.'

'Great!' said Colin, looking surprised and pleased at once, his blue eyes fixed on hers. He had stopped outside the post-room, and now gestured to the door. 'Mind if I check my pigeonhole first? I'm expecting a note from my tutor.'

'No, go ahead.' Tessa checked hers, too, discarding all the usual bumph about societies and meetings, Christian rallies, political crusades, appeals for cash and time. There was just one letter for her in a stiff white envelope, which must have been delivered by hand, since she'd already scoured her pigeonhole after both the morning posts. She ripped it open, stared at the two words dashed off in splodgy ink: 'Phone me.' Nothing else, except an impatient, drunken 'M', and an Oxford number jotted underneath. She could hardly hold the letter, her fingers numb, as if the paper were a sheet of ice which had frozen her whole hand. Colin, still riffling through his mail, suddenly looked up at her, his face registering alarm.

'What's wrong?'

She shook her head, her voice and throat immobilized as well.

'Tessa, what's the matter? You look as if you've seen a ghost.'

'Nothing.' She forced the word out, forced her lips to work. 'I've . . . got to make a phone call.'

'It's not bad news, I hope?'

'No. Just . . . unexpected.'

'Would you prefer to call the party off? We don't have to go if you'd rather . . .'

'I'm not too sure.'

'Tell you what – I'll wait for you in my room. You make your call, then come up and tell me how things are, and we'll take it from there – okay? We can always skip the supper, or grab a bite en route.'

'All right. But you go on, though. I need a sec to think things out.'

'Are you sure you're okay? I mean, can't I help or – ?'

'No, honestly. I'm fine. See you in ten minutes.' She stood watching him drift off, too anxious to exult. Michael might have ordered her to ring him simply to tell her it was over, to confirm his weeks of silence, make the break official. It *was* an order, wasn't it – that terse and lordly 'Phone me'? She unfolded the letter again, hoping it might have changed, expanded to three pages of contrite explanation, plus some ardent, grateful outpourings about their Saturday together and how he'd thought of nothing else, despite his illness, or his mother's fall, or his summons to a funeral at the other end of England, or . . .

No. Just half a line.

How dared he take that tone, leave her high and dry for twenty days, then insult her with two words? She damned well wasn't going to phone. Let him stew! She'd go back to her room instead, tart up in her favourite dress, dazzle Colin, seduce the Irish poets.

Anger seemed to empower her feet, release her from inertia. She raced across the quad, hurtled up the stairs, tugged her clothes off, washed and changed in minutes. She dug out some dangly earrings, squirted perfume on her wrists, then frowned at her appearance in the mirror. Her hair was greasy, badly needed trimming, the fringe so long it was falling in her eyes; the eyes themselves shadowed by dark circles. Both were Michael's fault. He'd prevented her from sleeping, made her too despondent to bother with trivia like haircuts. She tied a bandeau round her head, scooped her hair on top, tried to fix it firmly in place with clips and coloured combs. At least it looked flamboyant, if not exactly soignée. She darted down the stairs again, stood dithering at the bottom. She'd totally forgotten to ask Colin where his room was, would have to trek back to the porter's lodge to find out.

'Staircase eleven, room fourteen. And you look very smart tonight.'

'Thanks,' she said, fiddling with a swathe of hair which had already come adrift. Paul was her favourite porter, often paid her compliments.

'Going somewhere special?'

'Yes,' she grinned. 'The Naked Lunch Society.'

'Rather you than me. It's too late for lunch and too cold for stripping off. But have a good time, anyway.'

'I will.'

She jogged back the way she'd come. Staircase fourteen was the one right next to hers, though she had never noticed Colin coming out of it. Nice that they were neighbours. She must work at the relationship, not let herself be led astray by trivial things like height, or carroty hair. And talking of hair, she could phone the salon now. They worked late on Friday evenings. Maybe they could fit her in tomorrow; then, if Colin asked her out again, or planned something for this weekend, at least he wouldn't mistake her for what her mother called a 'Dulux dog'.

She ran on to the JCR, where there were two phones in the basement; sorted through her purse for change. Three tens should be ample, even if they kept her hanging on. She dialled the number, listened to the ringing-tone shrilling, shrilling, shrilling. It sounded peevish and indignant – seemed to be reproaching her for troubling busy people. She was about to put the receiver down when a male voice answered, one she didn't know.

'Yes, hello?' it said abruptly.

Her own hello was softer, more or less inaudible. She swallowed, tried again. Her hands were clammy, her whole stomach somersaulting.

'I want to speak to Dr Michael Edwards. Is he there?'

6

'CHRIST! TRISTRAM, WHAT was going on? You look completely pissed.'

'I *was* completely pissed! That was our last day. See Jo there in the corner? She stripped down to her birthday-suit and tried to have it off with a campy Greek waiter who was more interested in boys.'

'He wasn't,' Jo protested, snatching back the photograph. 'And I only took my top off – nothing else.'

'Wait!' yelled Peter. 'I haven't seen it yet. Is that Michael in the hat?'

'No, Michael wasn't there. He was lying down in a darkened room, recovering from the night before.'

'Balls!' retorted Michael, ripping open a packet of nuts and pouring them down his throat like coals down a chute. 'I'll have you know I was reading a good book.'

'What, *Tropic of Cancer*?' Peter asked sardonically.

'No, *Winnie the Pooh*.'

They all laughed, save for Tessa. She felt totally excluded from this group of bantering medics, half of whom had just returned from a holiday in Greece – windsurfing in Vassiliki. Their tanned and glowing faces, Michael's in particular, had reduced her to a silent, seething fury. She'd been imagining him on his sick-bed, feverish and pale, or grim-faced at his mother's grave, or coping single-handed with some emergency at the hospital, taking over from a stricken colleague, renouncing food and sleep in order to save lives. And instead he'd been larking in the sun, skimming over rumbustious waves beneath a Cambridge-blue sky, or drinking himself silly with a bunch of naked nurses. She glanced round the room again, still hadn't got their names straight. Jo was the brunette and Jennifer the dumpy one, but that leggy blonde reclining on the sofa – who was she, for God's sake? Michael's new goddess, the girl he'd sipped and guzzled on some deserted Ionian beach, or rescued when she'd fallen off her surf-board? Peter was still pawing her, but that didn't mean a thing. Girls seemed interchangeable in this haphazard Headington flat.

The flat itself had shocked her – the clutter and the mess, dirty dishes piling up, clothes flung on the floor, beer spilt on the carpet, cigarette-burns on the once attractive furniture. Even now, Jo was using a pot-plant as an ashtray, and Tristram struggling to peel an orange with neither knife nor plate, juice spurting everywhere. He was the one who planned to do obstetrics, though she shuddered to think of him delivering vulnerable babies with that dirty scruff of beard, which barely hid the acne on his chin. Nobody had mentioned patients, and when they'd talked about the hospital, it had been mainly to complain, Michael more than any of them. He'd been ranting on about social workers ('cretinous and meddling'), GPs ('second-rate dropouts opting for an easy life'), psychiatrists ('all bonkers') and geriatricians ('more half-dead than their patients – need pensioning off en masse'). The only doctor he admired was his own consultant, the famous Thomas Thornton, who, apparently, could do no wrong. Tessa was beginning to feel as jealous of Sir Thomas as she was of the blonde goddess, especially now that Michael had steered the conversation from sea and surf back to blood and guts.

'I was in theatre with him yesterday, and he stitched in a valve in less time than it takes old Braithwaite to scrub up. He's a real virtuoso, with this incredible technique. And you'd never believe . . .'

Tessa switched off, took refuge in her orange juice. She had refused the beer and wine, having already drunk more than enough with Colin – nearly killed herself cycling up Headington Hill an hour or so ago. She should have stayed with Colin, not told him all those lies; might be letting her hair down at that party on the barge, instead of sitting like a lemon with a group of virtual strangers. Even Michael seemed a stranger, using terminology she couldn't understand, and still extolling the skills of his boss.

'I don't know whether you realize, Tristram, but he's pioneering a method of repairing aortic aneurysms with material from a donor-bank of human tissue, rather than using gortex. The implications are mind-blowing, especially for congenital heart disorders. And you should have seen him yesterday! He had this impossible septal defect, which no one else would touch, and he simply . . .'

'Cut the crap, Michael,' Tristram interrupted, swallowing one last orange-segment, before wiping his hands on his creased and baggy trousers. 'You talk as if you spend all day in theatre. I've only been three times in five weeks. Most of the time I'm slaving on the wards, taking endless boring bloods and endless boring histories, and so are you, if only you'd admit it, instead of trying to convince Tessa here that you're Thornton's second-in-command.'

Tessa looked up in surprise, noticed Michael flush; his dark brows shuttering down over piqued defensive eyes. Certainly he had given the impression that he spent at least half his time with a scalpel in his hand, or conferring with Sir Thomas over their latest joint emergency.

'*And* we're paid a pittance,' Peter interjected. 'A friend of mine went straight from school into a job in advertising, and he's living like a king now. *I've* trained for bloody years, and still can't face my bank manager.'

Tristram spat out an orange pip, flicked it on the floor. 'And no doubt your advertising friend pigs himself silly every day on expense-account lunches at some gourmet restaurant, while we poor glorified ward-clerks are lucky if we find the time to grab a roll and butter in the hospital canteen.'

Tessa felt still more confused. Was Michael just a ward-clerk instead of an up-and-coming surgeon, and how could he earn a pittance when he drove that flashy car, indulged in four-course breakfasts at luxurious hotels, and had just returned from what sounded like a pretty pricey holiday in Greece? Perhaps his doting mother gave him an allowance – a bonus for an archangel – or he had private means, or . . . ? There was so much she longed to know, so many conversations they hadn't had – might never have, if he was always so elusive. He had scarcely said a word to her this evening – well, nothing really personal or meaningful, just asked her a few vague questions about what she'd been doing with herself since they last met. She could hardly confess that her every waking thought had been focused on his absence, so she'd prattled on about Eights Week and all the college bops and parties; let him think she'd been living it up, as *he* had. She should never have phoned him in the first place, let alone dropped everything and come racing round the minute she'd heard his vintage-claret voice. She felt completely out of her depth – a naive and awkward student among a bunch of cool professionals, who had salaries (however low), experience, commitments, patients in their care. She was also overdressed, dolled up in her glad rags, while they wore casual gear – or uniform in Jo's case.

She glanced across at Michael, who was wearing red tonight, a brilliant scarlet sweater, which clashed with his red wine, emphasized his suntan, set off his dark hair. He made Colin look anaemic – pasty-faced, unhealthy. And yet Colin had been a tower of strength, offering instant help in her 'emergency' – could he lend her money, or make her tea before she left? – support and comfort, in return for craven lies.

The tall blonde suddenly erupted from the sofa, tugging her brief mini over bronzed and shapely legs. 'Sorry to break up the happy party, but Pete and I simply must push off. We're meeting Roger in the pub, and we're frightfully late already. Why don't you all come too?'

'Good idea!' said Michael. 'We're running low on booze here, and I could do with something to eat.'

'I'm on nights, so count me out,' groaned Jo. 'Though I wish to God I was back on that Greek island, with nothing to do but laze in the sun and . . .'

'And take your clothes off,' Tristram grinned.

'Oh, don't start that again. Will I ever live it down?'

'No,' said Jennifer. 'You won't. And we'd better put our clothes *on*. It may be hot in Vassiliki, but it's freezing cold in Headington. Just listen to that rain!'

'Tessa, where's your coat?' Michael shook the last few peanuts from the bottom of the bag, then licked the salty crumbs up from his palm.

'Outside.'

'I'll fetch it. The pub's only round the corner, but you don't want to get drowned.'

She followed him into the hall, so she could inform him *sotto voce* that she didn't plan to join them, would cycle back to college, catch up with some work.

'But you've only just arrived.' He swung round to face her, obviously put out. 'I've got loads and loads to tell you.'

'If you mean about your holiday, I think I've got the gist already.'

'What's that supposed to mean?'

'Listen, Michael, you might at least have mentioned the fact that you'd be away for several weeks.'

'Ten days. And if we're going to argue, I suggest we do it in private, rather than embarrass all my friends.' He strode into his bedroom, pulled her after him, then slammed the door behind them both.

She leaned against the wall, keeping a safe distance from the bed, and trying to sound reasonable, controlled. 'Never mind how many days. That's not the point at issue. You completely disappeared, without a . . .'

'I sent a postcard – two, in fact – one of a taverna near our villa, and one of the whole bay.'

'How odd. They never arrived.'

'Are you calling me a liar?'

'No, I'm merely saying that I didn't get your cards – or any hint or warning that you'd be away at all. The last thing you told me was . . .'

There was a sudden hammering at the door, a hail of shouts and catcalls, as the others trooped out into the hall – was Michael bloody coming, and could he get a move on, they hadn't got all night.

Michael changed his voice to breezy, shouted through the door. 'We'll join you in the pub, okay? We've got a spot of business first.' He grimaced at the inevitable taunts about the nature of their 'business', then sat down on the bed, his tone now petulant. 'Look, I *couldn't* tell you, Tessa – there simply wasn't time. It was all a spur-of-the-moment thing. Tristram had organized this villa party with Joshua and Pam and a few other bods we know, but I wasn't all that keen myself, told him to count me out. Then one of the group cried off, just a day or two before the flight, and there was a bloody great kerfuffle about finding a replacement, preferably a guy, to keep the numbers equal – all that sort of crap, so in the end I let them talk me round. I was damned lucky in a way. It's usually a problem getting locums at short notice, if you decide to go away without planning it in advance. But I knew this fifth-year student who was almost begging on his hind legs for the experience. So he was happy, I was happy, and . . .'

'And *I* was quite delirious.'

'There's no need to be sarcastic.'

'I feel sarcastic. Can't you see that I was worried?'

He shrugged. 'I assumed you'd got my cards.'

'Perhaps you forgot to post the blasted cards. They're probably basking in the sun, or lying in a darkened room, recovering.'

He grabbed her by the wrists, almost shook her in exasperation.

'Listen, woman, never mind the cards! The posts are lousy anyway, and half of Greece is usually on strike. What's important is I missed you – thought about you every fucking day. Why the hell d'you think I phoned you the minute I got back?'

'Tristram said you got back a week ago.'

'Christ Almighty, Tessa, I do have a job, you know.' He let her go, sank down on the bed.

'Okay, okay, you're busy. I understand.'

'I wonder if you do? I've worked a hundred and seven hours since our plane touched down last Thursday. The weekend was so pressured, any good the holiday did was entirely cancelled out. I came close to cracking up, if you really want to know. We kicked off on Saturday morning with an emergency at eight – a guy with multiple stab-wounds which only just missed the heart – then we had a slow death in intensive care, and by Sunday midnight we were still admitting patients for Monday's list. And for that marathon stint I actually earned less per hour than the bloody hospital cleaners. *They* get time and a half on Sundays, while we poor suckers are only entitled to a third of our usual rate. Anyway, I won't bore you with the horrors of the system. I can see it doesn't interest you.'

'Look, it does, of course it does. It's just that . . .'

Her voice was swamped as he continued with his outburst; face now turned away from her, hands yanking at the duvet. 'This is the first sodding day I've had time to get my breath back, and what do I do but brave that lousy traffic in the town, to leave a note at Balliol for some ungrateful bloody bitch who accuses me of lying.' He thrust his fingers through his hair, then let his back and shoulders droop, as if he'd suddenly lost heart, had no more powers of argument.

The silence in the room seemed a more vehement reproach than the fury of his tirade. She rubbed her wrists, which were hurting still; edged towards the bed. 'I'm sorry, Michael, honestly. I missed you too – a lot.'

'Did you? I'm surprised. You sound as if you've hardly had the time.'

'What d'you mean?'

'Well, Eights Week and your college ball, and all those trendy parties. Even if I'd been kneeling at your feet, would you really have been able to tear yourself away?'

'Oh, I'd have fitted you in somehow,' she said airily, relishing the fact that even the swaggering Michael Edwards could be jealous. 'Why don't you kneel now?'

'Kneel to a woman? You must be joking. *You* kneel.'

'No!'

'Go on.'

'Why should I? You were the one who suggested it.'

'Okay, let's both kneel. We'll kneel to one another.'

They subsided to their knees at exactly the same moment, Michael watching Tessa warily, as if frightened she might cheat. A yard or two of carpet stretched between them, a dingy pinkish carpet, patterned with blowzy flowers. Again at the same moment, they began walking on their knees, one towards the other. Their mouths met first, and joined. The kiss was very slow. Everything was slow – his hand sauntering down her throat towards her breasts; the drone of a car dawdling past the house; his stealthy tongue loitering in her mouth, gliding over her teeth, nudging at her lips. It was so different from the picnic. He seemed to be treating her as fragile, something precious which might break. Yet she felt as strong as Magog, empowered by the delirious fact that he still wanted her, desired her, had thought about her 'every fucking day', fought traffic jams and downpours to leave a note for her in college. And it wasn't simply words. The proof was his great corduroy erection, champing at her groin, the corrugated velvet chafing through her dress.

'I'm boiling,' she whispered, shrinking back from the clutches of his sweater, which seemed to be mumbling her as well with its fuzzy scarlet tongue.

'So am I.'

They caught each other's eye; burst out laughing for no reason they could think of, except the absurdity of still having all their clothes on. She unzipped her dress, pulled it off, while he eased the tight-necked jersey over his head.

'The suntan really suits you, Michael. How far does it go down?'

'Not around my bum, alas. They're still surprisingly strict in Greece. Even topless is forbidden, let alone bottomless.'

'We're not in Greece,' she challenged, hand moving to his belt. She helped him slide his cords down; the mahogany tan dulling to light caramel on the private strip between his navel and his groin. Shouldn't he be paler there – almost white, as he had been at the picnic? She could see him lying in the lecherous Vassiliki sun, as naked as the sultry blonde beside him, her thatch a platinum candyfloss, with Michael's hand exploring it. Dr Michael Edwards didn't obey pettifogging rules about sunbathing with nothing on, or screwing randy nurses.

She suddenly pushed him to the floor, climbed on top, skewering herself on his traitorous tanned prick, then thwacking hard against him, building up an angry lunging rhythm. He immediately picked up the rhythm; his prick so deep inside her, it seemed to be anchored like a limpet, so that he was butting every fold and crevice, every hidden cranny. Neither said a word. She hadn't energy to speak; needed all her stamina to keep slamming, circling, slamming; he following every movement, like her shadow or her double.

She leaned right back, hands stretched out behind her and taking all her weight; knees hurting and uncomfortable, pressed down on the floor. The pain was nothing, lost in fiercer pleasure. He was now reaching forward to slick her with a finger, and the two matched but different probings – one shallow and one deep – were creating an unbearable momentum, in which she must either explode or stop. She arched even further back, so that there was more of her to touch, felt his finger slip inside, almost to its hilt; knead and fret, like a second, smaller prick. She was crying out for him to stop, with great yammering choking gasps, but the word 'stop' meant nothing, nothing, and suddenly all the wild sensations clashed and seethed together, and she slumped forward on his chest, still whimpering and pleading, 'Stop stop stop stop stop!'

'Christ! I love your comes, Tessa. You make such a marvellous racket. You must have woken the whole village, including all the corpses in the graveyard.'

She laughed, still half-ashamed, and uncramping all her limbs now, stretching like a cat. '*You* didn't come, though.'

'How could I, when you kept yelling out "Stop! Stop!"?'

'I really meant "Go on!"'

'Crazy girl.'

'I'm sorry.'

'Don't be sorry. It was pretty damned fantastic. You felt incredible, you know – all plumped up and moist inside, and sort of closing round me like a demented sea anemone.'

She turned over on her side, hand ruffling his dark pubic hair. 'But you're still stiff.'

'So what?'

'Well, shouldn't we . . . ?'

'In a while – no rush. Let's lie down on the bed. This floor's too bloody hard.'

'I haven't got the strength to move.'

'So shall I pick you up?'

'No fear!'

Michael struggled to his feet, grabbed his sheepskin coat, which lay crumpled in a corner – looked as if it had been left there since May Morning. 'Here, lie on this. The carpet's filthy dirty.' He laid it fleece side up, rolled her gently on to it, sprawled out again beside her.

'It's all tickly,' she observed, taking hold of one of the sleeves and stroking it against her breasts to contrast the two textures.

'Does that turn you on?' he asked, obviously intrigued.

'Mm . . . It does a bit.' She yawned indulgently, spread her arms and legs apart, luxuriating in the softness of the fur. The clips had fallen from her hair, which was escaping from the bandeau, tumbling round her shoulders. She tugged the headband off, tossed it on to Michael's naked chest. He picked it up, wound it tightly round his prick, as if to keep it still erect.

'You're beautiful like that,' he said. 'All heavy and shagged out, and showing everything you've got. No – don't close your legs. I want to take a look.' He knelt up on the floor, spread her thighs again, both hands reaching down. 'You've got these quite amazing labia, which stick out like little wings – except they're almost hidden by this wild and woolly fuzz. What a bush! Look – it even strays halfway up your stomach.'

'Yes, I know. I hate that.' She made a face, tried to push his hand off. 'You're meant to use these creams and things to strip the straggly hairs off, tidy it all up.'

'You dare! If you don't like it, turn over on your front.'

She heaved over, closed her eyes, whacked but cock-a-hoop. All the things she disliked about her body, Michael seemed to cherish. This morning she had felt a mess – lumpen, plain and stupid – now she was voluptuous, and probably a genius. She especially loved the way he'd been with her in her come – not a separate being, distanced and apart, but participating, merging, so that every move or noise she'd made had been somehow his as well. Always before, she'd felt frustrated and depressed that however close you were to someone, there were still barriers and boundaries, demarcation lines you couldn't cross. She had never managed to slip out of her skin and merge with Rob or Gavin, so that they'd become one flesh, one soul. But Michael broke through barriers, ripped off separate skins.

Suddenly she tensed. His finger had edged between her buttocks and was exploring that intensely private part of her which even Michael mustn't touch, which nobody had ever touched, which was totally proscribed.

'Relax,' he urged. 'You're so tight I can't get in – not even with a finger.'

'No, not there. I . . .' It was difficult to speak. Her bottom was humped up, her voice muffled by the sheepskin, and he was now using not his finger, but his tongue. The sensations were extraordinary – the hot tongue sidling in, lapping round the rigid ring of muscle, trying to expand it, force it to release a little, then boring further in. She had never associated that area with pleasure, only with locked doors, bad smells, crude jokes. But the pleasure was exquisite, almost indescribable. And now his bristles had come into play as well, rasping at her skin; the tiny stroppy prickles magnified to rapiers as they snagged and scoured against her. She was crying out again, no longer saying 'no'; no longer saying anything, but making high shrill noises, eyes screwed up, hands clenched. She heard a plane rumbling overhead, the windows shaking as the noise accelerated – booming, roaring, blotting out her own cry, then dying down down down, as she too sagged, subsided.

'You timed that well,' said Michael, sinking back himself. 'Pretty powerful sound-effects.'

She kept her face pressed against the coat, didn't want to look at him, or joke. What he had done was incredibly important – accepted her in total, no part of her too intimate to be labelled out of bounds. Even her liberal mother could be coy about the 'dirt-chute', but Michael had abolished all idea of dirt, all crudity and shame.

'Are you all right?' he asked. 'I didn't hurt you, did I? I restrained myself deliberately, only used a finger. But once you've loosened up a bit . . .' He laughed and slapped her rump. 'God, Tessa, the things we're going to do together! We're made for one another, d'you know that?'

Yes, she whispered silently. I do.

'I'd better have a wash,' he said. 'And I think we need a drink – a very long and cold one. Be an angel, will you, and rustle up something from the fridge.'

73

'Okay.' She sat up slowly, shook her tousled hair back. 'But could I borrow a dressing-gown?'

'What for? We're on our own. And I like to see your ass bare, and all that marvellous flesh, the way it slightly ripples as you move.'

'But supposing all your friends barge in?'

'They won't. Only Josh and Tristram live here. Josh is still on duty, right through to the morning, and once Tristram's got his bum on a banquette and a Guinness in his fist, he won't be back till closing-time. Actually, I wouldn't mind a beer myself, though I bet he's scoffed the lot. See if you can find some juice. The kitchen's two doors down. Ice in the freezer, glasses in the sink. You'll have to wash some up.'

It seemed strange washing glasses in the buff, and she could see her naked breasts reflected in the window-pane. The nipples were erect still, as if awaiting their next course. It astonished her that Michael hadn't come yet, seemed intent on thrilling her, rather than snatching his own pleasure, then losing interest, sloping off. 'The things we're going to do together,' she repeated to herself. 'We're made for one another.' She could see a picture in her mind of some snowy-bearded God, creating not Adam and Eve, but Michael and Tessa; shaping their voluptuous limbs and wild dark matching hair from a speck of dust and spittle, then leaving them to play, naked and for ever, in a garden full of passion-flowers.

She was almost surprised to see a tea towel in her hands instead of lotus or hibiscus – and a very grubby tea towel, fraying at the hem. Michael and his fellow doctors were clearly neither natural cooks nor cleaners. There was more dirt around than food, and all she could find in the battered though capacious fridge was a half-empty carton of orange-juice, three tomatoes and a hunk of mousetrap cheese. The freezer part was encrusted, frozen solid, so that she had to chip the ice trays out with an egg-slice and a knife – cold work, with nothing on.

'I think I need a hot drink after that,' she grinned, brushing ice-strands off her breasts, as Michael sauntered through the door, swathed only in a towel.

'Help yourself. We've even got some decent coffee – or we did have yesterday.'

'A common or garden tea-bag will do fine.'

'In that yellow jar there, right next to the kettle. Actually, we should be drinking champagne! I haven't told you yet, but I've got

74

this marvellous job – the two-year rotation at Newcastle. I kick off with a six-month stint in casualty, then for the following six months I'll be working for a brilliant bloke who's moved up there from Bart's – a real whizz who's in the news a lot, and has just brought out the latest tome on prosthetic valve replacements. And the rest of the time, I'll be doing general surgery in their brand-new theatre suite. It's an extremely big catchment area, so I'll get every sort of case – not just all the routine stuff like hernias or appendectomies.'

Tessa slumped down on a kitchen stool. The only word she'd really heard was 'Newcastle', which was the other end of England, almost into Scotland, an eternity away. She could see the map unfolding in her mind, the mocking miles of motorway stretching on for ever. Even the coach fare would eat into her grant, be more or less impossible to raise.

'I'll be madly busy, swotting for my fellowship, as well as coping with the job itself – which is why I'm glad I'm starting off in casualty. You see, it works on a shift system with a one-in-four rota, and that means far less extra unpaid work and a more structured sort of day. In *this* job, we're all over the place and can't make definite plans, but up there it should be easier, because when we're off we're off.'

He plugged in the kettle, then poured himself some juice. 'I must admit I'm relieved. I'll need that time for flicking through my text-books and getting the old neurones back in shape. They also give us study-leave and . . .'

Fine, thought Tessa, wonderful – three hundred miles between us, and his precious new free time already earmarked for revision, rather than for her.

Michael dropped an ice cube, scooped it from the floor into his glass. 'Tristram's got a job as an anatomy demonstrator at Guy's, which gives him practically half each day free. He keeps telling me what a fool I am, going straight for a surgical rotation. The first part of the new fellowship exam is pretty bloody tough, you see, so we're all a bit het up. But in my opinion he's the fool – wasting a whole year – besides the fact that a demonstrator's job is boring boring boring. I'll be in the thick of things, involved with real live bodies, not cutting up corpses. Hold on! The kettle's boiling. Bung a tea-bag in that mug and I'll fill it up. Sorry there's no milk. It was Tristram's turn to buy it, but the lazy sod forgot as usual. Sugar's in the bag there. Shove some extra in, to make up for the milk. Right – you can toast me in Typhoo now.'

'Congratulations!' she stuttered out, then did her best to concentrate while Michael expanded on the advantages of Newcastle – the cardiothoracic centre (which offered the widest range of treatments in the entire United Kingdom); the wealth of other experience he'd get in general surgery; the first-rate teaching, the buildings, the equipment; the beauty of the countryside, almost on their doorstep. 'It sounds great,' she faltered lamely – that countryside so far away, it seemed out of focus, blurred in chilly mist. Yet Michael had edged closer, slid an arm around her shoulder, while he moved on to the details of his work in A & E – the hours he'd be on duty, the convenient closeness of the motorway, which would hurl car-crash victims straight into his arms.

'When do you actually start?' she asked, recoiling from the pile-ups, and examining instead the way the hair grew on his chest. It seemed a waste of his bare body to have it pressing close while his whole attention was on CT scans and ventilators.

'August the first. And I won't get finished here till the fucking night before. The system's bloody bonkers! Theoretically, one contract ends at midnight on July the thirty-first, and the next one starts at eight the following morning. And I've got to pack up all my gear, drive two hundred and fifty miles, and then clock on, bright-eyed and bushy-tailed, at Newcastle bloody General. As for sleep, forget it!'

She tried her best to sympathize, but continued to be distracted by his nakedness, his dark and tangled pelt. The hair was longer on his chest, curly on his stomach, more downy on his back, though with a rougher swatch just across his shoulders. His pubic hair was darker still, a black impenetrable thicket, which seemed to call attention to his prick, insist she looked at it.

He noticed the direction of her gaze, steered her hand there too. 'Hey! Why don't you come up with me – spend a week or two up north? I get a hospital flat, and no one knows or cares whether I bring a friend to share it. I'll be up to my eyes – that's the crazy system – but if we choose a time when I'm not on nights, at least we can make up for it in bed. And there'll be loads for you to do while I'm on duty. I know people say Newcastle's a dump, but there are some very decent bookshops, and half a dozen cinemas, and several theatres, including the Theatre Royal, which even puts on Shakespeare when it's not awash in musicals . . .'

Tessa wasn't listening. Who cared about the Theatre Royal, when she would have Michael to herself in bed? She'd be living in his flat, part of his new life, there when he got back each evening. All the different images were swarming in her head – she and Michael making love from dusk to reeling dawn, breakfasting together, hiking in the Cheviots, driving to the open pounding sea. She flung her arms around his neck, kissed his face all over. 'Oh yes, yes, yes – yes, *please.*'

He laughed. 'So I'm to take it you approve of the idea?'

She nodded. 'Approve' was a paraplegic word, a feeble car-crash victim. 'Adore' would be more accurate – exulting, crowing, sending up a fifty-gun salute. He had mentioned just a week or two, but couldn't she extend it, make herself indispensable, an asset, an attraction which he couldn't do without? Her second year at Oxford didn't start till mid-October, so she'd be free of any ties. Even her mother wasn't expecting her, since she'd planned to stay in Juxon Street for most of the vacation. They had to pay the rent there from the beginning of July, whether they actually took up residence or not, so she'd more or less decided to get a job in Oxford and avoid the disadvantages of home – the intrusive noisy lodgers, the constant mess and clutter, and having to play gooseberry to a canoodling Ken and April. According to her mother's letters, the romance was blossoming. She was happy for their sakes, but now she had the chance to cultivate her own romance, a world away from that cramped and dreary semi in a soulless suburban street.

She should be able to get a job in Newcastle – waitressing, or bar work, or maybe even coaching. She'd have to earn enough to pay her Oxford rent, but there were no other major outlays. Michael had his car, which would save the expense of fares, and he'd probably buy the food. She could pay him back in lots of ways – transform his flat, for instance. She'd always been good at making things artistic, and a hospital flat in Newcastle was bound to need a face-lift, if not the kiss of life. Perhaps he'd invite her each vacation, come to need her there. The Oxford terms were only eight weeks long, which meant she had twenty-eight free weeks a year – six months to spend with Michael. She glanced around his kitchen. It no longer looked so slovenly. She'd been far too harsh and critical, ignored the high ceilings, the basic fine proportions of the house; dwelling on its shortcomings because she was angry with its tenant. She drained her tea, toasting not just Michael now, but the two of them together, in their new life, new flat, new roles.

Michael tipped the last few drops of orange-juice directly from the carton into his mouth. 'Another thing I plan to do is take up parachuting. A mate of mine has been doing accelerated free-fall at this marvellous place in Alnwick, which is spitting distance from Newcastle. He's always raving on about it – how he's learning turns and back-loops, and jumping from twelve thousand feet – so I thought I'd have a bash myself. I don't know whether it turns you on, but we could try a weekend course together.'

She stared at him, incredulous. Parachuting seemed as exotic, as astounding, as forming a new colony or hunting unicorns, and way beyond her means. It was the sort of hobby Charlotte might take up, subsidized by 'Daddy'. Michael must mean *he* would pay; knew she had no money of her own.

'But how will you find time?' she asked, still not daring to believe it might actually come true. Michael's leisure was as rationed as her cash.

'I'll make time. And anyway, I'll need a break from slogging – something really different which gets the old adrenalin going.'

She spread her arms out like a bird, went flapping round the room, too hyped up to keep still. Parachuting seemed the perfect symbol for the way her life was taking off. She was flying high, winging to new places, spiralling and soaring, defying gravity. 'Oh, Michael,' she exclaimed, pretending to crash-land at his feet. 'I can hardly wait!'

'Well, we've still got a bit of free-fall to catch up with in the bedroom, but if you keep bopping round like that, with those marvellous bouncy tits of yours jiggling up and down, I won't be able to wait myself, and I'll shoot my load all over the kitchen floor.' He removed his towel, thrust his pelvis forward in a body-builder's pose. 'See what an effect you have?'

She sheathed his erection in both her hands, excited by the way it twitched and swelled beneath them; seemed another, separate Michael, as hot-blooded as its owner.

'Quick!' he urged. 'Tea-break's over.'

He pulled her into the bedroom, leaned against the wall, legs apart and braced. 'Kneel on the floor between my feet. No – you're not quite high enough. Fetch a couple of pillows and kneel on those. That's it.'

She was aware that he was bossing her, but was willing to obey – happy to do anything now she knew they'd be together.

'Edge in a bit closer, and rub your nipple up and down my prick. Fantastic! Now the underside, along that little puckered seam there.

78

God! It feels exquisite, very cool and light. Now try to push the nipple into the tiny little opening in the tip. I love that – it's a turn-on. Are you all right? You're looking a bit off.'

She nodded, steered her nipple back into the slit. She wasn't 'off', just amazed at all the different things two people could do. And it needed concentration, to keep penis-tip and nipple in close contact, to make sure the pressure was just right – deep, but very light.

'Don't stop. It's magic! You're a natural, Tessa, honestly. I could come like this, you know. Except I won't. I'm saving that for later.'

She squashed both breasts together, made her cleavage into a second cunt, so he could butt and thrust between them. It was strange to see his prick so close, to watch its every movement, instead of it being out of sight, submerged. Suddenly, it was moving to her mouth, and he was leaning down to cup his balls, push them right against her lips. 'Try these,' he said. 'They're rather good to eat.'

She kept her mouth tight shut, felt daunted and uneasy. They looked so ugly – large and lumpy, streaked with coarse dark hairs. Yet how could she refuse, when he'd kissed every part of her? She closed her eyes, tried to do as he directed; slide the left one into her mouth, hold it very gently there, as if it were a bird's egg and she mustn't break its shell; then knead it with her lips.

'That's wonderful, stupendous! Now try to get them both in.'

She tried and gagged; was terrified of choking, didn't like the taste and feel of these very foreign bodies in her mouth; the tangled hairs rough against her tongue; the flesh saggy and yet bloated, both at the same time. But she had to admit it gave her a real sense of power to see him so aroused, hear his sudden exclamations, as he praised her skills, her body, told her she must have been a courtesan in another, earlier life.

His prick was swelling, preening, nudging right against her face, begging for its turn. She could no longer ignore it, though she was sure her mouth would be too small, that it would cram and swamp the confining space, and still insist on more. Already, she was retching as it plunged against her throat.

'Keep going! It's quite brilliant. But use your teeth. Bite hard.'

She was thrown by his demand. The sex-books all advised you to be gentle, to shield your teeth behind your lips, not to bite at all; warned you how you could hurt a man, how sensitive he was.

'Harder! You won't hurt me. I can scarcely feel it yet. Yes – better – even more.'

She used her teeth more fiercely, shrugging off the sex-books. Why not play the role of courtesan, the one she'd been in a former wilder life? Delilah wouldn't gag, would relax her throat, breathe deeply. And Jezebel would enjoy herself, not keep worrying and holding back, doubting her own skills. Why not savour the experience of him filling her whole mouth, the strange taste of his prick – part salty, part stale pee; his wild intoxication, as he lunged and shouted out? He must be coming, surely, when he'd reached such fever pitch. She had never had a man come in her mouth, but Delilah wouldn't spit him out; would encourage him, suck harder, focus on his pleasure, not on her own fears.

He suddenly whipped out, pulled her to her feet, and half-carried her towards the bed. 'Lie down on your back,' he ordered. He immediately slammed in, kneeling up above her. 'Put your feet up on my shoulders – yes, right around my neck.'

She felt him lock in deeper, as she raised her legs, arched her pelvis up. He laughed, swept all her hair back. 'You great lascivious thing, you, shimmying like that! You *were* a whore – that's certain – probably at the court of Cleopatra.'

He could no longer talk, was thrusting far too furiously, then wrenching out again; sliding down her body, replacing his wild prick with his even wilder mouth. She remembered the sensations from the picnic, except this time they were fiercer still, and she was crying out, grimacing, about to come herself, when he forced back in once more, now pressing down on top of her, his thighs heavy on her own. He rode her for a moment, sweaty-hot and spurring, then abruptly changed position, again alternating prick with mouth. The two were very different – prick bludgeoning, mouth lapping – though she barely had a chance to delight in one, adjust to it, before he switched again, building up a crazy double rhythm, which skirled to a crescendo.

'Come on, come on!' he shouted. 'Come *with* me, Tessa. Now!'

She hardly heard the words. She had turned into an animal, one which clawed and bellowed, one which shook its mane, reared up.

'Oh, beautiful!' he shouted. 'Oh darling darling darling! You amazing greedy slut. I love you. I adore you. I just can't tell you how miraculous it is when a woman comes at exactly the same time.'

She fell back underneath him, but he shifted one last time, lay with his chest between her thighs, hair tickling on her belly. She could feel his heart beating far too fast against her cunt. *She* had made it pound like that – overtime and frantically. The source of life and happiness had moved down between her legs; powered by Michael's heartbeat, kindled by his prick. Her own heart drummed in time with his, echoing his words: he loved her, he adored her; she was 'darling' three times over – miraculous, in short.

She was also very sore, though the steady rhythmic pulsing helped distract her from the fact. But when he finally sat up, she groped down with her hand, felt the skin tender and inflamed. 'You must need a special razor, Michael. Your bristles are so tough they're more like little arrowheads.'

He kissed her as apology. 'It must be twelve or fourteen hours since I last shaved. I suppose I should shave twice, but even once is such a bore. Hold on – I'll fetch some ice.'

She tried to stop him, wanted him to stay there, joined to her by sweat and sperm, elation and exhaustion. But he'd already bounded to the kitchen, returning with a beer-mug filled with ice-cubes. He touched one against her cunt; the cold a stab of pain.

'It's already damn near melted in just two seconds flat! You're such hot stuff, my darling, you can even thaw an ice-floe. Look! The second one's a sliver.'

'And dripping everywhere.' She loved the way he didn't care about the mess; loved that 'darling', and even more the 'my'. And the icy water was exciting in itself, trickling across her labia, running down her thighs. He kept applying ice-cubes, no longer as a compress, but to titillate her now, slipping them right in and down, laughing when she winced.

'What's it like, for heaven's sake? I'm not sure I could bear it on my prick. I envy you, you know. I'm sure women have more pleasure. They've got more bits and pieces.'

She bent her legs right up, to try to trap the ice, stop it sliding out. 'You didn't do too badly yourself.'

'No, but once I've come, I've come. Whereas you could go on endlessly, I bet. In fact, why don't I bet? If you come again, I'll buy you dinner out.'

'I'm too flaked for dinner out.'

'Well, breakfast out tomorrow, then.'

She half-sat up. 'D'you mean it?'

'Of course I do. I mean everything I say.'

She reached down to still his hand, needed a brief respite to take in what he'd said. Breakfast out would mean she'd stay the night with him, share his bed, his flat. She needn't wait till August; could watch him sleep, watch him clean his teeth, even watch the battle of the bristles.

'Well?' he asked, impatient.

'You're on,' she said, moving the ice a fraction, so it was perfectly placed to help her win the bet, then smiling, lying back.

7

TESSA SQUINTED AT the alarm clock for the hundredth time since midnight. Still only three o'clock. The illuminated hands looked ill – a jaundiced sickly green – as if they'd caught some deadly virus, which had slowed them down, made them creep and hobble. She wished she could slow down herself, but she had turned into a fairground – roller-coasters swooping through her stomach, dodgem cars colliding in her head, music blaring out, competing with the snap of rifles, the slam of coconuts; coloured lights flashing on and off.

'Roll up! Roll up!' the gypsies yelled. 'Try your luck. Win a prize.'

She'd won every prize there was, though even the trophies refused to sit inertly on the shelf, but kept glittering and shimmering, spinning with the room. She wasn't pissed – far from it – or only on weak tea and Michael Michael Michael Michael Michael. She couldn't say his name enough, longed to shout it from the tallest tower in England; tell the breathless world that he was all-star, superfabulous, alpha-double-plus. If only he'd wake up. It was agony to keep so still, when she itched to jig around the room, and her voice was tripping over itself, wanting to babble and effuse, pour out a Niagara Falls of words. Strange how quiet he was. She had imagined him a restless sleeper, fidgety and tossing, maybe even shouting out in some dark dramatic nightmare. But he'd barely moved a muscle, and his breathing was so faint she kept fearing he was dead. Everything was tranquil, save for her – the hushed garden, sleepy street, dark and silent flat. The last few nights she had also lain awake, sleepless from sheer misery because Michael hadn't phoned. Now she was jangled by sheer joy because he'd rung every bell she had.

She stroked the lumpy duvet, which was privileged to spend each night caressing his naked body. She worshipped all his things – loved his twisted toothpaste-tube, which had lost its cap and was leaking from the middle; his Family Deodorant, '20% free'; his moulting toothbrush and grubby smelly towels. She'd had a bath before she went to bed. The water had been tepid, the bathroom cold and draughty, but she was Cleopatra, immersed in torrid asses' milk.

She ran a hand across her breasts, then down between her thighs. She was no longer overweight, but voluptuous, majestic. She and Michael belonged together because both of them were big – big in appetite, ambition, achievement, expectation. They had joined all the famous lovers of literature and history; the new Lancelot and Guinevere, Hero and Leander. She kept thinking about Heloïse, wishing she was in the room, so they could laugh and talk together, compare their sensational men. Did Abelard come like Michael did, with those explosive trumpeting cries; had he kissed his mistress in forbidden secret places; sucked ice-cubes from her cunt? No, they'd hardly have ice-cubes in 1117 – though she felt so close to Heloïse, the centuries had rolled back, and she'd *become* her, in a sense, standing in that Paris house with her uncle, Canon Fulbert, being introduced to the dazzling scholar Abelard. He was thirty-five, she only seventeen – a far more daunting age-gap than between her and dazzling Michael.

But both she and avid Heloïse were very willing pupils. She loved that section of the *Historia Calamitatum*, where Abelard described the lessons as '*interspersed with more words of love than words of philosophy; more kisses than construed sentences*'. And the next few lines had always turned her on. She could recall them almost word for word: '*Sometimes, to allay suspicion, I went so far as to strike her – not in anger, but in love; not in hate, but from affection. The blows were sweeter than the sweetest of all perfumes.*' She'd recite the passage to Michael in the morning, and perhaps he'd copy Abelard, beat her with sweet blows.

It was obvious from the *Letters* that Abelard and Heloïse had been pretty phenomenal lovers – totally abandoned, willing to try anything. Were lots of people like that, or did the so-called average couple settle for much less, trot along contentedly with 'Rob-and-Gavin' sex? And if the first was true, then why was life so drab? Shouldn't people be hosanna-ing, whooping in the streets, grinning stupidly all day; bits of their bare bodies flying off, exploding, from the violence of their comes? Take the dons at Balliol. Nothing seemed to turn them on, save finding a long-lost manuscript, or meeting a fellow scholar who was the world authority on Beowulf, or had an interesting new viewpoint on a minor skirmish in the Wars of the Roses. What about their skirmishes in bed?

She'd been swapping beds all night – from Headington to Newcastle, then on to Scotland and the Highlands, travelling several thousand miles in Michael's zizzy car, while the clock-hands scarcely crawled. They'd been hurtling along motorways, hair streaming in the wind; switchbacking on mountain passes; overtaking all the timid Sunday drivers, breaking every speed limit. And she'd done so much parachuting, she was already an instructor, helping Michael open up the 'chute as they jumped hand in hand from Everest, harnessed front to back. They had made love as they floated down, forced into extraordinary new positions, and having to be quick – which was also new, and wonderful.

She rolled over on her side, her body nudging Michael's. How could she wait till August, when just one night was lasting a millennium? Perhaps they could go sooner, if only for a weekend. He could show her round the hospital, let her see the flat. His car should eat the miles up. They might do Headington to Newcastle in four hours, even less.

'Michael,' she whispered; had to wake him up.

'Mm?'

'Are you asleep?'

'I was.'

'I thought I heard you say something.'

'Well, I was talking in my sleep then.' He stretched and yawned, shook himself, sat up. 'What in God's name did I give away? I hope it wasn't anything incriminating.'

'You said I was the most amazing bloody woman you'd ever met in all your life.'

'Liar!'

'So it isn't true?'

'Kiss me and I'll tell you.'

'Well?'

'That didn't count. I need a longer kiss.'

'Only if you shave.'

'No fear! It's still pitch-dark. I'll shave at seven, and not a jot before.'

'Seven? Why so early?'

'I told you. I'm on duty.'

'You didn't tell me.' She tried to quash a twinge of apprehension.

What about their breakfast out? She'd had it at least twenty times in fantasy – scrambled eggs with caviar at some posh upmarket hotel; a picnic breakfast lying on her back, with Michael filling both her mouths; breakfast in a workmen's caff, with black pudding and fried bread. It wasn't really the food she wanted, whether snobby or plebeian, but more of Michael – and the all-important assurance that he kept his promises.

'Ssh. Go to sleep,' he murmured, sounding half-asleep again himself.

'I can't.'

'Yes, you can. In exactly half a minute you'll be out like the proverbial light. Dr Edwards says.'

'So how did you sleep?' Michael reached across to turn the alarm clock off. Light was filtering through the curtains, dappling the drab walls.

'I didn't.'

''Course you did.'

'Not a wink.'

'So you disobeyed my orders?'

She nodded, shook her hair free.

'The penalty's a kiss.'

She climbed on top, complied.

'Christ, Tessa, let me go! I can't do my ward-round with a hard on.'

'Your ward-round?'

'Yes. Eight-fifteen sharp. And the registrar's a real stickler for time, so there'll be all hell to pay if I'm late. Can you put the kettle on?'

She didn't answer, couldn't trust her voice to hide its disappointment. She could hardly argue with a ward-round, yet if he broke his word on minor matters, then how could she be sure she'd ever get to Newcastle?

'And make the tea really strong. I feel half-dead this morning.'

Half-dead, when she was soaring on cloud nine? – cloud ten, eleven, twelve, in the middle of the night – although now she'd nose-dived back to rocky treacherous earth. 'Breakfast out' had shrivelled to a cup of tea and a hunk of mousetrap cheese, eaten on the run.

She pulled her clothes on miserably, didn't want Tristram to find her in the altogether, if he strolled in to make his own tea. She had heard him coming back last night – a crash, a belch, a muttered curse

86

– then silence once again. She ought to wash, but Michael had already commandeered the bathroom, and she didn't feel he was over-keen to have her share the basin or his private morning rituals.

She buttoned up her dress, finger-combed her hair, which looked a total mess, as limp as she was feeling. She slunk into the kitchen, washed three cups, hunted for some bread – which she found with the saucepans, underneath the sink – put it on to toast, while she removed six clammy tea-bags from the chipped and lidless pot.

'Can I smell buttered toast?' asked Michael, breezing in, still naked, but now shaved and spicy-scented.

'Yes. I made some extra for Tristram, in case he . . .'

'Tristram never eats, and we won't want it either. We're going out for breakfast. Or had you totally forgotten?'

She put the teapot down, had already poured their tea. 'But you said you had a ward-round.'

'Which is why we're having breakfast in the hospital canteen. I reckon that still counts as "breakfast out", although I must admit it'll be mainly stodge and grease, rather than strawberries and champagne.' Michael picked his cup up, blew on it, then swigged. 'But to show you what a splendid chap I am, I'll throw in a second breakfast, a proper ritzy one. You can have it on credit, an IOU, which you can hold me to, as soon as I'm less busy.'

'Oh, Michael . . .'

'What?'

'I love you.'

'No you don't. I've told you that as well. Now, hurry! We're leaving in five minutes, and I loathe unpunctual women.'

She ignored her own tea, darted to the bathroom, borrowed deodorant and mouthwash, then skewered all her hair on top. She frisked back to the bedroom to secure it with the bandeau, found Michael in his shirt and pants; the brawny, hair-fleeced, long brown legs slightly braced as he fiddled with his tie. She knelt between them as he'd instructed her last night, head tipped back, mouth open.

'Hussy! Fucking whore! Christ, I wish we had more time. You should have woken me in the night.'

'I did.'

'You're right! I must have been a total fool, or only half-awake. Okay, you can hold me to another come, on credit. I seem to owe you quite a lot already. Now, get up from your knees, before you drive me wild, or get me sacked for neglecting all my patients.'

She felt pretty wild herself, as they drove up to the hospital – wild with crazy joy again. He didn't break his promises, but honoured them twice over, which meant the 'week or two' in Newcastle could spin out to a month or two, then maybe Christmas, Easter, and a second blissful summer.

She was astonished at the difference in the hospital. She had seen it only once, arriving on her bike in a grey remorseless downpour, and shrinking from its ugliness – the white-tiled squarish blocks like some monstrous public lavatory. Now it was shining in the early morning sun, and the man at the reception desk smiled instead of scowling, as she followed Michael through the door and up the stairs, and into the canteen.

Michael slowed his canter to a jog-trot, waited until she'd joined him at the counter. 'I'm afraid it's really grotty here. And it always smells of curry and fried onions, even at tea-time, when they're serving currant buns. Eggs and stuff for you?'

'Yes, please.'

'And fillet steak?'

They laughed.

'Right, grab a tray, and some knives and forks. Oh, hell! There's Princess Pam.'

'Who?'

'Pamela Griffiths-Wharton. You met her at the flat last night – with Pete. Peter Foster-Clarke. They're more or less engaged. Pete and Pam, the double-barrelled prats.'

Tessa stared at the blonde goddess, although she no longer looked a goddess, with her hair scraped back, and her figure swamped in an over-large white coat. 'Why's she wearing that white coat? I thought she was a nurse.'

'No, a doctor, though a lousy one. I can't stand her, to tell the truth. Let's dive into that corner and maybe she won't see us.'

Tessa bit into a mushroom, relishing its taste. Nothing smelt of curry. The breakfast was delicious, and her pleasure was completed by the fact that she didn't have a rival any more. In the middle of the night, she had pushed the blonde off several beetling clifftops, but now she could first-aid her, offer her sweet tea. Easy to be magnanimous when Michael couldn't stand the woman.

She loved the fact he'd made her part of his world; brought her here to eat her eggs and bacon among the white coats and

88

the uniforms. Admittedly, the place was almost empty – only the odd nurse coming off a night-shift, two or three dishevelled-looking doctors, and a group of porters relaxing in their shirtsleeves. And it wasn't exactly the Ritz, with its polystyrene ceiling and moulded plastic chairs, but, as he'd said himself, it was still 'breakfast out' – another helping of Michael, another promise kept. She totted up the score: two breakfasts now, one brunch, one picnic lunch, one dinner out, one supper in – last evening – and one whole night together. By the time she returned to Oxford in October, the numbers would have rocketed to a hundred meals, a hundred thousand comes.

She glanced around the room again, eager to absorb every tiny detail, store them in her mind – the plastic plants, the stained and shabby carpet, the blue stripes on the curtains, the deep scratch on their table where the Formica had been gashed. She adored this place – scratches, stains, the lot – because it was Michael's milieu, part of Michael's life. She beamed at Princess Pam, who had spotted them at last, and was waving a languorous hand.

'Yes, look! We're still together,' she wanted to announce – not just to Pam and Pete, but to the whole eight-storey hospital. 'I spent a marvellous night with him, and we plan to share a pad in Newcastle.'

If only Pat and Debbie could see her – realize how many miles she'd travelled since the shallows of the sixth form. There she was, sitting with a real live doctor – soon to be a surgeon of international fame – who could hardly wait to lure her to his bed again. She returned her gaze to him, watched him gulp his coffee. Everything he did was a source of fascination: the way he ripped open a sachet of sugar (his fourth or fifth, at least), and sprinkled its contents directly on to his tongue – as if to add more sweetness to the coffee in his gullet – then brushed his lips with the back of one broad hand.

'Must dash, Tessa – sorry,' he said, jumping to his feet, but still savouring the sugar, licking a few remaining grains from the corners of his mouth. 'You sit tight and let the grease go down.' He scrabbled in his wallet, slipped something into her hand, closed her fingers over it. 'Here – buy another breakfast, my darling greedy girl. Or take a taxi back. I don't want to leave you stranded here all day.'

She pushed his ten-pound note away, embarrassed, disconcerted. Fine to be a Jezebel, a sensuous Cleopatra, but not a vulgar little tart who expected cash down on the table. And why shell out for a taxi, when she could take the bus for 70p? He was collecting up his things now, about to dash away, his white coat slung around his neck, a smear of orange marmalade glistening on his shirt-front. 'Hold on a second, Michael. When are we going to meet?'

'Well, next week's quite impossible. And I'm away at the weekend. And the weekend after that, I'm on duty again. I swapped rotas with a mate of mine because his sister's getting married. Which means I'm off the following one – June the twenty-second. And with any luck, I'll be finished about five-ish on the Friday afternoon, so I could call for you at college and we'll zoom off to the country, spend the whole weekend together.'

Tessa put her cup down, anxiety and jubilation clashing in her head. 'That Friday's the last day of Mods.'

'Perfect! You'll be panting for a break. I'll pick you up from Schools, and we'll have dinner in the Cotswolds, to celebrate your First. And now I've got to dash. If I'm not on the ward in exactly half a second, Clive will blow his top.'

'Celebrate your First,' she repeated in a daze, watching Michael hurtle to the door, a piece of toast half-eaten in his hand. So he assumed she'd get a First; wasn't just a whore, but a whore with brains, with intellect. The most she'd ever hoped for was a fairly decent Second, but he'd just thrown down a challenge, and, so far, she'd met his challenges with no demur or hesitation. If he was busy for the next three weeks, then she'd be busy too. She would slave at her revision, spend every waking moment in the library, ask her tutors for extra help, re-read Charlotte's essays, get up earlier each morning, and not waste time in the bar.

She drained her tepid tea, trying to drown the mocking little voice which was telling her sardonically: 'However hard you slog, you still won't do it. You haven't got a first-class mind. You need to be bloody brilliant for a First, or at least to have attended a bloody brilliant school.'

'You're brilliant,' Michael said, though he had vanished through the door, must be halfway down the stairs by now, 'absolutely brilliant.' Okay, so he was referring to her mouth around his prick, but he'd also called her clever – brainy, gifted, Mahatma Tessa Reeves. He believed in her, so she couldn't let him down. He himself had high ambitions, planned to be the next Sir Thomas Thornton. 'Sir Michael' sounded great – classy and yet casual. And if she got her First in Mods, it would be one important step towards becoming not just worthy of him, but becoming the future Lady Edwards.

8

TESSA EMERGED FROM the gloom of the Examination Schools into the dazzle of the High Street – a self-assertive sun blazing down on the huge crowd just outside, who had come to meet the examinees with champagne and flowers, streamers and balloons. She stopped, momentarily confused, searching for a face she knew. John had promised he'd be there, to revive her and Vicky and Rob and co with a bottle of cheap bubbly. He was reading geography, not history, and so had finished his exams the day before. Two of the second-year historians had also said they'd come, and another rather scatty girl who'd done the costumes for the play. She heard someone call her name, swung round, expecting John – instead encountered a bouquet in rustling cellophane, with a beaming smile above it.

'Colin!'

'Tessa!'

She let him kiss her, relieved that Michael had been delayed, wasn't there to see the extravagant red roses, reclining on green fern, nor the fervour of his rival's hug. The ginger frizz was tickling her left ear; his own ears flushed a nervous pink with pleasure and excitement. She had hardly seen poor Colin in the last three pressured weeks, but he'd obviously assumed that once the exams were over, he'd be allowed back into the picture. She was thankful when a rakish John (wearing striped shirt and red bow-tie) broke up the embrace with an ejaculating bottle of champagne. One of Vicky's schoolfriends had also rolled up in triumphant style, with Veuve Clicquot and a box of Belgian chocolates. There was no sign of Charlotte, who'd left the exam room a good five minutes early and must have rushed off on her own, to escape the inevitable post mortem on the papers. But the two second-year historians had now found them in the crowd, and were struggling with the cork on their own Sainsbury's sparkling wine. They all stood swigging from the bottles, cramming their mouths with nougatines and truffles – except for Richard, who was too busy warding off attack. His elder brother – a biologist at Queen's – had come to meet him not with wine, but with two giant aerosols of shaving foam and a three-pound bag of flour. His dark hair had already disappeared beneath a white meringue of foam, and was now curdling to a sludge as they pelted him with flour.

The university proctors, in their bowlers and dark suits, were attempting without much success to move everybody on. Rob ducked away to avoid them – and the flour. His girlfriend, Kathy, had spotted him from the other side of the road, and immediately zipped between the cars, throwing away her ice-lolly to leave both hands free to hug him. 'Well, how was it?' she enquired, displaying a hectic orange tongue.

'Crap!' said Rob. 'I couldn't answer anything.'

'Yeah, the paper was piss-awful,' Richard muttered through his foam-and-flour coating.

'What did you think, Tessa?'

She shrugged. 'Not bad.' It wasn't done to gloat; would only sound presumptuous and cocksure if she babbled on about getting all the questions that she'd hoped for, writing faster than she'd ever done before, feeling almost taken over, as if someone else had been sitting at that desk, thinking more coherently than she could ever do herself. The same had happened in yesterday's exam, despite her clammy hands and churning stomach, her lack of sleep and constant queasiness. It was Michael who'd inspired her, Michael who'd dispelled her nerves, infused her with new confidence and with his own superior skills. As soon as she'd walked into the examination hall, she knew that she could do it; knew she *had* to do it – for his sake. She still felt high – high from adrenalin, achievement – and also still felt sick; pushed away the bubbly when the bottle did the rounds again, refused another chocolate.

The crowds had brought the traffic to a standstill, and the hot and harassed policemen trying to get it moving again were hampered in their efforts by a barrage of eggs and flour. A few bemused tourists were taking photos of the students, or picking up souvenirs – champagne-corks and flower-heads from the gutter.

'Why are they wearing penguin suits?' asked an overweight onlooker in a garish Hawaiian shirt.

'They're not,' said Vicky. 'That's subfusc.'

'Come again?'

'Subfusc. Formal academic dress. It's compulsory for exams.'

'And bloody stupid in this heat,' whinged Richard, struggling out of his flour-spattered black gown and rolling it into a ball. 'I almost died in there, dressed up in this funeral gear.'

'I've got my shorts on underneath,' Vicky grinned, whipping off her tight black skirt to reveal scarlet satin hot-pants. The tourists rushed to record her for posterity, while Colin edged up close to Tessa.

'You look really great,' he said.

'Thanks,' she muttered awkwardly. She could hardly tell him that she'd taken so much trouble with her outfit for Michael's sake entirely, since, until his lunch-time phone-call, she had assumed he'd be picking her up. Her attempt to turn subfusc (which literally meant dark and drab) into something rather special had obviously paid off. Her blouse was crisply white, her grosgrain skirt a treasure from a stall, her tie a chic black velvet ribbon, unlike Liz's tatty bootlace. Liz looked creased and rumpled altogether, as if she'd slept in her brief skirt and used her gown to stuff a pillow – but then she wasn't meeting Dr Michael Edwards.

Tessa repositioned the roses, to allow her to see to cross the road. The bouquet was stiff and bulky, cumbersome to carry. She only hoped she'd manage to dispose of it – and Colin – before Michael's car drew up. It would mean lies again, alas. She hated lies, and they seemed unfair to Colin, who'd been ungrudging and supportive when she'd told him she'd decided to work flat out and ditch her social life. She hadn't said a word about her dream of getting a First, for fear of evoking pitying looks, or scornful comments made behind her back. Nor had she mentioned Michael – not to anyone. They'd only gab and gossip, fail to understand how exceptional the whole thing was, how shattering, intense; how far removed from the usual low-key couplings which puttered on or petered out in college.

'Hi, Tessa!' yelled a panting voice. 'Sorry I'm so late.' A skinny blonde in dungarees chopped off at the thigh pounded up to join them – Anne-Marie, the girl who'd made the costumes for the play. She handed over a single rose, its stalk swathed in silver foil. 'Oh dear! Coals to Newcastle, I see.' She cringed in mock-dismay at the dozen lusher blooms.

'No. It's gorgeous, honestly. And I can wear it in my hair – look!' Tessa tucked it in her hairband, secured it with a grip. The scent was wonderful – musky, honeyed, rich – in keeping with her mood. She was thrilled her friends had all shown up; that despite her being so unsociable of late, they still cared enough to bother. She drank in the whole scene; wanted to include it in the photo-album she kept hidden in her mind; record each heady detail – the brightly coloured streamers contrasting with the black and white of subfusc; the gleaming pavement wet with spilt champagne; a boy brandishing a huge cigar trying to smooch a girl with a double strawberry cornet and matching pink balloon.

'Shall we wander back to college?' Liz proposed. 'Buy some wine, dance naked in the quad?'

'Okay,' said Rob. 'But let's grab a pint in the pub first. I'm sweating like a pig in this get-up.'

'Well, take it off, then!' Kathy quipped, proceeding to undress him.

People were still hugging, swilling beer and wine; two boys using their mortarboards to clout each other on the backside. But the crowds were slowly thinning as students sauntered up the High Street arm in arm, or headed down the other way to Magdalen.

'We could go back to my room,' John suggested. 'Roll a huge great spliff and get stoned out of our minds.'

'We can always do that later. I vote we start with a few beers in the King's Arms, then make tracks back to college and get absolutely wasted.'

Tessa murmured her approval of the plan, so she wouldn't seem a killjoy, though she had no intention of getting pissed or trashed, and must also keep a constant eye on the time. Michael had rejigged the arrangements and was now collecting her from Balliol at 'seven-ish'. It was only twenty-five to six, so she didn't have to worry yet, especially as his 'seven-ish' would probably mean eight-thirty. Three days ago she'd gone racing up to Headington to meet him at the hospital. At least, that had been the general idea when he'd phoned her out of the blue and suggested that they had a drink. She had never changed her clothes so fast, never cycled at such a breakneck pace, especially not uphill; the 'drink' escalating in her mind to a meal, a midnight punt-ride, a whole astounding night with him. After two hours twenty minutes, tears had taken over from elation. She'd spent the first excited hour pacing up and down in a fever of impatience, then collapsed exhausted on a bench, still trying to convince herself that everything was quite all right, and he'd turn up any moment.

After another interminable wait, she'd finally been informed that Dr Edwards had been unavoidably detained, and would not be free that evening after all.

'Please don't let anything go wrong tonight,' she prayed. 'No emergencies or haemorrhages, no clots or sudden deaths. It's our first weekend away together and I can't bear anything to spoil it.'

She walked four abreast with Colin, Liz and Richard, swinging up the High, then turning into Catte Street and along to Radcliffe Square. The towers and spires looked picture-book, as if the city had made a special effort to beguile and charm the tourists, display itself at its perfect summer best; the golden stone basking in the sun, the clouds themselves valeted and spruced, any wispy tatters hoovered from the sky. She could never take this city quite for granted, despite the fact she'd been here a whole academic year and should be much more used to it, even blasé like the rest. Instead, she was more conscious of its deeper layers and levels, its private treasures shut off from general view – priceless books in libraries; secret gardens; even secret genius – some future Einstein or Shakespeare burning the midnight oil in his shabby student room. And all those strange medieval rituals which outsiders never saw – the Latin songs, and sconcing; the Boar's Head Feast at Queen's; the Saint Catherine's Night Dinner at Balliol, when the Loving Cup was passed from hand to hand; the ceremony at All Souls to celebrate the first year of each new century, when the fellows paraded round the quad in full academic dress, and holding lighted torches. When she heard about such rites, she always felt a frisson of excitement, aware that she was part of something venerable and awe-inspiring. Of course, she had to hide her feelings, don her usual mask, but she was slightly more accustomed now to the split between her private and her public selves, to relishing in secret what she shrugged off with her friends.

It was an added gain that she shared the place with Michael; that both of them were woven into its fabric, part of its huge history. She suspected he might scoff as well, if she ever broached the subject; knew he saw her as naive. If only she could get her First, it would help to bridge the gulf between them, make her more his equal. Her thoughts kept sneaking back to the gloom and grind of the examination hall, running through the papers. She'd been forced to rush the final question; had chosen the one on history and biography, rather than history and anthropology, because she could then include both Abelard and Guibert, yet if she'd only had more time, she could have expanded the whole issue of subjectivity in history, brought in the example of . . .

She broke away abruptly, dumped the roses in Colin's arms, and went dashing down the steps to the garden of St Mary's church, driven by an urgent wave of sickness. She was about to throw up any second, and couldn't bear to do it in full view of her friends. She crouched down on the grass, head bent over the flowerbed, heaving, retching, but unable to bring up anything but a trail of slimy dribble. She felt dizzy and light-headed, but it couldn't be the wine – she'd only had a sip or two. It must be simply stress. She'd been working far too hard, had barely slept last night, stayed up till three revising, then begun again at six. Everyone felt lousy at exam time. One girl had worn dark glasses the whole week, because she'd been bursting into tears so often, her eyes were red and puffy. And another girl had fainted, twice, the day before her finals.

She wiped her mouth, took a few deep breaths. She'd be all right tomorrow, once life was back to normal. Michael would restore her. They could lie in bed all day – if not exactly resting, then with their minds on something other than exams.

Her legs were still unsteady, but she made herself get up. She must rejoin her friends, allow their cheerful banter to distract her from her symptoms. She walked slowly up the steps and began to cross the square, suddenly stumbled on an uneven patch of cobblestones. She stopped, bewildered, pressed both hands to her head – an insinuating voice was resounding through her skull, stunning her with the force of a physical blow. *Be careful, lass. If you eat a piece of this, you'll fall pregnant within the year.*

She stood stock-still, the word 'pregnant' seeming to echo round the square, eclipsing any other sound or thought. She realized with a sickening dread how familiar the word was; how it had been festering in her mind for the last few frightening weeks, despite her refusal to acknowledge it. But her present bout of nausea seemed to clinch her fears beyond all doubt; confirm the morris man's grave warning, which she had laughed off at the time. She could taste his treacherous cake again, its moist and spicy sweetness cloying in her mouth. She had eaten it on this very spot, in Radcliffe Square, on that overcast May Morning – the morning she'd met Michael. And she had fallen pregnant the first time they'd made love, at that picnic in the woods.

She groped back to the garden, so that she could sit down on a

97

bench; too shattered to do anything but slump. '*No!*' she said out loud, trying to push away the images swarming in her mind: cells dividing and dividing to form a new life, a threatening and unwanted life, feeding on her own. She shook her head irritably, as if arguing with some invisible opponent. It couldn't happen – not to her. It was always other girls – careless, feckless types who didn't take precautions. *She* was on the pill. Okay, she had stopped taking it for just two paltry days, or maybe three at most, but only because it seemed so bloody pointless when she'd broken up with Rob. As soon as she'd met Michael, she had started it again; even swallowing the ones she'd missed, as a sort of extra safeguard. Then she'd gone back to the doctor for her next six months' supply, and had taken one religiously every single morning. Her last period hadn't come, but the GP had changed her prescription, put her on a newer brand, so she'd assumed that was the reason. She remembered reading somewhere that on certain types of pill, some women had no periods at all, so why should she . . . ?

'Tessa?' Vicky called, her voice anxious yet impatient as she jumped the three steps in one bound. 'Ah, *there* you are! I couldn't see you anywhere. Why on earth did you dash off like that? Poor Colin's doing his nut!'

Tessa dragged herself up from the bench, gave a wan ghost of a smile. 'I was just feeling a bit sick.'

'Bad luck! You probably pigged too many chocolates, and what with the boozing and this heat . . . Are you okay now, or d'you want to sit and rest a bit? I'll stay with you, if you like. We can always catch the others up.'

'No, I think I'll be all right. I could do with a glass of water, but I can get that in the pub.'

The rest of their crowd had disappeared, except Anne-Marie and Colin, who were waiting by the Bodleian. Colin made a beeline for her, as if to reclaim his rights. 'Whatever's the matter?' he asked, passing the roses to Vicky so he could support her with an arm. 'You're as white as a sheet. Are you sure you're not going down with a bug?'

No, she thought – not a bug, a baby. The unspoken word set off a second surge of panic, more intense than the first. A child would ruin everything – her career at Oxford, her relationship with Michael. She couldn't even tell him. He'd be horrified, incredulous, maybe even angry. He'd asked if she was on the pill, and she'd told him yes, she was. He'd imagine that she'd tricked him, been completely irresponsible. She'd have to get rid of it – except if she wanted an abortion, she'd be sent to the John Radcliffe – Michael's hospital. His flatmate, Tristram, planned to do obstetrics. He might actually examine her, ask her who the father was. And, anyway, she wasn't sure she even believed in abortion. They'd had a debate on the subject at the Union, at the beginning of last term, and she'd found herself feeling more and more uneasy. Most of the girls who'd spoken had stressed the woman's right to choose, but she herself had sat in wavering silence, plagued by doubts, misgivings; maybe influenced by her mother, and by a vague suspicion that half the people there were spouting theories they hadn't followed through emotionally.

'You're very quiet,' said Anne-Marie.

'Just tired,' she said, only now aware she'd missed every word of the others' conversation.

'It's a good thing you're not going to a ball, then.' Vicky gestured towards Wadham as they stopped outside the pub. A pink-striped canvas awning had already been erected at the entrance to the college, and several vans were parked outside, unloading trestle-tables, potted palms, crates of beer and wine. A minibus had also just drawn up, and was disgorging a dreadlocked reggae band – six brawny men in jeans and vests, hauling out their sound-system.

Tessa barely registered them, more concerned about the uproar in the pub – the mass of jostling bodies spilling out on to the pavement and blocking the main door. She was tempted to skulk off, escape the racket and the crowds, the yowls of laughter, drunken cheers and shouts. But Vicky had cleared a path for her, using the roses as a cudgel, and Colin was already asking if she'd like a brandy for her stomach.

'No, I'll stick to water, thanks.'

They found the others at a table in the corner; Rob already draining his first pint; Sally with her shoes off, her grubby feet up on Richard's lap. Tessa squatted on his chair-arm. No one seemed to notice she felt ill, especially as she made an effort to chip in the odd remark, while continuing her anguished speculation underneath. How could she survive the whole weekend with Michael, and not give anything away? Or was she over-reacting, jumping to conclusions, without any solid proof? She'd only missed one period. Her second one had been due just yesterday. Okay, it hadn't come, but that was actually a blessing. She didn't want stomach cramps in the middle of exams.

She had probably delayed it by sheer determination. But now the papers and the stress were over, it would start at any moment.

There was a sudden burst of laughter from their table. John had spilt his Guinness on Sally's feet, and Anne-Marie was scouring them with a beer-soaked handkerchief. 'I know bathrooms are in short supply in college,' she grinned. 'But your feet are quite disgusting, Sal. Have you washed them yet this term?'

Sally jabbed her in the belly with a still damp and smelly foot, while John stood up to order another round. 'Aren't you drinking, Tessa?'

She shook her head. 'I've had too much already.' Safer to pretend she was a bit the worse for wear. Her friends could deal with that, whereas pregnancy would appal them. They couldn't help her anyway. Term was over, and everyone was going down tomorrow or the next day. Some had gone already – those who hadn't had exams – and there was nothing left of Oxford save an aching gap of empty time until the next term began in mid-October. It hadn't felt empty till today, but all her busy happy plans now seemed meaningless. She couldn't go home – couldn't face her mother – but neither could she beetle off to Juxon Street, or join Michael in his new hospital flat; couldn't make a single move until she knew she was all right.

She jerked up from the chair-arm, counting figures in her head. If she had conceived that day in Foxlow Woods, she'd be almost twelve weeks pregnant by the time she left for Newcastle on 31 July. She could hardly expect Michael not to notice – a fully-trained doctor, who must have done his stint in gynae and obstetrics. Perhaps it showed already. She was so ignorant, so clueless, she'd no idea what the symptoms were – except sickness, which she'd got.

'D'you need some air?' asked Colin, who was still hovering at her side.

'No, just the loo,' she said. She squeezed her way through the close-packed groups of students; their numbers recently swollen by an overspill from Wadham, who had breezed in for a drink before the ball – girls in sculpted silk creations, men in evening dress. How could anyone even contemplate going to a ball, stuffing themselves with steak and smoked salmon, dancing the night away? Still more inconceivable that she'd once enjoyed those things herself. In the last few minutes, she had become another person: one incapable of eating, queasy at the thought of drink, and whose mind refused to shift from abortion clinics, labour wards.

The noise was overwhelming – a roar which seemed to close above her head. She was foundering in it, choking; her own weak voice submerged by the boom and bray around her. She staggered down the stairs and along the passage to the toilet; the cool quiet of the basement a relief and an escape. She bolted the loo door, pushed her skirt right up, to get a full view of her stomach. It had never been exactly flat, and looked no different now – certainly no bigger, no suspicion of a bulge. But her breasts felt full and tight. She had blamed that on the pill as well – this peculiar new brand which had stopped her periods had swollen up her boobs. She unbuttoned her blouse, eased one breast from its bra-cup. It was larger, definitely, more solid and compressed.

She sank down on the toilet-seat, suddenly burning with resentment towards Michael. He should have used a condom, then he'd have saved her from all this. Okay, the sex had been spontaneous, and they'd both been carried away, but all the same, he had been irresponsible. The day after the picnic, she'd found herself reflecting on it – surprised and even shocked that a doctor, of all people, should disregard the warnings about safe sex. She'd been thinking then in terms of AIDS, not pregnancy, and however crazy it might sound, pregnancy actually seemed more threatening than a terminal disease, because it was more real and more immediate.

She touched her swollen breasts again; her bitterness now tinged with self-reproach. Was it really fair to blame Michael, when it was equally her fault? Women could carry condoms just the same as men, and if she was stupid enough to miss her pills, then . . .

'Tessa? Are you in there?' Vicky's voice again.

'Yes,' she faltered. 'I . . . I'm still feeling a bit off.' Couldn't she confide in Vicky, blurt it out right now, the whole confused and ghastly mess?

'Everyone's heading back to college,' Vicky shouted through the door. 'Colin says he'll wait for you, but I'm afraid I've got to dash. That guy I met last Saturday has just asked me out to dinner. He drives an MR2, so I'm hoping that the restaurant will live up to the car! See you in the morning – okay?'

Tessa heard the door slam before she'd said goodbye, then rapid footsteps fading into nothing. No one cared a jot. They were all bound up in their own lives – their plans, romances, pipe dreams. She'd been just the same, ignoring Colin; totally preoccupied with

Michael and her First. Yet poor Colin was still there, waiting for her patiently but fruitlessly. She'd better fabricate some reason why she wasn't free this evening; be as decent as she could to him, at least till seven-ish.

She was still embroidering her explanation as she and Colin walked into the garden quad, joined the others on the lawn. Someone had bought wine, which they were gulping from the bottles, passing them from hand to hand – those who weren't already semi-conscious. Tessa sprawled out on the grass, closed her eyes against the sun, though she could still see the college in her mind: the majestic flight of steps leading up to Hall; the ancient twisted mulberry tree, a cool four centuries old; the green dome of the Sheldonian, just showing above the wall – the ceremonial theatre where successful students were granted their degrees. If she turned out to be pregnant, she'd miss that grand occasion; would lose everything she treasured here; chuck away her future, every hope she'd cherished since she was an intense and high-souled twelve.

'Swine!' yelled Richard, as Sally trickled wine between his shirt-buttons. The two began a wrestling match; laughing, swapping insults; Richard grabbing Sally's hair, while she dragged off his shirt. Tessa half-sat up, forced her mouth to smile, envying their horseplay. How extraordinary that people could still laugh, lark around like kids. She looked beyond her group of friends to the stately college buildings; let her eyes track slowly from the steep-pitched chapel roof to the heraldic shields in the windows of the library, as if seeing the whole place afresh – no longer as an unencumbered student, but as the mother of a child. She could think of no environment less suited to a baby – a male-dominated academic forcing-house, where prams and nappies would be not just an irrelevance, but somehow in bad taste. And the whole 'me-first' student culture was alien to motherhood – the drink, the drugs, the deafening music, the late nights, the cult of self-absorption. Yet that inappropriate baby could well be growing by the minute; taking possession of her body like some alien yeast or mould; insisting on its right to live, oblivious of the fact that it could only be a burden.

'Okay, you win,' groaned Richard. 'But give me back my shirt, Sal.'

'Come and ge–t it!' Sally taunted in a sing-song voice, then pranced away, Richard in pursuit. Anne-Marie joined in, caught the crumpled shirt which Sally threw her, and tied it like a sash around her middle.

Tessa watched them stonily. She was so tired she could weep. The term had been a gruelling one – first, all that hideous worry over Michael, then the non-stop slog for her exams. She just hadn't got the energy to cope with all the extra hassle of a baby; to try to be a supermum, as well as a voluptuous courtesan, and a high-achieving student. Oxford was bad enough in any case, expecting undergraduates to excel in every field – to be actors, journalists, socialites, budding politicians, as well as slaving in the library half the day, and gutting books like fish. Add a kid to all of that, and she'd probably have a breakdown.

Well, she'd simply have to steel herself to go through with an abortion, though that option, too, had almost as many drawbacks. They cost a fortune, didn't they – the private sort which would bypass the John Radcliffe? Or could she get one on the National Health if she returned home to Dr Cunningham? But that would mean confessing to her mother – endless talk and agonizing; April telling all her friends, even total strangers in the pub, as she'd already told them about her 'brilliant daughter's' A-levels, as if she was the only girl in England who'd ever got to Oxbridge. And, anyway, April opposed abortion totally and vehemently; always took the pro-life view – for her own subjective reasons. 'You're the living proof it's wrong, Toots. If I'd have pulled the plug on you, I could have been killing the next – what's her name? – Joan Austen.'

Murdering Michael's baby would be worse. Could she really flush his genes and skills and talents down the drain? Yet if she didn't, then she'd lose him; lose her trip to Newcastle, her two years here in . . .

'I'm going for a slash,' John announced to no one in particular, as he heaved himself up to his feet.

'Me too,' said Lynn, following him across the grass.

Tessa watched them go. Maybe Lynn could help. She was a kindly tactful sort, and already twenty-two; had come to Oxford after dropping out of another course at Bristol – might know about abortions, at least advise her what to do. She ran to catch her up, but Lynn ran faster, hurtling down the steps to the basement of the JCR. 'I'm bursting,' she explained, as she slammed the toilet door.

Tessa slunk into the second toilet, rehearsing what she'd say. She'd have to get a move on, collar Lynn the moment she came out. It was already nearly seven, and she hadn't even changed yet. She'd better have a pee herself, ready for the drive to Chipping Campden. She pulled her pants down, stared at them in shock. They were stained a brownish-red. Her period had come!

She clutched the cistern, as if physically to restrain herself from soaring through the roof. A hundred full-term babies had just been ejected from her stomach, and she was so light she could take wing. She had her pee, then peered into the toilet-bowl to make absolutely sure. Yes, a few more drops of miraculous blood had stained the water red. She scrabbled in her bag for a Tampax; had never put one in with such a sense of delight. She washed her hands, bounded through the door and up the stairs, leaving Lynn still primping at the mirror. She was eager now to make up for lost time – join in the celebrations, grab her share of wine. But first she ought to go and see if Michael had arrived. He wasn't meant to stop outside the college, and she had visions of him fuming at the wheel, or running down some obstreperous traffic warden. It was only five past seven, so extremely unlikely that he'd have even left the hospital, but . . .

'Michael!' She dashed up to the car, kissed him on the lips with more fire and force than she had ever shown before.

He reeled back in the driver's seat, pretending to cower beneath her assault. 'Christ! I've got a hard on. You're a highly dangerous female, Tessa Reeves! Let's forget the Cotswolds and go straight up to your room.'

She backed away, her mood abruptly changing. What was triumph and relief for her, for him would be a bloody nuisance – literally. 'My . . . my period's just started,' she muttered, looking down, blushing as she said it. Rob had hated periods, found them messy and embarrassing, always avoided sex with her till they were well and truly over. Michael hadn't commented at all. Was he angry, disappointed, about to cancel their weekend?

'Look, I'm sorry,' she began.

'What for?'

'Well, the mess and . . .'

'Damn the mess! Who cares? Most women are more horny when they're menstruating, and since you're already the most horny girl I've ever had the amazing luck to meet, it should be an experience.'

She pressed her open mouth to his, in an encore to the first kiss;

hardly caring that she'd attracted a small audience – two college porters and at least half a dozen tourists, all riveted by the scene. She was rejoicing in three miracles: she wasn't pregnant, Michael wasn't late, and she was the most horny girl he'd ever had the luck – no, amazing luck – to meet.

9

'THOU SHALT NOT KILL!'
   'ABORTION: THE FIRST CHILD-ABUSE!'
   'DON'T THROW YOUR PRECIOUS BABY IN THE RUBBISH-BIN!'
Tessa dodged back out of sight behind a clump of bushes, still
staring in horror at the placards. Nobody had warned her about
pickets – a group at least ten strong – one frightening-looking woman
in a long black shiny mac, clutching a huge crucifix; the others with
their accusing banners, or crude squares of painted cardboard: 'THE
SLAUGHTER OF THE INNOCENTS'.
   She could hardly bear to look at the gruesome colour photographs
of bloody foetuses; tiny tadpole-babies who appeared to be in tears,
wiping their blind eyes. Another placard was held by a small boy
– a child of only five or six, with curly white-blond hair – whose
message read: 'DON'T MURDER ME'. How could she walk past the
group, brave their shouts, their pleadings? Yet she was already late
for her ten o'clock appointment; had lost her way when she came
out of the station, forked left instead of right. If only Charlotte had
come with her, as she'd promised at the outset, but Charlotte had
left for Italy at dawn; would be sipping cappuccino on the terrace
of her grand hotel, tucking in to warm croissants and chilled melon.
Tessa put her bag down, leaned against the fence. She herself had
eaten nothing since a bowl of soup last night. She longed for a dry
biscuit, a cup of sweet strong tea, but the clinic had insisted that she
fast from midnight, and drinks were forbidden as well as food; even
plain water strictly taboo.
   She checked her watch again. Nearly 10.15. If she didn't book in
now, they might postpone her operation. She had a sudden grotesque
vision of herself swelling up and up, until she was nothing but a grossly

distended uterus, a bulging mass of cells remorselessly expanding. She pressed her stomach gingerly, barely able to believe that it didn't show at all yet, and that she was still at what the doctor called a very early stage. The word 'early' seemed a mockery, when she'd been waiting, waiting, waiting for the last interminable fortnight – agonizing, counting days, whilst forced to pretend to Charlotte's stilted family that she was simply enjoying a restful stay in Sussex with her friend. Better to face the pickets than endure another minute of that stiff and sleepless nothing-time, in which her whole attention had been focused on her body – her periods, or lack of them, her morning sickness (often bad throughout the day), her tender, bloated breasts. She took two nervous steps along the street. A dowdy matron in a drab beige anorak had seen her and was closing in. Tessa felt a hand snap round her wrist, a damp and clammy padlock, which contrasted with the warm and friendly voice.

'We're here to help you, Mother. Don't let them kill your baby.'

Tessa stood rooted to the spot, staring down at the pavement, noticing the pattern of its tiny cracks and fissures. She had been called a mother, made a mother – an instant and official one; the blob of frogspawn in her womb transformed into a living breathing child – a child she was about to kill.

'If you come along with us, dear, we can help you sort things out – even find you a place to stay, if you've no one else to turn to.'

Tessa hesitated. She was all alone; Charlotte's house now locked and barred until the family returned in late July. She had agreed to stay at the clinic overnight – hadn't any choice, in fact, since there was nobody to fetch her, and she wasn't officially registered with a local Brighton doctor. Then, first thing in the morning, she'd turn tail back to Oxford, lug her stuff to Juxon Street – another empty lonely house.

She raised her eyes to the woman's face, a wrinkled and wind-roughened face, but sympathetic, kind. 'But how can . . . ?' she began, breaking off uncertainly as the small blond boy came skipping up, exclaiming over a ladybird which was crawling up his arm. She'd have given almost anything to swap her life with his – to be that young, and a male, so that there would be no chance of getting pregnant; to be more interested in ladybirds than in the placard he'd let fall.

There was a sudden undignified scuffle, as another male pushed his way into the group, a taller and more brawny one in a dark blue uniform. Tessa tried to shrink away, but he was striding straight towards her, his face looming into close-up, his voice a husky baritone as he asked if she had an appointment at the clinic. She could feel herself tugged in two directions, answering with two voices, stepping forward, flinching back. She heard a squall of protests; glimpsed the woman with the crucifix raising it above her head like a gleaming dangerous weapon. She shut her eyes, entered a strange dream-state in which her legs were paper, her spine a piece of string, yet she was still somehow moving forward – through a gate, along a path, up some steep stone steps – half-carried by the dark and solid stranger. Once she'd regained her senses, he had already disappeared, and she was standing in a shabby room she recognized. She and Charlotte had waited here a terrifying hour, when she'd attended for her initial consultation; Charlotte taking charge, while she'd been just the anatomical specimen – the womb they'd poked and prodded, the blood and pee they'd scrutinized.

This time, the place was busier – at least a dozen people squashed up on the scuffed grey vinyl chairs, including a girl with her whole family in tow: an infant in a pushchair, a toddler with a toy giraffe, and an embarrassed blue-jeaned husband, who was trying to soothe the baby. Its shrill and fractious whining seemed to affront the silent room; all other voices stilled, as if the notice on the wall said 'No talking', not 'No smoking'. Even those in couples were totally subdued; every face a mask. Several girls were sitting on their own – a thirty-something yuppie in a smart designer suit, picking at her scarlet-painted nails; an Indian in a sari, with a sallow haggard face, and a spiky-haired teenager whose bulge was clearly visible, despite her baggy smock. No one else looked pregnant – their condition hidden, secret, as if they were here to see the doctor about some trifling cold or rash.

Tessa chose a seat in the far corner, trying to compress herself to nothing; aware of several pairs of eyes swivelling towards her, surveying her as the latest mild distraction. She kept her own eyes on the carpet, a cheap brown hessian affair, badly stained and worn. Everything was cheap – except the price of the abortion – the skimpy net curtains which barely screened the neglected waste of garden; the dog-eared magazines on the battered fake-wood table. It could have been the foyer of a second-rate hotel, except that above were wards, not bedrooms, and beyond her not a restaurant, but an operating theatre.

She tried to steer her mind away from anaesthetics, suction tubes, but soon became obsessed instead with the turmoil of the last two weeks, starting with the Sunday when she'd returned from her weekend with Michael. Outwardly, it had been a huge success, and they'd enjoyed the most fantastic sex, scaling new exquisite heights together. But while Michael had relaxed, recharged, she'd been secretly distraught; the whole occasion ruined for her by the fact that the few drops of blood she'd welcomed on the Friday evening had amounted to no more than that. The doctor had explained it when she'd seen him four days later; referred to it as 'spotting', which he said sometimes occurred in pregnancy at the time a woman's period was due.

Michael had dropped her at the college at five-ish on the Sunday afternoon, and she'd run straight into Charlotte – not the usual cool self-confident Charlotte, but panicking and close to tears because her parents had been due at three, to take her home to Lewes, and she was sure they'd had an accident. The two of them had decamped to Charlotte's room, where they'd sat drinking tea – then vodka – and she'd found herself somehow pouring out her own fears over the second glass of Smirnoff. When the Harvey-Taylors finally showed up, unharmed but three hours late, she had returned with them to Sussex – a friend and guest in their eyes, but actually a patient. Charlotte knew this 'super place' in Brighton: a nursing home called Langham Park, which had been set up eighteen months ago and offered slightly lower prices than its long-established rival on the other side of the town. She had accompanied a schoolfriend there, last Christmas, and so was familiar with the whole grim business – except that she made it sound not grim at all; assured her it was nothing, that you were in and out in half a day; and that she'd take her and collect her, then drive her to the Ciao Bella, to celebrate with *escaloppe Milanese*. 'But you'll have to get a move on,' she'd insisted. 'We're leaving for Lake Como on the morning of the eighth.'

'I've booked you in for the morning of July the eighth,' the doctor had informed her, refusing her request for an appointment in late June, since the foetus was so tiny, there was a risk that they might miss it if they operated earlier.

How could he refer to it as tiny, when it filled her every waking moment; had stifled all her usual concerns, including Oxford and her work, even supplanted thoughts of the more important doctor in her life? If only Michael had been with her through the nightmare – imbuing her with courage, helping her decide – instead of miles away, both physically and emotionally. She envied the girl opposite, whose boyfriend was right next to her; his arm around her shoulder, their two feet nuzzling toe-caps. Yet the wretched girl looked desolate, her face red and blotched from crying, as if she realized she was ultimately alone; that once they summoned her to theatre, there'd be no boyfriend to play footsie, or whisper words of comfort while she lay unconscious on the slab. Wouldn't it be better if they could all share their fears, their stories, instead of sitting in this rigid isolation? Twelve unwanted pregnancies in one claustrophobic room. She could almost sense the ripples spreading out – all the parents, partners, friends involved, their shock or guilt or anger; the terror of the girls themselves. She watched the lucky candidate who'd been called up to the desk. Lucky? The poor kid was underage – not to mention foreign – a confused and blushing schoolgirl, wearing sneakers and white socks, stammering out replies in broken English.

Tessa could feel the girl's bewilderment added to her own; the pain and tension in the room inflating like the pregnancies themselves. If they didn't call her soon, that 'tiny' foetus would develop to full-term, and she'd give birth here, in public, while everyone continued to sit in passive silence, pretending not to notice. The longer she waited, the more queasy she became, yet also more empty and dry-mouthed. The toddler was eating a Crunchie bar, totally absorbed in it; had torn off the whole wrapper and smeared chocolate down his clothes. Her gaze kept straying back to him; each drooling bite intensifying both her hunger and her sickness. And his lanky blue-jeaned father was unashamedly swilling coffee, which he'd fetched from the drinks machine outside. She watched him sip and swallow, trying to remind herself that she was in fact extremely lucky, not just in having Charlotte – who'd turned out to be an angel in disguise – but in living in the enlightened 1990s. She should thank her lucky stars that she hadn't been around in the days before legalized abortion. She had heard all sorts of horror stories about potions made of gunpowder or lead; 'fallen women' pitched into the workhouse, or landing up in mental homes or prisons; back-street botch-ups which resulted in infection – if not death.

All she had to face was a ten-minute operation by a fully-trained professional in the most hygienic of conditions, and with no hint of shame or stigma. Yet she was still ashen-faced when she walked up to the desk – at twenty-five to twelve – still icy cold with nerves when she was shown into the ward; told to leave her things there while she went to pay her fee in a cramped and stuffy box-room on the top floor of the house.

The woman guarding the cash-box was hard-voiced and flinty-eyed, and dressed in a white coat, as if extracting money was a medical procedure. Tessa longed to have her mother there, so that she could cling to her hand – that plump, hot hand, spiky with cheap rings, which had smoothed the blankets, tucked the sheets, spread jam on bread, or Savlon on grazed knees, and which could lead her out of danger now, down the stairs and through the door. Instead, she was a prisoner here, subject to her gaoler. She perched uncomfortably on the edge of a hard chair, wrote out her cheque as slowly as she could, then fumbled in her handbag for her card.

'I'm sorry,' said the woman, as she glanced at it. 'This card only guarantees a sum of up to fifty pounds, so I can't accept your cheque.'

'But I . . . I'd no idea. I mean, I thought you . . .'

'The instructions are printed quite clearly on your form.' The woman was speaking slowly and deliberately, as if dealing with a foreigner, or a halfwit. 'We do take cheques, but not above the limit of your card. After that, you have to pay in cash.'

'But I . . . I haven't any cash.' Tessa emptied out her purse – just a fiver and a few odd coins.

'You'd best go straight down to the bank, then. You'll find all the main branches in the town. Turn right at the corner and . . .'

Tessa stared at her aghast. The pickets! She'd have to pass them twice again – on her way out, and coming back – quite apart from losing her original appointment time. Once she'd returned from her long trek to the town, she was bound to find the waiting-room crammed and overflowing, worse than it was now. 'Look, please,' she implored, 'can't we phone the bank from here? I've got the money, honestly. I paid it into my account last week. My father wrote me out a cheque and . . .'

'I'm afraid a phone-call won't be any use. A rule's a rule, and I'm not allowed to change it. I need cash down on the table.'

'You've got enough, for God's sake!' Tessa shouted suddenly, gesturing to the cash-box, piled high with fivers, tenners, a wad of twenty-pound notes, and several ostentatious fifties. She strode to the window, stared down at the tangled grass, the weed-infested beds. Langham Park indeed! The name suggested the gracious lap of luxury, not this sordid dump. The whole thing was a racket – clinics making money from desperate panicked girls; raking in their profits like the biggest of big businesses. She'd read the statistics, knew the damning figures: seven hundred abortions performed every single day; two hundred thousand every year – and that was just in England. It was millions in America – billions if you counted them in dollars. Even counselling cost extra at this clinic, plus any drugs they pumped into you, if anything went wrong. Yet Charlotte had convinced her how 'reasonable' it was; had cautioned her continually about going National Health – the already long delays made longer still by medical men with consciences (mainly born-agains and Catholics), who deliberately postponed appointments until the girl was past the legal limit. Maybe Charlotte was exaggerating, but she hadn't dared to risk it, although she'd been worried sick about how to find the money. Finally, as a last resort, she'd been driven to approach her father and beg him for a loan (ostensibly as payment-in-advance for the house in Juxon Street).

'How on earth can they demand so much when you're only renting it?' Dave had carped suspiciously; both he and Tessa uncomfortably aware that never in her life before had she asked his help, either financially or otherwise, let alone on this gargantuan scale.

In the end, he'd given her a cheque – an outright gift and not a loan – which she'd guessed was a sort of guilt-offering for his eighteen years of absence. Twenty minutes later, she'd banked it in the Croydon branch of Barclays, a stone's throw from his house, then returned to Charlotte's place, feeling a racking combination of shame, relief, and misery.

Well, now she'd better go and draw it out again – in banknotes – watch that voracious cash-box overflow; her father's first and only gift paying for a death.

She turned the corner and walked slap into the wind, a vindictive wind blowing off the sea, and letting fly at everything – churning up the waves, buffeting the gulls, ripping through her lightweight cotton dress. She struggled on, head down, cursing the idiot cashier who'd made such a fuss about handing over the money. Apparently, her father's cheque had taken several days to clear, because she'd paid it in in Croydon, and all the witless man could do was bleat and stall and waffle, then pass the buck to someone else. The second chap had explained to her that he'd have to ring the Oxford branch, to check on her account, but the line had been constantly engaged. She'd finally lost patience, told him she was slipping out to get a breath of air, and would he kindly have the money ready the minute she got back. A breath of air! This was a force eight, the waves crashing on the shingle with a mushroom-cloud of spray; assaulting the West Pier – a tatty ruin, cut off from the mainland like a wrecked and sinking ship. 'HELP ME!' begged a notice tacked across its crumbling roof. 'SAVE ME', cried another.

'Help me,' she repeated, but her words were blown away, lost in the dull booming of the sea. She slumped down in a shelter, beside a frail old woman in a floral-patterned frock, her pink scalp showing through the thistledown of hair.

'Cold,' said Tessa, 'isn't it?'

The woman didn't answer. Deaf, perhaps, or foreign, or simply scared of strangers. She *was* a stranger here, a foreigner who didn't speak the jolly native language. Brighton was a Fun Town where people came in groups or gangs, bought naughty postcards and sticks of rock, shrieked with laughter when their Kiss-Me-Quick hats blew off, or the wind groped beneath their skirts. No one was alone, except the winos and the grey-heads, the stupid pregnant failures. She gazed out at the sea. Why did people call it blue, when it was a dirty sludgy grey; or come here for sun and swimming when there was a red flag flying on the beach announcing 'DANGER! NO BATHING ', and the idle (or despairing) sun hadn't bothered to get up?

She shambled to her feet again, couldn't stare her life away, like the bag of bones beside her, or the gin-befuddled tramp sprawled out on the promenade with his Gordon's and his dog. She turned back the way she'd come, passing vast impersonal hotels – rows and rows of bedrooms, where couples would be making babies, only to destroy them once the holiday was over. People coming and going like the waves. Nothing permanent or meaningful. Seven hundred babies murdered every day. Easy, if you had the cash. So many people shrugged it off – Charlotte wasn't the only one. Several girls who'd spoken in the Union debate had dismissed the whole process of abortion as just another method of contraception, and one strident women's libber had likened it to 'yanking out a decaying tooth'. Strange that it should cost so much to pull one rotten tooth.

Her pace quickened as her thoughts returned to money. She must jog back to the bank, and prod those dozy cashiers into action. She hurried on until she reached a second pier – the Palace Pier – a playground, not a ruin. There was a funfair just beyond it – the main attraction a huge Viking ship swingboat rocking back and forth, the kids on board screaming with excitement. Everything was lurching: the fairground rides, her stomach, the roller-coaster sea itself – brown-speckled adolescent gulls bobbing on the swell.

She stood fighting the wave of nausea, her attention drawn to the family in front of her: two small girls tweaking at their parents' sleeves, trying to lure them on to the pier. She found herself following, so desperate to belong to someone that she was quite prepared to fall in line as their third and youngest child. She was forced to abandon them, however, when they stopped to buy King Burgers; the reek of grease and onions too much for her poor stomach. Every sort of food-stall had been set up on the pier – shellfish next to doughnuts, curry-flavoured samosas outsmelling fish and chips. No one else was fasting – children sucking lollies, old men guzzling whelks, a Sikh in a turban licking sugar from his fingers. She felt suddenly enraged with them, indignant at the raucous hurting colours – bilious yellow popcorn, brash pink sticks of rock. Oxford was a grey town, tasteful and fastidious, wouldn't dream of flaunting these racks of lime-green flipflops, those red and silver windmills whizzing round and round. This whole place was a con – a racket, like the clinic. A wonder they didn't charge you for the view, or even for the wind, jacking up the price as the gale-force grew in strength, like they charged more for abortion, the later you left it.

She stopped outside the 'Palace of Fun', a huge covered central area full of video games and slot machines, where the lights were thankfully low, and she could escape the wind and glare. Yet the instant she stepped inside, she was assailed by noise instead – whoops and bleeps from the machines, the clatter-jangle-chink of coins, and a pounding manic rock-rhythm blaring from the amplifiers. The place was packed with bodies, everyone intent on winning – or destroying; faces creased in concentration as they shot down spaceships, blew up planes, steered Ferraris round the race-track, wrestled, boxed or bombed.

She fed her five-pound note into the change-machine, picked up her cache of coins, chose a game in which she had to gun down aliens, tiny writhing figures with bloated heads and green stick-arms and legs. They looked familiar, somehow, floating in space with their blind but staring eyes. They had to be exterminated – that she did remember – and as soon as possible. It was easier and safer if you didn't wait too long; didn't waste weeks dithering, while they grew bigger by the hour.

'Zap, zap!' went her guns, and another three collapsed, exploding in a puff of scarlet smoke. Three a minute, wasn't it, seven hundred every working day? She could kill far more than that; her finger jabbing at the button so fast that it was aching. Who cared about the pain? The aliens felt pain, but you ignored it or denied it; refused to hear their anguished cries when the suction-tubes blew them into bits.

'Bang-bang!' Another four blitzed. She was becoming quite an expert. Two hundred thousand every year; a million in America; sixty million in total, if you counted every country in the world. It was so quick, so easy, all over in ten minutes. Her five pounds was almost gone, but that was fair enough. Destroying things cost money, and these tiny fragile aliens were more complex than they looked. They weren't just globs of tissue, or pictures on a screen – and not at all like rotten teeth – but had heartbeats, brainwaves, livers, lungs, which must be pulverized, destroyed.

She could hear the heartbeat now, a weak but steady throb-throb-throb, pulsing from the machine. It had to be snuffed out before it grew louder and more powerful, became the roar of Life. There was enough noise as it was – the music stabbing, strident, punching through her head; a cascade of coins rattling from a fruit-machine; a boy's shrill laugh as he pocketed his winnings. Her finger hit the button with even greater force, smashed a dozen hearts. The only problem was that she was running out of cash, but the bank should have her money ready, so she could play the game a second time – for real.

'All sorted out,' the cashier smiled, as he handed over a wad of crisp new notes.

'Thanks,' she said, whipping through the door, across the road, then right, and up the hill. There wasn't a second to lose – she'd hung around too long. She felt stronger and more hopeful with the money in her hand, and anyway she'd proved that she could do it – anyone could do it – just close your eyes and kill. Even the nausea had completely disappeared, leaving her hollow and half-starved. She tried hard not to notice all the cafés; every other door she passed a restaurant, tea-shop, snack-bar. Well, it would all be over soon, and she, too, could sit and stuff herself, or at least beg some tea and toast.

She peered up at the sky, which looked grey and leaden, threatening heavy rain. Already the first drops were spattering on her face, increasing very suddenly to a vicious drenching downpour, which stung her legs, glued her flimsy dress against her skin. She had left her mac in the clinic, which was still a good half-mile away. There was no shelter anywhere. The shops were all behind her, and the trees were few and skinny, so she dived back to the nearest café – a sandwich-bar and takeaway – stood shivering in the doorway, explaining to the waitress that she wasn't allowed to eat or drink, but could she stay there till the rain eased off?

''Course you can. Sit down, dear.'

She chose a bench-seat near the window, so that she could watch the weather, make a move the minute it cleared up. Her hair was dripping down her neck, her cheap brown sandals squelching. It would be almost a relief to strip her clothes off and slip on a white gown; allow the anaesthetic to waft her to unconsciousness, disconnect her brain. She'd been awake and worrying too long.

The small boy sitting opposite was drinking a milk-shake, slurping through his straw. Her eyes kept flicking back to the tall glass ringed with chocolate-froth, the rich dark colour of the shake, the effervescent bubbles blinking on the top. Far from feeling queasy, her mouth was actually watering – the first time in three weeks. She felt an almost-lust for something chocolatey. Perhaps it was a craving, the sort pregnant women were always meant to get. She called the waitress over. 'Do you do milk-shakes to take away?'

The woman nodded, reeled off a list of flavours.

'Chocolate, please – a large one.' That would provide some sustenance for after the operation. As far as she remembered, the clinic laid on meals, but no doubt they'd cost extra, like the drugs. It would be far more economical to bring in her own snack, rather than paying through the nose for half an ounce of chicken and a teaspoonful of trifle.

The boy was draining his glass with a tantalizing gurgling noise. She turned her back, so she wouldn't have to watch him – watched the rain instead. It was slackening off now, definitely, so she paid for her milk-shake, then hurried up the street again, not stopping till she reached the clinic. The residential road was quiet, the pickets gone – thank heaven – just a few odd pamphlets dirty in the gutter. She picked one up, leafed through it. *'At eight weeks, all the organs are present and the milk-teeth are just forming.'*

Rubbish, she thought irritably, tossing it away. Why should foetuses have teeth, when, even after they were born, their only food was milk and slops? The whole thing was a pack of lies – like the way those gormless pickets had called her 'Mother'. She couldn't be a mother. Mothers didn't kill. Mothers nursed and nurtured. Mothers also looked after themselves; made sure that they ate properly, so their unborn babies' milk-teeth could develop.

She sat down on a low stone wall, the brown bag from the café cradled on her lap. She could hear the counsellor's voice again – that fusspot at the clinic who had run through the instructions what seemed like twenty times. 'Now remember, Tessa, it's essential that you fast from midnight. If you eat or drink a single thing, however small, then we won't be able to operate. You do understand that, don't you?'

'Yes,' she said, 'of course,' then plunged the straw through the lid of her milk-shake, and drained it without stopping.

I O

TESSA OPENED HER eyes, glanced at the alarm clock. Ten to nine. She turned over on her back, startled by the eager morning light, luxuriating in the fact that it was Saturday, and sunny, and her first day off in a month. There was no need to get up, no need to do anything except lie there and recover from the long hours waitressing each day, the late nights babysitting, the Sunday morning coaching – a twelve-year-old called Duncan who needed help in basic grammar, as much as history. She shut her eyes again, tucked the duvet right up to her chin. She and the baby would enjoy a lie-in until noon. They deserved it after four weeks' solid slog.

She placed her hand across her stomach, which was just beginning to swell, though no one else had noticed. She couldn't feel him move yet, but according to the books, he would already be swimming and somersaulting; could turn his head, curl his toes, swallow, squint and frown. She had made her own calendar of pregnancy, so that she could tick off all the weeks – sixteen now – which meant twenty-three to go. He would be born in early February – an age away from the hot and sultry August they'd been sweltering through – lawns parched, tourists wilting, the first yellow leaves blemishing the trees. Even at this hour, the sun was surprisingly strong, butting at the curtains, trying to barge in.

She already felt at home here, having done her 'House and Garden bit', as Alexandra called it. Hardly garden – that was still a jungle – but her bedroom did look good, especially compared with Alexandra's bare white walls and Liz's cluttered tip. She only wished the loo wasn't downstairs; hated the long trek when she was half-asleep, or worse still, in the middle of the night. A pregnant bladder seemed an irritable demanding thing, always whimpering for a pee like a badly trained dog. It was whining at this moment, so she struggled out of bed and down the stairs; made herself a cup of tea before returning to the bedroom. She drank it by the window, with her feet up on the bed, re-reading for the hundredth time all the cards and letters she'd received since mid-July. She started with the postcard showing a fourteenth-century Book of Hours, which was signed Ruth Sylvester, and said how gratified she was to hear of Tessa's First in Honour Moderations, and might she offer her congratulations? Tessa sat savouring her tutor's stilted phrases, still hardly able to believe that they were actually addressed to her – the prat from Emberfield.

She'd been even more incredulous when she'd scanned the list in Schools and seen her name right near the top – as few as thirty in Class I, out of a total of three hundred, and only a dozen of them females. She had rushed to phone her mother, dashed off a note to Michael; received more congratulations – a boxed satin card from April, complete with scarlet bow, and from Michael a Victorian postcard of the Tyne. She treasured his four cards – one for every week in August – each only a few scribbled lines, and more or less illegible, but proving that he missed her, that his bleeding wrecks of patients hadn't pushed her from his mind.

He'd gone up north alone, in fact, having decided it would make more sense if he sussed the job out first; checked on his surroundings and the condition of the flat before she joined him there. Two weeks ago, he had phoned to say he'd settled in, the flat was fine, he'd even bought a double bed, and it was high time that they christened it. She'd been tempted to drop everything and catch the next train up, but was still in such a turmoil about admitting the existence of the baby that she'd postponed the trip, pretending to be ill. She had agonized since then, changed her mind from hour to hour, then finally sat down and written him a letter – the most difficult exhausting letter she'd composed in all her life. That had been two days ago, so now, at last, Dr Michael Edwards was aware he would be a father in five months.

'Tessa! Are you deaf? There's someone on the phone for you. It bloody woke me up.'

She dashed downstairs again, flinging an apology to the disgruntled Alexandra, but too keyed up to feel guilt. It must be Michael phoning. He'd have got her letter and would want to talk things over, tell her his reactions – shock, delight, annoyance, pride – or a mixture of all four – or maybe even fury and suspicion. She picked up the receiver, out of breath, hands sweaty.

'*Who?*' she said. 'I'm sorry, it's a bad line. Oh, I see. This morning. No, that's fine – I'm free. I'll see him at ten-thirty, then.' She subsided on the sofa with a sense of total anti-climax.

'What's up?' asked Alexandra, who had hung around to eaves-drop.

'Bang goes my lie-in! That was Mr Collingsby – Duncan's father – asking if I could come today, instead of Sunday.'

'You should have told him to get stuffed.'

'I can't. He pays too much. Ten pounds an hour's a fortune, compared with my slave wages in the café.'

'You're telling me!' Alex mooched into the kitchen, to switch the kettle on, then banged about with plates and cups. 'I'm doing the late shift at Freud's tonight, but the sods don't pay me extra for working after midnight. Want a cup of tea?'

'I've had mine, thanks, but I'll join you for some breakfast. Or are you going back to bed?'

'No. I've got too much to do – all my washing, for a start. And Julie's coming round at twelve, with half her flaming family, so I'll have to buy some food and stuff.'

'I'll get it, if you like. I'm going past the shops.'

'But you did it last time – and the time before – lugged back half a ton.'

'I'm just building up my credit for when I've had the baby. It'll be your turn then. You can wash the dirty nappies.'

Alex made a face. 'Won't you use disposable?'

Tessa shook her head. 'Can't afford it.' She went to fetch the bread, then turned on Radio Oxford to fill the awkward silence. She knew what Alexandra thought – that she couldn't afford to have the kid at all, not in any way – was crazy to attempt it, or imagine she could continue working for a degree with a squalling new-born infant soaking up her money and her time. Both Liz and Alexandra had been stunned, not only by the bombshell of her pregnancy, but also because she was adamant about staying on at Balliol, making as few changes as she could. She'd tried to convince them she could cope – convince herself as well. She'd discovered there were special grants for single-parent students, and though she had to admit that time would be a problem, finals were still two years away, and the second year was supposed to be a doddle, compared with the rigours of the first. Of course she did have doubts – full-blown terrors, sometimes – but there was no alternative. She could neither kill her child nor chuck in her degree.

'Has the postman been?' she asked, in an attempt to change the subject.

'No, he's always late on Saturdays. I suppose you're itching to hear from whatshisname?'

Tessa nodded, reflecting once again how peculiar it was that Alexandra seemed totally incapable of remembering Michael's name, whereas for her that name chimed endlessly, setting up reverberations, ripples; was branded on her body, tattooed into the skin. But then Alex wasn't keen on men; looked butch herself with her cropped dark hair and heavy khaki combat gear. The word 'heavy' seemed appropriate in several other ways – heavy features, heavy jaw, heavy sullen moods. Yet they'd grown closer in the last few weeks – thrown together by circumstance, as the only two who had moved into the house yet. Liz was living at home until September, and Vicky was on holiday in Greece, so she and Alexandra had no other available company. They'd even started confiding in each other, enjoying late-night chats, when wine or sheer exhaustion encouraged them to drop their guard. Tessa was relieved to have found an ally when she'd more or less lost Charlotte, who'd been indignant to hear that after all her efforts and her parents' hospitality, the 'patient' had absconded from a clinic she had personally recommended. The memories were galling still – Charlotte's scorn and huffiness, the way she'd banged the phone down with the briefest of goodbyes.

Another person she'd upset was Colin. He'd written to her several times, suggesting that they met, and she'd eventually confessed in a short but sheepish reply that there was another man in her life. Colin's own six-page response had been an outpouring of regret and self-reproach, unredeemed by its Tennysonian imagery. She felt highly apprehensive about meeting them both next term – Colin wretched, Charlotte curt – and herself swelling unequivocally each day.

Though the new academic year still seemed a million miles away from this hollow summer Oxford. Without its tide of students the town had lost its heart and purpose, and become a sort of stage-set for an audience to gawp at – those hordes of Japs or Yanks who were deposited en masse by daily plane and coach, with their programmes and their opera-glasses. The main actors (dons and students) had departed on their holidays, or gone back to their homes, but the spectators still poured in to applaud the empty stage.

Balliol, too, was utterly transformed, and had been playing host to conferences for a good part of the vac – management consultants prowling through the library; quantity surveyors conferring in the quad. At present it was closed; even its own students were allowed only as far as the post room, then chivvied out immediately, like dangerous intruders. She'd felt a certain indignation not just at being excluded, but at living out at all; losing her two rooms in college, which she'd come to feel she owned. Though there were advantages, as well. College life could be really claustrophobic – the non-stop gossip about who was shagging whom; the casual way that anyone and everyone could knock on your door and expect to swan in for a chat, regardless of how busy you were. She was beginning to enjoy sharing a whole house with just one other person; far removed from Sloanes like Charlotte, or those ex-Harrovian hippies who spent their time in college posing as East Enders, so they wouldn't offend against the canon of Balliol's fervent anti-elitism.

'You did actually post that letter, then?' Alexandra asked, intruding on her thoughts. 'I was sure you'd lose your nerve.'

'So was I!' said Tessa, who had actually forgotten the all-important letter for at least two-and-three-quarter minutes. 'I stood by the pillar box for what seemed like a good hour, with it poised halfway through the slit, but I just couldn't let it go. And even when I did, I instantly regretted it, and hung around for ages again, wondering how the hell I could get it back.'

'You're mad!' Alex heaped her branflakes with brown sugar, sniffed the milk to check it wasn't sour. 'I only hope you demanded your rights. He ought to pay his whack, you know.'

'Well, no, I . . .'

'Christ, Tessa, you're pathetic! I'd bloody make him sweat. And some girls would go much further and expect not just commitment, but even marriage and . . .'

'He *can't* get married, Alex, not at this stage. A wife and baby would put the kibosh on his career. He's incredibly ambitious, but he's got years and years to go yet. He hasn't even taken his primary FRCS.'

'And how about *your* career? A babe-in-arms is hardly going to help you.'

Tessa didn't answer. Of course she wanted marriage; had fantasized about it long before she knew that she was pregnant. But it had always been a future prospect – a rosy, hazy future, when she'd got her own degree, and Michael was established – the two of them miraculously unencumbered by jobs, responsibilities, or bills, but making endless love in moonlit woods. The baby had changed everything, brought her down to earth, forced her to think practically about Michael's life, as well as hers. She couldn't inflict a child on a busy SHO sweating it out in casualty, often working nights and always with emergencies, who hardly had a minute to himself. Great to be his courtesan, his astounding brazen mistress, but not a bloody millstone round his neck.

She picked up a stray branflake from the table, crumbled it to dust. 'I couldn't get married anyway, not if I go on with my degree. I can hardly commute from Newcastle to Balliol.'

'Have you told the powers-that-be yet – your tutors, or the Dean?'

'No fear! I don't intend to. I'll just turn up next term and carry on as if nothing's any different.'

'But surely it'll show by then?'

Tessa shrugged, crushed a second branflake with something close to anger. She'd dumped all these painful issues in the cellar of her mind, and now Alexandra was trying to drag them out again, expose them to the light. She turned the radio right down, sagged back in her chair. The jokey announcer was getting on her nerves, and even the sun seemed intrusive and insensitive, showing up the dirt in the messy, jumbled kitchen.

'They may insist you take a year off,' Alex pondered. 'I mean, there's no crèche or anything. Oxford's positively medieval when it comes to things like nurseries.'

'I know,' said Tessa shortly.

'Would your mother help at all?'

'I haven't told her.' Tessa studied the cereal packet, pretending to be engrossed in the amounts of vitamins and minerals provided by an average portion. There were a score of different reasons why she wished to spare her mother – and also spare herself from a tidal wave of advice and speculation, lamentation, drama.

'But you won't be able to hide it for much longer. Anyway, I thought you said she was coming up to stay.'

'Yes, she is – next week.'

There was silence for a moment – just the sound of Alexandra's spoon scraping the last branflakes from her bowl. 'Tessa . . .' she began again.

'What?'

She had pushed the bowl away now – preparing her next onslaught, Tessa guessed.

'Look, if Lord Muck says he won't cough up, I'll chip in with something. It can't be much – I'm in debt up to my eyebrows – but I can probably help in other ways. I mean, I don't mind babysitting when you've got lectures or tutorials, and I'll even wash your rotten nappies, though only if you're really pushed.'

Tessa shook her head, too choked to speak. Grouchy Alexandra was offering help – and cash – yet her overdraft was already pretty hefty, and unlike well-heeled Charlotte, she didn't come from a three-car, three-bathroom home. Her father was an insurance salesman who'd just been made redundant, so she was obliged to work herself during the whole of the long vacation.

'Tessa, listen will you? Liz and me and Vicky have already had a chat about it, and we've agreed we'll all muck in, do a sort of rota – you know, looking after the kid, giving it its bottle, or whatever the fuck they have. That way, you won't be landed with the whole caboodle. Hell! There's no need to *cry*, mate. It was meant to cheer you up.'

Tessa gave Alex a brief, embarrassed hug, then fled upstairs to her room. She *was* cheered up – more touched than she could say, yet tears were streaming down her face – tears for all she'd lost: Michael, marriage, security, the name Edwards for her child. She had asked for absolutely nothing in her letter – no money and no ties. It had required great strength of will; taken days of heart-searching, and, in the end, she'd been influenced by Heloïse. Yet how could she explain that she'd let herself be swayed by the arguments of a precocious female scholar who'd lived more than eight hundred years ago, and who had languished in a nunnery for most of her tormented life, after the trauma of her own affair? Alex would dismiss her as a nutcase.

She picked up her copy of the *Letters of Abelard and Heloïse*, which she kept on the bedside table, close to Michael's cards. It should have been packed away by now, along with Saint Bernard, Guibert, Suger and the rest. She had finished with the whole subject of Early Gothic France; would be moving on in her second year to something completely different – nineteenth-century English History:

Peel, Disraeli, Gladstone. Yet Heloïse continued to obsess her; had become so important in her life – almost a physical presence – it would be impossible to consign her to the bottom of a suitcase. She sometimes actually found herself involved in conversations with her, discussing love, or loneliness, or asking her advice, as if she were a loving elder sister, or a soul-mate. She would rather die than admit it to her friends. It seemed so bizarre, so childish – if not downright mad – to be communing with a minor historical character on the syllabus, but she had never felt more sane, in fact. The pregnancy had grounded her, brought her face to face with stark realities. It had also provided a further link with Heloïse. The parallels between them were uncanny – both roughly the same age, both students, and both tall, both pregnant out of marriage, and both shatteringly in love with a selfish, headstrong, yet charismatic man. And it was precisely because of Abelard's great gifts that Heloïse had opposed his offer of marriage; couldn't bear to shackle him with sordid duties and petty obligations, which might dull his restless brilliance.

She sprawled out on the bed, began flicking through the *Letters*, looking for that section of the *Historia Calamitatum* where Abelard reported her selfless reasons for refusing any legal tie.

'*Think of the situation marriage would inflict on you*,' Heloïse had protested. '*What harmony can there be between scholarship and running a home, between a desk and a cradle, a book and a distaff . . . ? Is there anywhere a man who, with his mind on Scripture or philosophy, can endure the wailings of a new-born child?*'

She re-read the words, as she'd done umpteen times already. If you changed 'desk' to scalpel, and 'Scripture' to surgery, they fitted Michael perfectly – which is why she'd paraphrased them in her own letter. The more she reflected on Heloïse's brand of love, the more she was attracted by its unselfishness, high-mindedness – the refusal to involve a philosopher of genius in an infant's sick and shit, or drag his mind from God to cots and colic. Heloïse had loathed the thought of being not a helpmate but a burden, of preventing his huge talent from benefiting all mankind, not one mere wife and child. Didn't the same apply to Michael? Once he became a leading heart-surgeon, he'd be transforming lives, even saving lives – unless her own demands distracted him.

The whole nub of Heloïse's case was *not* to make demands; to spurn rewards, security, and give instead of take. Tessa leafed on through the pages to find Heloïse's reply to the *Historia*, written years after the love affair, when she was abbess of her convent and so vowed to a life of total celibacy. Yet though she had renounced sex, she still burned for it in secret; still hungered after Abelard, who was more her god than God. That only proved how great had been her sacrifice, to renounce not just the world, but the man who was the world to her. In her letter, she complained to her once-lover that he'd failed to grasp the essence of her argument – that she had preferred love to marriage, freedom to chains, and had sought nothing for herself except the chance to please and serve him. *'The term "wife",'* she had confided, *'may seem more sacred or more binding, but another term was always dearer to my heart – that of your mistress, or even of your concubine, your whore . . .'*

How extraordinary it was that Heloïse had used those words – Michael's words – which must have sounded blasphemous in the mouth of a chaste nun. And there were other similarities between them. Heloïse was probably illegitimate – there was no mention of parents, and she'd been brought up by her uncle – and though she herself had April (with Dave vaguely in the background), she was also what was bravely called a love-child. Yet she mustn't push the analogy too far. Twentieth-century attitudes were so completely different that it was unfair – and unhistorical – to see her own predicament in terms of Heloïse's. Despite all the angst and heartache, her situation was simpler altogether, and she had far less to lose. No one would entomb her in a convent, or remove her precious child, and once Michael realized she was no threat to his freedom, was there anything to stop them resuming their relationship?

The noise of a car backfiring in the street outside suddenly blasted her back to the present. She'd be late for Duncan Collingsby if she didn't get a move on. She put her favourite book away; wrenched her thoughts from Heloïse to the Tudor Revolution, and how she'd teach her dozy pupil to memorize the sequence of Henry VIII's six wives. She peeled off her nightie, sorted through her clothes for a chic but loosish dress, which would help her play the part of a well-paid history tutor whilst concealing any suspicion of a bulge. She brushed her tangled hair, recalling how she'd let it fall like a yashmak over Michael's thighs, the last time they'd made love, then wound the strands around his stiffening prick, binding them together. They *were* bound, inextricably – and most especially by their child, who was already half his birth-length, could breathe, digest and pee, and was about to sprout his own hair. She owed it to the baby to be calm. The first weeks of his life she'd spent in storms of tears or rage, so now she must seek to cultivate an inner peace and harmony – whatever Michael said in his reply.

She deliberately slowed her movements as she dressed and made the bed, then strolled downstairs to check the fridge and store-cupboard and scribble a brief shopping-list, and was finally turning out of Juxon Street at exactly 10.15. She loved the street, with its brightly-painted houses and their obstreperous front gardens where flowers and weeds battled for supremacy; the faint rumble from the local factory, which Alexandra bitched about, but *she* found reassuring. This particular patch of Oxford was called Jericho, and though only fifteen minutes' walk away from the centre of the town, it seemed a separate village, with its Bohemian atmosphere, its own small shops and restaurants, the picturesque canal.

She crossed Walton Street – its thoroughfare – glancing to her right, as always, at the Radcliffe Infirmary, a few yards further down. It had been built two centuries earlier than the John Radcliffe in Headington, and was another reminder of Michael, since he'd worked there for a while. It seemed strange that he was no longer sharing Oxford with her, and a week ago she'd been missing him so badly, she had cycled up Headington Hill to visit the JR, as if the mere fact of her returning to his former territory might somehow bring him back.

She had wandered into the foyer of the maternity department; been halted in her tracks by a white-draped showpiece crib, complete with doll inside. The doll was stiff and waxen – eyes shut, face impassive – dressed in a white bonnet and old-fashioned lacy gown. 'PLEASE DO NOT TOUCH', the notice said, and she'd backed away obediently, though the image of that torpid form had lodged deep in her mind. If only her own baby were just a sleeping doll – not alive, not growing every hour. Her spirits had sunk lower still when she looked up at the blackboard with its chalked-on visiting times, most prefaced by the tag: 'Husbands and partners only'. She *had* no partner, no one to support her when she finally went into labour; no one to accompany her on her ante-natal visits, like these couples flocking through the door; men arm in arm with their pregnant wives or girlfriends. She had followed them downstairs, stared in horror at the grossly swollen bellies; the lurid posters warning of the risks involved – rubella, diabetes, toxoplasmosis. This was not her world, but an alien and frightening one, in total contrast to normal student life, where the only major worries were finishing your essay or wondering if the bank would increase your overdraft. She had blundered blindly out again, ignoring the receptionist, who was eyeing her suspiciously. Since then, she had resolved to keep clear of all such clinics. Heloïse had managed without people poking and probing her, or alarming her with scare-stories.

Today, she felt much stronger; easier in her mind now she'd got her letter off to Michael, and cheered by Alexandra's change of heart. She was not alone – not really – had generous friends, a job; wasn't a poor skivvy living fifty years ago, who'd be sacked without a penny's compensation for daring to be pregnant out of marriage, or marched weeping through the streets as an example to the rest. It was true she had felt a certain shame, an instinct to apologize, hide herself away, but that was going to change. She'd accept her pregnant state, be proud of it, even flaunt it; maybe hunt down a maternity dress in the trendy second-hand shop she'd discovered recently, just two streets from the house. She'd drop in there on the way back from the Collingsbys', return to Alexandra not just with cheese and wine, but with her first designer smock.

The noise and laughter could be heard from three doors down – a full-scale party at their house, judging by the din, which had overflowed outdoors. Tessa walked down the side passage, saw three small boys rolling in the unmown grass, and various mothers, aunts and cousins reclining on a picnic rug, quaffing plastic cups of wine.

'Ah, the grub!' said Alex, striding out to meet her. 'I hope to God there's enough. Julie said her family, but this is more like an army. At least they brought a stack of booze, so we can save ours for the next invasion. Grab yourself a glass. You look completely knackered.'

'Let me just dump this lot first. The bottles weigh a ton.'

Alexandra followed her into the kitchen, started unloading all the bags. 'Oh, by the way, that letter's come. The writing's so appalling, I thought it wasn't ours at first, and was about to bung it back, but then I saw the Newcastle postmark.' She fetched it from the mantelpiece, stood peering at the stamp.

Tessa had to restrain herself from snatching it away. Alexandra's hands were dirty, and the envelope was already stained and creased. How dare she mess it up like that – something so important, a precious part of Michael? Yet she almost dreaded opening it; wasn't quite prepared. It had come too soon, caught her unawares, despite the fact that she had thought of nothing else since she'd dropped her own letter in the post-box. Michael must have written back immediately, sat straight down and dashed off his reply. Her hand was shaking as she reached out for the envelope; droplets of cold sweat snailing down between her breasts.

'Well, open it – go on.' Alex moved in closer, consumed with curiosity, evidently expecting to be regaled with all the details.

'I . . . think I'd better change first. I'm boiling in this dress.' Tessa bolted up to her room, stood by the window, tracing the first line on the envelope – the exuberant looping T; the 'Reeves' little more than a boisterous blotchy doodle. What Alex had disparaged as 'appalling scrawl' had become something she respected: confirmation of Michael's hectic schedule. A calligrapher might have time to cross his t's or dot his i's, but a surgeon was too busy fighting death.

She slit the letter open with a nail-file, didn't want to tear it, when it was something she would keep for ever. One of the children in the garden was screaming that he'd grazed his knee – expiring, by the sounds of it. How could she read the most crucial letter of her life with those anguished yells resounding through the neighbourhood?

'Hi, Tessa!' Julie called, suddenly catching sight of her and waving with her empty glass. 'Come down and join the party!'

'In a sec,' she shouted back, gazing beyond Julie to the ancient deserted cemetery which adjoined the Juxon Street back gardens. She sometimes went there for a stroll, or to escape the hubbub of the town, though Alex thought it ghoulish to take one's recreation in a graveyard. It was really like another garden – a secret place guarded by tall trees, full of shrubs and tangled flowers, and much quieter in late August when the factory shut down. It would be the perfect spot to read her private letter. She had never met another living soul there, and even some of the locals didn't know of its existence.

She crept down the stairs as quietly as she could, hoping to sidle out unnoticed.

'I thought you'd gone to change,' Alexandra challenged her, emerging from the kitchen.

'Yes, I had,' said Tessa. 'But . . . but I left something at Duncan's, so I'm just going back to fetch it. They'll be out all afternoon.'

'Poor you! It's a bloody pain in this heat to slog up there again. Has your bike still got a puncture?'

'Two!' Tessa escaped into the street, the letter burning in her hand. She felt decidedly less harassed as she closed the gates of St Sepulchre's behind her, entered her green sanctuary. Today it seemed especially lush, as if it had laid on all its bounty to celebrate the fact that Michael had replied so quickly, not kept her in suspense. Swags of glossy elderberries galaxied the bushes; a pair of peacock butterflies were courting in the sun, skimming from a blowzy rose to a burst of yellow ragwort. Even the weeds looked luxuriant and fertile – soft-lipped nettles flowering in the undergrowth; the frothy lace of hedge-parsley emitting its rank scent. She was glad she had left the party, didn't need all that raucous giggly company; had her own built-in companion in Michael junior. She always assumed he was a boy, and would be tall like both his parents – dark-haired, dark-eyed, and in every way exceptional. She was sure Michael would adore his son, once he'd recovered from the shock; see him as another (miniature) archangel; maybe even start planning his career – Eton, Christ Church, a professorship in surgery.

'Listen, kid,' she told him, pressing her palm against her belly. 'This is a letter from your father, and we're going to sit down here and read it.'

But the minute she sat down, she was up again and pacing, too nervous to keep still. The letter seemed untypical of Michael – four folded sheets instead of two scant lines. What could he be saying in all those words and words and words? – though in cool objective fact, it didn't matter. She had made her own decision, and didn't need anyone to sanction it, support it – not partner, mother, doctor or do-gooder. So why was she so agitated, unable even to walk straight, but lurching round in circles? Often, when she came here, she studied the inscriptions engraved into the stones – those she could still read, which hadn't flaked away or crumbled like their owners in the coffins. She had grown to love the graves, which seemed a reminder of the ones outside her college room, though these were even older – moss-encrusted, mouldering, wonderfully romantic. Or sometimes she picked flowers: tiny secret vetches, tall ragged-petalled daisies, a blazing scarlet rose. But today she couldn't concentrate, and her hands were full already – weighed down by four huge sheets of bronze.

A sudden bray of laughter exploded over the wall – Julie's party trespassing even here. Tessa veered away to the far corner of the cemetery, where she'd be safely out of earshot. She'd hide inside the long dark skirt of her favourite copper-beech tree, whose branches hung so low they seemed to enclose the tombs beneath them in a second mausoleum. She squeezed between the burnished leaves, entering a cool refuge, like the inside of a tent; the ground rough beneath her feet from last year's crackly beech-nuts; the smells of earth and leaf-mould. The noises here weren't threatening – rustlings in the twigs; the swoop and thresh of birds' wings; a squirrel's acrobatics as he shinned from branch to branch.

She forced herself to sit down, squatting on a dismembered plinth of stone. Its cross had broken off and was lying on the ground in a tourniquet of ivy; jagged cracks bandaged with green moss. She used it as a foot-rest, wiped her clammy hands before unfolding the four sheets, resting the letter on her stomach, so as to involve her child, as well. 'Okay, Michael,' she said to both of them. 'Here goes.'

She read the first page quickly, eyes devouring the words, then gradually slowing down, as if those words had sapped her strength. The third page slipped from her hand, seemed to be wilfully recoiling from her, fluttering to the ground. She let it lie where it had fallen, sinking back herself, peering through the branches at the ugly factory wall. Alex was right – this place was quite grotesque – a dilapidated cemetery standing next to an eyesore of a factory. How could she not have noticed those stained and broken windows, those dangerous-looking wires looped across the dirty brick, the air of desolation? And her 'romantic' graves were little more than ruins, dunghills for old bones. She had been wrong about so many things – the ludicrous and high-flown way she'd modelled herself on Heloïse; her fatuous naivety in regarding Juxon Street as home. The house was just a dump – and a prohibitively expensive one – full of rowdy strangers at this moment. It was time she went back to her real home, became a child again.

She returned the letter neatly to its envelope, then scrabbled at the parched and stubborn earth, trying to dig a shallow grave where she could bury it for ever. It belonged here in this cemetery, with dead things and abandoned things – and so did she.

He'd killed her.

11

'COME ON, JACK, get your finger out, mate. I've got a thirst like the Sahara, and you've not bought a round all evening.'

'Jack's not buying nothing. He's just blown his whole year's salary on that poncy BMW.'

'It's not a BMW, it's a Merc.'

'Hey, that reminds me of the one about the chauffeur and the schoolgirl. This rich bloke hires a chauffeur to take his youngest daughter to . . .'

Tessa tried to block her ears. She had moved seats twice already, but there were no quiet secluded corners in this vile suburban pub; nowhere she could escape the muzak and the fruit-machines, the beery guffaws drowning every punchline. She wondered how her mother could stand the ghastly place – the dreary decor, where everything was fake: pretend-wood panelling, leatherette banquettes, 'antique' pictures, circa 1990, olde-worlde carriage lamps from some modern hypermarket. Even the plants were plastic, as if nothing green and sappy could survive the smoky atmosphere, the reek of greasy food and stale spilt beer.

Everyone around her seemed to be laughing, telling jokes – a voluptuous hennaed female spilling gin and giggles on to her partner's cardboard pizza; a balding man with a boozer's red-veined face thinking it hilarious to remove his socks and shoes. A boisterous group was playing darts, every double-top greeted with a crescendo of cackles, cheers and shouts. She felt a completely different species from these flushed and practised drinkers – an alien, an intruder, who had no right to be here. If a creature from another planet should walk into the pub, he would pick on her immediately as the odd one out, the grey and silent one, with a great boulder lodged inside her. The heavy stone was pressing on her stomach and her voice-box, so that she could neither eat nor speak. She was drinking, though – a double Malibu and Coke – a present from her mother, who'd been too busy yet to do anything but hug her, kiss her, and express wonder and surprise at seeing her darling daughter in the flesh.

'Toots, you've made my day! I was beginning to think you were avoiding me, or maybe even ashamed of your old Mum. I mean, after getting that first-class degree, it's probably half a crown to speak to you.'

'It wasn't a degree, Mum – just my first official exam. I don't take my degree for another two years.'

'Never mind the name. It was first-class honours wasn't it? – just as I expected. I'd like to meet those big wheels at your college and tell them what you said to me the moment you were born. Well, you didn't speak exactly, but it was the nearest thing to talking I've ever seen in a kid two seconds old. You were still all wet and slimy, seeing as you'd only just popped out, but I'll never forget how you opened your huge eyes and gave the place the once-over. You looked just like you were about to put in a complaint – "I don't think much of this joint. I'm made for higher things."'

Tessa hadn't joined in April's laughter, too startled by the instant talk of birth. Was her mother psychic, able to pick up vibes from the stomach she'd concealed in a loose-fitting summer dress? No. It was purely a coincidence. There was nothing yet to show. But once her mother had stopped running round with plates of cottage pie, and could sit down for a minute without Sergeant Major Connie breathing down her neck, she would have to steer the conversation back to babies and maternity wards – except that this time it wouldn't be a laughing matter.

She sat sipping her expensive drink, aware of all the warnings she'd read about drinking during pregnancy. But a few mouthfuls of white rum were nothing like as lethal as the damage Michael had done. He had destroyed the baby somehow, so that she no longer felt pregnant, no longer even felt a woman – just a reject and a freak. She rummaged in her bag for his damp and dirty letter, which she had rescued from its grave. She kept reading and re-reading it, as if hoping that some miracle would change the words and sentiments when she ploughed through it for the twelfth or twentieth time. How terrible his writing was – sloppy, barely formed – an insult, in a way, to feel he'd spent so little trouble on making it less raw.

'All right, darling?' her mother asked, teetering up to Tessa's table in her scarlet slingback shoes, which were ridiculously high for waitressing and cramped her pudgy feet. 'I'm afraid Shirley's off sick tonight, so I'm busting a gut trying to keep up with all the orders. But we stop serving food at ten, so after that, maybe we can . . .'

She wheeled round as someone hollered for their scampi, lurched away with her loaded tray; hair tumbling from its lurex clip, skirt so tight it hobbled her. Tessa watched her put the plates down, then scrabble for a Kleenex and start dabbing at her nose, blowing surreptitiously when the customers weren't looking. Her mother must be suffering from another of her summer colds, which she caught every year unfailingly. She never seemed to have the time to look after herself or feed herself – too busy feeding others. She had dashed back to the kitchen, and was returning with two plates of egg and chips; her leopard-print blouse (fake, to match the pub) splattered with a second pattern of what looked like Bisto gravy. Yet even the most boorish of her customers received their food garnished with a smile, and her regulars got more – a fond pat on the shoulder, a saucy squeeze of the arm. April stinted no one but herself. There was a ladder in her tights, but tights cost money, and so did vitamin C, though it might have prevented her colds.

Tessa chewed the orange-slice which had been floating in her drink. Single parents married Tyrant Poverty – she knew that from her own case. She'd been shattered by the price of prams, even second-hand ones; the price of nappies, baby clothes. How dare her father live it up in Croydon, in a house twice the size of theirs! Okay, he wasn't loaded, but he did have a car, a video, and holidays abroad – all the things that Michael had as well. She thrust the letter back into its envelope, tempted to rip it into shreds. He had offered not to support their child, but to get rid of it instead. He hadn't put it quite so bluntly, but there was a whole page about his 'contacts', and 'not wasting any time', and how if she was worried about the money side, just to leave all that to him. She wouldn't touch his money – not for murder. She already had the cheque from Dave, which now seemed tainted, shameful, although her father hadn't known what it was for. She couldn't help wondering if he had offered cash to April, nineteen years ago; dashed off a similar letter, rejecting and denying her when she was still a helpless blob. It was only now that the trauma of her own conception had really hit home – fury with Michael curdling in her head with resentment towards Dave. How could she have repeated the whole unhappy saga? And the irony was worse when she reflected on the fact that April had sacrificed everything to give her daughter the chance in life she'd never had herself.

She had decided not to tell her mother about that part of Michael's letter. April would only brand him as a butcher – the term she used for anyone who advocated abortion. There was so much she'd have to censor: the Brighton clinic; the lies about her stay with Charlotte; the amazing, almost frightening heights she and Michael had reached together, the last time they'd made love. Her hand was sweating on the envelope, crumpling it to nothing, while the other hand longed to smooth it out. She might never get another letter, so maybe she should keep it as the last dregs and husks of Michael, a precious, sickening relic.

'Won't be long now,' April puffed, pausing for a moment with her arm on Tessa's chair. 'Things are slowing down, thank God, but that damn-fool of a dishwasher is playing silly buggers, so's I'll have to do the washing-up by hand. But once I've finished here, you can sneak into the kitchen with me, and we'll have our little natter over the sink.' She fished inside her blouse-sleeve for a damp ball of lilac Kleenex, mopped her nose again. 'Connie's on the warpath, but she's leaving at half-ten, so at least I can relax when she's pushed off. She gives me the heeby-jeebies, the way she watches me like a hawk. And she's told me to stop getting colds. I ask you, Tessa! – as if they're something I pick off the shelf at Tesco's – two tins of soup, one sore throat, and a stinker of a cough. I suppose she's worried about germs – some health inspector on the snoop, reading her the riot act – although I keep swearing blind it's hay-fever.'

'Mum . . .'

'What?'

'I love you.'

April leaned over to kiss her daughter's cheek; the middle button on her blouse popping open to reveal a strip of bosom, a flash of black lace slip. 'That deserves another drink! Same again?'

'No, thanks.'

'Well, how about a burger? Or we've got those turkey whatsits – though the only turkey in them is the picture on the packet. Or you could always have an egg. Mind you, even eggs is dodgy. I was reading in the *Mail* last week that male cocks are laying eggs now. They stuff them with these hormones and . . .'

'I've eaten, Mum, honestly.' 'Honestly' was a lie, but she was

135

well aware that anything she ordered would be charged (full-price) by Connie. Anyway, the thought of food sent shock-waves through her stomach, especially turkeyless turkey and 'male' eggs. The man opposite was tucking in to prawns, tearing off the shells and whiskers, then relishing each moistly naked body. His face had changed to Michael's – dark stubble, Latin eyes, full lips slicked with butter as he crammed in a bread-roll. There was another Michael next to him, mouth moustached with Guinness foam; the coarse hairs on his hands running right down to the fingertips, and tangled at the wrists. Everywhere she looked, Michael preened and guzzled – swilling whisky, stuffing whelks, leaning forward to paw the barmaid's cleavage, his own shirt open to the waist.

She tried to keep her eyes down, fix them on her beer-mat – Carlsberg Special Brew – but even that reminded her of Michael. He had drunk it in the hotel lounge, their last weekend together. She glanced up again, to the shields and shining silver cups displayed above the dartboard – silver cups for services in bed; shields to keep her safe, protect her from his poison-darts. Except they'd already found their target – stabbing through her womb, stinging in her bladder. She blundered to the toilet, wincing as she peed. If it hurt to pee, then it probably meant she was going down with cystitis – another hazard of pregnancy. She slumped back on the toilet-seat, suddenly noticing a graffito scribbled on the wall: 'CASTRATE P.H.A.!' Abelard's initials, with an H stuck in the middle – H for Heloïse, and horror. Abelard's castration had stunned the whole of France; appalled her when she'd read his own description of it.

She scratched at the initials with her thumbnail; couldn't shift the crude black biro, and didn't have a pen to cross them out. She fumbled for her lipstick, twisted up the cheap gilt sheath until she could see the scarlet phallus – a brilliant greasy red. Red was Michael's colour – the poppy-red of his favourite sweater, the crimson of his car, the hot red of his blood. Using the lipstick as a crayon, she drew a scarlet stroke right through the initials, then wrote 'M.E.' instead. The 'CASTRATE' looked too small now, not murderous enough, so she deleted it as well; began again, higher up, on a pristine stretch of wall. 'CASTRATE MICHAEL EDWARDS!' The letters seemed to scorch and sear, throbbing with the agony Abelard himself had felt – the pain and outrage, disgrace and disbelief, which he had poured out in his terror-crazed account.

Yet Abelard had also written that the punishment fitted the crime, and the same was true of Michael. She could see the victim writhing on his bed, hear his howls of pain, but suddenly the movements changed, and he was heaving, thrusting, circling with his thighs, teasing her by pausing, sliding almost out, then slowly, slowly in again; his cries no longer anguished, but ecstatic.

She looked up at the wall again, began frantically to rub the lipstick off, smearing it and smudging it, until the letters were illegible, but her fingers stained deep scarlet. At the basin, she scoured her hands with soap, watched the water running red, like blood. Even now, there was still a faint red tinge left – Michael's red, which would stain her life for ever.

She stumbled from the ladies' room, fought her zigzag way across the packed saloon bar, and out into the street, gulping down the darkness, trying to drown herself in black. She dived into an alleyway, a narrow faceless cul-de-sac which smelt of damp and cats; gradually slowing down her pace, regaining her control. Despite the dark, the air outside was still close and very muggy, as if this last stifling day of August was determined to extend itself, rather than be swallowed up by a cooler and more kindly month. She checked her watch – exactly ten. Two hours to go until the first of September. That was autumn, more or less, and then came ruthless winter – cold, dark, fading days; her baby's birth.

She trudged back to the pub, scanning the 'What's On' notice tacked up on the door. 'Drag Nite', 'Golden Oldies Nite', 'The Guv'nor's Birthday Bash'. All more work for April, who was now clearing tables, piling trays with dirty plates and lugging them into the kitchen. Singing as she worked, though – some happy carefree love-song. Wouldn't it be unfair – and even cruel – to break the bombshell news, capsize her mother's rosy mood by dumping a huge problem on her doorstep? April was euphoric because the affair with Ken was blossoming: the first of her romances to last beyond a few casual months. Had a daughter any right to destroy that fragile happiness?

She stood dejected at the door, gazing out at the dark confining alley, uncertain what to do. She'd planned to tell her mother in the hope of lightening her own load, and hungry for some sympathy and comfort; had spent half the bumpy coach journey imagining April magicking her pain away with a Band-Aid or a Bounty bar, a kiss, or bedtime story, as she had done in the past. Yet now it seemed . . .

'Right, love, Connie's buggered off now, so the kitchen's all our own.'

Tessa started at the throaty voice rasping just behind her; let April link her arm through hers and lead her back into the bar. She found herself shrinking from the noise – the clink and slam of glasses, the muffled roar of yakking mouths, shrill warbles from the games machines. She looked round at the faces, all cracked by stupid grins. Even the Toby jugs were smirking on their ledge above the bar, and on the walls Victorian Lolitas simpered in their fake-wood frames. She would have gladly wiped the smiles off those smug faces – Michael's most of all – the gloating smile he'd flashed her when she'd told him she adored him.

It was a relief to reach the quiet and empty kitchen, though under normal circumstances she would have been appalled by all the mess: worktops overflowing with unwashed pots and pans; giant catering packs discarded on the floor. She knew she ought to help, but felt exhausted, even dizzy. She mooched towards the only chair, watching April kick her shoes off, rub her aching feet.

'Mum, d'you want to sit down? You look as if you could do with . . .'

'No, you park your bones. It's odd, you know. I've been asking Father Christmas for a brand new pair of pins every year since you were born, and he keeps on sending soap or scarves instead. That's typical of men – *they* don't get the bunions.' She tied an apron round her waist, a comic one, printed with a suspender-belt and bra. 'Well I'd better make a start, I suppose, or we'll be here till kingdom come.'

She ran some water in the sink, then spooned the last scrapings from a dish of chicken curry straight into her mouth, followed by a few crumbs of apple pie. Dinner over, she soaked the dishes, squirted them with Squezy, then swung round to face her daughter. 'Now, tell me how you are, Toots. I want all your news, and especially how your birthday went. Maybe you don't realize, but it's the only one we haven't spent together.'

Tessa didn't answer, was aware of her mother's eyes on her. April hadn't yet turned back to her pile of washing-up, but was fixing her with the most intense and searching scrutiny she had received in nineteen years. Suddenly, she walked over, dish-mop in her hand, placed an arm on her daughter's drooping shoulders.

'You're pregnant, Tessa, aren't you? You're going to have a baby.'

138

Tessa tried to speak and couldn't. She could feel her mother's dry coarse hair tickling on her neck; the bolster of her bosom soft against her face; her arms a shield, a shelter.

'Don't cry,' said April simply.

Tessa glanced down at the wet spots shining on the lino, hardly believing they were tears. She'd been determined not to cry; dared not cry in case she couldn't stop. She cleared her throat, still groping for the words to express her relief and yet astonishment. How on earth could her mother know like that, when she hadn't so much as mentioned the subject? Was her stomach bigger than she thought; her breasts noticeably enlarged?

'H . . . how ever could you tell, Mum?' she blurted out at last.

'I suppose mothers have a sixth sense,' April said, mopping her nose and then Tessa's tears with the same soggy wad of Kleenex. 'And there's a different look about you, Toots – something in your face.'

Tessa gripped her hand, equally surprised by her mother's quiet acceptance – no hysterics or histrionics, no recrimination.

'Don't cry, my pet,' April said again, offering her the Kleenex box.

Tessa wiped her eyes, edged away a little. Her mother smelt of curry and cheap scent. 'I . . . I'm not crying because I'm pregnant, I'm crying about the father.'

'What about him, Tootsie?'

'Well, he . . . he doesn't want the baby, but' – she shrugged – 'I can accept that, just about. He's got his own ambitious life, and he thinks I tricked him anyway, because he made a special point of checking I was on the pill. What hurts is . . .' She broke off again, recalling Michael's letter – its cold dismissive phrases; the raging rabid jealousy she'd been fighting since she read it. She suddenly lurched up to her feet, let out a howl of fury. 'Mum, I still can't quite believe it, but he's been two-timing me from the first moment I laid eyes on him. He never said a word till now, but he's more or less engaged to someone else.'

April strode back to the sink, so indignant now herself, she started lashing at the dirty plates with her dish-mop, spitting out disparagements. The father of her daughter's child was a rat, a crud, a shitbag . . .

'*Don't*, Mum! I can't bear it. I love him. I still love him.'

'You can't love a man like that, Tess – a liar and a cheat.'

Tessa stared down at her hands. Michael had kissed those fingers, sucked each one right into his mouth; used his teeth to graze them, his tongue to circle their tips. He owned her body now and she couldn't wrench it back; couldn't stop loving him, whatever her mother said. However much he hurt her – physically or mentally – she knew it wouldn't change her basic feelings.

'It's not that Robert, is it? – the one you never let me meet? I knew there must be something odd about him.' April was still laying into plates, banging knives and forks down on the metal draining board.

Tessa shook her head.

'Well, just you tell me who the hell he is and I'll go straight up to Oxford and give him . . .'

'He's not in Oxford any more.'

'Where is he then?'

'He's . . . gone.' The word stuck in her throat – a terrifying hopeless word. She grabbed a tea towel, started drying up the cutlery, polishing each fork until her hand hurt. But he's coming back, she told herself; he must be coming back. He couldn't simply end things with a letter.

She was suddenly aware of the silence in the room. April had stopped her clattering, and was standing rigid at the sink, both hands in the water still, but doing little more than fiddle with the mop. Her rouged but shiny face looked tired and almost old; her lipstick smudged; the brave glitter on her eyelids melting into greasy silver creases.

'Listen, Mum, he's coming back.' This time she said it out aloud, as if speaking the words was enough to make it happen, and could dispel the utter wretchedness on her mother's wilting face.

'Yes,' she said, more brazenly. 'He's definitely coming back.'

12

'NOW THIS IS my treat, Tessa. I don't want any argument.'

'But you've only just . . .'

'No argument, I said. It's the first thing I'm doing for my grandchild – feeding its poor mother up. When *I* was sixteen weeks, I had a belly like an airship, and yours doesn't show at all yet.'

'So, how the hell did you guess then? You haven't really explained it yet.'

'Mothers simply know these things,' April said complacently, settling back in her chair. She reached out for the menu, an extensive one, swanking in a clammy vinyl cover; the same oppressive shade of burgundy as the squiggled carpet, the flock-patterned swirly walls. 'Now, what are you going to eat, love? The fried Pacific prawns are nice, although beef might be a safer bet – if it hasn't got mad cow disease. You have to be so careful when you're pregnant. Or there's always plain chop suey, or . . .'

'I've told you, I'm not hungry, Mum.'

'Well, how about some egg-drop soup? That's nourishing, but very light.'

'Okay,' said Tessa listlessly. The last thing she wanted was to be sitting in Yum Sing's at five minutes past midnight, but her mother had seemed reluctant to go home. She was having trouble with a lodger, so she claimed, although she'd tried to laugh it off, had looked a shade embarrassed, as if she were keeping something back. Could 'trouble' mean involvement, either sexual or emotional? Surely not, when Ken was on the scene?

They'd already spent an hour discussing the whole business of Michael and her pregnancy, before eventually escaping from the deserted Horse and Groom. She was tired now, even irritable; resentful

141

of the happy couples sitting all around her; one man forking noodles into his girlfriend's red-lipped mouth; another twosome clinking glasses and drinking to each other. Was Michael also toasting his engagement, feeding his new woman – that mysterious hateful female he'd known for seven years? According to his letter, they'd met originally at Christ Church when he was reading physiology. A brilliant girl, no doubt, and with all the social graces, who wouldn't let him down with her below-stairs accent or her uncouth comprehensive school. Strange he hadn't mentioned such a paragon before, if she meant so much, and had been earmarked as the partner of his future.

'I made it quite clear,' his letter said, 'that I wasn't free to love you, Tessa.' A blatant lie – he had never said a word. In fact the whole thing sounded devious; a string of trumped-up excuses to get him off the hook. His shadowy fiancée didn't even have a name, but was referred to merely as 'she'.

'She and I are both too busy to live together, so there's been no formal engagement, but I have to let you know that I'm totally committed to her.'

'Totally committed'. Those words hurt most of all. Michael was totally committed only to his career. She picked up her knife, made angry little slashes at the table. She had struggled with her selfish instincts, her longing to possess him; fought an inner battle with herself, until she was willing, even eager, to make Heloïse's sacrifice and refuse to tie him down. Instead, he'd tied himself down with marriage-bonds and manacles – the very constraints she'd done her best to spare him. The only things she'd asked for were regular discussions about the baby's health and progress, the occasional visit from his father – if and when he had the time – and the odd card or teddy bear.

'Shall we have the fried rice or the boiled, Toots? Or perhaps we'd better order both. That waiter's looking a bit cheesed off. He probably doesn't like us waltzing in so late, then hardly eating anything.'

Tessa shrugged. 'Chinese waiters all look pretty grouchy.' Even now after storms of words and tears in the sweltering pub kitchen, her mother hadn't really grasped how much Michael meant to her. Would anyone ever understand – or realize just how devastating it was to have to accept that the most momentous experience of her life had been, in his eyes, little more than a casual fling, something on the side? He'd been doubly unfaithful, not only to her, but also to the other woman, the one he'd promised total deep commitment. She felt sorriest of all for the poor rejected baby, who'd been offered not a teddy, but a coffin. Michael had even had the gall to say that he had no proof the child was his – a barb which really wounded, with its implication that she was as promiscuous as he was. And even her anxious shaken mother had seemed more concerned about Oxford – the appalling thought that she'd have to give it up – than about her losing Michael's son.

'It's a bit gloomy in here, isn't it?' April said, smoothing out the tassel on the menu, as if it too needed comfort. 'You'd think they were trying to save on the electricity.'

'I suppose it's meant to be romantic.' Tessa continued stabbing with the knife. Fine for all the other couples, drinking to their engagements or their special anniversaries; sharing food and lives. April must have forgotten the pain of being alone, now that she had Ken. The smugly happy pair of them were probably more or less engaged, as well, totally committed like Michael and his lovebird. Maybe Ken had popped the question in this restaurant, which was why April knew the opening hours, and could recommend the fried Pacific prawns.

'Ah! Here's the other waiter coming. At least he doesn't look as if he's buried half his family and divorced the other half. Now listen, Tessa, once I've given him our order, we've really got to talk.'

'We've talked.'

'No, we haven't – *you* have. That's fine. I'm not complaining. I needed time to take the whole thing in. It's a shock for me – of course it is – but what's done is done, I always say, and we've got to put our heads together and work out how we're going to cope. Just a sec – what was it you wanted – the chicken with cashew nuts?'

Tessa nodded. Who cared what she ordered? She could always push it round her plate, or offload it on her mother's.

April pointed to the number on the menu, to make sure the waiter understood. He looked small and weedy beside her; his pasty skin rebuked by her bright lipstick, which she'd reapplied, together with more silver on her lids. 'And the Pacific prawns for me, please. And we'd both like some fried rice, and a dish of those bamboo-y things, and two crispy pancake rolls and . . .'

'Mum!'

'Wait! We've got to have prawn crackers. And if this lovely man could find me some tomato sauce – not that soya stuff – then we'll all be home and dry.' April banged the menu shut, blew her nose, lit a half-squashed Silk Cut, then leaned back in her chair. 'Where was I? Yes, the baby. Now, what I'm going to do first is change my job – hand my notice in to Connie at the pub, and go back to hairdressing. I can take it with me then.'

'Take what with you?'

'The baby. I know you call it "him", but supposing it's a girl? In fact, now I come to think about it, it's bound to be pink bootees. My mother had six girls; my sister's got her Alice and Anita, and my Grandma, who I never met, had . . .'

'Mum, I don't know what you're talking about.'

'Well, Valerie's dead keen for me to go back to the salon. She phoned me just last month and told me I could more or less dictate my terms. I shall! I'll ring her up tomorrow, and say if she's no objection to a carrycot, or the odd poo or puke or grizzle, we're in business. After all, it'll only be in termtime, won't it, and that's less than half the year. And if the kid gets too much of a handful, well Val's mum lives over the shop, and she's nothing much to do all day except play kiss-kiss with her budgie. She'd probably jump at the chance of a little human company, even if it's not quite talking yet, or saying "Pretty Boy".'

'You mean, you'll . . . ?'

'It's the obvious way, love, isn't it? You can't give up your college place – it would break my heart, and Dave's – and I don't want my precious grandchild being bundled off to strangers, or stuck in some old musty library, with a load of corpses just outside the window.'

'But, I . . .'

'No "buts". And here's our food. Or the crispy whatsits anyway. I'd better save this fag for later.' She stubbed her cigarette out, let her fingers brush the waiter's arm. '*And* he found the ketchup,' she cooed at him flirtatiously, dousing her pancake roll with sauce.

Tessa refused her mother's offer of the sauce-bottle, a hideous red plastic object in the shape of a tomato. She couldn't concentrate on food, when so much was at stake. She had been offered a solution. Her child might not have a father, but he'd just found a willing grandma, one who'd called him precious, one who shared his genes. Wouldn't he be better off with his own relative, his flesh and blood, than with casual Liz or hard-boiled Alexandra? But could she really expect her mother to disrupt her life, return to a job she'd once described as 'one I like, but which doesn't like me'? April had a way with hair, and had always been a favourite with her clients, but the chemicals and bleaches brought her out in rashes, so that she had to work with blistered swollen hands. And the hours were much longer than at the Horse and Groom – not so late, admittedly, but all damned day from nine. Her mother would have thought of that – and relished it – more money for the baby. But was it fair to saddle her with all that fag and grind, duplicate the problems she'd endured already, nineteen years ago?

Tessa stared down at the tablecloth, which was a murky shade of pink, as if it had absorbed a tinge of burgundy from the surrounding sombre walls. A host of other doubts and fears were churning through her head. April would do anything to prevent her losing Oxford, but suppose she lost it anyway?

'Listen, Mum, there *is* a "but". Balliol may not have me back. They might insist I take a year off, or even drop out altogether.'

April made a strangled noise through her mouthful of hot batter. 'Over my dead body! And I mean that, Tessa Reeves. I'll lie down in that busy street right outside your college, if they start ordering you to leave. Anyway, they won't. Now you've got those first-class honours, you must be their big star, their strawberry on the gâteau. If they had the sense they're born with, they'd lay on a proper nanny for you, instead of wasting all that money on croquet-bats and boat-races and more books than any normal person could read in umpteen lifetimes. And while they're about it, they could root up those old tombstones, and find a cot and pram. Not that I trust nannies. Mrs Lawson had one, and she left a mite of just three months alone in a dark house while she went to meet her boyfriend.'

'Oh, Mum . . .'

'What?'

'You're an angel, honestly.'

'No, I'm not. I could never keep the wings on, and I don't think angels smoke – not Silk Cut, anyway.'

'Do you really think it could work?'

'We'll make it work. We've got to.'

'But what about . . . Ken?'

'What about him?'

'Well, if you're going out a lot together, who the hell will babysit? And anyway, he might object. I mean, you'll be busy enough slaving in the salon, without adding full-time Grandma to your list of jobs. He'll hardly get to see you.'

'That should suit him fine.'

'What do you mean?'

April pushed her plate away. One stray beanshoot hung trembling on her lip. She removed it, wiped her mouth. 'I'm afraid it's over, Tess.'

'Over? But . . .'

'No, don't say anything – or I'll probably cry my eyes out.' April riffled through her handbag for her compact, snatched an anxious glance in it, as if checking that her misery wasn't showing on her face. Then she licked her finger, smoothed her eyebrows with it, and sat up very straight; seemed to be making a fierce effort to compose herself, control her shaky voice.

'His wife came round last night, and there was a really nasty scene. That's why I was in such a sweat about going home this evening. She knows what time I get back from the pub, you see, and I was frightened she'd call in again, start effing and blinding, the way she did before. I didn't want to tell you, love. It's all so sordid, isn't it? Mind you, I had no idea she and Ken were close. He swore blind the marriage was over – kaput, he said – dead and buried, not a spark of life left in it.'

'Men!' stormed Tessa, breaking off as the waiter glided up, and began unloading all the dishes from his tray. She felt mad with him, as well, for no other reason than he was the same sex as Ken and Michael. Why should April always lose her chances, never find a partner who would cherish and pursue her, rather than sling her on the scrapheap? All the time she'd been pouring out her own woes, her mother hadn't said a word about how she was suffering just as much; but had offered help, support and love, while starved of them herself.

'Listen, Mum, we'll manage. We'll show the bloody pair of them! Who needs men, anyway?'

'That's the spirit!' April said, heaping rice on to her plate. 'And, whatever else, we mustn't let 'em stop us doing justice to our dinner. It's funny, Tess – the more miserable I am, the more I want to stuff myself. Last night I had a real old binge. I ate almost a whole chocolate cake, then I made some Ready Brek, and sat there, snivelling into it, with that woman's voice still squawking from the radio, though it was tuned to Des O'Connor.'

Tessa speared a chicken piece, helped herself to rice. No more snivelling from either of them. They must damned well toughen up, look after one another, show the world they could cope. And once the child was born, it would actually be a huge relief to let her cheerful mother take him over. She'd still have him more than half the year; wouldn't be like Heloïse, who had never seen her son again, once she was cloistered in her convent. And she'd still have Michael, in a way – more of him than that loathsome almost-wife. She was carrying his first-born; his genes and cells and temperament fused with hers in something that was part of him, however much he might struggle to deny it, or want to flush the child out.

'What are you going to call the little mite?' April was spooning overflowing rice grains from the table to her mouth.

'Michael.'

The silence felt uncomfortable. Tessa tried to fill it. 'Oh, I know you'll disapprove, but I've been calling him that for a good two months, and I can't bring myself to change now.'

'But what if it's a girl?'

'I'd better call her April.'

'I'll pray heaven it's a boy, then.'

'I'm certain that it is. I've got this sort of hunch. I'm so sure about it, I've already chosen his other names. He'll be Michael Peter Astrolabe.'

'Astra-what?'

'Astrolabe. It's the name Heloïse gave her son.'

'Heloïse? Who's Heloïse? Oh, you mean that funny little friend of yours we met when we were punting? I didn't know she had a son. She only looks about sixteen! And what a mouthful and a half to saddle the poor nipper with. Foreign, by the sounds of it. But then she can't be English herself, can she, with a fancy name like Heloïse?'

Tessa didn't answer. She'd told April about Heloïse several times before, but her mother's memory had off-days, like her feet. Astrolabe was certainly an odd choice – meant an instrument for measuring the height of the stars – and, as Ruth Sylvester had remarked, it was rather like christening one's child 'Telescope' or 'Computer'. But it must have had some significance for Heloïse – maybe a reference to the starry heights she envisaged for her son. The name also had the same initial letter as Abelard, and the same ring and rhythm to it, so perhaps she'd been hoping to create a second Abelard.

'Can I try a prawn?' she asked, deliberately changing the subject before her mother launched into a list of her own favourite babies' names. 'The chicken's pretty good, but it's mostly nuts and sauce.'

'Help yourself. I'm glad to see you eating. You should never starve the womb, you know. You weighed ten pounds-six when you were born, and the midwife said . . . She was Scottish, I remember, and had a husband back in Glasgow who used to duff her up. "Now listen, Mrs Reeves," she said . . . She always called me "Mrs", which I must admit I liked. "I've never seen a bonnier bairn, and I've seen plenty in my time." Which reminds me, Tess – I hope you're doing all you should – check-ups with the doctor, cod-liver-oil-and-thingummy.'

Tessa said nothing, simply bit into a prawn.

'In fact, now you've come back home, I think you ought to stay here, at least until you've had a little chat with Dr Cunningham. He was asking how you were, just the other day. I'll phone the surgery first thing Monday morning and fix up an appointment.'

'Oh, no, Mum.'

'Oh, yes, Mum.'

'Well, only if you let me pay for dinner.'

'No, I told you, it's . . .'

'Listen, Mum, you've spent all evening running round in circles for that pittance Connie gives you, and now you're spending twice as much on . . .'

'We hardly ordered anything.'

'Okay, let's order more. I want to celebrate. We'll have some wine, to start with, and this is definitely on me.' Tessa grabbed the wine-list, tried to blank out the high prices. She would spend her father's money, or some of it, at least. It pleased her sense of irony that Dave should pay for April's tipple, when he had stinted her so long. She called the waiter over, chose a sparkling white. She and April both deserved some fizz.

Once he'd brought it, poured it, Tessa raised her glass, turned her back defiantly on all the happy loving twosomes. There were other sorts of couples, equally devoted. 'To a fantastic generous grandma,' she said slowly. 'And the best mother in the world.'

'Now I *will* blub,' April flurried, dabbing mouth, then nose, then eyes, with another of her seemingly inexhaustible lilac tissues. She sipped her wine, clinked the glass to Tessa's. 'And I'll propose a second toast. To my grandchild – my very special grandchild, who may have knocked me for six and turned my legs to gravy, but is welcome just the same. Mind you, I hadn't planned on being a grandma until the ripe old age of forty. Never mind. I'll have to work on my grey hairs, buy a pair of granny-specs.' She picked up her prawn cracker, snapped it into pieces, stowed the largest fragment in her mouth. 'Where was I?

I'm so confused this evening, Tess, I keep losing track of what I'm trying to say.'

'You were about to drink a toast – I think.'

'So I was – that's it.' She gulped her wine again, then held the glass up, so that it caught the pinkish light. 'May Michael Peter Astronaut, or April Tessa Doodah be happy, healthy, and the image of its gorgeous brainy mother.'

13

TESSA STOOD BY the window, trying to breathe through the contraction – breathe slowly and deliberately, and not tense up her body. She kept rocking backwards and forwards, which seemed to help a little, though the nurse had advised her to remain lying down in bed. The pain eddied, shimmied, clawed her stomach, sent jolting shudders across her lower back, then withdrew and sighed away, like the backwash on a breaker. She took a sip of water, wiped her sweaty forehead. Only a few minutes' grace before the next contraction. They were more frequent now and stronger, although she was still alone – only the odd nurse popping in to ask her how she was, or check her pulse and blood pressure. The hospital had encouraged her to bring someone with her who could act as a companion – her mother, or a friend or neighbour; anyone she chose. She'd chosen no one. If she couldn't have the baby's father, then she'd rather be alone. She had also refused pethidine, or any other painkillers. She didn't want the pain killed; felt she ought to suffer it, as the baby had to do.

She could feel the next contraction already rolling through her body; did her best to ride it, but the rhythm of her breathing and the rhythm of the pain were somehow clashing with each other, jarringly out of sync. She waited until the spasm had passed, then tried to gain control once more, sponging her damp face, smoothing back her hair. Strange, that word 'control'. People bandied it about, yet you could control so little, actually – not your body, or the pace of labour, not men, or love, or fate.

She used the lull between the pains to look out of the window. A child was playing in the garden of one of the red-brick hospital flats; his mother pegging out her washing on the line. She watched the woman's calm unhurried movements, the way she stooped and stretched, shook the clothes out carefully, before securing them with orange plastic pegs. The child was digging in his sandpit, equally intent, pressing down the sand in his broken-handled pail. It astonished her that they could work and play so tranquilly, when her own body was in turmoil, her whole attention focused on her womb. They were only yards away from her in terms of simple distance – she could have hammered on the window and caused them to look up – yet there was a barrier between them far more solid than the pane of glass. She felt totally cut off from the outside world, the normal world, from people who could laugh and chat, turn out sand-pies, launder shirts and pants.

She gazed up at a huge grey cloud drifting slowly across the sky. She was cut off from that, as well; from the vast mystery of things, which again defied any semblance of control. 'Stop!' she wanted to shout – to the cloud, the world, her pains – but nobody would hear. Suddenly a real shout tore harshly from her throat, as she struggled through the worst contraction yet. She was clammy-cold and trembling, despite the stale fug of the room; longed for somebody to come, someone kind and motherly, who would hold her hand and make everything all right; tell her she was safe now, that the bogies had all gone. She could hear noises from the ward: footsteps tramping past her door, the rattling of a trolley, a burst of conversation, a barked order from a nurse. She hadn't realized they would put her in a side-room, treat her like a leper, somebody in quarantine who might infect the other patients.

She lumbered round the tiny room like a sick sheep in its pen, pulling at the skimpy gown which was gaping at the back. She remembered being twelve again, and too big for her clothes; even too big for the house – that cramped confining semi, which had quashed her huge ideals, when she'd believed that she could save the world – a new-minted Florence Nightingale fused with Martin Luther King. In the last three weeks, the foetus seemed to have grown and grown, until she had lost her personality, her intellect and brain cells, all her normal interests and concerns, and become nothing but a baby-growing machine. Her womb was no longer even her own, but had become public property; poked and prodded by a string of soulless doctors; scanned, screened, monitored and probed. And then the batteries of tests – urine samples, blood tests, checks on bowel and bladder, diet, weight and heart rate. Before her pregnancy, she had never given her health a second thought. Her body simply functioned – automatically, efficiently – and no one had shown the slightest interest in any of its processes. She preferred that state of things; hated revealing it to strangers, having every private cavity open to inspection, every function scrutinized.

She lurched retching to the basin as another fierce contraction shook her in its grip, combined this time with an urgent need to be sick. It was useless trying to concentrate on relaxation-breathing whilst also throwing up. Though there wasn't much to throw up – she hadn't eaten a mouthful since supper yesterday. She stood leaning over the basin, cross-currents of nausea guttering through her stomach, conflicting with the pain. The contractions were getting stronger all the time, now etched and scored with panic. She had never known anything could hurt so much, take over her whole body, disregard her totally, as if she were just a squatter crouching in the attic, with no say over what happened in the main part of the house.

She pressed the button by the bed, kept her finger over it. If someone would only sit with her, distract her from herself, chat about the weather, the headlines – anything. She realized how unwise she'd been to have refused her mother's help; to have told her so insensitively that she could manage on her own (upsetting her into the bargain). But it had been difficult to make the right decision, especially in advance. It had seemed wrong for April to be there – taking Michael's place – suffering for no purpose. Yet if she'd known how harrowing it would be, she would have clung on to her mother for dear life.

A nurse appeared – an Indian – one she hadn't seen before. She'd glimpsed so many different faces in the last six or seven hours, but none of them had stayed long enough to become a friend or ally. And most of them were foreign, which only increased her isolation. Impossible to communicate when their English was so hard to understand, and when they were so rushed off their feet, they had no time to spare in any case. It was all she could do not to scream or swear; tell the harassed lot of them that she'd reached the end of her tether and couldn't bear another minute's pain. Instead, she lay down quietly on her back, and let herself be inspected yet again – her gown shoved up to her armpits, while clumsy fingers groped between her legs.

'You've quite some way to go yet,' the nurse observed, as she removed her surgical gloves.

Tears slid down Tessa's face, tears of disappointment and frustration. She had assumed that it was nearly over, that she'd deliver in the next half-hour, and the terrible ordeal would end. They had given her some pessaries first thing in the morning, and she'd already had contractions since early afternoon; had breathed and paced, breathed and rocked, even puffed and panted while tapping out the rhythm of a tune, as another means of dealing with the pain. Yet, apparently, all that effort and exertion had been to no avail, and she still had hours more to endure. How could one small baby take so long to be born? It was as if her body were reluctant to expel him; had decided to hold on to him, shield him from more trauma. There had been so much waiting anyway, in these last few interminable weeks – waiting for appointments, waiting for results, sitting like a sack on hard uncomfortable chairs, with rows of other wombs, prattling, knitting, swelling all around her.

She rolled over on her side, in an endeavour to evade the pain, which was shooting through her back now, fanning out in jerky waves.

'Why not have some pethidine?' the nurse suggested, handing her a box of paper hankies. 'There's no point suffering for the sake of it. Shall I go and ask the doctor to write you up for some?'

Tessa shook her head, torn between her desire to stay alert and the sudden lacerating spasm gnawing at her back. 'Yes, okay,' she muttered, embarrassed by the shameful tears still streaming down her face. They, too, appeared beyond control; had turned on like a tap, regardless of the fact that she had resolved to keep her dignity, not to cry or scream.

She felt more frightened when the nurse had gone, leaving her alone – alone with this wild beast of pain, a sadistic dangerous animal which tossed her on its horns, attacked with teeth and claws. She was utterly defenceless, lying on her back again, while the beast reared and snorted over her, crashing its great hooves through her naked gut and groin. And the fear itself brought more fear. Suppose she went to pieces, became hysterical, or violent? And suppose the doctor didn't come? They were understaffed – she knew that – and the nurse had vanished what seemed like hours ago. She could hear herself calling out, yelling for them both, imploring them to hurry. The voice didn't sound like hers – a distraught demanding bellow, growing louder and more agonized as nobody responded. She shut her eyes, prayed to die; tried to shift her thoughts from terror to escape. She must heave the window open, jump down to that garden, change places with the woman hanging out the clothes. How incredible to be that free – free to do the washing, free to scrub a floor, free to have a body which wasn't kidnapped, taken over.

'Please help,' she kept on pleading, although nobody could hear. 'Please come, please someone come.'

Maybe better to give up, let the wild beast win, stop fretting about what people thought, or how badly she behaved. Typical of her to have to bend over backwards to get a First in labour, to prove she wasn't inferior; that a dunce from Emberfield could do as well in childbirth as the cream of Balliol. She no longer even cared, just collapsed back on the bed and allowed herself to scream; lay hopeless and inert, nothing moving but her mouth. Suddenly, three faces were looming over her – cold hands on her belly, a needle in her thigh. She fought the needle, fought the hands, but someone held her down.

'Relax now,' said a deep male voice, one with a strange accent, guttural and harsh. Everyone was foreign, everyone an alien – Michael, too – far away in the remote and foreign north.

'Relax,' the voice repeated. 'Take a few deep breaths.'

She gasped and spluttered as she struggled to obey; trying to remember how she breathed in normal life – calmly and unthinkingly, without this choking panic. A nurse was holding her hand – a different nurse, a tall blonde English one – her fingers cool and comforting; her long hair smelling faintly of some lemony shampoo. Tessa clutched the fingers, used them as an anchor; longed to bury her face in the hair, block out all the hospital smells.

'That's better,' smiled the nurse. 'The injection won't take long to work. Just try to put your mind on something else.'

Tessa made a conscious effort to leave the pain behind. She arranged herself more comfortably, then slipped away to Brittany, where Heloïse had given birth in Abelard's family home: a farmhouse in the peaceful Breton countryside. They must share each other's labour; commiserate with one another that neither had her lover there – Abelard in Paris; Michael up in Newcastle. But at least Heloïse had been attended by Abelard's sister, Denise – a kindly soul with children of her own. Tessa closed her eyes, to make the scene more vivid, shut out the twentieth century. The fair nurse had become Denise – soft-hearted, sympathetic – and her brood of children were playing in the room; a snug and homely room, far removed from an impersonal hospital ward. Denise had prepared a sleeping-draught: a potent home-brewed herbal tea for curing agues and fevers. Already it had made her drowsy – heavy-lidded, heavy-limbed – so that all the griping torment was stealing miraculously away. She was falling into sand; must have joined the little boy in the sandpit just outside, and had nothing else to do now but turn out golden sand-pies in the warm caressing sun.

*　　*　　*

154

'It's raining,' someone said.

Tessa felt her body – wet – ran a finger down her face and neck. They were damp as well. How odd that it should rain indoors, and without her even noticing. Except that everything was blurred, so perhaps she wasn't inside any more. She forced her eyes to open, saw a doctor leaning over her – black hair and eyes, white coat.

'I'm Dr Mahendra,' he announced, the small teeth very sharp and bright as his mouth split in a smile.

She didn't answer, knew the man was angry, and that the smile was just a mask – something he strapped on to cover up the black hole of his face. She wished he wouldn't press so hard. He was hurting her so badly she could feel things grinding and tearing. She tried to knee him off, but couldn't make her muscles work. Perhaps he'd tied her down. He looked powerful and well-built, with an athlete's brawny shoulders and broad hot hairy hands. The hands were thrust between her legs, jabbing and molesting. Michael must have sent him – too busy to come himself, but making sure that she was punished in his absence. Michael was resentful, furious that she'd tricked him; had been hostile since the day they first met. He'd cursed her that May Morning, almost run her over. She could hear the rain once more, drenching down in that narrow Oxford lane; striking at their naked bodies as they lay in Foxlow Woods. He had sown the baby then, spat it like a grape-pip right into her stomach, then blamed her when it grew.

'I'm sorry,' she said wearily, 'I didn't know. I thought that I'd be safe.'

A female voice was answering. Tessa shrank right back. That was his fiancée, so she must pretend she hadn't heard. 'G . . . go away,' she stammered, but the woman wouldn't move; had gripped her tightly by the wrist and was breathing in her face. There was nothing she could do. The woman had more power. She was Michael's woman, so of course she would be strong.

'All right,' she yielded. 'He's yours. You've won him, and I've lost. But I still love him more than you do. I love him more than anyone – more than my own life.'

Everyone had gone now, leaving her in the dark. She was frightened of the dark; had to find her mother. She stumbled out of bed, half-crawled across the floor, attracted by a chink of light shining from outside. She limped along the passage, uncertain where she was, her bare feet damp and clammy, sticking to the lino. She blundered through an open door, towards something white and solid, put her arms around it. Her mother had a long white nightgown – or had done years ago – a warm and cosy nightie which smelt of home and safety when she pressed her face against it. So why was it so cold now, cold and hard and shiny? And why was no one speaking, breaking the cold silence? Her mother always clucked and soothed if she woke from a bad dream, unsnarled the tangled blankets, brought her a hot drink.

A shriek ripped through the night. Tessa blocked her ears. Perhaps it was another child, fighting through a nightmare on its own. All the mothers had been sent away, or maybe they were dead. The screams were getting louder, then fraying into hopeless racking sobs. She had screamed like that herself, though she couldn't remember why.

'Tessa! What are you doing out of bed? I told you not to move. If you need to spend a penny, you should ring for a bedpan. Now you're in the toilet, you'd better go, but next time wait – d'you hear?'

Tessa peered up at the figure standing over her; couldn't make much sense of it. That was no one's mother – not in a blue uniform, with that peculiar white cap, and a voice which rasped and scratched. She let herself be helped on to the lavatory, clinging to the uniform, so she wouldn't fall or faint. She tried to pee, but nothing seemed to happen. She had forgotten how to do it, or perhaps she hadn't learned yet. It was something very difficult, and she hadn't got the knack. She could hear a tiny trickle dribbling into the pan, though she wasn't really sure whether it was hers or someone else's. She stood up again, still leaning on the uniform. She'd like to ask where her mother was, but the stranger seemed annoyed, marched her down the passage, returned her to her cell.

'Don't go,' said Tessa timidly. 'I'm scared.'

'What of, for goodness' sake?'

Tessa didn't answer, just watched the woman straightening up the bed, covering the water-jug, chivvying the curtains until she'd removed the gap in the middle.

'What's your name?' asked Tessa. A name might help, make things safe, more real.

'Nurse Bailey.'

The name sounded familiar, though she couldn't remember why. 'Bailey,' she kept repeating, until suddenly it clicked – Deborah Susan Bailey – her once-best friend from school. Debbie had a baby of her own, which had somehow come between them, undermined their friendship. Babies had such power: broke up close relationships, drove your man away.

'Have *you* got any children?'

'No, I haven't, dear, and is this an inquisition? I'm sorry, but I can't stay chatting here. Sister's gone off sick, and we're short-staffed as it is. We've just had a new admission, and . . .' She gave a final tweak to the curtains before stumping out, still talking to herself.

'Goodbye,' called Tessa, but the door had closed already. No one had tucked her in; no one read a story. Her mother always read the one about the Goose-girl and the Prince.

The screams were still re-echoing, even through the door. She lay there listening to them; knew they were her own screams. She was howling for her mother.

'Mum,' she sobbed. 'Come back.'

'Nearly there!' the staff nurse said. 'It'll be coming any minute now, so draw your knees up and open your legs wide.'

Tessa did as she was told. She felt something slide away from her, something slimy, precious, which slipped into the clumsy metal bedpan. That was no place for her baby, mixed up with the shit.

'All over,' said another voice. 'Now, how about a nice hot cup of tea?'

Tessa shook her head. 'I want to hold my baby.' If she didn't grab him straight away, he'd be flushed down the toilet, or chucked out with the rubbish. They'd already removed the bedpan and were trying to smuggle it out of sight.

'Best not,' the staff nurse burbled. 'He's not a very pretty sight, and you don't want to upset yourself. You've been through quite enough.'

'I want to hold him,' she repeated, her voice imperious. She had been a child too long, patronized and bullied. She was a mother now, the mother of a son.

'Well, let's just clean him up first.'

'No, I prefer him as he is.'

She could hear them whispering; knew they planned to cheat her, daze her with some drug or pill, weaken her resolve. But she was strong now, very strong. All the pain was over, the nausea and delirium, the dishevelled tousled night. It was daylight now, and sunny; a late September sun flickering on the yellow leaves outside.

'Now listen, dear,' a new voice coaxed, a wheedling winceyette voice. 'Doctor told you, didn't he, that your baby couldn't survive? They're just too small to live, you see, at only twenty weeks. And your wee chap was handicapped, which is why you had to lose him in the first place. I'm afraid he's passed away already, pet, so wouldn't it be better if you left the little mite with us, while you try to get some sleep?'

'No,' she said, 'it wouldn't.' She sat up very straight, used every ounce of strength she had to overrule and silence them. They were all lying, anyway, all hand in glove with Michael – about to kill her child, but pretending he'd been born dead, to justify themselves.

The wheedling one had started up again, her voice dripping like warm syrup. 'Why not leave things be, dear? At least your baby's peaceful now, and he didn't feel a thing. It was kinder in the circumstances, to agree to let him go. I mean, he couldn't lead a normal life, so you spared him all that suffering. What you need is a chance to rest and . . .'

Tessa pushed the nurse away; kept her arm out, like a barrier, to prevent her sidling back again. 'I'd like everyone to go,' she rapped, astonished by her boldness. 'And I'd like my baby – now.'

She mustn't take her eyes off them, or they'd bamboozle her, deceive her. She could see them swaddling something in a sheet. Probably just a con – a sheet wrapped round a nappy. They placed the bundle in her arms, but she hardly dared to look at it, still suspecting some base trick. She held her breath, made herself glance down, her whole body flooding with relief as she glimpsed a tiny face. It was stained deep red, as if flushed from its exertions; the weak eyes not quite focused, the lashes barely formed – but still her son, her first-born.

'Michael,' she said softly, trying to welcome him with her voice. His eyes were open, so how could he have 'passed away', as that creepy nurse had claimed? He needed rest and care, that's all, to make up for what he'd suffered. At least she was alone. Everyone had shuffled out, as if persuaded by the strength of her conviction. She listened carefully, to make sure they weren't outside the door, waiting to burst in again. No – she could hear their footsteps fading into nothing; a last low voice also swallowed up in silence. She tugged crossly at the sheet. They'd pulled it tight on purpose, to make it difficult to undo; were still determined to frustrate her. But she was equally determined to see her baby naked, to lie beside him, skin to skin, so they could be fused and bonded, as all the books advised. At last she succeeded in unravelling the sheet, and sat gazing at her son, startled by his size. He was a scant eight inches long, although the lump on his back was very large and red, almost half the size of his head.

'*I* don't mind the lump,' she told him. 'It was only all the others who made such a fuss about it. You're beautiful to me.'

She held his hand – a perfect hand – all the tiny fingers there, even the beginnings of the nails. She wished he'd grip her own finger, but he was lying terribly still; his scraggy legs bent back, his skin transparent, streaked with threads of blood and waxy mucus. She would clean him up herself, didn't want him roughly handled by careless hard-pressed staff. He was already bruised and marked, his frail limbs blotched with purple, as if he'd injured himself in trying to be born. She would bathe him very gently, rub ointment on the weals; but there wasn't any rush. First they needed time to get to know each other, lie peacefully, enjoying the warm sun. If he'd been born when he was due, on the second of February, it would be wintry cold outside, the trees bare skeletons. But it was still only early autumn, and everything was glowing gold – fiery leaves, glinting sun, burnished bronze chrysanthemums underneath her window.

She lay back against the pillows, with him snug against her breast. He was warm and very light; couldn't be a burden to her, which was the word they'd used last week. They'd used so many callous terms – handicapped, retarded, possibly deformed. Lies again, exaggeration, blowing up minor problems out of all proportion. Michael and the doctor here must have stage-managed the whole thing; simply seeking an excuse to do away with an inconvenient child.

'You're no trouble, are you, Mishka? – the easiest baby anyone could want.'

She placed her nipple in his mouth, but his head slipped sideways, one arm dangling down. Michael's son should be a guzzler, but perhaps he was too tired still. 'I'll feed you when you're hungry,' she said, marvelling at his dainty feet, each toe a miniature replica of her own.

She shut her eyes, let herself relax. The sun was very comforting, like a kindly nurse who had time to stay, distract her, play a game of chequers on the bedspread. If only it were stronger, though – warm enough to insulate her baby, prevent him catching cold. Perhaps she'd been mistaken to unwrap him. He was already losing heat, needed cosseting and pampering while he was still so small and vulnerable. She swathed him in the sheet again, then pulled the bedclothes right up to her chin. She was shivering herself; couldn't understand it, when the room was almost stifling, and there were three thick cellular blankets on the bed.

It was not good for her to shiver like that, because she couldn't keep the baby still; couldn't even talk to him now her teeth had started chattering. She touched his face – much cooler – felt a rising surge of panic. It was desperately important to keep new-born infants warm. If she wasn't a good mother, they'd snatch him from her arms, cremate him with the trash, flush him down the sluice. They were coming for him now – heavy footsteps tramping down the passage, tap-tapping through the door.

'No,' she begged. 'Don't take him. He's perfectly all right. He's fast asleep, that's all.'

'You need some sleep yourself, pet. Just lie back on your side, so we can give you a wee jab. That'll make you nice and woozy, so . . .'

'No!' Her shout took them by surprise. 'Just one more minute, *please*. He must be christened first.' She sat up, leaned across, until she could reach the jug of water standing on the bedside table. She dipped her fingers in it, then uncovered the bald head, let two drops flick gently on the scalp. She was struggling to recall the words; had heard them used in a television programme, one she'd watched with April, not that long ago. She must imagine April with her now – not as mother, but as godmother – declaring her support for the baby; repeating with the priest that the child had passed from darkness into light. That was all-important. Light meant life, survival. She only wished she didn't feel so shaky, that she could perform the rite with dignity, not stumble over the words. The names came first, that she did remember. The priest in the programme had pronounced them slowly, solemnly, stressing every syllable. She tried to do the same, ignoring everything around her, looking only at the baby in her arms.

'Michael, Peter, Astrolabe,' she said, pausing with each name, letting each resound. 'I baptize you in the name of your dead father – Michael Peter Edwards.'

14

'PLEASE, I'D LIKE to feed my baby now.'

'Now, come on, Tessa, try to eat your own food. You've left all your chicken pie, and that lovely strawberry ice-cream has gone and melted into a puddle.' The nurse picked up the small glass dish, offered it to Tessa, with the wafer and a spoon.

She shook her head. 'I've got to feed him first.'

The nurse sat down by the bed. 'Look, your baby wasn't well, dear, so we . . . we . . . had to take him away.'

'I know you did, but now I want him back. I realize you're all busy, but if you could just tell me where he is, I'll go and fetch him myself. I don't want to be a nuisance.'

The nurse said nothing, simply took the tray and closed the door behind her.

Tessa sagged back on the pillows. She still felt weak and soggy, as if her body had been used as a football – people kicking it and hurling it, spattering it with mud. She had also lost all sense of time, except it seemed always to be dinner-time – people coaxing her to eat or drink, while her baby lay starving in some remote part of the hospital, hidden or imprisoned. The door clicked open once again, but she didn't even bother to look up. It would only be another tray, or a cup of tea or Ovaltine. It was wicked for her to stuff herself, when her child was losing weight.

'Are you awake, my dear?'

Tessa squinted through her eyelids, saw a grey-haired man in a three-piece suit, standing at the door. Everyone kept 'dear'-ing her, but it didn't mean a thing. They were all strangers and all liars, just pretending to be kind so they could conceal the truth about what they'd done to her baby.

The man walked over to the bed, offered her his hand to shake – a well-groomed, white-cuffed hand. 'I'm Dr Haines, the consultant paediatrician. Mr Lawson-Scott asked me to come and see you.'

She didn't answer; was still taking in the names. Mr Lawson-Scott was the consultant gynaecologist. She had seen him very briefly: a plump man with a plummy accent, and three inches of white cuff. Michael's boss at Oxford had probably looked the same – Sir Thomas Thornton – primped and prinked and manicured, in his expensive suit and made-to-measure shirt. Michael would be a consultant himself in another dozen years or less. He was already halfway there – had the accent and the background, the breeding and the cash.

Dr Haines pulled up a chair, brushed the speckled vinyl seat, as if he feared it might be dirty and spoil his immaculate clothes. 'I understand you're finding it rather difficult to accept that your baby's dead.'

'He's not dead.'

'Look, my dear, I'm afraid he was never capable of independent life. He wasn't sufficiently developed or mature – not at twenty weeks.'

'I'm not your dear,' said Tessa.

'I beg your pardon?'

She pulled at the fringe on the bedspread; wished the man would go away; also wished she could keep her thoughts from Michael. Newcastle had never seemed more distant – a far-flung island, completely inaccessible.

Dr Haines was frowning, patting down a strand of silver hair. 'Now, remember when you had the scan – or two scans, wasn't it? – you could tell from the pictures on the screen that he wasn't a healthy babe.'

Tessa locked her hands together, squeezed the fingers tight. Even the memory of those scans could make her sweat and shake. The machine purred into action in her head. She saw herself lying on the couch; her proud delighted grin as her baby sprang from womb to screen, and she watched him jerk and flicker in fuzzy black and white.

'He seems a very active child,' the radiographer had smiled.

Of course, she'd thought. He's Michael's son.

But then the radiographer's voice had taken on a guarded tone, as she muttered awkwardly, 'I'm afraid there may be a bit of a problem.'

Odd, the words they used. 'A bit of a problem' was something trivial – a double-booking at the hairdresser; the coach from Oxford running late – not your baby's health at stake; not a brutal sickening shock which blitzed your life apart. It had never crossed her mind that her baby would be anything but healthy. That first scan, at sixteen weeks, was simply a routine one, given to all pregnant women, however fit they were. The second scan was different; the words themselves growing darker and more complex – hydrocephalus, myelomeningocele – words she'd never come across before.

Dr Haines cleared his throat, brushed a speck of nothing from his suit. 'And it was your own decision, wasn't it, to terminate the pregnancy? No one forced it on you.'

Tessa kept her fingers tightly locked, did her best to concentrate on the hardness of her knuckles, the dampness of her palms – anything to distract her from the horror of the last few weeks. All the words were wrong again. 'Terminate the pregnancy' meant kill a living child. And 'decision' was eight letters concealing days and days of agony. How could anyone decide in such a hideous dilemma? Though her mother had, without much hesitation – had cried bitterly for half an hour, then pulled herself together and declared that she was committed to the baby, whether handicapped or not; and would even tend a vegetable or stump. Abortion was murder, and murder was wrong, and that was her last word on the subject. But other things were wrong – allowing an innocent child to suffer all its life, especially Michael's child, who should be energetic, free as air, not confined to a wheelchair or dribbling at both ends.

Another complication was that no one had seemed certain just how serious the problems were. She'd had the second scan at nearly nineteen weeks, but that was still too early for any exact prediction of whether Michael junior would be brain-damaged, incontinent, or only slightly affected by the lesion on his spine. There were also operations which might put things right, offer him the chance of a fairly normal life. But everything was speculative, hedged around with maybes; couched in terms which were cruelly imprecise. Yet if she postponed the decision for even one more month, it would be too late to end the pregnancy, and she might be sentencing a helpless child to a gruelling round of operations.

Dr Haines shifted uneasily on his chair. 'And I understand from Mr Lawson-Scott that you talked the matter over with at least two counsellors before agreeing to come in.'

'Yes,' she said. 'I did.' She might just as well have saved her breath.

The counsellors were kind, but they couldn't grasp the fact that she was trying to decide for Michael – the father of the child – as well as for herself and for the baby. Michael didn't want a kid at all; would totally reject an imperfect second-rate one, let alone a simpleton. And since the child was part of Michael, she'd be inflicting pain on him as well. Both of them might blame her – Michael senior hating and resenting her for producing something defective, and baby Michael turning on her savagely after a life of deprivation. She'd been particularly distressed by a book she'd read on spina bifida children – how even as toddlers they could be in and out of hospital, or stuck in plaster casts; how they often grew up isolated, cut off from normal kids; obliged to cope with colostomy bags, or calipers, or frightening-looking things called shunts inserted right into their heads. If Michael landed up like that, or with stunted twisted helpless limbs on a body ridged with surgery scars, might he not be bitter about her blithe assumption that he would opt for life at any price?

In the end, she'd decided she should suffer in his stead. By going through the pain and loss herself, she'd spare both Michaels, and also spare her mother, who might not have the strength to continue caring for a stump.

She could hear the doctor's velvet voice droning softly on, but she ignored his actual words. All doctors were the same, swathing murder in pretty lacy shawls, or making it less heinous by using medi-speak. At last, he groped up to his feet, offered her his hand once more, like some prize for good behaviour. She hadn't screamed, or cried; had hardly even argued with him.

Alone again, she lay staring at the wall. Too easy to blame doctors. It was time she faced the truth. If her child was dead, then she was the one who'd murdered him, or at least sentenced him to death. She hated that word death; had to keep denying it, though the effort was exhausting her. Life and death were wrestling in her head, each begging for acceptance, each refusing to give way. Three days ago, she had felt the baby move – the first time in her pregnancy – just a tiny flutter, but for her an avalanche; a desperate deafening roar of life, reminding her that the child was still developing, that she could save him if she chose. She hadn't chosen; hadn't even achieved her aim of sparing him from suffering. By twenty weeks, a foetus could feel pain, could even cry real tears. All through her labour, she had heard him weeping silently, flinching with the pain of each contraction – futile pains, since they were ejecting him to death. That nurse had claimed he hadn't felt a thing, but that was just a lie, another hypocritical attempt to whitewash the whole process, save everyone embarrassment.

Tears were running down her own cheeks, but she felt too crushed even to fumble for a Kleenex, simply let them fall. Only when she heard footsteps at the door again did she mop her face with the sheet; then immediately lay back once more; eyes shut, feigning sleep. She couldn't bear more sessions with counsellors, consultants; more glib and empty words. There was no one in the world she could talk to in the way she craved; no one who could understand the subtleties, the cruelties. Her mother's stance was far too cut and dried, and Michael didn't even realize that his child was handicapped. She had sent him just the briefest note, saying she'd arranged to have the termination which he had advised in his own letter, though not explaining why. Her Oxford friends were also in the dark, but even if she told them the whole story, what possible help could they be? She felt decades older than them all; knew she'd left them miles behind, become a mother and a murderer while they were still carefree undergraduates.

The door opened, but she made no move; lay impassive, with her head turned to the wall. She was used to people barging in and out – cleaners with their silly chat, nurses bringing trays or drugs, the registrar sparing her five seconds, but calling her 'Annette'. She had wondered who Annette was – another girl who'd killed her child? One birth in five was now aborted, or so Tristram had remarked once. Did that make it better, make her guilt less sharp? She could see the pile of foetuses – tiny wrinkled bodies with half-formed limbs or dangling heads – thrown out with the offal, sharing the same waste-bin as infected kidneys, diseased appendices. Tristram carped about abortions, not on any moral grounds, but because he saw them as a waste of time.

'They're a bore, an utter pain,' he'd groused. 'You could assist on ten a morning, and not learn a bloody thing.' She loathed his callous attitude; had come to loathe hospitals in general – Tristram's world and Michael's – though the way they talked of hospital life you'd have assumed it was a glamorous round of parachuting, wind-surfing, OBEs and knighthoods, not a constant daily battle with disease and death and handicap.

'Ah, you *are* awake! I wasn't sure. I'm sorry to disturb you, dear, but I thought you'd like to see these flowers. They're really something, aren't they? I mean, such a huge great box! And they've come all the way from abroad.'

'Abroad?' Tessa rolled over to scrutinize the cardboard box, which was three feet long, at least, and weighing down the woman's arms.

'Yes, Madeira, so it says. And there's a great long word above it which I can't make head or tail of. I think it must be Spanish. Got a friend there, have you?'

'No,' said Tessa, frowning. 'And how d'you know they're flowers?'

'It says so seven times, and in ever so many languages – flowers, *fleurs, flores, Blumen,* and a few more I can't pronounce. Whoever sent them must have a bob or two. And just look at all those stamps! They must have cost a pretty penny too. There's half a dozen largish ones, and a whopper with a peacock on. In fact, I'd love those for my grandson, if you're not wanting them yourself.'

'Okay,' said Tessa listlessly, still wondering who had sent the box. Only two people who knew she was in hospital – Michael and her mother. Could Michael be abroad? Had he gone away deliberately? That would get him off the hook, provide him with a good excuse for not being by her side. He'd know full well he ought to come, but he'd detest the very thought of it, and do anything he could to avoid the inconvenience. Madeira would be perfect at this time of year, with all the tourists gone, but the sun still strong and generous. A romantic place to take his almost-wife. They could swim and sunbathe – naked – feed each other in candlelit tavernas, then return to their hotel and . . .

'Now, if you sit up, I'll put it on the bed.' The woman was still gushing over the box – its size, its weight, and how her Kevin would be thrilled to bits with the fancy foreign stamps. 'And I'd better help you open it, though I think we're going to need a pair of pliers, or at least some decent scissors. I'll see if Sister's got some, and while I'm gone I'll fetch a vase – or three. They've sent a whole flower-bed by the looks of it.'

Tessa watched her waddle through the door, praying that she'd stay away. She didn't want anyone to help her open Michael's flowers, least of all this prattling nosy parker – a voluntary worker called Winnie, who had breezed in twice before and asked a string of prying questions. She wormed up out of bed, found her own scissors and a nailfile, levered up the staples on the box, then slit through tape and string. She wrenched the cardboard lid off, caught her breath as she stared down at a dozen showy orchids, each separate stem encased in moistened cotton wool, then double-wrapped in polythene and foil. She had never seen such flowers – fabulous, exquisite, and far too flauntingly extravagant for her small and shabby room. There were several different kinds – some pinky-purple ones with sensual petals and a sweetish fondant scent; a few smaller yellow-green ones, which looked too stiff and waxen to be real, and some which had a fever – their open mouths a livid red, their petals flushed, their furred tongues blotched and swollen.

She reached her hand out, but drew it back uncertainly; somehow couldn't bring herself to touch them. They seemed threatening, almost hostile, as if they resented their surroundings; were more at home in luxury hotels, or prima donnas' dressing-rooms – prima donnas themselves, pampered and voluptuous. The pink ones had deep pouting lips – female lips, flirtatious lips, mouthing to the bees that they were desirable and fertile, oozing luscious nectar.

She sank down on the bed, unable to tear her eyes away from these rare outlandish flowers, which seemed to hypnotize her, affect her mind and body like a drug. She remembered Charlotte's father telling her a story about some extraordinary species he'd seen in the Bahamas, which burst into exotic flower just one night in the year, conducted its whole sex-life between midnight and dawn, then withered by the morning. Hundreds of white sphinx-moths had rushed from bloom to bloom, he said, reeling from the heady scent of foot-wide flowerheads, weighted down with pollen; their whirring wings only silenced as the sun came up, and the flowers vanished like a mirage. Her sex-life with Michael had been very much the same – passionate, dramatic, but confined to one brief spell, and leaving her shrivelled and condemned.

She poked her finger into a soft pink lip, surprised how gaping-deep it was, how it seemed to close around her flesh, even throb and grip. She shut her eyes, saw Michael's woman opening, opening; a rare outlandish species oozing precious nectar, with Michael as her tiger-moth. She stroked a fleshy sepal, felt it moisten and respond. The slut was more than ready for him, exposing everything she had – secret curves and hollows, distended inner lips. She was probably just as greedy at table as in bed – slurping, scrunching, using teeth and tongue.

All the flowers had tongues, some of them protruding, some inflamed and mottled. She seized a purple one, its gaudy petals

167

pockmarked, its stem naked, tacky-smooth. She crushed the centre
to a pulp; her fingers sticky from the festering yellow discharge. Sex
could make you ill – bloat you and infect you; seed new malignant
growths which had to be cut out. She ripped the whole flower off its
stalk, mangled it between her palms. How dare they send her flowers
– the rutting randy pair of them; cancelling out their guilt with some
sweetener from a hothouse. Flowers were for achievement, for birth
and celebration, not for pain and death. If they felt a need to pay
her off, then they should have sent a wreath.

She picked up a greenish orchid which already looked defunct –
ominous, anaemic, and with no trace of any scent. She snapped its
stem in half, plucked off its jaundiced petals, one by furious one; then
flung the debris back into the box and rammed the lid on top. She
plunged towards the door, the box across her shoulder like a baby;
one hand cradling it securely at the bottom. Emerging from her room,
she cannoned into Winnie, who was just returning with two vases and
a shrill lasso of questions. She struggled free, ran on along the passage,
not daring to pause for breath till she was safely in the toilet with
the door locked. She laid the box down on the floor, removed each
flower in turn and tore it into pieces. She stuffed the wreckage in the
toilet-bowl, pulled the plug between each one, impatient with the slow
protesting cistern. She really needed an incinerator or waste disposal
unit. There must be one around – scores of them, most probably.
That's what hospitals were for – destroying living breathing things
before they'd had a chance to bloom.

At last the box was empty, save for some crumpled tissue paper.
She tossed that in the sanitary-bin, with the bloody smelly towels,
then limped back to her room. There was no sign of either Winnie or
the vases. Thank God, she thought, as she fumbled for a pen, found
a scrap of paper.

'NO FLOWERS,' she wrote in capitals. She should have thought of
that before, had it printed in the obituary column of the *Telegraph*
or *Times*. It was what you often said for death, and Michael read
The Times.

'Toots, how are you, darling? I've been sweating blood about you –
didn't shut my eyes all night, wondering if . . .'

'I'm fine.'

'But you look so pale and drawn. And what a dreadful poky room!
You'd think they could afford some decent curtains after all we pay

168

in taxes.' April inspected the thin fabric, then plumped down in a chair, drew it up beside the bed and squeezed her daughter's hand. 'Oh, Tootsie . . .'

'Mm?'

'I just don't know what to say.'

Tessa chewed her thumb. The silence seemed to close above their heads, leaving them both foundering. Her mother was never lost for words, carried sacks of them around with her, as if she'd bought a job-lot at a special price, always at the ready to fill a silence or forestall a deathly hush. But today she'd left her words at home, or mislaid them on the bus.

'How's work, Mum?' Tessa asked, at length, trying to plug the hole herself, a hole expanding dangerously after three – three hundred – minutes.

'Busy, busy, busy.' April undid her shiny mac, to reveal a tight ribbed sweater in a hectic shade of pink. 'But never mind all that. How's *you* is more important.'

'I'm okay.'

'But what happened? Did you . . . ? I mean, the doctor said . . .'

'D'you mind if we don't talk about it?'

'But I must know how the . . .' Her mother's voice stumbled to a halt, sounded hoarse and out of practice.

'Tell me all your news, Mum. That'll cheer me up.'

'News? I haven't any. It's only been a day since I last saw you.'

'A day?'

'Well, a day and a half. In fact, I was worried sick I'd never get away.'

Tessa stared down at her hands. A day and a half was totally impossible. She might have lost all track of time, but she was very well aware that a lot of it had passed – heavy, creaking, hurting time, deliberately sadistic as it trampled with slow feet. Anyway, mirrors didn't lie, and the glass above her basin showed her she had aged – her face thinner and more haggard, her hair straggly, with no shine. She tugged a limp strand from its clasp, wound it round and round her finger. She must keep busy, not sit twitching like her mother. April's hands were restless, denied their usual cigarette; empty hands, fiddling with her handbag, plucking at the squiggles on her skirt.

'How . . . how's Connie?' Tessa tried again.

'Off sick.'

Another clotted silence. April must be ill herself, Tessa thought uneasily, as she wound the strand still tighter, pulled it till it hurt. If somebody was sick, her mother always recounted the symptoms in duplicate or triplicate, along with the diagnosis, prognosis, and her own unorthodox but vigorous views on remedies and causes. But instead she was sitting tongue-tied on her stiff-backed wooden chair; the only sound the choked gasp of her handbag as she snapped it open and shut. Outside the window dusk was falling, and the murky waning twilight seemed to have seeped into the room, made it damp and chilly, bleached the once-bright colours. Even her mother's fuchsia top was fading and unravelling.

Suddenly, she seemed to snap to attention, as she looked searchingly around the room, eyes and face alert now. 'Didn't they send the flowers?'

'What flowers?'

'The orchids. I told the bloke to make sure they were delivered today, so they'd be here to cheer you up. The postage cost me double, but I said blow the cost, just so long as they arrive on time. They even put me through to Mr Big. Well, his real name's Geoff, and he's only five foot five, but I'm going off the point. He's Ken's big brother – big moneywise, at any rate. He runs this huge great nursery in Madeira – a really swanky joint it is, or so everybody says. I met him at that party on Ken's boat, when he was over for a week or so, and he was rabbiting on about his plants, while all the others were talking bows and sterns. None of your boring old chrysanths, he said, but exotic things like canna lilies or birds of paradise. I thought orchids would be best, though. He told me they had class. "Yes," I said. "Like my Tessa. And mind you get her name right." I spent an age spelling out the hospital address, and, would you believe, they've still botched the whole thing up.' April jerked her head so crossly her earrings twirled and jangled – fake gold-and-diamond teardrops which twitched again protestingly as she released her hips from the groaning wooden chair. 'I'd better have a word with Sister – find out if they've come.'

'No, don't, Mum, please. She's . . . she's busy.'

'Yes, that's the trouble, isn't it? Too damned busy to unpack a box of flowers. If I don't get her off her butt, those orchids will be dead before you've even seen them.'

'They're . . . dead already.'

'Dead? They can't be! They cost me an arm and a leg.' April's elaborately pencilled eyebrows were drawn down in a frown. 'I bet he's diddled me, that Geoff! He must have heard I'd broken up with Ken, and decided to get his own back by sending you duff flowers. What a rip-off, Tessa, when I told him you were ill and all. "Geoff," I said, "she's really going through it, poor kid, so can you pick her out something extra special." I'll give him special! I've a good mind to phone him here and now – tell him what I think of him, *and* his rotten orchids.'

April was already halfway to the door. Tessa tried to make her voice reach, inflate it from a croak. 'Mum . . . *don't.*'

April stopped, swung round. 'I'm blowed if I'll let him get away with it. I mean, it's a flaming racket, isn't it? Didn't you keep the flowers, so I could see just what he sent?'

'N . . . no.'

'Why not, for goodness' sake? It makes it much more difficult. I can't complain if I haven't any proof. Did Sister get a peep at them?'

Tessa shook her head.

'Well, someone must have seen them. Or do they leave you on your own all day, expect you to fetch and carry when you're still bleeding and in shock? If I don't complain about the orchids, at least I'm going to tell them you need proper looking after. You should be home with me, love. I wouldn't let you gallivant around, disposing of dead flowers.'

Tessa watched the tears splash on her hands. She hadn't meant to cry. It was shaming, hurt her eyes.

'Toots, my pet, what's wrong? Don't fret about the flowers. I won't say another word about them, not if it upsets you. I just wanted to do something sort of . . . different – you know, to show I cared. I mean, you're off your oats at the moment, so chocolates would be daft. I did think of fruit at first – one of those posh hampers from Fortnum and Doodah, but fruit's still food, and if your poor stomach's playing up . . . Then I thought I'd buy you a nice nightie, but that didn't seem right, either. I realize how strung up you've been, and I didn't want to put my stupid foot in it, upset you even more. But orchids seemed so dignified, sort of halfway between birth and death, if you understand my meaning. I went to that florist down the road first, and she suggested roses. I ask you! Roses! How tactless can you get! It was only then I thought of Geoff. Mind you, I had a little private blub before I picked the phone up – what with memories of Ken, and that party on the boat when we were still talking love and marriage, and he all but popped the question while we were chugging past the

Greenwich whatsit . . . Tessa, *darling*, you mustn't cry yourself. Look, it doesn't matter, not a fig, I swear. I'm only rambling on like this, because . . . because . . . I . . . I don't know what to say about the . . . baby.'

'I killed them, Mum.'

'Killed what?'

'The flowers.'

'Of course you didn't, pet. Geoff sent duds, to spite me.'

'No, he didn't. They were perfect. Perfect, and I killed them.'

'You can't kill flowers. You're just tired, that's all, and muddled. It's time I took you home. I'll go and speak to Sister, tell her . . .'

'No! You're not to tell her!' Tessa's voice was rising, a siren now, a requiem. 'Don't tell anyone. Nobody must know. I'm just telling *you*, that's all. You've got to listen, Mum. You've got to hear exactly what I've done. I killed them, like I killed my child.'

15

TESSA STOOD RIGID on the pavement, buffeted by bad-tempered crowds of shoppers; people bumping into her, or trying to force their prams past. She had never seen so many prams – pushchairs, buggies, baby-slings. She had shopped here all her life, yet never noticed babies. And all the stores she knew so well had changed in just one day. She'd been to Boots a thousand times, bought shampoo or soap or hand-cream, lipstick or deodorant, but those had disappeared, leaving the shelves new-stocked with baby-foods, feeding bottles, nappies. Smith's sold books and stationery – or had done till today. Now there were only baby magazines – *Mother, Right Start, Nursery World* – all with perfect infants on the front. She had leafed through them for half an hour, searching for a bruised child, or a scrap with crippled legs; a baby with a lump on its back, or an enlarged and swollen head. But, without exception, they were normal chubby specimens, and most were smiling broadly, enchanted by the camera, or chuckling to themselves. Those smiles had seemed so vulnerable; the infants blithely unaware that there were dangerous people waiting to destroy them – abortion clinics, doctors, Mr Lawson-Scott.

She made herself walk further on, surprised by the new shops: toyshops, pram-shops, shops for nursery furniture. And had Mothercare been there before? – she couldn't remember passing it. She stood just outside the door, immediately feeling more at home as she peered in through the glass. There were the women she'd sat beside in the ante-natal clinic, or met in ultrasound; girls whose lives centred on their wombs, who carried someone else around inside them. She had become so used to carrying her child, she felt completely empty now; missed their daily dialogue. She had talked to him so often – in the bath, in bed at night; trying to tune in to him, establish a deep bond

– it was proving hard to stop, to remember there was no one there. Her insides felt so hollow, they must have ripped out everything – not just the baby, but her womb itself, all her sexual organs. She never wanted sex again – couldn't have it anyway, no longer had the parts. Though in reality her stomach had blown up, seemed to have bloated after the termination and stayed that way, regardless. She was wearing her maternity dress, since only that was loose enough, didn't constrict her round the waist. And in Mothercare, it would make her just another pregnant woman, shopping for her baby gear on a Saturday afternoon.

She slipped in to the shop, instantly assaulted by the day-glo colours, glaring lights, by the babies, babies, babies, all around her – pictures of them on the walls, glossy posters six feet high; rag-dolls modelling baby clothes; real ones grizzling from their prams. She turned her back on the gaudy pinks and yellows, veered towards the section labelled 'Newborn', where the gowns and shawls and bootees were all in restful white. The clothes seemed quite ridiculously large, even those in starter sizes, but a small baby would grow into them. She could see him growing as she moved to the next rack, hunted through the pram-suits marked 'Age One'. She wanted something dignified, not splashed with frogs and bunnies, or plastered with cutesy slogans, which turned babies into jokes. She chose a simple blue suit, then progressed to toddler sizes, found a pair of denim jeans identical to Michael's Levis, but made in miniature.

Another mother was sorting through the school clothes – smart grey trousers, pleated navy skirts. Tessa watched her silently. Michael's child would be top of any class. She had sometimes pictured him at school, winning all the prizes, going on to Oxford (though torn between Balliol and Christ Church). And he would probably be athletic – a rugby blue, a cricketer. She selected some school shorts, age four, and a couple of white shirts, then picked him out a football jersey and a pair of low-cut swimming-trunks to match his sporty father's. She peered at the price on a pair of shiny wellingtons, so small they looked like toys. Those would keep his feet dry, and they were brilliant singing red – Michael's red . . .

'Are you okay?' a saleswoman was asking, a grey-haired dumpy matron who'd been filling shelves just opposite.

Tessa nodded, fumbled for her handkerchief. She cried several times each day now, but the tears meant nothing much – just her hormones playing up, the staff-nurse had explained.

174

'And don't you want a basket, dear?'

Tessa took the one she offered, piled all the garments into it, then left it on the floor. She wouldn't need them yet.

She drifted back to the 'Newborn' racks, passing a poster of a craggy dark-eyed father bathing his small son. Both of them were smiling, the baby's hand stretched out to the man's huge soapy one; dark hairs on the father's thumbs; longer, coarser chest-hair showing at his open neck, running down to his navel, further down to . . .

'Excuse me,' someone snapped. 'I'm trying to get by.'

Tessa squeezed herself against the wall, to make room for the pushchair – a twin one, with two boys in. Michael. Michael. She looked up at the advertisement above a rail of broderie-anglaise gowns, trimmed with lace and ribbon. 'Get Yourself Another Little Treasure,' said the words.

She shook her head. 'I can't. The other Michael's left me.'

She unhooked the smallest gown, took it to the till; stood behind a couple who were queuing arm in arm, the woman's head tipped towards her partner's, their fingers clasped and locked. Tessa turned away, and was immediately accosted by another pregnant woman in the queue – a petulant-looking girl, evidently keen to share her gripes. The shops were all so crowded, the clothes overpriced and shoddy, and as for her bad back, it was playing up even more than when she'd had her first baby.

'Is it *your* first?' she enquired, raking through her shopping-bag for a shabby plastic purse.

Tessa nodded, kept her eyes down.

'And when's it due?'

'The second day of February.' Tessa could suddenly see the trees outside being stripped of all their leaves – their autumn bronze and russet replaced by naked grey. She could sense snow in the air, the sky pregnant with it, lowering; the ruthless February wind blowing helpless birds off course, snapping brittle trunks. Her fingers were so cold now she could no longer hold the nightgown, let it fall as she blundered from the till. The baby-posters on the walls seemed to be swelling as she lurched towards them, every pore and wisp of hair magnified to threatening size. The violent blues and purples of the playsuits had been transformed into fierce strobe-lamps, flashing on and off; colours from some freaked-out manic rock band, resounding through the shop. And all the time the noise was getting wilder

– frantic scarlet baby-screams stabbing through her skull – dying infants accusing her of murder.

She bolted from the shop; stood outside, breathless, shaky, battling for control; eyes fixed on the pavement – its stains, its snaking cracks. When, at last, she dared look up, she was surprised to find the trees still gold, the sky a hazy blue; relieved to see no half-formed bloody foetuses. She had come out to buy her Oxford stuff – folders, binders, file-paper – things for the new term. She must fight the choking panic, return to Smith's, and work strictly through her list. They had warned her at the hospital she might feel strange at times – not just tearful, but moody, out of sorts. 'Keep busy,' they'd suggested, which is why she'd come out shopping in the first place.

She struggled down the crowded street, dodging prams again. Four hundred thousand babies were born every single day, in all the different countries of the world. Tristram had tossed out that statistic once, and the figure had lodged firmly in her mind, but now she could actually see them in the flesh – dusky ones and dark ones, jostling on all sides; some with oriental eyes, or frizzy Afro hair, but still none deformed, none handicapped. Mr Lawson-Scott had asked her, with his well-bred smile, if she was worried about the future, about the chance of giving birth to a second abnormal child. She had produced the child already – a whole brood of freaks and monsters, who were delivered in her nightmares; some with faceless faces, some with double heads.

She stumbled into Smith's, picked out her pads and folders, and a birthday card for Liz. She would see her in three days, when she returned to the house in Juxon Street in time for the new academic year. She had already phoned her friends, told Vicky, Liz and Alex the same brief and simple story. She had suffered a miscarriage after tripping down some steps. No – she wasn't hurt; yes, she'd more or less recovered from the shock, and planned to take them out for a pizza and a pint her first night back in Oxford, to thank them for their support. That meal would be a turning point, her symbolical new start. She must keep away from babies – both the subject and the reality – erase the past five months, and look only to the future: her second year at Oxford, with loyal and generous friends, and her own new first-class status. She might even be awarded a scholarship, or so Alex kept insisting. They were very often given to those who got a First in Mods, though the idea seemed far-fetched to her, the sort of thing that happened to the ex-Marlborough types, the thoroughbreds.

But if it actually materialized, it would mean she'd be entitled to buy a scholar's gown, and she had to admit that prospect did appeal. Gowns were very rarely worn, in fact, especially not at Balliol, which was notoriously anti-traditionalist – but it would still be a mark of privilege, a tangible proof (to herself as much as anyone) that she couldn't be so clueless after all.

Her new tutor, Robin Bowden, might also treat her with slightly more respect. He was an authority on Gladstone (who'd published seven books and countless highbrow articles in the *English Historical Review*), and he'd already told her at the end of last term that he intended to teach her on her own, without a partner. The thought had quite unnerved her, but if she looked at it more positively, she could turn it to her own advantage. No Charlotte overshadowing her, hogging all the limelight, maybe telling tales about that bonehead Tessa, who'd needed constant nannying to achieve a First at all.

She chose another card – an arty one for Charlotte, which might help to heal the breach – then found some fancy writing-paper marked down to half-price. All she needed now was a cheap jotter for her lecture-notes. She traipsed back to the school section, and came face to face with Michael. He was grinning from a showcard, tripping down the street in his shiny scarlet boots, with his cap askew and his satchel on his back. And there was his proud father waving from the garden gate – tall and dark and hunky, of course – with a smiling wife beside him. Tessa slammed her basket down, raised her fist to the man's handsome smirking profile. 'Look, you've left me, Michael – right? Left me for that woman. And I refuse to let you wreck my life any more than you've done already. So get off my back, for God's sake!'

She turned into her narrow treeless street, scrabbling in her handbag for her key, then pausing for a moment to wince at the front door, which was painted in canary-yellow and had a doormat saying 'OH NO, NOT YOU AGAIN!' – her mother's little joke. Before she'd gone to Balliol, she'd scarcely thought about her house. It was merely home – the place she'd always lived in – overstuffed with April's clutter, and often smelling of the lodgers: their pipes, or socks, or suppers. Neither of the present two smoked pipes, but Eric liked his kippers, and liked them almost charred. Frank was less ambitious, lived on Pot-O-Noodles, but he burned joss sticks (rather than fish), and sometimes the combined aroma of sickly musk and scorching kipper pervaded the whole house. In the past she'd tended to shrug it off, but this last year she had found it really rankled, because she was seeing it through Charlotte's eyes, or Ruth Sylvester's, or, latterly, through Michael's. She could just imagine Michael's place, that mansion in the Quantocks, where his ex-fashion-model mother lived. She had always hoped to meet the stunning Zoe, whom Michael had sometimes mentioned with a mixture of affection and respect, but now those hopes were dashed. Instead, Zoe would be entertaining her brilliant son's fiancée, delighted at his choice of such a charming creature; a highly suitable daughter-in-law for a woman of her standing.

Tessa inserted her key, tried to close the door on Zoe, Michael, Michael's wife, so they wouldn't see the cramped dark hall, or notice that the front room was strung with Eric's washing, rather than housing a chiffonnier, or a Bechstein baby grand.

'Hello, love,' the lodger called, emerging from his room with a load of dirty underpants. Saturday was washing-day for Eric, party-day for Frank. 'How's tricks?' he asked, x-raying her parcels with his sharp, miss-nothing eyes, which matched his wiry greyhound body, his beaky nose, thin face.

'Okay.'

'Been spendin' all your cash, I see.'

'Yes.' She shrugged. 'Plus some I haven't got.'

'Mind if I monopolize the sink?'

'Go ahead. I shan't be using the kitchen for half an hour, at least. I've got to sort out all my Oxford gear.'

'Your mother said you was goin' up together, on the gad.'

'Yes – Tuesday morning, early. She's taken the whole day off, and I've promised to show her round the colleges – those she hasn't seen already – and maybe we'll go punting again and . . .'

'Well, don't you overdo it, love. You still look like death warmed up.'

'I won't.' Tessa escaped into her room, the largest in the poky house, the so-called master bedroom. Typical of April to take the tiny box-room for herself, give her daughter all the space, while Frank cooked and snored and clattered in between them. He was out today, thank God, or he'd be doing his cross-questioning bit again. Eric was single, Frank divorced, and neither had enough to keep him busy. Both regarded April as a substitute wife and mother, so she herself was 'family' and expected to keep them up to date with all her news. Her pregnancy had stunned them, sent a frisson through the house, but her subsequent 'miscarriage' had clearly lacked conviction. That was probably April's fault, since she was the world's worst liar, who believed that even white lies would be punished with a thunderbolt.

Tessa switched her thoughts from Frank and Eric to considering what she'd need to pack, and how much she could lug with her on the coach. Half her gear was still in Oxford, but even so, her wardrobe seemed cram-full. Her clothes were in a mess. She'd lost all interest recently in ironing ruffled blouses or revamping junk-shop skirts. She made a washing pile, an ironing pile, then began to sort her books. Her copy of the *Letters of Abelard and Heloïse* was lying on the chest of drawers, still not packed away. She was hardly going to need it once she was immersed in the high politics of nineteenth-century England, and focusing on Robin Bowden's Gladstone. All the same, she was unwilling to discard it when she'd thumbed its pages so frequently, marked so many passages, and when Heloïse herself had become so much a part of her life. She'd been thinking of her recently with a new understanding, empathy. Each of them had lost her lover, then been parted from her child; forced to renounce their babies at such an early stage that there was no chance of being a proper mother, or watching them grow up. Yet, in her letters, Heloïse was silent on the subject of her son, as if the absence of his father was by far the crueller loss.

Tessa leaned against the wardrobe door, opened the book at random.

'It was lust, not affection, which bound you to me; crude desire, not love. So that as soon as your desires were extinguished, any show of feeling disappeared as well.'

She sank down on the bed, jolted by the words. Was it a coincidence that the book should open at Heloïse's first impassioned letter, and especially just that section where she was reeling off reproaches, accusing Abelard of using her, grabbing what he wanted, then callously losing interest? It was as if Heloïse had burst into the room and was dictating the exact reproof she should write herself, to Michael. She'd been shattered that he hadn't got in touch with her, hadn't penned the briefest line asking how she was. As a doctor, he must be well aware of all the pain and trauma of a late abortion, yet he'd totally ignored her, was probably far too busy advancing his career. Like Abelard, nothing seemed to concern him except his private worries and personal ambition, his achievements and his setbacks. His new world now excluded her, as Abelard's had excluded both his wife and son. Yet every time she'd tried to express her bitterness and anger, hurl him words which scorched the page, her pen had stumbled to a halt, and she'd found herself still aching for him, pouring out a different sort of passion. Heloïse had felt the same, torn between recrimination and sheer tormented longing.

Tessa leafed back through the letter, addressing every word to Michael, as Heloïse was urging her. *'I have always loved you with a love which knows no bounds'* . . . *'You, the sole cause of my sufferings, alone have power to bring me consolation. You only from whom all my sadness springs, can restore me to happiness, or at least afford me some relief.'*

She closed the book, let it slither from her lap on to the floor. There would be no relief from Michael, no comfort, consolation. She had vowed to forget him, and instead she was entreating him, as Heloïse had Abelard, for the favour of a letter, a few begrudged and lying words. If he couldn't write spontaneously, and write with real concern, then she had best accept his silence, assume he had abandoned her. It was time she stopped her wavering, her living in the past; took to heart the hospital's advice, and made a positive effort to keep busy. She could start by doing her washing – something practical and physical, which would distract her from her brooding introspection.

She ran downstairs to boot Eric from the sink, but found the kitchen empty. Only his faint smell remained – sweaty socks, BO. She hunted through the cupboard for some Air-Fresh and some stain-remover. Her nightdress was still bloodstained – the one she'd worn in hospital – despite April's vigorous attempts to get it white again. She had a go herself, but the brown mark wouldn't budge, so she left it soaking while she made a cup of coffee. The break would do her good. She was feeling weak and empty, having eaten almost nothing since a slice of toast at breakfast. And supper would be late. Her mother was helping with a wedding reception, and not expected back till nine; had tottered out in her highest heels, with a showy white carnation in her hair.

Tessa took her coffee through to the sitting-room, slumped down on the sofa. Even with her mother out, she was still surrounded by her – her poppies on the curtains, her roses on the chairs; her favourite ashtray in the shape of a coffin; her 'Home Sweet Home' tapestry framed in mahogany veneer – a special offer from the *TV Times*. The only reading matter was her pile of *Woman's Realm*s, and half a dozen lurid-covered paperbacks propping up the coffee table (which had lost a leg a year ago and never been repaired). Tessa

crooked her knees, remembering how the sofa had once seemed huge
– a playground – when she was a child of four or five. Now she had
outgrown it, as she had outgrown her bed upstairs – everything too
small. In just ten days, she'd be sitting in her new tutor's room with
its lofty ceiling, its expanse of Persian carpet, its impressive book-lined
walls – learned tomes from floor to frieze. There'd be towering ancient
trees outside the window, not wet sheets on a washing-line; a bronze
bust on the mantelpiece, instead of a china pig-in-boots.

She sipped her mug of Maxwell House, trying to transform it into
the finest Tio Pepe, served from a decanter in silver and cut glass.
She was suddenly impatient to be back, missing not the college sherry
or the priceless Persian rugs, but her friends, her crowded timetable,
her vital sense of purpose – following a structured course, striving for
a goal. She'd been lonely in this house, with her mother always out
working, and even as a child she'd had to get her own meals, or live
on crisps and Mars bars. Her Oxford friends were blasé about meals
in Hall, skipping them, disparaging them; unable to appreciate that
for someone like herself it was a treat and not a bore to sit down
at a regular hour with good company, three courses, even swarms
of kitchen staff to do the washing-up. She must keep dwelling on
her blessings, not her loss. If she'd been around in Heloïse's time,
she might well have died in labour. Thousands did, apparently –
according to Sylvester – and about a third of all babies born then
were either dead at birth, or succumbed to some infection in the first
week or two of life. It was essential that she kept things in proportion,
instead of drowning in self-pity and forgetting those who'd suffered
more than her. There were no safe and sterile terminations on the
twelfth-century National Health. Abortion was a sin and a crime,
and if the process didn't kill you, then you were severely punished
afterwards with years of stringent fasting.

She spooned half-melted sugar from the bottom of her mug. She
too had been fasting for the last few days – not through any sense
of penance, but because she couldn't face the thought of food. That
must change as well. She drifted back to the kitchen to find a biscuit
or a hunk of cheese, to plug the hole till supper. First, she checked
the nightdress, which was still brown-stained and murky, the cooling
water flecked with scum. Impetuously, she hauled it from the sink,
dumped it wet and slimy in the dustbin round the back, then rammed
the lid back on. She would never wear it anyway: it was tainted and
polluted, an immediate cruel reminder of the hospital. This was her

symbolic break with doctors – with Lawson-Scott, the registrar, even useless Cunningham, who had blathered on about vitamins and good fresh air, then suggested that she bought a pet – a goldfish or a golden hamster to replace her precious child.

She strode into the house again, reached up for her vitamin pills and slung them in the waste bin. She had decided to chuck everything connected with her pregnancy – the childbirth books, the larger bras, her hospital appointment card, the stupid droopy dress she had on now. It was ridiculous to wear a sack when she'd lost a stone in weight, and if her waist was still not back to normal, then a loose skirt would solve the problem.

She went upstairs to change; scoured her room for anything which might still tie her to the baby; then moved on to her mother's room, grimacing at the mess – the bed unmade and strewn with clothes; open drawers disgorging tarty underwear; make-up jars without their tops, and the carpet barely visible beneath a flotsam of discarded odds and ends. Her own face was staring back at her from half a dozen photo-frames – Tessa as a baby, Tessa as a toddler, Tessa fat and spotty in a cheapo grey school skirt. There was also a faded childish drawing tacked up on the wall, with 'My Mummy' scrawled below it in greasy limping crayon. 'My Mummy' was a giant, with primrose-yellow hair, joints of beef for hands, and one eye a good inch higher than the other. The giant seemed sad and haggard, as she'd been looking recently. Tessa touched the white-chalked face, the grimly down-turned mouth. It was too easy to forget that April had also lost a child – her first grandson, whom she'd championed, fighting for his right to life.

She turned back to the dressing-table, picked up her mother's knitting, which had been abandoned in mid-row – a tiny lacy baby-coat in what April called sky-blue, though few skies were quite so blinding. She yanked it off the needles, tugging at the stitches until every row unravelled, then consigned it to the dustbin with all the other relics. For her mother's sake, as well as her own, she had to clear the house of every last reminder.

She bolted the back door, to put a symbolic barrier between the contents of the dustbin and her new determined self. She would hoover the whole house next, then prepare a proper meal – not boring eggs, or beans on toast, but a lavish three-course dinner, which she'd have waiting on the table for her mother. The fridge was pretty bare, so she'd have to go out shopping first, to stock up on the basics.

She dragged upstairs – third time – to fetch her coat and bag; was beginning to feel weary, daunted by the steps. Suddenly, she doubled up, clutching at the banister as violent pains shuddered through her stomach. She could feel something hot and wet gushing down her legs. She bunched her skirt up, stared in horror at the spew of blood. It had already soaked her pants and tights, and was now seeping into the stair-carpet, overlaying the drab beige cord with a lurid blotch of crimson. She pressed both hands between her legs, trying desperately to staunch the flow, but it simply poured between her fingers, as she watched in mounting panic.

'Eric!' she shouted, collapsing where she was. 'Help me! Help me, quick! Ring 999, for God's sake, and call an ambulance.'

16

TESSA TRUDGED FROM Chestnut Close to Beechwood Avenue. The street-names lied, as usual. No chestnut trees, nor beeches, only unkempt gardens. She stopped to look at one. A green-eyed gnome sat grinning on a rockery, his fishing-line dangling over hard-baked barren earth as he fished for stones and pebbles. The flower-beds were all empty, save for one clump of chrysanthemums – ragged flowers, fading from their former fiery bronze; their petals tipped with brown, as if they'd been singed. She walked on down the avenue, hands thrust in her pockets. She had come out without her gloves, forgetting how the weather had changed; how raw and cold the mornings were; a damp mist clinging to her hair, like the first sour breath of winter. April called it autumn still, but half the trees were bare, and the other half yellow-tinged and sickly. She had shuffled through a fall of leaves on her way up to the shops; envying the children who'd run laughing, crackling through them, kicking them waist-high. They'd been relishing the scrunching noise, snatching up the brightest ones, not brooding on the death of summer's green. The streets were now deserted, the children all at school, the commuters in their offices, students in the lecture-halls, or – more likely – still in bed.

'Michaelmas,' she said out loud, stopping once again to touch the fading purple daisies which bore that loaded name, the same name as her stolen Oxford term. It *had* been stolen from her – by illness, Dr Cunningham, those poisonous pills he'd given her: anti-depressants which had made her more depressed. 'Give them time,' he'd wheedled. 'They always take a while to work, and sometimes – yes – you do feel worse, but it's worth it in the end.' She had done as he'd advised, given them time, and lost Oxford in the process.

She snapped a purple head off, crushed it in her hand. Three days ago had been official Michaelmas Day – the feast of St Michael and All Angels. She had celebrated privately, imagining both her Michaels were still with her, not torn away and lost – her lover in her arms, leaning down to kiss her swollen stomach, and so acknowledging his unborn child. The baby would be twenty-five weeks now, if they'd left him in the womb – growing eyebrows, toenails, kicking really vigorously, almost able to survive if he was born.

'Tessa!' called a cheery voice, breaking in on her thoughts. 'How nice to see you, dear.'

Tessa cursed silently as she watched the small brown figure bustling across the road – Mrs Hughes, the squat and shabby mother of her former schoolfriend, Pat. She was tempted to bolt for home. The wretched woman was bound to ask why she hadn't kept in touch, hadn't phoned or visited for what must seem an age.

'Long time no see!' Mrs Hughes' clammy hand had snailed into her own. 'Our Pat was talking about you just the other day. But I hear you've been in hospital?'

'Yes,' said Tessa briefly, wondering who the hell had told her. One of April's customers, most likely. Her mother had finally abandoned all pretence of any cover-up, and entrusted the whole story to Connie at the pub and Val at Hair Affair, so half the county was probably now aware of it.

'So what exactly was the matter, dear?'

Tessa glanced with veiled hostility at the pale pinched face closing in on hers. Mrs Hughes was nothing like her daughter – a mouse in size and colouring, whereas Pat was raven-haired with the dimensions of a drinking straw. Yet both were nosy parkers. Pat might have been her friend for seven years, but there was no denying the fact that she was a bit of a Paul Pry, and now her avid mother was pumping out the questions in the same insistent way, demanding every detail. Which hospital had it been, and how long had she stayed in, which doctor was she under, was she taking any tablets, and had she had to have an op?

'I had a haemorrhage.'

Mrs Hughes pounced. This promised more diversion than some routine tonsillectomy. Tessa filled her in. No point trying to hide the drama of the last few months, as she and April had originally agreed. Who cared anyway? If the Hugheses liked to tittle-tattle, well, at least her case would provide a bit of spice; contained all the key ingredients of scandal, shock and horror.

'You see, I'd developed an infection,' she concluded, 'which suddenly flared up, so they gave me antibiotics and then a D and C. They discharged me after forty-eight hours, but I was still running a high temperature, so I stayed in bed at home. The doctor came in every day and . . .'

'Dr Cunningham?'

Tessa nodded; tugged her woolly scarf both ends, until it was sawing at her neck.

'He's a real love, isn't he? Your mother recommended him to us.'

Tessa didn't answer. April's matiness with Cunningham was beginning to get her down. All those earnest chats they'd had about the patient's state of mind had left her anxious mother not less concerned, but more. Cunningham wasn't a 'real love', but a misery, a creep, a bumbling old woman, due for pensioning off, and if she and April had both kept well away from him, she might be back in Oxford now, discussing life or literature over coffee with her friends, rather than wandering round these dreary streets alone.

She backed away from Mrs Hughes, who had edged so close she could smell her frowsty breath; see the mouse-like whiskers on her chin. There was probably a mouse's tail coiled beneath her corsets.

'So when are you going back to college, dear?'

'Next year.' Every time she said it, Tessa felt the bitter sense of irony. She'd been utterly determined not to take a year off just because she was pregnant; to miss nothing but a scant few days while she actually gave birth; then to hand the baby over to her mother, while she herself continued with her history course. Yet here she was at home without any real excuse: no pregnancy, no baby, no reason save depression. The irony was double. The more she loafed around with no work or sense of purpose, the more depressed she became.

'January, you mean?'

'No, October,' Tessa shrugged, mumbled some excuse about being late for an appointment, and walked abruptly off. She couldn't face more questions – not about Balliol – Mrs Hughes prattling on about how she'd miss her friends, be obliged to start again with a group of total strangers, maybe lose her drive, her whole appetite for study. If only she could change her mind, but she'd told the college categorically that she simply couldn't cope; rejected all their overtures. She'd had her chance and lost it – even lost her scholarship. Robin Bowden had phoned her at home to tell her she'd been awarded one; used it as a bauble, the bait to lure her back.

'You don't have to take a whole year off,' he'd pointed out in his upbeat plummy voice. 'Couldn't you settle for two weeks or so, come back late and catch up on the work you've missed? I could always send you a reading-list, so you can make a start at home.'

His breezy tone had riled her. He was talking as if she'd had a dose of flu, or had lost her voice, rather than a baby. Anyway, she felt far too weak and hopeless to tackle her degree work. Even the news of the scholarship had failed to lift her mood – only made things worse, in fact. They'd expect much more of a scholar; would be pained and disappointed to see how changed she was; how her brain had all but addled under the onslaught of the pills. And Dr Cunningham had fuelled her fears by stressing how she'd suffered a severe shock to mind and body, and so mustn't overtax herself. She needed proper rest, he said, and a chance to convalesce.

She had informed the college that she was following his advice and departing for a restful month in Broadstairs. It was just a fabrication to get them off her back – neither she nor April had any cash for holidays. She had dished up the same story to Alexandra and Vicky when they'd offered to come down and visit her at home. It would be more than she could bear to have to listen to their thoughtless talk about essays and tutorials, parties, college plays. She had already lost her revamped room in Juxon Street – another girl had grabbed it, moved in all her gear. And her student grant would be on its way back to the authorities – her last links with Oxford severed for eleven months.

She peered over her shoulder to check on Mrs Hughes. The mouse was still standing on the pavement, whiskers twitching, watching her, no doubt. She darted round the corner to evade her beady eyes, turning into Mount Street, which should have swapped its name with Chestnut Close, since there were conker trees in plenty here. Some were stripped and naked; others thick with leaves. Did the naked ones accept their lot, she wondered, not rail at fate, or envy the still-clothed ones, the Alexes and Vickys? And if they did protest, who would hear or care; who restore their foliage? She toiled on up the hill, beneath a heavy sky. The mist was clearing now, but had left a bleary greyness in the air, which seemed to seep into her body, remove the colour from her cheeks.

'Penny for the guy,' intoned a scruffy kid, squatting on the pavement beside the most rudimentary guy she'd ever seen: a lumpy half-stuffed faceless sack, with a hat stuck on its head. She tossed him 20p, panicked by the lightness of her purse. If only she felt well enough to begin to earn some money of her own. Cunningham had suggested that she apply for Income Support, but she hadn't yet got round to it, loathed the thought of spending futile months addicted to anti-depressants and social security.

She ambled past the library, its scuffed door locked and barred. They were working shorter hours these days, due to lack of funds, and any book she wanted seemed never to be there. Her mind leapfrogged to Oxford once again – seven million volumes in the Bodleian.

She veered right towards the Health Centre, which had been built some eighteen months ago and housed six GPs and every sort of clinic from Well Woman to Toddlers. She had never been inside, merely damned the building as an eyesore – one more reason to slate her dismal suburb. For all his other shortcomings, Dr Cunningham did at least see his patients at home – a stately Edwardian house in mellowed brick, with a front garden full of flowering shrubs, and a cosy wife who let you in.

She slowed her steps as she passed the concrete monstrosity, glancing at the large framed board which listed all the doctors – Dr Alan Reynolds, Dr Malcolm Barr, Dr Anne McNeil, Dr Michael Edwards . . . Dr Michael . . . ! All the blood which had drained from her face now came scorching back. Her body was on fire – crackling, blazing, exploding in bright tongues of flame, convulsed by heat and light. She reached a hand out, touched the letters gingerly, to make sure that they were real. Yes – Michael's name, written there by fate – not a trick or mirage, not a mere coincidence, but deliberate and intended.

She stumbled up the concrete path and through the plate-glass doors, making straight for the reception desk. She cleared her throat, tried to calm her breathing, so she wouldn't sound too agitated.

'I'm registered with an Oxford doctor, but I've just come to live down here, so I'd like to change to Dr Michael Edwards.'

She was astonished at her voice – its confidence, its coolness – even more surprised when they handed her a form. She had half-expected problems: some stuffy fusspot bureaucrat telling her she couldn't change, or announcing smugly that Dr Edwards' list was full. Instead, a cheerful smile, a few brief and simple questions, and, yes, if she wanted to save time, she could fill the form in straight away and return it to the desk.

Her hand had never moved so fast, pausing only at the entry

'Any other surnames you have had'. She was tempted to write 'Edwards', since she had taken Michael's name in spirit and in fantasy. But she left that section blank, dared not risk a snarl-up. She was already worried about Cunningham, but it was true that she was registered not with him, but with Dr Pryce in Oxford, and treated as a temporary resident when she came home on vacation. Anyway, there was no earthly reason why you couldn't change GPs, and doddery old Cunningham had almost reached retirement age, so she'd have to find a new doctor at some stage or another.

She handed in the completed form, and was walking to the door again, when she suddenly heard a female voice call Dr Edwards' name. That meant he must be there, just yards from her, and breathing the same air. She swung round, saw a sheepskin – Michael's coat, identical – even down to its grubbiness, its air of wealth and squalor mixed. She kept her eyes fixed on the buttons, choking back a savage disappointment. She was aware his face was wrong, yet knew she must adjust to it. He was wearing glasses, though of course he didn't need them. Michael's sight was perfect, and he never had his hair cut short. But those were trivialities. This man's hair would grow, and he probably took his glasses off as soon as he got home. At least he was quite tall – not Michael's six-foot-three, but a good head higher than herself. She couldn't tell the colour of his eyes, but preferred to remain in ignorance. It was hard to accept too many aching differences.

He was talking to a blonde, a flashy type in skin-tight jeans, who was jangling with cheap jewellery. Tessa felt her fists clench as she watched the girl make up to him – flirting, pouting, running puce-tipped fingers through her mane of brassy hair. She forced her eyes back to his coat; suddenly saw that winding Oxford lane again – her own sprawled and shaken body lying in the road, with a sheepskin standing over it. It was his coat she'd registered first: that snobby coat which had become a sort of partner in their affair. She could feel it soft against her back as she lay naked on its furry side, their last weekend away; Michael thrusting into her, his sperm and her wild wetness mingling on the fleece. She had even sewn the missing buttons back, not as an unliberated hausfrau, but because she wanted the coat perfect. She checked them now – all there – the sleeves, like Michael's, a fraction short; the same odd stains and blotches.

She tensed. The coat was moving, actually bearing down towards her, making for the door. She stood back to let it pass, then immediately dashed after it.

'Excuse me,' she called frantically, jogging to keep up. 'Are you Dr Michael Edwards?' She had to be completely sure. There might be other Dr Edwardses – not Michaels, not his surrogate.

He stopped, whole stance impatient, brow creased in a frown. 'Yes, I am, but I'm in a devil of a hurry.'

She smiled with sheer relief, doubly reassured now. Of course he was hard-pressed – harassed, pressured, always fighting against the clock. 'I'm sorry, I won't keep you. I just wondered if you were on this evening.'

'Yes, but fully booked.' He turned on his heel, stalked towards his car.

She had already stored his words away in the treasury of her head – tetchy and short-tempered words, like Michael's. She tried to assimilate the rest of him – his faint smell of musky aftershave, the creases in his neck, the dark stripes on his sober tie, the way his hand had fidgeted. She felt worried by his eyes, which were blue, and very pale blue, not Michael's Latin black. And his voice was *vin du pays*, not vintage claret. But at least the walk was right – a vigorous, determined stride, which declared he was a busy man who hadn't time or words to waste. She already knew his car would be red, and was relieved when she confirmed it – a maroonish Citroën estate – not as bright or racy as a crimson open-top MG, but still unquestionably in the red range. She listened to the engine coughing into life, breathed in its exhaust-fumes, trying to cram them down her throat, so that they'd be absorbed into her bloodstream, become part of her whole system. Once he'd pulled away, the huge car-park seemed deserted, though there were other cars, insipid cars, boring beige and black. She plunged back to the surgery, stood queuing at the desk behind a windbag hypochondriac and an old man on two sticks. At last, it was her turn.

'I want to make an appointment for this evening, with Dr Michael Edwards.'

'I'm afraid he's fully booked.'

'I know – he told me just a minute ago. But he said I was to go back to reception and ask if you could kindly squeeze me in.'

'Overbooked, in fact.' The receptionist was frowning as she scanned the list of names and times on the already crowded page. 'You could see another doctor, though. Dr Barr is free.'

'No.' The word came out like a croak. If only she had the talents of a poet or a barrister, to overwhelm, compel. 'It must be Dr Edwards,' she said desperately.

The woman still seemed hesitant, even slightly hostile, her plastic biro jabbing at the page. It was all Tessa could do not to snatch the pen herself, cross out every name on Dr Edwards' list, and substitute her own.

'*Please*,' she entreated, fighting back her tears. 'He said he didn't mind. He knows it's really urgent.'

'Okay, come at ten to six.' The woman's tone was grudging, and she was shaking her head, as if she resented having granted the concession. 'But you may have to wait – I warn you.'

Tessa watched her write 'Miss Reeves' in a tiny squeeze of space, appraised each stunted letter before she backed away. Even then, she hung around to take in Dr Edwards' world – the shiny walls, low ceiling, rigid polystyrene chairs. She knew them well, had seen them all before – at the John Radcliffe at Headington.

She drifted out, glancing at her watch. Seven and a quarter hours to wait. But she was used to waiting for Dr Michael Edwards, and now she almost welcomed it. She had a goal, a purpose, something solid in her timetable.

She dawdled down the path, which was bordered by a narrow strip of flower-bed, planted with low shrubs. She hadn't even noticed it before, despite the vibrant colour of the berries and the leaves – sunshine-yellow, tawny gold, crimson lake, vermilion. She plucked a spray of fiery leaves, stuck it in her buttonhole. Her mother was right – it wasn't deadly winter yet, but still blazing vital autumn.

17

TESSA LINGERED BY the board again, the doctors' names now swallowed up in bonfire-scented darkness. She savoured autumn's smells – ripe conkers, rotting leaves, smoke and mist, decay – let her hand run slowly across the centre of the board where Michael's name was written. He and all the other doctors had taken the Hippocratic Oath. She'd looked it up in the library, just three days ago, when she'd been mooning round the reference section with nothing much to do. The words had disconcerted her. 'I will give no deadly drug to any, though it be requested of me, nor will I counsel such, and especially I will not aid a woman to procure abortion.'

Strange, how many broke it.

She meandered slowly down the path, still trying to kill time. It was only half past five, so she was twenty minutes early. But she'd deliberately set out before her mother was expected back; had no wish to be delayed, or enmeshed in awkward questions. April had left Connie and the Horse and Groom for Val and Hair Affair. Another little irony. She was doing what she'd planned to do as official working grandma, but instead of caring for a new-born baby boy she was looking after her strapping full-grown daughter. She had also started a new system of 'family meals', which meant Frank and Eric sat down with them, four evenings out of seven, and shared their chicken pie or Irish stew.

'It'll be much more fun for all of us,' her mother had declared, though what she really meant was, 'It'll bump up the housekeeping, now Tessa's lost her grant.' She was also clearly hoping that it would provide some life and company for a dejected daughter too much on her own.

'You can help me with the cooking, Toots. It'll do you good, give you a new interest.'

Everyone was determined to do her good – suggest hobbies, interests, ways of filling voids. Well, she'd made the pudding for tonight, peeled the potatoes for Frank's chips (which he regarded as the staple of any dinner worth the name, including curry or spaghetti bolognese), and laid the too-small kitchen table. She'd disguised it with a lacy cloth, added paper napkins twisted into swans, then set about her own disguise. She'd washed her hair, sponged and ironed the outfit she'd been wearing on May Morning – the day she first met Michael – and spent two hours on her face. She examined her reflection now in the heavy plate-glass doors. Her eyes looked bright, intense; made more dramatic by their clever stagy make-up, which concealed the dark circles underneath them. She had swept her hair on top, sprayed herself with scent, chosen a gold pendant which hung low between her breasts and so emphasized their curve.

She did her best to calm herself as she walked up to the desk, feeling very much the same as when she'd ventured into Balliol the first day of her first term – keyed up, elated, petrified. She gave her name to the receptionist, though it sounded odd, as if she and 'Tessa Reeves' were no longer quite connected. She had lost contact with a lot of things, including some parts of her body.

She was told to take a seat, chose one in the corner by the fish-tank, so she could re-appraise her appearance in its glass. She opened her book, but made no pretence of reading; observed instead the slumped or sniffling patients in the waiting-room. How many of that blank-faced mob were on Dr Edwards' list? None, she hoped, shuddering at the thought of him touching them, or intimately concerned with them, knowing all the details of their bodies and their lives. She must dismiss such thoughts; think only about him; keep trying to convince herself that all the niggling differences didn't need to matter – the straight Hovis-coloured hair, which had none of Michael's bouncy dark exuberance; the pale eyelashes, thin lips.

Suddenly she tensed. A mother with a baby was making for her corner, about to take the adjoining seat.

'No!' Tessa mouthed, too late. The woman had sat down, the baby now so close she could smell its smell; hear its fractious chunterings as it fidgeted on its mother's lap. It turned its head to look at her, becoming unnervingly and unnaturally still as its piercing gaze transfixed her. There was no affection in the scrutiny, no suggestion of a smile. The baby was accusing her.

'Yes,' she whispered, 'I killed him.'

She shrank away, trying to break the contact, but the blue-stone stare still penetrated – paralysing, chilling, shrivelling everything inside her to a parched and barren waste. She was terrified that other eyes would turn on her as well; every patient in the room aware of what she'd done. She fixed her whole attention on the goldfish, longed to be that simple – an ounce of freckled fin and tail swimming round and round. If only the weed-caressing water would close above her head; drown her thoughts, regrets.

'Miss Reeves?'

She jumped. It was only five past six. She had hardly waited any time at all; didn't feel prepared; her mind confused – a ferment of uncertainty and doubt. She was directed to the corridor, made her way along it as slowly as she could, passing other doctors' rooms; seeing Dr Edwards' name with an arrow pointing to the right, and then – again – stencilled on his door. She knocked.

'Come in.'

The voice was different – pleasant, not cantankerous. She kept her eyes on the brown carpet, walked the hundred miles to the chair, only then daring to look up. Dr Edwards was smiling.

'Ah, you're the new patient. I don't think we've met yet, have we?'

Yes, she wanted to shout, we have, of course we have. But she merely shook her head. He hadn't recognized her, but was it any wonder? When she'd dashed after him this morning, she'd been wearing an old tracksuit, with her greasy hair scraped back in a rubber band.

'Do sit down.'

She sat, relieved to have a chair-seat underneath her. There was too much to take in – the smile, the teeth, the patterned navy socks, the rough tweed of his jacket, the fact he looked much older than he had done just this morning. And then the room itself: carpet, curtains, desk – photo on the desk – photo of a woman on the desk, a woman and a baby. She couldn't take her eyes off it. He was too old to have a baby; must be nearly forty, and the woman, too, was in her lateish thirties, yet holding an infant of only a few months. She was nothing like she'd imagined Michael's wife – not glamorous or statuesque – but her rival, none the less.

'So what can we do for you?' Dr Edwards was asking.

Tessa clasped her hands together, locked the fingers tight. *We.* He'd said we. Which must mean him and Michael. Write to me, she answered. Make love to me. Come back.

194

Her eyes were glued to the photograph. The woman's hair was short, neither straight nor curly, but with a slight apologetic kink to it, and a shade darker than her husband's. The baby had no hair at all, just like her own baby.

'How can I help?' Dr Edwards shifted on his chair. The impatient note had crept into his voice again. He crossed his legs, the trousers straining slightly, pulling at the thigh; one foot jiggling restlessly.

Tessa cleared her throat, switched her gaze from the baby's head to the doctor's polished brogue. The patterned holes in the toecap were watching her with their tiny lashless eyes. 'I . . . read this piece in . . . the *Observer*,' she began. The words were beginning to come – words she didn't know were there – but crippled, stumbling, forced to limp and creep. 'About . . . drinking when you're pregnant.'

'Are you pregnant?'

'No.' She dragged her hands apart, sat on them to keep them still. Interruptions made it very difficult. 'They . . . said it could cause birth-defects, things like spina bifida.'

He shook his head, about to contradict her.

She raised her voice. 'It *can*,' she insisted. 'I know that. You see, it happened in my own case.' All the drinks she'd swallowed so unthinkingly were reeling in her head: the Harvey-Taylors' gin – Dutch courage for the abortion – the champagne she'd swilled with Michael their last weekend together; the wine she'd ordered at Yum Sing's, when she and April were toasting a baby already damaged by her carelessness.

'They're stricter in America,' she said, breaking off as she recalled the chilling facts. She knew those facts by heart now, since she'd read the piece a dozen times, at least. When she'd finally put the paper down, her hands were blackened from the newsprint, the whole of her unclean. She struggled to control her voice, to convey the gist of the article as dispassionately as possible, as if she were taking part in a Balliol debate.

'If you drink when you're pregnant in the States, you can actually be prosecuted, or even land in gaol. They call it child abuse. One woman had to go through labour handcuffed in a cell. And another girl, who was only eighteen and a half . . .' The sentence petered out as she watched the tears slide slowly off her chin. They'd be ruining her make-up, her disguise. He'd see her for what she really was – a murderer, destroyer.

Abruptly, she flinched back. He was leaning forward across the desk, reaching out to strike her, punish her for her crime. No. His hand was making contact with her own; warm fingers closing round it. She was dreaming this, hallucinating. It was utterly impossible that Michael should be touching her. She stared down at the hand – its broad and fleshy fingers, well-groomed oval nails, the knuckles slightly reddened, a faint scar on the thumb. She shut her eyes, so that she could relish its firm grip; the confidence it gave her; the incredible sensation of bare skin against bare skin. She could see his naked body now – hair-whorled, thrusting, hot – feel it pressed against her thighs, wet with sweat and sperm. He was asking questions – questions about her pregnancy – but they completely failed to register. All she was aware of was this overwhelming miracle: she was joined and merged with Michael once again.

'Pass the spuds,' said Frank.

'They're not spuds, they're chips.' Eric picked one up in his fingers, bit off its greasy head.

'They was spuds once, wasn't they?'

'Yes,' said Tessa. 'This morning. And filthy dirty spuds. It took me half an hour to scrub the grime off.'

'Well, I usually buy frozen,' April flurried. 'But . . .'

They cost more, Tessa filled in for her silently, feeling still more guilty that she'd just used her mother's money to buy wine. Yet she had to do something to mark this day as special. She refilled all four glasses before telling them her news.

'I've got a job,' she announced.

Frank's and Eric's voices clashed, as they chimed in simultaneously: what, where, congratulations, and how much was the pay?

'Well, it's only babysitting, but it may lead to something else.'

'Babysitting?' April frowned, stressing the first syllable. 'Do you think that's a good idea, pet, when . . . ?'

'Yes, I do – don't worry, Mum.' She'd need to convince not just her anxious mother, but Dr Edwards too. He hadn't given her the job yet, and she hadn't even suggested it. The idea had only come to her when she was walking back from the surgery. She had to find some means of meeting his wife and child, gaining access to his house, and babysitting seemed the perfect way. The only problem was that he might consider her unstable, too disturbed to look after his small son. If only she hadn't cried like that, hadn't mentioned babies. But then he wouldn't have held her hand, kept it clasped within his own

196

for nearly two astounding minutes – a hundred seconds by the clock, but six wild months if she reckoned by her own time – as long as she'd known Michael. And even when he'd let it go, he'd still stayed close, moved his chair in nearer hers, his whole face concerned and softened.

'Well, good idea or not,' said April, forking in her last few peas, 'how come you found a job at all, when you said you'd only gone out for a walk?'

Tessa forced herself to release his hand, which had crept towards her own again; the fingers easing down between her knuckles, one sensuous thumb feathering her palm. 'It was just a stroke of luck,' she said. 'I was wandering down Beechwood Avenue, going nowhere in particular, when I bumped into Mrs Hughes and we stopped to have a chat. I told her I was looking for some work – something simple to tide me over until I'm feeling a bit better. She said she knew this local doctor . . .' The lies slipped out so easily, Tessa knew they were dictated to her, and that by repeating them in public, she'd make them true, make the job materialize. She explained the doctor's problem to her mother – how his usual trusted babysitter was moving to the other side of London, so he was desperate to replace her. 'Mrs H rang him up the minute she got home, said she'd known me years . . .'

'Well, I hope it won't mean missing evening meals. You're losing weight as it is.'

Tessa didn't answer, just glanced around the table. How could this be a family? Frank and Eric were too old for brothers, and completely wrong as fathers. Frank was wearing a red sweatshirt which said FIT, FUN AND FORTY, AND ENJOYING BEING NAUGHTY. He was fifty-one, in fact, and totally unfit; carried his substantial paunch with an air of almost pride, often patting it, or talking to it, as if someone lived inside, squeezed between the kippers and the chips. The hair on his head had mostly disappeared, but hairs sprouted from his ears and nostrils in vigorous compensation, and his eyebrows were 3-D, jutting above blue but bloodshot eyes.

She watched him roll a cigarette, his podgy fingers surprisingly deft; tongue flicking out to moisten the frail paper. Nice to have a real family – brothers who resembled you, and could discuss the things you cared about; a father who was there; whose toothbrush nudged your own in the cracked mug in the bathroom, and whose books were on the shelves – books you'd bought together, strolling down to Dillons, arm in arm. Did Dr Edwards have brothers – brown-haired, blue-eyed brothers with broad and well-groomed hands? Was his father cultured – a professor, a headmaster? Did he . . . ?

'Hell! I'm missing "Star-Gazer".' April kicked her chair back, tuned in the kitchen radio. 'She's a marvel, that Astrid! You should have heard her last week. There was this chappie who rang in, and she told him she was picking up that he'd had a dreadful shock. She didn't know him from Adam, but she could feel the vibes, you see – I mean, before he'd had a chance to say a word about his life. He was flabbergasted, I can tell you – practically in tears – said yes, his wife had had a heart attack two months ago.'

Tessa cleared the plates away, dumped them in the sink. 'Oh, Mum, you're so gullible! You could say that to almost anyone and they'd be bound to find some truth in it – come up with a "shock" to fit the bill.'

'Dead right!' said Frank. 'I've had three big shocks this week alone. The horse I backed last Saturday came in second-last, my ex-wife's found another bloke, and . . .'

'Ssh!' said April. 'She's talking about Fate. Oh, heck! It's that man who phoned in last time, the one with AIDS, whose mother booted him out. Fancy doing that to your own flesh and blood!'

Frank exhaled a curl of smoke. 'You can't say "ssh" and talk yourself.'

'Want to bet?' said Eric.

Tessa fetched the pudding and started doling it out – apple crumble and custard. She had failed to get the lumps out of the custard, and the crumble had burnt black along the sides.

'You've got to be more assertive, Wayne, refuse to take that shit.' Astrid's voice was breathy – transatlantic drawl overlaying Jewish cockney chutzpah. 'Anyway, your luck's about to change, dear. I can see a break in the clouds. Do the initials FRB mean anything?'

MPE, Tessa repeated to herself. Could Dr Edwards' second name be Peter, and had he been to Oxford, or trained at the John Radcliffe? She longed to know, to fill in all the blanks. It seemed strange – and quite miraculous – that he was living a mere mile away; probably sitting down at this moment at a polished antique table, about to eat his own meal. Were there other children, older ones, perhaps a nanny or au pair? That would put the kibosh on her plan. Except even a nanny would need days off, and holidays. She must meet whoever worked for him, become friendly with them, trusted by them, so she could suggest herself as substitute. She could easily get references from the babysitting job she'd had at Oxford; even a brief note from her tutor or the Dean, vouching for her character. It might take a little time, but time she had, in unlimited supply.

'Kids need time and patience! Kids need healthy food! But what kids *don't* need is caffeine. New Taste-Rite Cola gets its kicks naturally – kicks without the risks!'

April retuned; spent half her radio-listening life avoiding the commercials.

'Hold on!' protested Eric. 'I was gettin' really interested in that bit about the poltergeist. Is Astrid a psychic, or . . . ?'

'She's a bit of everything. And she says she's been re-in-thingummy – re-incar . . . – you know, had previous lives. One of them, she was Astrologer Royal at the court of Cleopatra. But the programme's nearly over now, and I must catch Radio Two. They're giving out the winners of last week's competition, and I've got this hunch I've won.'

'I suppose you can feel it in the vibes,' quipped Frank, removing a shred of loose tobacco from his lip. 'What's the prize, anyway? A hundred grand, or a silver-plated Porsche?'

'No,' said April. 'Four tickets for "Come Dancing".'

'Count me out,' Eric muttered with a grimace. 'I can't stand those poncy types who spend their whole lives prancin' round in sequins, practisin' the cha-cha.'

Dr Edwards didn't dance. Tessa knew that in her bones. His hobbies would be sedentary, refined – chess, perhaps, or bridge, or the more demanding type of crossword puzzles. He would preserve his vital energies for work – healing, saving, the laying on of hands.

'*I* went to an astrologer once,' Frank chipped in, stubbing out his cigarette, and making a foray into his crumble. 'The real kosher kind with a black cat and matching wig. She told me everything would fall apart in 1987. I sweated blood, lost a stone, couldn't sleep for worrying – and all that happened was our sodding garden shed collapsed in the great hurricane.' He spat out half a clove, which he'd bitten inadvertently, removed a further fragment from his tooth. ''Course, they say it weren't a hurricane, though it beats me how a common or garden storm could fuck up fifty million trees and . . .'

'Fifteen million,' Eric interrupted.

'Fifty million, fifteen million – what's the difference? Once it's millions I lose count.'

'You wouldn't if it was pound notes on the table.'

'How d'you count trees anyway?' Frank prodded his pudding more warily, as if it were a minefield strewn with clove-explosives. 'I can't imagine some busy civil-service bloke traipsing round every piddling patch of backyard and adding up the trunks.'

'Don't be daft,' snapped Eric. 'They . . .'

Tessa got up to make the coffee, ignoring their yak-yak. She'd just had a new idea. She could embark on a different sort of study-course, a degree in Michaelology – researching everything she could about the second Dr Edwards: his background, education, interests, hobbies, tastes; what family he had – siblings, children, in-laws. She peered through the dark window-pane, which looked out on the blank brick wall of the Hardwicks' house next door, and a stretch of their own battered wooden fence. It would still be history in a way, and easier to handle than her history course at Oxford. Now that she was distanced from it, she felt increasingly pissed off with the way that course was taught. You had to tackle far too many subjects, and race through them so fast, the whole thing seemed disjointed – a skim across the surface with no depth or continuity. Yet, despite the range of topics, there were huge areas you never touched at all. The earliest period you could study began in AD 285, but what about BC, and what about world history? Oxford was so insular, it could blithely turn its back on entire continents and dynasties, to examine in the minutest detail one single session of the British House of Commons, or one minor skirmish in the English Civil War.

But more dodgy than that was the whole vexed question of historical truth. Recent history was so bogged down with documents you could hardly fight your way through the morass, whereas in early medieval times the problem was the opposite – such scarce or scrappy sources, you were often reduced to guesswork. And those who'd written the accounts were bound to be subjective, peddling their own pet beliefs, or driven by some personal obsession. And because they were exceptional types – members of a small, cultured elite – their views would be a world away from those of Mr Nobody, who'd just got on with living his life, rather than recording it. She'd probably have learned a whole lot more about the turbulent twelfth century from Joe Bloggs, peasant, than from Abelard, philosopher. Sometimes, when she'd struggled through his dazzling dialectic, she'd been amazed at how he'd sweated blood over subjects like the Trinity, which later generations would dismiss as mere abstractions. He'd stated categorically that a belief in the Trinity was natural to all men, but

200

such a notion would be laughed out of court in the agnostic twentieth century. Yet for him it had been truth, which only went to show how 'truth' was . . .

'What on earth are you up to, Toots? You don't have to pick the coffee beans, you know. Maxwell House do that. All you need is a teaspoon and four mugs.'

She started at her mother's voice, only now aware that she hadn't even filled the kettle, and was still standing at the sink with the cold tap idly running. 'Sorry, I was thinking.'

'Thinking's bad for the brain,' Frank warned. 'Which is why my own grey matter is in such A-1 condition.'

'One of my clients told me you lose loads and loads of brain cells every single day – billions in a week, she reckoned, just flaking off like dandruff.' April spattered cigarette ash on to her debris of burnt crumble. 'So it's a flipping miracle I'm still compost mental at the age of thirty-eight, 'cause I can't have had that many in the first place.'

'It beats me how they count,' mused Frank. 'It's like them trees again. I mean, d'you wire up everybody's heads, or rake through all the clippings at the barbers'?'

Tessa burst out laughing, startled at the sound.

'What's the joke?' asked Eric.

She shook her head, spooned coffee into mugs. There wasn't any joke, but she suddenly felt better. She had narrowed down her own research, given herself a project, a Special Subject more significant and relevant than the ones on offer at Oxford. No more need to mooch about the streets, or kill time watching 'Neighbours'. She could start tomorrow: planning her new project, deciding how she'd structure it, what sources she would use – local papers, other patients, babysitting agencies, the medical *Who's Who*.

April got up from the table, squeezed her daughter's hand. 'I'm so glad you're feeling better, love. It's the first time you've laughed in weeks.'

Tessa slid her hand away, pretending she was busy making coffee. It wasn't that she balked at April's blisters – though her mother's skin had already reacted badly to the chemicals and hair-dyes – she was simply intent on preserving Dr Edwards' traces. He had held that hand, made it sacrosanct, and she didn't want his fingerprints overlaid with April's; their potency diluted. She had decided not to wash the hand till morning, and was even trying not to use it, though it had proved extremely difficult to eat breadcrumbed chicken legs with just a fork.

She kissed her mother's cheek instead, to prevent her feeling hurt. 'Look, you make the coffee, Mum. I want to go upstairs.'

'What for?' The anxious look returned to April's face. 'I don't like you sitting moping on your own. That's why we're having meals together.'

'I loved the meal, Mum, honestly, and I haven't time to mope. I've got work to do – important work – and it needs my total concentration.'

18

TESSA PACED UP and down Tregunter Road, always stopping short
of Dr Edwards' house. It was too dark to see it anyway, but she'd
patrolled this street so often she knew exactly what it looked
like – a detached mock-Georgian house built about five years
ago, with pretentious columns flanking the front porch, a double
garage painted blue, and a driveway made of blue-grey patterned
bricks. All the houses were identical – all prosperous, all spruce, all
carbuncled with burglar-alarms and screened by lofty evergreens to
maintain their privacy. She had never been inside, and was finding
it impossible even to open the front gate, let alone go up and ring the
bell. Somehow, though, she would have to rouse her courage in the
nineteen minutes left to her – Mrs Michael Edwards was expecting
her at seven.

It had taken her a month – a frustrating, often hopeless month,
in which she'd been told ad nauseam that most GPs maintained a
firm divide between their patients and their private lives, and were
unlikely to employ someone to work for them at home who might
turn up in their consulting-room next day. Once she realized that,
she had deliberately kept away from Dr Edwards' surgery, hoping
he would forget her – temporarily at least – forget her name, her
face. Instead, she'd focused on the wife, discovered that she didn't
work; had just one child – a baby of nine months; attended an
evening class on Wednesdays called 'Our Island Heritage', and
belonged to a babysitting circle composed of other local mothers,
who used a voucher system. That last had really crushed her. How
could she offer herself as child-minder, when she wasn't married and
had no children of her own? She'd be totally excluded from such a
narrow circle on grounds of age and circumstance alone. She had

refused to admit defeat, however. Eventually she'd find a way to penetrate his house – or Fate would help her do so. She was aware that there were forces she barely understood, regulating everything, steering her, however indirectly, towards her goal – and Michael. And time had proved her right. By researching all the members of the babysitting circle, she'd found one she knew already – Mrs Alice Webb, who'd taught her French at school, and had always been both friendly and supportive. She had gone to see her teacher and given her a carefully edited version of the truth – playing down the trauma of her pregnancy, and stressing the fact that she was now fully recovered and in urgent need of work. Mrs Webb had promised help; spoken to her closest friends in the babysitting circle, two of whom had employed her straight away. She had poured her heart and soul into those jobs; knowing that the word would spread that she was punctual to the dot, capable, adaptable, and someone they could trust. Soon she was being called upon several nights each week, and always doing more than was expected. Every time she washed the sheets when a baby had been sick, or worked through piles of washing-up once her charges were in bed, she was doing it for Mrs Michael Edwards – doing it with passion and commitment, because she knew if she was patient, the longed-for summons would come.

And yesterday, it had come – relayed through Mrs Webb. Was Tessa free on Wednesday? A lady called Joyce Edwards had an evening class that night, and her doctor-husband was going out as well. Alice couldn't do the job herself, but she'd given her ex-pupil a glowing testimonial.

'Thank you,' she had stammered, pretending to be looking for a pencil, to jot down the address. She knew it perfectly well, of course – even the post-code engraved into her skull.

'What's she like?' she'd asked, in a studiously casual tone, trying to make it sound an afterthought.

'I barely know her, Tessa, though she seems a decent sort. I've only been there once, and that was way back in the summer. It's a really lovely house, though, and the garden was a picture. Roses by the cartload!'

Tessa shivered. The roses would be dead by now, killed by last month's frosts. It was the first week of December, and too cold to hang around. She forced her feet to carry her to number twenty-seven, pausing at the gate to calm herself, compose herself, practise sounding casual and detached. Dr Edwards had already left – thank God. She'd watched his Citroën pull away a good half-hour ago, the smug purr of the engine seeming to express her own relief. His wife wouldn't know she was a patient, would greet her as a stranger.

'Ah, Tessa! Do come in. I've heard such a lot about you.'

Tessa shook the friendly hand, tried to return the smile. It was more difficult to meet the eyes – her rival's eyes, but affectionate and welcoming. Joyce Edwards looked a mess – dressed in baggy skirt and dreary blouse, with no make-up but a smear of coral lipstick – but, as Mrs Webb had said, she was clearly a good sort, and that fact was quite unsettling.

'The kitchen's just through here. Do make yourself a drink. I've left the tea and coffee out, and some fruit-cake in that tin. And if you'd like to watch the television . . .'

Tessa followed the slight figure – no voluptuous curves, no height, but boyish hips, a bustling walk, and a ladder in her frumpy patterned tights. They were trekking through the ground floor of the house, and Tessa could feel herself assaulted by a wild succession of colours, shapes and smells; tantalized by furniture and rooms – too much at once and every item resonant, because these were Michael Edwards' things. Everything she passed belonged to him, or had been touched by him: his fridge, his cooker, hi-fi, chairs, his photo on the mantelpiece, his white cat on the sofa. She was so overwhelmed to have been admitted to his house, at last, her steps were slow and hesitant; her voice struggling to form sentences – politely paltry words about the house, the cat, the cold spell. It was hard to talk at all when she required every ounce of self-control to stop her hands from reaching out and scooping up possessions – souvenirs of Dr Edwards, keepsakes to take home. Anything would do, however paltry: a brick, a tile, some fluff from the new carpet, a few combings from his hair.

Joyce had already gone ahead and was standing on the staircase, beckoning Tessa up. 'And now you must meet Jonathan,' she said. 'He's had his bath, so all you'll need to do is give him his bottle and settle him down in his cot. He likes his bedtime routine – you know, a story, or some nursery rhymes, or you could show him a few pictures in his book.'

Tessa hovered outside the nursery door, building up her reserves of strength before she dared to enter. It had been hard enough looking after other babies, when each one only emphasized her loss, but Dr Michael Edwards' child would be the most difficult of all. She made herself walk over to the cot, met the solemn gaze of lustrous dark brown eyes – Michael's eyes – the luxuriant lashes casting shadows on the cheek. The baby's hair was also dark, not Hovis-brown or Joyce's brown, but the same full-bodied shade as hers and Michael's; hair already wayward, refusing to lie flat.

'This is Tessa, Jonathan,' Joyce was saying as she picked the baby up, repeating the name Tessa, as if addressing a much older child. 'Tessa's come to look after you. Are you going to say hello to her, give her a nice big smile?'

Jonathan didn't smile, just stared at her like the infant in the waiting-room – a direct unflinching scrutiny. She couldn't find a word to say, but stood self-conscious, begging him to accept her, pleading with her eyes and outstretched hand. Jonathan ignored the hand, his face crumpling in a whimper, and clearly on the verge of tears.

'Here,' said Joyce. 'Could you hold him for a moment, while I straighten up his cot?'

Tessa feared her arms would break. The baby was quite light, in fact, but he was weighing down her body with turmoil and emotion. She subsided on the nursery chair, every nerve and muscle tense as she prayed he wouldn't scream. He was resisting her in other ways, squirming on her lap, arching up his back, jabbing with his hands and feet, struggling to get down. She tried to reassure him, to settle him more comfortably, make her arms a shield and a support. His solid warmth seemed an extension of her own, as if they'd become one flesh and blood – Michael's blood, fierce and energetic, pumping through his veins. He was dressed in a fleecy stretchsuit in cornflower blue, which set off his dark hair. His mouth was small but mobile, his eyebrows well-defined; the watchful eyes beneath them never leaving hers. He was calmer now, but still wary and suspicious, unsure if he could trust her.

Joyce retrieved his teddy from the floor. 'I'd better get a move on. Our teacher's a bit of a dragon, so I don't like being late. Tell you what – I'll go and heat the bottle up, and leave you and Jon-Jon to get to know each other. I'm afraid he's a bit of a Mummy's boy. Come on, chicky, aren't you going to smile for Tessa?' She beamed at him encouragingly as she crossed the room to the door, her footsteps tapping down the stairs, then fading into silence.

'*Michael*,' Tessa said, emphasizing the name, as Joyce had done with hers. It was essential that he learnt it, forgot that stupid Jon-Jon and demeaning names like chicky. 'I'm not Tessa, I'm your mother.'

'Mama,' said the baby.

Tessa sat motionless, scarcely believing what she'd heard. The child's face had relaxed at last, the mouth no longer trembling and down-turned. He reached out for a strand of her hair, clenched it in his fingers, clamping them so firmly round it, she couldn't prise them free. He seemed fascinated by the hair, gazing at it, pulling it, tugging really hard. She welcomed the sharp pain. The two of them were joined now, anchored to each other. '*Mummy*'s hair,' she told him.

'Mama,' he repeated.

She felt tears prick her eyes – tears of joy, relief – but fought to hold them back. A grown-up's tears were probably frightening for a baby. 'And Mummy's hands,' she added, wiggling one to show him. He released her hair to grasp a finger, seemed equally intrigued by it; giving it his full attention, eyes intent, enthralled.

'Mama,' he insisted.

'He calls everybody Mama!' Joyce laughed, reappearing at the door. 'It's the only word he's managed yet, and he likes to try it out.'

Tessa didn't answer. Joyce was simply ignorant, couldn't understand.

'Though actually, he's quite advanced to be saying even that. The tot next door is a whole month older, but she's still not got beyond a few basic grunts and squawks. Right, here's your bottle, Jon-Jon. Tessa's going to give it to you while Mum pops out to learn about the Vikings.' She slipped the teat into his mouth, then backed away unobtrusively. 'That'll keep him quiet. When he's finished, you can have your little story-time, then he should drop off to sleep. If he wakes and cries, just pick him up and cuddle him. I don't believe in leaving them to shriek.'

Tessa muttered some reply, hoping it sounded coherent and responsible. But she had no wish to talk, to dilute this almost-miracle – Michael on her lap, feeding from her, close to her, accepting her as mother.

Joyce gave a jaunty wave. 'Okay, I'm off. Good luck! I've left the Institute number on the table in the hall. If there's any problem, you can phone me there, and I'll shoot back straight away – it's only up the road. I'm sure you'll be all right, though. I've heard marvellous things about you.'

Tessa frowned, embarrassed. Joyce was speaking the wrong lines; should be distant and aloof, not full of eager praises. Once she heard the front door close, and the splutter of the car exhaust, she was aware of all her tension draining magically away. Now she was restored at last, as Michael's mother, Michael's wife – alone, in charge, unchallenged. The baby's lips were clamped firmly round the teat, his eyes tight shut, one fond hand still clutching her finger. He sucked noisily, voraciously, with his father's greed and zest, only pausing to give tiny snorts of pleasure. She shared that pleasure, even echoing the noises, so bonded with the baby that she seemed to be swallowing the milk herself, savouring its sweetness, her stomach gently swelling and distending. It was vital they were fused, to make up for the weeks of separation, the brutal way they'd been torn apart, lost to one another for so long.

She watched the level of the milk creep slowly down and down; every mouthful lulling him, as if it contained a tranquilliser. He was no longer threshing on her lap, but peaceful and contented. Once the bottle was finished, he pushed it away, stared up at her with burning eyes, trying to communicate. She, too, had things to say.

'Michael, darling, I hope you'll understand, but there's something that I . . .' She broke off, glancing nervously around, as if scared that she was being watched; felt strangely guilty as she laid him on the changing table and started taking off his clothes. But she had to see him naked, examine every inch of him, to make sure that he was normal.

The stretchsuit peeled off easily, though the nappy was more difficult, and she was worried when she removed his vest that he might bellow his objection. But he lay serene and uncomplaining, as if he understood how wonderful it was for her to see him as he'd been when he was born, clothed in nothing but his warm and living flesh. She touched the dimpled creases in his knees, his plumply rounded belly and soft pink pudgy feet – feet which looked too delicate for walking, and should be put in a glass case. She turned him on to his stomach, ran her hand lightly down his spine. Of course there was no lump – she had dreamed it in some cruel horrific nightmare. Her and Michael's baby would be perfect – exquisite, well proportioned, without the smallest blemish. She gazed in fascination at the tiny unshelled mollusc of his penis; so different from his father's, so innocent, quiescent. She stroked it with a finger, startled when it stiffened slightly. She had no idea that babies had erections, but this was Michael's son – his expression one of blissful

208

self-absorption as she continued gently kneading it. They were even closer now – not just bonded – intimate.

She would have gladly spent all evening fondling his bare skin, but Joyce had said he liked his bedtime routine – a story or a nursery rhyme – and he might start getting restive if she didn't stick to it. She dressed him with great care, making sure she put his clothes back exactly as she'd found them, then sat him on her knee again, reached out for his rag-book. She flicked swiftly through the pages, tossed it to one side. He didn't need those silly cosy pictures of teddy bears in overcoats, or bunnies with blue ears. Better to tell him a real-life story – the story of his father – explain exactly how they'd met: that dramatic near-collision in the street – not a chance encounter, but something planned, intended. And her pregnancy was part of it. She had only missed a couple of her pills, yet even so she'd fallen pregnant the first time they'd made love; conceived a child who now united them, fused their genes, their cells.

When she'd finished her account, the baby repaid her with a smile – a radiant, delighted smile, which she accepted as a priceless gift. It changed his face completely – the eyes brightening as they widened; the mouth relaxing open, showing his still milky tongue, and two tiny teeth at top and bottom. And then the smile became a yawn – a yawn so huge, he gasped for breath.

'You're tired, Michael, aren't you? I mustn't keep you up.' She laid him in his cot, tucked the blankets round him, stooped down to kiss him goodnight. She lingered over the kiss, inhaling his clean-baby smell of milk and soap and talc; admiring the peach softness of his cheek. His eyes were already closing, another gaping yawn pulling his small face apart.

'I'll pop back in a little while, to check that you're all right. And you mustn't worry when I leave – it's only for a day or two. You'll be seeing a lot of me from now on. I'll take every single chance I can of coming here again.'

His eyes were shuttered by the lids; one tiny hand flung out, defying the restricting sheet. She touched the hand, closed her fingers round it. 'Sleep tight, Michael's son.'

She switched off 'Tomorrow's World'. It was impossible to concentrate, or even to sit still. Dr Michael Edwards had sat in this same chair, punched these same buttons on the television. His feet had lapped the carpet, his hands plumped up the cushions. The whole room was wild and charged with him, yet she somehow couldn't reach him. There was a barrier between them, like the fish-tank in the waiting-room – a screen of glass preventing her from diving into the water, pressing close to gill and fin. And the glass was slightly warped, distorting everything she looked at, blurring lines and shapes. She realized she was hungry – hadn't bothered to eat before setting out from home – and had exhausted herself in the last nerve-racking hour or so by continually running upstairs to check on Michael. She was beset by constant fears that he was dead, or maybe trapped in some horrific dream, or wet, or sick, or dirty. Though every time she'd tiptoed in, she'd found him quiet and tranquil, breathing peacefully, his nappy clean and dry. 'Goodnight,' she'd said a dozen times. 'Sleep well.'

If only she could follow his example – relax, let go, flop out. Instead, she was pacing restlessly around, found herself wandering into the hall, traipsing up and down from kitchen to front door. Perhaps she'd make a coffee, sample the fruit-cake. She mooched back to the kitchen, studying the row of mugs hanging on the dresser. Which one did Dr Edwards use? Would he prefer the chunky earthenware to the blue-rimmed porcelain? Probably both of them had pressed against his mouth, felt the touch of his lips. She longed to be those mugs; to be anything which shared his life or had access to his body – thought enviously of his toothbrush, which could penetrate much further in, mingle with his saliva, taste the heady remnants of his wine. She ran upstairs to the bathroom, locked the door behind her. Here were still more intimate things – wooden bath-brush, yellow sponge. Had they scrubbed his back and thighs, crept between his legs? And the shaving soap and razor she found in the small cabinet – daily they must caress his face, smooch his damp flushed skin. She sat down on the toilet seat, where he too had sat, this morning – private, making smells. She even loved the smells. There was no part of Michael Edwards she would ever shrink from or reject.

She pounced on a blue sponge-bag on the ledge below the window; discovered Joyce's things – her tampons and her diaphragm, a tube of contraceptive gel. She re-zipped the bag immediately. The images it seeded drove her almost mad: Joyce and Michael copulating; their naked bodies entwined. She stole into their bedroom, surprised to find the bed so neat; the prim white lacy counterpane concealing the stained sheets and heaving rumpled blankets she'd been seeing in her mind. If only they had twin beds, to keep them separate and apart. She loathed the room – every item in it. Joyce had imposed her taste on him: pink carpet, floral curtains, ruched and frilly lampshades. There was nothing of him left – only his grim smile in their gilt-framed wedding photo. She approached it with a mixture of distaste and curiosity. Joyce's spaniel eyes were fixed on him adoringly, as they stood arm in arm in a rose-bower; her disaster of a hat – another rose-bower in itself – almost overshadowing the stiff bouquet she was holding like a truncheon. She didn't look much younger, so the photo must be recent. Had he tired of her in bed yet? Did they do it every night, even when she had her period? And how did . . . ?

Her thoughts were interrupted by a sudden noise outside. A car was drawing up – not Joyce, at half past eight. She peered out through the curtains, saw Dr Edwards' Citroën, nosing into the garage. She fled downstairs to the sitting-room, arranged herself on the sofa, trying to look natural, as if she'd been there quite some time. She grabbed the December *Ideal Home* and started leafing through it, cheeks scorching hot, heart thumping in her chest. Supposing he was angry to see a patient in his house? Or perhaps he wouldn't recognize her. She was dressed simply, almost austerely, in a plain grey skirt and pastel blouse; had deliberately left off jewellery and make-up. She could hardly breathe as she listened to his key turn in the lock, his heavy footsteps tramping down the hall.

'Joyce!' he called. 'Where are you, darling?'

The apologies and explanations which had been forming in her head shrivelled in an instant. He didn't even know that she was here; was expecting to be greeted by his wife. The fierce pain of that 'darling' was still stabbing through her skull, resounding and resounding like a strident peal of bells. She fought an urge to climb out through the window and make a quick dash home. Instead, she went to meet him, forced a cautious smile.

His own smile died, replaced by an uneasy frown, then the penny dropped and he shook his head in mock-exasperation at himself. 'Stupid of me! I'd totally forgotten you were coming. I probably scared you, didn't I, barging in like that. I hope you didn't think I was a burglar!'

'No,' she said, intoxicated once again by the bulk and warmth of his sheepskin coat, its astounding dangerous closeness.

'Joyce did tell me – twice – that you'd be here, but, even so, it slipped my mind. Do sit down. How's Jonathan? I hope he's been no trouble.'

'I haven't heard a peep from him.'

'Good!' He removed the coat, then stretched out on the sofa, easing his collar and tie. 'How are you, by the way? I thought you might come back to see me in the surgery – you know, as we arranged.'

She stared down at the carpet, embarrassed and confused. So he did know who she was, remembered all the details of her case. Was he concerned about his baby, frightened she had harmed it – the girl who'd killed her own child? Could he tell she'd touched its genitals? Would he round on her in fury?

'I'm fine,' she reassured him, her traitor voice unsteady. 'Back to my old self, in fact.' She must make him see she was completely fit and healthy, conscientious, trustworthy – more than that – indispensable. Now they had this chance to talk without doctor/patient constraints, they could drop the cool formality and proceed to a more friendly footing. She was already halfway there: admitted to his house, sitting on his chair, so close to him, she could touch his hand.

'Good,' he said again, glancing at his watch, then heaving himself up to his feet. 'Well, perhaps you'd like to get off home, now I'm back myself. There's a bit of mist building up outside, so it's probably wise to make a move before it thickens into fog. Have you far to go? Beech Close, isn't it?'

'No,' she said. 'Clifton Road.'

'I'd offer to take you in the car, but we never leave Jonathan on his own. My wife's very strict about it – always telling me these horror stories about babies choking to death the minute you turn your back . . .'

He laughed – a hollow laugh, she felt. He didn't want to talk, didn't even want her there, couldn't wait to get shot of her. And yet it might have been so different. She realized that she'd missed her chance, answered the wrong way. He had asked her how she was, and that should have been her cue. If she'd treated the question seriously, she might still be sitting close to him, filling in the minutiae. The answer could have taken her all night – starting with her head, and progressing through her body, including every limb and organ, every cell and function – her blood pressure, digestion, the coursing of her blood around the veins, the beating of her heart, the condition of her skin. 'How are you?' was the most vast discursive question in the world, and she'd simply shrugged it off, rebuffing his first overture.

'Shall I fetch your coat?' he asked.

She nodded and stood up, extracting a last sad snatch of pleasure from the sensation of his hands brushing against her shoulders as he helped her put it on. She'd give anything to keep them there, to turn round and feel the hunger of his body, lose herself in the blaze of his embrace. But he had already stepped away, was hanging up his own coat on the fancy wooden stand.

'Goodbye, then,' she said flatly.

'Hold on a sec. We owe you something, don't we?' We. The married we this time – him and Joyce, him and Mrs Edwards.

'No, honestly, don't worry. I've only been here an hour and a half.'

He ignored her protests, fumbled for his wallet, and as he pulled a banknote out, she glimpsed a photo of his wife, flaunting in the centre section, behind a transparent square of plastic. She reeled back as if he'd hit her; could almost feel his clenched fist in her stomach, or smashing her front teeth. If Dr Michael Edwards carried photos in his wallet, then *she* must be the face in them; *she* the one nestled close against his body, soaking up its heat, accompanying him everywhere, lulled by the rhythm of his breathing and his heartbeat.

He pressed the note into her hand, then opened the front door. 'Goodnight,' he said. 'And thanks.'

She stepped out into the cold and dark, felt herself swallowed up in mist, dissolving into damp and clammy nothingness. She wheeled back, close to panic; had to see his solid smiling face again; the rectangle of saving light which framed it in the doorway. Both had disappeared; the door slammed shut, the face now lost, as he rejected and abandoned her.

19

TESSA TRUNDLED HER trolley round the corner, stopped once more at the baby foods – tins and jars of purées, dried milks, Farex, rusks. She glanced at her watch – ten o'clock exactly. She'd been wandering round the supermarket since it opened at 8.30, but still no sign of the Edwardses. Last Saturday they'd arrived at nine, and having trailed them for a good half an hour, she'd contrived a 'chance' meeting at the checkout; told them that she always shopped at Sainsbury's. In fact, Tesco's was marginally cheaper, and certainly much nearer, but she wouldn't meet the Edwardses there, so she'd changed her usual shopping habits and now toured Sainsbury's daily.

She trudged further down the aisle to the baby soaps and nappies, hoping nobody was observing her on the internal security system. She'd be a prime suspect for a shoplifter, loitering here so long, especially as she kept peering over her shoulder, and must obviously seem nervous and strung up. Maybe Mrs Edwards had done her shopping yesterday, and was now relaxing at the Leisure Centre, which had a pool and saunas – and also ran a crèche. Since she'd learned Joyce was a member, she had returned there several times, either hanging around outside, watching people come and go, or venturing in to ask for information. She knew there was an infants' swimming session at eleven on a Saturday, so she might catch sight of baby Michael if she went there straight away, stationed herself in the foyer. It was ten days since she'd seen the baby, so her anxiety was growing. She had told him she'd be back in just a matter of a day or two, but she'd had to break her promise. It wasn't up to her – she had to wait for a phone-call from the Edwardses, asking if she could babysit again. She hadn't heard a word from them, so she assumed they didn't want her; maybe even disapproved of her, and were now deliberately avoiding her by shopping at the corner store.

She drifted towards the till, took her place in the long and straggling queue. Everyone around her appeared to be in families – fathers pushing trolleys, toddlers cadging sweets; the man in front trying to stop his baby son from using the Air-Fresh as a teething-ring.

'Hello!' called a voice – Joyce Edwards' voice – soft and slightly girlish.

Tessa's hands tightened on the trolley, her grip so fierce it hurt. She hardly dared look round, but when she did, her hopes were dashed in an instant – the woman closing in on her had an upswept curly chignon and gold-framed spectacles, not limp brown hair and doggy Bournville eyes.

'How are you, Mrs Johnson?' she asked dutifully, trying to hide her disappointment. She had worked for Michèle Johnson just last week – not babysitting, charring – had also cleared the garden, washed the car, and shampooed her two bad-tempered dogs, as well as half the carpets in the house. She took every job she could now, in the hope that Mrs Edwards would hear about her skills, employ her as a cleaner or a gardener, if not as trusted nanny.

'I'm fine, my dear, but Zsa-Zsa's in a sulk. We changed her basket, but she doesn't like the new one. She did a poo-poo on the bedroom rug, to show us how put out she was. What a stroke of luck to bump into you like this! I've been searching high and low to find your phone number – I know I put it somewhere, but my desk is such a mess. I was hoping you could come again next week – say, Tuesday? You did a grand job on those carpets!'

'Yes, of course,' said Tessa, adding silently: Please tell Mrs Edwards how good I am at cleaning; how long I spent cutting back those creepers in the garden; be sure you let her know I'm careful and reliable.

She picked up a *Family Circle* from the rack beside the till. There was an article on baby-care – how to stop the pain of teething. Michael had more teeth to cut, including the large and painful back ones. 'What time do you want me?' she enquired of Mrs Johnson, already counting hours. By Tuesday morning, it would be more than three hundred since she'd last laid eyes on Michael.

She finalized the arrangements, paid for her mini-pack of Kleenex and her small tin of baked beans, then set off for the Leisure Centre. Several sporty-looking types were jostling through the doors – muscly men in satin shorts, girls in tracksuits, children with their swimming things. She couldn't really understand how they found the time for leisure. Her own life seemed packed with myriad tasks, and when she wasn't doing jobs for other people, or scouring streets and shops in pursuit of both the Edwardses, then she was working on her Michael thesis, widening its scope. Yet if they had a part-time vacancy here for a waitress or a pool attendant, she must somehow squeeze it in, since it would afford her one more chance of seeing baby Michael.

She ventured in to the foyer, which was already wreathed with tinsel; a huge decorated Christmas tree glittering in its scarlet tub. She dreaded the thought of Christmas Day. The Edwardses would be closeted at home, their doors locked and barred to the outside world; the surgery deserted; even Sainsbury's and this Centre closed, so there wouldn't be the slightest hope of seeing either of the Michaels. She faltered to the desk, embarrassed to discover that the girl on duty was the one she'd bothered several times already. At least on this occasion she was asking for a job, and not for her fifth consecutive membership form.

'I'm sorry,' said the girl, 'but the man who deals with staffing doesn't work weekends. You'll have to come back Monday.'

'I see,' said Tessa, frowning. 'Look, I don't want to be a nuisance, but I wondered if there was any chance of having a quick look at the pool – just to . . . ?'

'No, sorry,' said the girl again. 'Only paid-up members are allowed past that green door. You were going to join, weren't you?'

Oh, sure, she thought bitterly – if I had two hundred quid to spare, and nothing better to do than loll naked in the sauna or stretch out on a sun-bed.

A woman pushed in front of her, to book a facial in the beauty salon and something called a mud-wrap, handing over a small gold card with 'Privileged Member' stamped across the top. Another doctor's wife no doubt, splurging all her husband's cash. Who ever met a doctor on the breadline? They were always filthy rich; made their money killing babies, or yanking out women's wombs and ovaries. Doctors were beginning to disgust her, especially Dr Edwards, who had clearly told his wife not to let her in the house again. They couldn't be away. She checked on them twice daily; stealing past their house each evening to make sure the lights were on; then visiting the Health Centre every weekday morning, hiding in the bushes so that she could watch the doctors arrive. Dr Edwards was often the first, and always in his sheepskin. It was affecting her quite badly – that curdling mixture of longing and resentment the merest glimpse of him could rouse in her; the way she had to stop herself from racing after him and begging for a word. She was sometimes tempted to book appointments every day, except she'd no wish to be his patient. The relationship she craved was seductive mistress, beloved wife.

She backed away from the desk, her eyes fixed on the entrance. Mothers and babies had begun trickling in for the swimming class – one girl wearing an exotic fox-fur jacket; another sporting thigh-length calfskin boots; no one dressed by Oxfam. How smug they were, with their plush lifestyles, wealthy husbands, their children in the pink of health. They took it totally for granted that the expensively-dressed bundles in their pushchairs were flawless little specimens, not deformed and stunted corpses.

No child escaped her scrutiny, even those muffled up in shawls and woolly hats. All she had to do was scan the eyes, and so far none were dark enough, none wild and bright and intense enough.

Half an hour limped by. Most babies' eyes were blue – boring blue, anaemic blue, frustrating maddening blue. She was compelled to admit defeat; let the door slam shut behind her, grimacing at the cold. She decided to go home, make a cup of coffee to warm her from inside, but her feet refused to co-operate and were already steering her a different way – in the direction of the Health Centre. Dr Edwards wasn't on – she'd double-checked last night – and the Saturday morning surgery was always very brief, with just a skeleton staff. But something might have changed: another doctor gone off sick; an accident, emergency, which would keep it open longer. No. The doors were bolted, and there was no sign of life at all; only garish Christmas streamers mocking her grey mood. She dared not try Tregunter Road, nose around his house again. She'd been snooping there so many times, his neighbours must have noticed by now, and might well have got suspicious, even alerted the police. Dr Edwards made her feel a criminal – a woman with designs on him, always skulking, spying – yet all she actually wanted of him was his attention and his love.

She set off for home once more, calling in at his newsagent en route, in the hope he might be there, perhaps cancelling a paper or paying the account. The shop was full of kids, riffling through the comics, squabbling over sweets, their voices shrill and yobbish. She was praying for another voice, deeper, more refined. She hung around a while, to give him time – after all, he was busy and committed, like herself. She'd changed her own newspaper from the *Guardian* to the *Telegraph*. Although she didn't like its politics, it pleased her to be reading the same articles and features at perhaps exactly the same moment as Dr Edwards read them. She had also switched to the Edwardses' brand of coffee, gladly paying almost half as much again, so that she, as Mrs Edwards, could drink the same brew as her husband.

She made one last tour of the shop, bought herself a Twix for lunch, then dawdled down the road, still looking back, looking back, watching for that dark red car. She had never noticed Citroëns till last month, but now she saw them everywhere; the two inverted Vs in front like a tiny secret symbol, sending out a shock-wave, a thrill of recognition every time she spotted it. There was even one parked in her own street, though not a red estate. She turned in at the gate, greeted by the blare of Eric's radio. It was difficult to work at home on Saturdays, with both the lodgers insisting on loud musical accompaniment to their often noisy chores. At least Frank wasn't busy with his power-drill, only cooking curry.

'Hallo, treasure! You look as if you've lost a tenner and only found a safety pin. Want to try my chicken vindaloo?'

'No thanks.'

'You're as bad as Eric, you are! He's bought these slimming biscuits for his dinner, and he's so thin already, you can't hardly see him sideways on.'

'I'll try some later, Frank. I'm busy at the moment.'

'Busy working on your book, I take it?'

'What book? What d'you mean?'

'Your Mum said you was writing your memoirs. And if you plan to sell the film rights, make sure I'm played by Arnold Schwarzenegger.'

'Okay,' she said, 'you're on.' She gave him the thumbs-up sign, then closed her door hurriedly on a burst of wild applause. She wasn't keen on television game-shows, but was forced to listen second-hand every time Frank tuned in to 'Find Your Fortune'. It was all the more frustrating because she'd tried so hard to turn her room into a place for serious study – a hushed and solemn shrine, like the Camera or the Bodleian. She had put away the frivolous things – her Walkman and her cuddly toys, the dried flowers on the windowsill, the posters on the walls – leaving the room as austere and bare as possible, so that she could apply herself to work without distraction.

She sat down at her desk (keeping her coat on, to save the cost of heating), then spread out all her papers and her file-cards, to plot her graph of Dr Edwards' life. She had already sorted all the random facts into different labelled sections and could begin to see his biography taking shape: his schooldays at Bourne Hall; his training at Birmingham Medical School; followed by three years at the Leicester Royal Infirmary; his first job as a GP in a well-heeled Leicester suburb, and his eventual move to the south. There were still a lot of gaps, and the whole period in Leicester was shadowy and un-fleshed-out, but she'd done pretty well, considering all the obstacles. The people she'd approached had often been wary or tight-lipped, and she'd had to invent sound convincing reasons for her enquiries, to allay their fears, coax out more information. She'd phoned the General Medical Council and the Royal College of GPs; talked to local patients and two of the Health Centre receptionists; tracked down a hospital porter at Birmingham, who'd been there thirty years or more and remembered Michael Edwards as a student. She'd sent for brochures from the hospitals he'd worked at, and also from Bourne Hall – a so-called minor public school, which was housed in a Rothschild mansion and charged astronomical fees. Money had never seemed a problem for the Edwardses. The father had been rich – another Michael Edwards, who'd made his pile in property and left most to his son.

She was working on an index of all the names and places she'd come across so far, and kept jotting down any other sources she could check. She had managed to arrange her life so that she was alone for most of the day; going out to babysit when the others in the household were expected back from work, and missing 'family' meals whenever possible. Tonight she was sitting for the Wentworths – a doddle of a job, since there was only one docile child, who'd already be asleep in bed by the time she arrived at eight. It would save her from an evening of her mother's interrogation: when was she going to find a nice reliable boyfriend who had no other irons in the fire? Why was she only picking at her food, and what was wrong with toad-in-the-hole, pray, when she'd never turned her nose up at it before? And was it really healthy to be so anti-socialist, stuck up in her room for hours on end?

Sundays were the worst. It was hard to escape at all then, and everyone was in; three separate radios often playing at full blast, and

April insisting she sat down to lunch and tea. She didn't want her mother to see her Dr Edwards thesis, so she locked it in a drawer each evening, pretending she was still working for her degree. Actually, nothing could be further from the truth. She'd come to the conclusion that history was a sham. How could anyone be expected to take in such a Niagara Falls of facts – chronicles and archives, battles, treaties, statutes? And there wasn't a hope in hell of understanding the past without at least a grounding in loads of other subjects – things like anthropology, sociology, geography – not to mention several foreign languages, and a grasp of economics. The average student would be pushed to cover such a tough assignment in fifty years, or a hundred, let alone the paltry three that Oxford meted out. She was currently investigating the history of one single man, and that was daunting enough, but at least she had some hope of getting to grips with it, and there was less distortion and deceit. A lot of so-called history had been churned out as propaganda, to give people what they wanted – victories and heroes; a reassuring rubber stamp for the dogmas of the age; and also to provide boundaries and structure for those terrified of foundering in a tidal wave of purely random events. She was far safer studying Dr Michael Edwards, limiting herself to one essential subject, ignoring every other period save the forty-one-and-a-quarter years from his birth in Loughborough in September 1950, to the official nine-month birthday of his son, which must have been last Tuesday.

She laid her pen down, bitter once again at her exclusion from the Edwardses' house. Michael might have cut another tooth by now, learned another word, be struggling to stand up or take a step, and she wouldn't know, wouldn't be at hand to witness his achievements. She abandoned her graph, turned instead to the huge stack of local newspapers she had collected from the houses round about. She had told her friends and neighbours that she'd decided to write a history of the area and needed all the information she could lay her hands upon. Some old crones had papers going back a decade, so she hadn't found the time yet to gut each and every one. But she'd combed through several dozen, her eyes alert for news of Dr Edwards – snippets, photos, maybe awards he'd won or controversial views he'd aired, or reports about the Health Centre – its construction, its official opening, or even . . .

A sudden gale of laughter erupted through the wall. Frank had left his door ajar while he popped out to the bathroom. The bathroom door was also open, so she could hear the sound of his peeing – a long and very public performance – overlaid with the breathy voice of the quiz-master.

'That's it, Wayne and Cheryl, give each other a smackeroo! You've got through to our fantastic final round, and that means a chance of winning our incredible, fantabulous holiday of a lifetime on the sun-kissed island paradise of . . .'

The holiday destination and the flushing of the toilet were both swamped in a fanfare from the band. Tessa cursed the flimsy walls, unwrapped her Twix and bit into it angrily. Television was such a waste of time. Even the news seemed increasingly irrelevant – simply the fodder for more history: wars and cease-fires, strikes and famines, coups, assassinations. She found it hard to concentrate, if she listened to it at all. Michael always hogged the headlines, and the other items were merely frills and padding. So many things seemed to have lost their point or meaning: the cinema and theatre, food and drink, her friends. Both Alexandra and Vicky had invited her to stay – Alexandra in Juxon Street, Vicky at her Weybridge home – but she'd refused their invitations. She'd already frittered too much time away at Balliol, yakking in the bar, or acting in pathetic plays, or writing childish pieces for half-baked magazines. She simply hadn't known what life was all about – its gravity, its dangers.

The phone was ringing in the hall. She dashed downstairs before Frank could pick it up and start haranguing the poor caller. Pat Hughes had rung last week and received an earful about dog shit on the pavement and Pakis in the classroom before Frank finally bellowed up to her 'Tess! It's that girl you said you didn't want to speak to. Shall I say you're out?'

She prayed it wasn't Pat again. She was in no mood for a chinwag, and would only be embarrassed if her friend suggested meeting – didn't really care if she never saw Pat in her life again, despite April's constant cluckings about how important it was to keep up old acquaintances, and not shut herself away in her Eiffel Tower.

'Hello? Who? I'm sorry, the line's gone rather faint. Oh, Mrs *Edwards*! Yes, I'm fine.' She clung on to the wall, feeling dizzy and disoriented. Just hearing the name Edwards could set off instant symptoms – queasy stomach, pounding heart. And Joyce Edwards sounded anxious, which made her fear the worst – gruesome pictures of some emergency or accident flashing through her mind. Was baby Michael ill, Dr Edwards bleeding or unconscious? She listened for a moment more, before letting out a sigh of sheer relief. Her fears were all unfounded. The only casualty was the girl they'd booked to babysit, who'd just rung up to say she had a temperature.

'So I wondered, Tessa, if you could possibly help us out? We're going to this party, you see, and it's a really early start.'

'Tonight, you mean?' asked Tessa, hoping against hope that the answer would be no.

'Yes,' said Mrs Edwards, adding a babble of apologies. 'I know it's terribly short notice, and you're probably booked already, and . . .'

'No,' she said, 'I'm not.' She broke off in desperation, searching for solutions. Could she split herself in two, phone Peggy Wentworth and tell her she'd collapsed with flu, or that a really painful abscess had erupted in her mouth? Or maybe she could blame the . . .

'Hello? Hello? Are you still there?'

'Yes, sorry, Mrs Edwards. I just . . . er . . . dropped the phone. Look, tonight's no problem, honestly. I've got nothing planned at all. Yes, any time you like. Half past five is fine – see you then. Goodbye.'

Now *she* was the one with a temperature, so sweaty-hot and feverish she could hardly even think straight. She tried to make a mental list, sort out all the things she had to do – wash her hair, choose her clothes and iron them, phone her mother at the salon and beg her to come to the rescue, then get on to Peggy Wentworth and ask her if she'd mind if April did the babysitting instead. She couldn't let the Wentworths down, or word might filter back to Mrs Edwards that she was casual, unreliable.

She dialled the salon number, to be told her mother was busy with a perm, so could she call back later. She rushed upstairs to find a suitable outfit – something fairly low-key and restrained, but which would still set off her figure, attract Dr Edwards' notice. She'd dressed too drably last time, and too glamorously when she'd seen him in the surgery. This all-important third time she must get it absolutely right – strike the perfect balance between artlessness and artifice.

Frank's door was on the jar again, and she stopped to watch the game-show exulting to its climax – hysterical clapping and cheering from the audience, a final triumphant flourish from the band. She broke into a grin as she realized the applause was all for her. She might be jittery and flustered, torn between hope and dread, but she'd still won tonight's Big Prize – the incredible fantabulous prize of a whole evening with her son.

20

'I'M AFRAID WE'RE fearfully late,' said Joyce. 'I haven't even dressed yet. My mother popped in unexpectedly – told me it was a flying visit, then stayed half an hour. Michael! Tessa's here. Could you show her Jon-Jon's food and stuff, while I put my glad rags on?'

'I'm feeding him already,' Dr Edwards shouted from the kitchen.

Tessa tensed at his brusque voice. She'd imagined how he'd meet her at the door, welcoming and smiling, maybe even touching her – an eager grateful hand-clasp, or a light brush of her arm. But he hadn't even called hello; sounded decidedly unfriendly.

'Well, perhaps you could take over, Tessa?' Joyce suggested, pausing in the hall. 'My husband's changed already, and I don't fancy going out with him if he's got sicked-up baby food all down his front!' She laughed, and slipped upstairs, her silky blue-flowered dressing-gown fluttering out behind her.

Tessa hung her coat up, hardly believing what she'd heard. How could anyone not fancy going out with Michael Edwards? *She* would accompany him anywhere, whatever the state of his clothes. She gripped the wooden coat-stand, as if to brace herself; needed a few seconds to rehearse her opening lines. But when she sidled into the kitchen, all her amusing casual greetings foundered in her throat as she stared at the figure sitting at the table. He was totally transformed, the rich black of his dinner suit enhancing his pale eyes; his shirt so dazzling white it made her own seem grubby; his hair blow-dried, much fuller and more elegant than usual. He had taken off his glasses, which changed his face dramatically, removed a sort of barrier between them. But he refused to meet her eyes, and his 'hello' was quite unspirited, lacking in all warmth. He hadn't even risen to his feet, just muttered some excuse about being busy feeding

Jonathan. She switched her gaze from father to son. Michael – not Jonathan – was squirming in his high chair, obviously resenting the intrusion and his interrupted meal. His mouth began to pucker, heralding a scream.

His father tried to circumvent the scream by slipping the spoon between the baby's lips, but he pushed it peevishly away, let out an anguished wail.

'Damn!' said Dr Edwards. 'We were just beginning to make some progress and now he's playing up again.'

'Shall *I* feed him?' Tessa offered, the 'damn' smarting like a wound.

'Okay – have a go, but I shouldn't think he'll let you. He's teething at the moment, so meals are merry hell.'

Of course he'll let me, Tessa countered wordlessly, as she sat down at the table, pulled the dish towards her. 'What's he having?' she enquired, peering at the pappy greenish sludge.

'Puréed avocado.'

She fought a surge of anger. Avocados, indeed! Ordinary kids made do with Marmite sandwiches, while the Edwardses threw their cash around, had to be superior. The whole luxurious kitchen seemed to mock her mother's bare one – the panelled units in solid oak, not tatty peeling plastic; the peacock-patterned floor-tiles in place of scuffed brown lino; the microwave, the television, the ostentatious freezer. But it wasn't just the affluence – she was angry for more tortured reasons: because Dr Edwards seemed so cool and distant; had dressed up not for her, but for some exclusive fat-cat party. He hadn't even noticed her own clothes and hair and make-up, despite the hours she'd spent on them. And what hurt most of all was the still screaming cantankerous baby. Every time she tried to move the spoon towards his mouth, he'd turn his furious face away, and bellow even louder. She felt horribly embarrassed. Dr Edwards would conclude she was quite useless; had no maternal gift at all. Yet it was probably his own fault – somehow he'd turned their son against her, had spent the last ten days feeding him not avocado purée, but dollops of mashed prejudice, sieved and buttered lies.

The child was now so frantic, he was straining every muscle to escape from his high chair – writhing, twisting, stiffening his whole body when she tried to coax him back. Dr Edwards suddenly jumped up, released the baby from his strap and sat him on his knee. The screams abated instantly, as Michael clung on like a limpet, head against his father's neck; blocking Tessa out. She felt utterly rejected, even close to tears; pretended to be busy mopping avocado off her skirt.

Dr Edwards grabbed the dish impatiently, as if annoyed at her temerity in moving it. 'Pass me another tea towel, will you? I'd better stuff a bit more into him, and I don't fancy ending up with green all down my shirt. You'll find some clean ones in that third drawer on the right.'

She passed one over, watching the baby's mood change from querulous and bawling to simperingly affectionate. He snuggled against his father's chest, clutching at his shirt with flirtatious, chubby hands, his hostile back towards her. Dr Edwards responded in his turn, ruffling his son's hair, chucking him under the chin, stroking his soft cheek with the back of one broad finger, putting on a special voice, much softer and more captivating than his usual impersonal tone. 'That's better, Jon-Jon, isn't it? You're Daddy's little cherub now.'

She looked on with helpless misery; the superfluous spectator playing gooseberry to their love-scene. She could hardly understand the strength and sheer confusion of her feelings. She longed to have the baby on her own knee, nestling close and loving her, but she also craved to be the child herself; to feel Dr Edwards' adoring arms cradling her small body, his finger brushing gently down her face. She tried not to watch as he picked the teaspoon up again and cajoled his son to eat, making little smacking noises, murmuring endearments. He had never used such words to her – coquettish, almost erotic words, oozing love and tenderness. How fantastic to be fed, to have someone so involved with your every sip and swallow, to praise your every mouthful. Dave had never fed her as a baby – he wasn't there – and neither was her mother, who'd returned to work only three weeks after the birth. She supposed someone must have given her her bottle, stopped her mouth with a rusk, but she couldn't remember anything about it. April wouldn't have had the money to pay a proper child-minder, so it must have been an odd bod, or some neighbour popping in. Dave had fed his younger daughters – she'd sat and watched him do so – the perfect doting father to Lucy and Elizabeth, but not to his first-born.

She kicked her chair back suddenly, mumbling something half-inaudible about going to the loo, though what she needed to excrete was black and clotted anger – more anger than she had ever felt before.

Dave, her father, hadn't been in touch with her since June. He knew about her pregnancy, her illness, loss of Oxford, yet he'd not bothered to pick up the phone or scribble a brief line. Her mother had passed on a few vague and jolly messages from him, but he hadn't found the time to contact her himself; must be just too busy stuffing avocado purée into Daddy's little cherubs, Lucy and Elizabeth. And what about Michael up in Newcastle? She'd done her best to expel him from her mind, claw and tug her thoughts back when they kept trespassing up north, but she couldn't seem to stamp out her resentment. Perhaps he and his new lovebird had conceived a child by now. Was he feeding the smug bitch, so as to fatten up the embryo swelling in her womb – tempting her with mangoes and whipped cream?

She turned on the cold tap, rinsed her hands in a spurt of freezing water, hoping it would douse her rage. She banged the cloakroom door behind her, then stood peering up the staircase, but there was no sign of Mrs Edwards. Couldn't she be ready on time, when she had nothing else to do but swan around the Leisure Centre, or have coffee with her well-heeled friends after a little cultural chit-chat on the Vikings? April had a full-time job, yet *she*'d be bathed and changed, knocking at the Wentworths' door on the dot of eight o'clock.

She took a cautious step towards the table in the hall, which was piled with gift-wrapped packages; edged a little closer, so she could read the tags and labels: 'Happy Christmas from all at Yew Tree Cottage – and thank you for your help.' 'With kind regards from Alicia de Courcy.' 'Merry Christmas, Doctor, from the Crawfords.' Presents from his patients – those three thousand hated rivals on his list. Or perhaps Alicia de Courcy was a more intimate sort of friend, and her 'kind regards' meant passion and desire. The name itself was loathsome – exotic and pretentious – the sort of dangerous woman who could easily ensnare him. Dr Michael Edwards had so much in his life – not just seductive patients, but relatives and friends, hobbies, interests, duties, parties, meetings. How could someone like herself be of any consequence, when she was just a speck, a pin-prick, in his crowded timetable?

She heard a sudden noise, a footstep on the stairs, fled back to the kitchen. The baby had now finished his green pap and was playing with the spoon, gurgling at his father; the two of them absorbed once more in love-talk, oblivious to anyone's existence but their own. '*Michael!*' she was crying, to both of them, all three of them – the Michael up in Newcastle, the Michael in this kitchen, and to her precious traitor baby – but none of them could hear; none was even aware that she was speaking.

'Well, how do I look?'

Tessa swung round to the door. Joyce had just come in, all dolled up in a fussy chiffon number in an unpleasant shade of green – a cross between dank pond and mushy peas. Yet the dress had cost a bomb – you could tell that from its cut and style, the way the fabric hung. And her jewellery was the real McCoy, not junk. Somehow Joyce herself was lost, though; her scrawny figure and undistinguished features unable to compete with designer frocks, or pearl and emerald chokers.

Dr Edwards eased the baby back into his chair, so that he could paw and kiss the beauty queen. 'Lovely, darling – perfect! That soft green really suits you.'

Tessa turned away. His hands were still caressing Joyce's naked arm and neck, his lips lingering on her cheek. 'Perfect' he had called his wife, yet not spared a single glance for her own russet-brown culottes-suit with the white blouse underneath. Okay, it wasn't *haute couture*, or even very trendy – she had found it in the Cancer Shop a year or more ago – but it showed her curves off, emphasized her legs, which she'd tried to make still longer by wearing high-heeled boots. The boots were also second-hand, but they laced up to the knee, and even grudging Eric had admitted they were sexy, while Frank had suggested she take over from Madonna, and had asked if he could sign up as her manager? She doubted if Dr Edwards had even noticed that she *had* legs; he was too enamoured of his wife's, which looked leprous in their green-tinged tights, and hardly varied in shape and girth from the ankle to the knee. The only thing which distracted him, broke up the sordid clinch, was renewed screaming from the baby. He prised himself reluctantly from bare neck and chiffon flounces, to fetch a banana and a yogurt for his son.

'Can't Tessa give him those, Michael? We're frightfully late already, and it's a good hour's drive to Haslemere.' Joyce took the pot of yogurt from him, squeezed his hand a moment. 'Why don't you get the car out, darling, while I explain the drill to Tessa? They'll think we're never coming if we hang about much longer.'

You're the one who's been hanging about, Tessa thought resentfully, while she took in her instructions – outwardly the model of politeness, but inwardly tormented by the 'Michael' and the 'darling', the squeezing of the hand. Those were *her* prerogatives, not Joyce's.

228

'Could you be an angel and feed the cat as well?' Joyce was bustling round now, tidying things away. 'There's some minced chicken in the fridge in a jar with "Nellie" on it. My husband ruins that damned cat, cooks free-range chicken for her, would you believe – as if he hadn't got enough to do! I used to buy Kit-E-Kat, but Nellie won't touch it, now she's developed a taste for cordon bleu. Right, we really must get off. Don't cry, Jon-Jon poppet, Tessa's going to give you some lovely yummy pudding.' She kissed the baby, babbled her goodbyes, added a last word about not picking up the phone if it rang, as it was connected to an answering-machine. 'I'm afraid we won't be back till late. I do hope that's all right. It'll be after midnight – maybe nearer one.'

'No problem,' Tessa smiled, wishing she could persuade Joyce to make it later still. Dawn would be just fine – or even teatime the next day. There was so much she longed to do for Michael, but hadn't had the chance yet: get him up in the morning, give him breakfast, cook him lunch; bath him, wash his hair; wheel him in his pram to the shops or baby clinic; have other mothers compliment her on the beauty of her son. But most of all, she simply wanted to look at him – admire his perfect body. Once Joyce had gone, she'd have him to herself, could make a start on undoing all the falsehoods, trying to win his trust again.

She waved them off, closed the door behind them – *her* door, her sumptuous house – then returned to Michael, who was sobbing inconsolably. He must have thought she'd left him, departed with the Edwardses. 'You're all right now,' she soothed. 'Mummy's here. She'll never go away.'

She sat down at the table, removed the yogurt lid. She'd better finish feeding him, so that they could have some precious private time doing nothing but get close. She dipped the spoon in, held it to his mouth. He lunged at it in fury, trying to push her arm away, jerking back his head. She scooped yogurt off her blouse – and chin – then licked her finger, grimacing at the taste. No wonder he recoiled at such unappetizing sharpness. The yogurt was unsweetened – Joyce had said that she never gave him sugar in any form at all, and forbade all sweets and chocolate. Couldn't the poor child have a flavoured yogurt, or creamy strawberry mousse?

She tried him with the banana instead, breaking off a chunk and slipping it into his hand. He stopped screaming for a second, while he examined it suspiciously, then flung it on the floor. She held out another larger piece, which he mangled in his fingers, then smeared across his face and clothes, even in his hair. He seemed to be defying her deliberately, spurning her maternal love, along with everything she offered him, or maybe subtly punishing her for having been away so long. Perhaps he needed comfort – the comfort of a bottle and a teat, which might console him like a dummy, especially if she held him in her arms. Joyce had left the bottle ready, so all she had to do was check the temperature, then transfer him from his high chair to her lap. But he had other ideas, started fighting her with fists and feet, so that his flailing legs got entangled in the chair-tray, and even when she lifted him clear, he was still shrieking almost hysterically. It was impossible to feed him when he kept swiping at the bottle, as if his one desire was to knock it from her hand. It banged against her lip and teeth – the sudden stinging pain reminding her of *his* pain. Perhaps he was just trying to convey to her in the only way he could that his teeth were hurting terribly and he was desperate for some help.

'Forgive me, Michael darling. I'd forgotten you were teething. Let's take you up to bed and give you your nice medicine, then maybe you'll be able to get to sleep.'

She carried him upstairs, laid him on the changing-table, to remove his nappy, which was soiled and soggy-wet. But he kept twisting over on to his side, spreading browny-yellow gunge all over both of them. Finally, she peeled it off and dropped it in the nappy-bin; wrinkling her nose at the smell, but at least glad Joyce used disposable. Now she had to clean him up – clean herself as well. Joyce had told her not to bother giving him a bath, just to top and tail him. It sounded very simple, but in his present fractious state, anything she tried to do would be met with fierce resistance. She also realized with dismay that she'd left the Wet-Wipes out of reach, and he'd wriggle off the table if she so much as turned her back. She was a total bloody idiot when it came to handling babies – she should have collected all she needed first, before taking off his nappy. She picked him up, praying that he wouldn't pee while she darted round the room, groping clumsily for clothes and towels, with him slung across her shoulder.

His piercing screams had reached a new and frightening pitch by the time she laid him down again and started dabbing at his bottom. She had trouble fastening his nappy, because the adhesive tabs kept sticking to his skin, instead of to each other. Putting on his clean white suit was still more difficult. His legs were threshing so violently, she couldn't seem to guide them into the openings, let alone do up the fiddly poppers. She laid him in his cot, half-dressed, while she went to fetch his medicine, though he fought her even harder when she tried to force some in. She was crying now herself, her tears making damp-stains on the sheets. This was her own child, rejecting her, repulsing her, treating her as someone feared and hated.

By the time she'd tucked the blankets round him, she felt thoroughly exhausted, as if she'd battled through a long campaign in some cruel and bloody war. He'd stopped his bellowing, at last, but it didn't feel like victory, only a temporary truce. She knew she ought to sit with him until he finally dropped off – read him a story or sing a nursery rhyme – but was too overwrought to try. He'd expressed no pleasure or relief in seeing her again, hadn't called her Mama, hadn't acknowledged her at all; simply shrieked for her to leave. Someone must have poisoned his mind, turned him totally against her.

She switched the light off, closed the door, hoping for five minutes' peace. Downstairs in the sitting-room, she eyed the glass decanters on the sideboard. Joyce had told her to help herself to anything she wanted, and though she'd actually been referring to the bread and cheese and pâté left out in the kitchen, surely a thimbleful of sherry wouldn't hurt? She hunted for a glass, silencing her conscience with Dr Edwards' own words. When she'd confessed to him that she'd killed her baby through boozing irresponsibly, he'd contradicted her, saying there was no proven link between alcohol and birth defects, and pointing out (after her frenetic vow never to touch a drop again) that the odd drink couldn't hurt, might even be relaxing. Well, she needed to relax after what she'd been through; needed calming medicine as much as baby Michael had. She poured herself an inch or two, drained it at one gulp, enjoying the warm glow as the liquor kissed her throat, then filled the glass up to the top. There was no sound from the nursery, so she could take a well-earned rest. She'd browse through Joyce's glossy magazines – pick out a new spring wardrobe, or make the big decision about whether to winter in Antigua or Mauritius.

She unlaced her boots and kicked them off, removed her jacket, shook her hair free from its restraining clips and slides, then settled in the rocking chair, close to the log fire. There were Christmas cards on every ledge and surface, but they were no longer any threat. All those loving messages had been addressed to her and Michael. She was Mrs Michael Edwards now – the 'perfect' cosseted wife, who had *Vogue* and *Harpers* delivered every month, and a house cram-full of chocolates and champagne – offerings from those grateful loathsome patients. She reached out for the king-size box of Milk Tray, open on the coffee table, and was about to help herself, but Mrs Edwards' pampered hand turned back to her own workaday one, as she realized that the box was hardly touched. There were just two empty spaces, both together on the right, so Joyce would probably notice if she found a few more gone. Maybe she'd even left the box out as a sort of test or trap, a way of checking on her new employee's scruples. Safer to stick to paper food – luscious colour pictures of Christmas-party treats: choux-pastry swans swimming on a glistening lake of caviar; quince and brandy sorbet served in melon-halves.

Fifteen minutes later, she tossed *Harpers* on the floor. She had more important things to do than compare crayfish tails with lobster claws, or decide which caterers to choose for her next glitzy charity ball. She went to fetch her bag, then crept upstairs, turned the handle of the Edwardses' bedroom door. She stood nervous on the threshold, sniffing Joyce's smells – nail-varnish remover and a sickly flowery perfume which drowned carnation with sweet pea. Joyce's things were everywhere, but there were no shirts or ties in evidence. Was Dr Edwards tidier than his wife, or did Joyce stifle him?

She marched over to the bed, lifted up the pillows to find a low-necked turquoise nightdress snuggled up to a pair of blue pyjamas. She wrested them from each other's arms, slung the nightie to the far end of the room, right beneath the window, so that it would lose its clammy heat. Next, she delved into her bag and removed the stiff brown envelope which she'd brought from home deliberately. She laid it on the bed, then took down the Edwardses' wedding photo from its pride of place on the chest of drawers. She released the tiny metal pins which secured the ornate frame, and inserted her own photograph behind the cardboard backing – one taken very recently with Frank's new Olympus Trip. The photo showed her smiling, smiling in quiet triumph. It would wait here in the bedroom, invisible but potent, until such time as she destroyed the one which hid it; claimed her rights as Dr Edwards' bride.

She looked in on baby Michael, who was now peacefully asleep, then tiptoed down the stairs again. Somehow she must find a way to replace that photo in the wallet, too, so that she'd be with her husband – inseparable – whenever he went out.

She refilled her empty sherry glass, drifted to the kitchen with it and started clearing up the mess. She was about to return the yogurt to the fridge, but stood lost in thought, the fridge door half-ajar, its cold breath raising gooseflesh on her legs. Dr Edwards had held that yogurt carton; also held the teaspoon she'd just lobbed into the sink. Why destroy his fingerprints, wash them off with Squezy? She retrieved the spoon, then sat down on his chair. That, too, bore his traces; the last remnants of his body-heat seeping into her skin. No – she wasn't sitting on a chair, but on Dr Edwards' lap; nestling close against his chest, one tiny hand stretched up to touch his cheek. And he was feeding her with yogurt – sweetened yogurt, creamy yogurt, melting on her tongue – as he praised her and encouraged her for every eager mouthful. And now he'd put the spoon down and was dipping his broad fingers right into the carton, holding them against her lips, so she could suck the yogurt off. His fingers tasted strange – of mango mixed with Brie – but they were strong and stiff and comforting, and he had moved his face so close to hers, she could see each pore and bristle, smell his ardent breath. No one else existed in the world – just Daddy and his little girl – and he had nothing else to do in life but wait on her, delight her.

He had picked up the banana now, and was inserting it between her lips, pushing very gently, so she'd open her mouth, let him ease it in. 'Chicky,' he was murmuring, 'Daddy's pet, Daddy's little darling'; adding secret love-words in a language all their own. The banana tasted ripe and sweet as it spurted down her throat; liquefying, overflowing, oozing from the corners of her mouth. He scooped the drips up, held his hand against her lips and let her lick it clean again, while he admired the soft pink lappings of her tongue.

She swallowed the last morsel, clutching at a strand of his hair and gripping it as tightly as she could. If she didn't keep him captive here, he'd rush back to his hospital in Newcastle, or desert her for those patients on his list. She must tell him she was hungry, demand those other pappy foods which Joyce had said were suitable for babies – *fromage frais*, soft cheeses, lightly scrambled eggs. She shut her eyes, could taste the eggs already. He was giving her her breakfast, tempting her with fingers of crustless buttered toast, and still there at lunch, at tea: her guardian, her protector, her devoted doting father – ignoring the bleep which summoned him to casualty; refusing to pick the phone up when his frantic patients rang.

Not only was he feeding her, he had cooked for her as well – tender free-range chicken in a jar with her own name on. She went to fetch it from the fridge, heard a yowl from Nellie, who'd just strutted into the kitchen; could smell her dinner and was demanding to be fed.

'*No!*' said Tessa. 'I'm the only child he's got. There was never any Nellie, or Lucy and Elizabeth. He spent all that time and trouble cooking it for me.'

The cat continued pleading, rubbing up and down against her legs, tail erect, ears twitching. Tessa turned a deaf ear to the cries as she clambered back on Daddy's lap, let him slip the spoon between her lips. The chicken wasn't fresh, tasted slightly tainted, as if it had hung around too long, but she tried to concentrate instead on the skills of his deft hands, the comfort of his arm across her back. The cat was jealous, mewing really plaintively, about to spring up on her knee and muscle in on the petting and the stroking, share the dazzling warmth of Daddy's body. Tessa pushed her off, but she refused to stop her pestering.

'All right, Nellie, you can have some milk instead – but only on condition you leave the two of us in peace.'

She poured some into a saucer, then stood stock-still, the bottle in her hand. *She* should have a bottle, and Daddy ought to give it to her. That would really bond them, make him almost her mother. Michael's bottle was lying on the table, where she'd left it. No, not Michael's – Tessa's – and prepared for her by Daddy. His arms were wrapped around her, holding her securely; her head in the crook of his elbow, her sparrow weight supported. She was no longer baby Michael's age and eating solid foods, but a new-born infant only capable of suckling. He slid the teat into her mouth, smiling at her, worshipping. She sucked, but nothing happened; tried again, but only got the merest meanest drop. She clamped her lips more firmly, using all the force she had, but it was still no more than a droplet, a grudging trickle of unsweetened tepid milk. It was Joyce's fault that there wasn't any sugar in it – she was rationing and depriving her, as she rationed baby Michael. She understood his anger now, the wildness of his screams. You could suck and suck, and still be ravenous. She yelled with indignation as she tried to grab the bottle. Someone else was feeding her – not her skilful father, but some clueless bungling stand-in, who must have blocked the teat, and was reducing her to tears of helpless rage.

Or was it Michael crying? She could hear louder and more frenzied screams, confused with hers, but resounding from the nursery. She stumbled up the stairs, found him desolate, like her – starved of food, affection. She carried him into the sitting-room, sat down in the rocking chair, trying to turn its steady rhythm into the rocking of a mother's arms, which would soothe her and console her, lull Michael back to sleep. But he was demanding food, not sleep; his gaping mouth howling out its emptiness – an emptiness she shared; a wild voracious hunger which seemed to stretch back nineteen years.

Angrily, abruptly, she seized a chocolate from the box, bit off half and gulped it down, holding out the other half to Michael. Instantly his yelling stopped as he transferred it to his mouth; at first wary of the taste, then chewing with a passion when he realized it was good. Despite the enthusiasm he brought to it, the chewing was hard work. He didn't use his teeth, but chomped fiercely with his gums, pushing his ecstatic tongue up against the roof of his mouth, then licking chocolate off his lips; pink tongue-tip darting in and out.

'That was vanilla fudge, Michael. Delicious, wasn't it? How about another – caramello, this time?'

She found two caramellos, watched the baby copy her as she popped one in her mouth; his whole face alive with interest and excitement, his total concentration on the workings of his mouth. They were cruel, the Edwardses, prohibiting all sweet things, when he was obviously so fond of them. She could see them at their party, pigging themselves while they deprived their famished child; piling their plates with mince pies and meringues, then droning on about the unhealthiness of sugar.

Michael's mouth was bulging; chocolate slobber seeping out, which he pushed back with his hands, or daubed across his face, his neck, and the cushions on the chair. His white suit and her frilly blouse were also smirched with brown, but she no longer even cared. Why shouldn't they be messy, permitted to indulge themselves, and kick aside the rules for once? 'Bed at seven,' Joyce had said, and it was getting on for nine. Perhaps she'd keep him up all night, make the most of him; pay the Edwardses out for keeping him away from her, telling him gross lies.

He released his breath in a sigh of sheer contentment, as he sucked his coated fingers; his dark eyes fixed on hers, all but speaking to her as she rooted through the box again, checking the list of centres. She must be very careful not to give him any nutty ones, which might choke him or be difficult to swallow. *She* would eat the nougat, the brazil nut, almond cluster, and leave him the soft creams. She picked out a strawberry whirl, smiling as he snatched it from her hand. He could hardly wait to try it, his mouth still drooling caramel as he squidged it in his fingers, then lapped up the pink filling. She could see his father in him – sensuous Michael senior, with his virtuoso mouth.

'I'm glad you like it, Michael. It was your father's favourite, too. He ordered strawberries for our breakfast the very first day we met.'

'Mama,' he replied.

She kissed his mouth, his nose, his eyes, squeezed him even closer, laughing with relief. At last he had forgiven her, acknowledged her as mother: the one who fed and cherished him, gave him what he needed.

He could wolf every chocolate in the box if he'd keep on saying 'Mama'. She was already ransacking the second layer, hunting for a special treat – something to reward him.

'This is Turkish delight, Michael. It's pink inside, like jelly – though I don't suppose you've ever tasted jelly. They're full of sugar, so Joyce would only make them for herself.'

The baby's face was solemn as he savoured the new taste; the palms of both his sticky hands pressed right against his face, to prevent any scrap escaping. He had been waiting for this moment the whole nine months of his life, and his pleasure was her own. She replaced her nougat and brazil nut in the box; no longer needed to eat. It was enough for her to feed her child – feed Michael Edwards' son. She offered him her favourite – a coffee hazel cream. The hazelnuts were chopped up very finely, so they shouldn't be a problem, yet he seemed a little hesitant, ate it with less gusto than the rest, smearing half the filling down his suit. Perhaps he didn't like the coffee flavour, which might be slightly bitter, more suited to an adult palate. She scrabbled in the box to find something sweet and bland, but he wouldn't so much as look at it, turned his head away, even pushed her hand off.

'Okay, we'll have a rest, Michael. There isn't any rush. I'm not feeling all that good myself. We've both been through a lot. Let's lie down on the rug and just relax.'

She struggled from the chair, and sank down on one knee, laying Michael carefully on the fluffy sheepskin rug. She stretched out close beside him, luxuriating in the caress of its soft fleece, in the warm glow of the fire, the flicker of the flames against her face. Michael's father kept returning – in the strawberries, the licked fingers, and now his sheepskin coat; in the tangled mix of memories surging through her head.

'You've got to meet your father, Michael, but I don't know how we'll manage it.'

The baby whimpered for reply.

'I'm sorry, Mishka, but it wasn't up to me. If I'd had any say in it, we'd be living together – the three of us.'

He was squirming on the rug, pulling up his knees, as if in pain, making little moaning noises; fists tight-clenched and thrashing at the empty air. Perhaps he wasn't comfortable lying on the floor, felt insecure, abandoned. She scrambled to her knees, about to move him to the sofa, when a gush of chocolate-vomit suddenly spewed out of his mouth and cascaded over the rug. She stared in disbelief. How could one small baby sick up such a flood? The rug was ruined, covered with a slimy curdled mess, some of which had dribbled on to the carpet – an expensive Wilton, naturally. She tried to scoop the puke up, averting her eyes from the undigested gobbets of congealing pinkish scum which clogged the murky brown. She would never get the rug clean; never get rid of the smell. And Michael hadn't finished yet – a second horrifying spurt eructing unexpectedly right across her hands.

She was retching now herself, could feel her stomach lurching to her throat. She dashed out to the kitchen, praying she would make it to the sink. Halfway there, she doubled back – couldn't leave the baby on his own. But in saving him from danger, she'd held on just too long; clapped her hand across her mouth – too late. She was already throwing up – yes, right there in the hallway, with Michael in her arms.

She slumped against the coat-stand, hardly daring to look up. The stylish blue-striped wallpaper was spattered; puke dripping slowly down it to the Persian rug below. Not even the coats had escaped – Joyce's pricey skiing jacket, Dr Edwards' Burberry, both flecked with glutinous grey.

She laid Michael on the parquet, subsided on the floor herself, like a beaten dog surrendering. The Edwardses would forbid her to set foot in their house again – and could she really blame them when she'd made such a shameful mess in it, made the baby ill? He was screaming in near-panic, spreadeagled on the wood. She too began to cry; listened to their mingled sobs, echoing through the hall. She knew she ought to clean him up, change his stinking clothes, then scour the place with soap and mop, but she felt too small and puny. Shouldn't someone else appear – someone stronger, older, who'd come running at their first faint cry for help? Why was there no footstep on the stairs, no reassuring bottle in her mouth? Mummy was out working, but Daddy must be somewhere in the house, sorting through his papers, or busy at his desk. She tried to make him hear, redoubling her wild screams, imploring him to stop his work, remember she existed. Her neck was hurting from the strain of trying to lift her head – a lumpish head which seemed too heavy for her body. And she couldn't get a grip on the shiny wooden floor, kept collapsing back as her small hands slid away from her. Her throat was hoarse, her nappy soiled, her whole body wet and cramped, but it was impossible to move until her father picked her up.

'Please come,' she begged. 'Please help.'

But he didn't answer, didn't come, and she only made her throat worse; her face now red and swollen; her nose so blocked it was difficult to breathe. Best to lie in silence, close her eyes, give up. She could scream all day, all dangerous night, but still he wouldn't hear.

Daddy wasn't there.

21

'PASS THE CRANBERRY sauce, Michael. Thank you, darling. The turkey's good, isn't it – moist for such a big one.'

Michael put his fork down, to caress his wife's bare arm. She had dressed for Christmas dinner in an Yves St Laurent skirt and cap-sleeved real silk blouse; emeralds round her wrists and throat, a gold ring on her finger. 'More sprouts?' she asked, offering him the Wedgwood dish.

Michael took a spoonful, and another roast potato. He was wearing a new suit in an elegant blue-grey, and a tie she'd chosen herself. They had opened their presents that morning, sitting by the tree, with the baby crowing on her lap, drinking in the atmosphere, the excitement of the day, the heady smells of mulled punch and mince pies. It was already nearly three. They'd not got up till late, enjoyed a blissful Christmas lie-in, after an electrifying night together. Every time she thought back to their lovemaking – its exquisite combination of tenderness and passion – she felt a thrill of triumph, almost disbelief.

She sat gazing at her husband, who had changed since she'd moved in with him. He no longer wore his glasses, so his eyes blazed naked-blue, and he had grown his hair, to please her. His hand was fondling hers on the festive Christmas table; a table she had laid herself with a white lace cloth, a frieze of scarlet crackers, and a vase of gold chrysanthemums. It was the best Christmas of her life, so far, and she had hours more to enjoy – hours of luxurious happiness. Nothing had been stinted, not food nor wine nor love, and the most precious of her Christmas presents was the gift of Michael himself. She had learned new skills, to surprise him – spent ages last week fiddling around in the kitchen, trying to get the hang of home-made

239

petits fours, and had mixed a Christmas pudding so full of rum and brandy it was reeling in its pan. She could hear it bubbling on the hob with an exhilarated sputtering noise which matched her own elation. She ought to go and turn it down, didn't want it boiling dry or burning.

She jumped up from her chair, wheeling back to Michael before she'd even reached the door. She just had to stroke his neck again, feel the silky texture of his hair. It was impossible to concentrate on cooking when she was so utterly absorbed in him, so distracted by the tiniest of details – the fact that one neat eyebrow was a fraction thicker than the other; the reddened criss-cross pattern of the small scar on his thumb. Last night, he'd chafed that thumb against her breasts, then lapped them with his tongue, and this morning he had . . .

The phone shrilled through the images, capsizing them abruptly. She darted over to answer it, rehearsing her hello. It might be one of Michael's colleagues inviting them for drinks, so she must sound gracious – the perfect doctor's wife.

'Is Lucy there?' a girl's voice asked – drawly and offhand.

'Er . . . no,' she said. 'She's not.'

'Is that Elizabeth?'

'No,' repeated Tessa, with a hint of irritation. Her turkey would be getting cold, and it was draughty in the hall.

'And it's not Antonia.'

She wasn't sure if that was a statement or a question, but she answered no, in any case.

'Who is it, then? Sorry – that sounds rude – but I don't know who I'm talking to.'

Tessa tightened her grip on the receiver, hoping its solidity would somehow be transmitted to her, stop her falling apart. People shouldn't ask her who she was. 'This is Mrs Michael Edwards,' she kept repeating to herself, but the name no longer sounded quite convincing. The girl at the other end was becoming confused and then exasperated, and finally rang off. Tessa stood listening to the accusing vacant whine, then replaced the receiver, glancing at her hand – no gold ring on her wedding finger, no emeralds round her wrist; only a grubby tracksuit sleeve, with a sweatshirt underneath.

She slunk back to the dining-room – nothing on the table now but a bag of crisps, uneaten, and a glass of diet Coke. She drained the Coke in one violent choking gulp. She was still his wife, still Mrs Michael Edwards – even if she didn't possess a Wedgwood dinner service, or shop at Yves St Laurent – and she would still spend Christmas with him, or part of it, at least. It was just a matter of waiting, and she was bloody good at that. She had waited up all night, passed the barren morning counting minutes, mooching round the cold and empty house.

The phone had started up again, but she let it ring this time; its relentless high-pitched warble jangling through her head. She prowled to and fro until it stopped, then snatched up the receiver – had to phone the surgery once more. She'd rung sixteen times already, starting at sick dawn, when it was still blurry grey outside, and the other houses in the street were swathed in sleep; their windows blind, their bulky hedges insubstantial shadows. Sixteen times she'd listened to those reassuring words; let her body soak them up, like brandy. 'This is a recorded message. The surgery is closed, but in case of emergency, please phone Dr Edwards, on . . .'

There were six GPs in the practice, but it was Dr Michael Edwards who'd been chosen as the duty-doctor for Christmas Day of all days. She'd found out only this week, but had realized instantly that it was a gift to her, a stroke of luck, and she had to change her plans, rearrange her own Christmas. It had proved extremely difficult, entailed lying and invention – the creation of a new and serious boyfriend who had invited her to stay.

'But can't you bring him *here*, Toots?' her mother had complained, after an initial spate of questions about who he was, what he did, and why in heaven's name she'd never said a single word about him until 8.00 PM on 22 December, especially if he meant so much? 'It won't be Christmas without you,' April had concluded, her voice harsh with disappointment.

She had explained her boyfriend's circumstances – the fact that he'd promised faithfully to spend Christmas with his own mother, who'd been widowed just three months ago. The lies about the husband's death had been the easiest of all. She could feel the rawness of the wound, the sense of loss and void. Nor had there been any difficulty in supplying the boy's name. It could only be one name – though her mother was upset by it.

'*Another* Michael? That's cruel, my pet.'

It seemed equally cruel to scupper April's Christmas, leave her with two lodgers who had nowhere else to go, a pair of maiden aunts, and a female friend bruised by a recent divorce. But she didn't have a choice – had to take her only chance of seeing Dr Edwards. If she was ill on Christmas Day, he would visit her, acknowledge her, spend time with her, alone.

'Alone' had been another problem. It would be horribly embarrassing for him to call with April there. Her mother would spoil everything, fussing round with cups of tea and her *Reader's Digest* medical lore, or – even worse – the lodgers might appear. She could just imagine Eric asking his advice about why he couldn't eat dried fruit without getting flatulence, or a well-oiled Frank clapping him on the back with a kipper-scented hand, and bombarding him with nudge-nudge wink-wink jokes. Yet she could hardly turf them out, along with two rheumaticky aunts, who'd only panic anyway if she was ill enough to be summoning a doctor. In the end, she had phoned her father, Dave, told him in the strictest confidence that she and her new boyfriend were itching to spend Christmas on their own, and since she'd heard from April that Dave and family would be in Bristol with the in-laws, she wondered if she could possibly borrow his house?

The 'yes' had been reluctant and a very long time coming. He'd probably only agreed in the end because he found he got a certain kick out of ganging up with his daughter against his former not-quite-wife.

'Mum thinks I'll be in Essex, you see, with Michael's widowed mother, and I'd prefer it if you didn't tell her otherwise.'

'Okay, Tess, you can rely on me.' Dave had given a conspiratorial laugh, which she'd forced herself to echo. It upset her, actually, to realize that her parents were still antagonistic to each other, despite the fact that they lived their separate lives. April had always done her best to rose-tint the relationship, present it as quite painless, but Dave's remarks had hinted at the petty animosities, the grudges and resentments, which must have festered beneath the surface for close on twenty years.

But at least she had got the house – an elegant attractive house she needn't be ashamed of when Dr Edwards called. He'd feel very much at home as he stepped into the hall, with its thick-pile carpets and gold-framed prints of Surrey; sauntered down the passage to the fitted modern kitchen – in fact, more at home than *she* was. Although her father lived relatively close, she very rarely visited, felt a virtual stranger sitting in his dining-room, and had never really mastered the lay-out of the house. She had trouble remembering where everything was kept – especially in the kitchen, where an array of identical cupboard-fronts concealed waste-bin, fridge and dish-washer, and even tracking down a teaspoon was a major undertaking. Dave's present wife and family were the legal and official one, so she and April must be something of an embarrassment, perhaps regarded as a brief impulsive youthful fling, which could now be filed away as 'Finished business'.

She had wandered round his territory, this morning and last night, trying to piece his life together from the welter of painful clues; Lucy and Elizabeth continually confronting her in their toys, their clothes, their photographs, their drawings proudly pinned up on the wall. His wife was also everywhere, outclassing April in her furnishings and taste – the latest Ian McEwan on her Victorian bedside table; a pile of concert programmes in what Dave called her den. Even her name – Antonia – had a certain quiet distinction, a gulf away from corny names like April. Three females in her father's house, all with classy names, but no trace of *her* – the eldest child – no sign she even existed. It also struck her as ironical that the longest stretch of time she'd ever spent there in her life should be when Dave was absent, a hundred miles away.

In the end, she'd turned it into Dr Edwards' house – no woman there but her; no child save baby Michael. It hurt too much to imagine him in his own house, so she'd been making (largely futile) efforts to wrest her mind from Tregunter Road; from him and Joyce in bed, exchanging gifts and bodies; him and Joyce sharing Christmas breakfast in their dressing-gowns. Those dressing-gowns kept gaping open, revealing Dr Edwards bare-torsoed, tanned, well-built; Joyce half-naked in an alluring skimpy nightdress; her skin still flushed from lovemaking. When he came to visit, she, too, would wear a nightdress; arrange herself in bed with her breasts spilling from the low-cut top; the erect excited nipples pushing through the lace. She had found the perfect rig-out in Antonia's chest of drawers – a creation in white satin, with a near-transparent top and the skirt slit to the thigh.

She checked her watch: only two minutes past three. She must wait till it was dark – no, wait until late evening – postpone the visit as long as possible, so that her day had point and purpose, and she had something to look forward to: a burst of hope at nightfall, to redeem the lonely pacing hours. Yet it was proving hard to settle; to stop wishing she were somewhere else – in Tregunter Road, or Newcastle, or even back at home. Her mother would be tuned in to the Queen; Frank making cracks about Royal Highnesses and corgis. She was seized by a sudden longing to be eating April's Christmas cake, instead of Smith's potato crisps; to be surrounded by familiar possessions, not intimidated by dark expensive furniture, outstared by hostile clocks.

She switched on the television, the strains of the national anthem just fading into nothing. A circus came on next – a troupe of Spanish trapeze artists in spangles and fake smiles, cavorting on the high wire. She could hardly bear to watch. Her own life was too dangerous – no strong man to support her, no safety-net below. But if she had stayed at home with April, she'd be just a performing animal – a poodle in a frilly skirt, walking on her hind legs or jumping through a hoop, in order to reassure her mother that she was as happy as those pictures in the current *TV Times*. They seemed an alien race, those beaming paper families who smiled their way through Christmas week, raised their glasses in non-stop bumper toasts, rollicked by the Christmas tree with their entrancing kids, cute pets. Her own friends were very much the same – or ex-friends, she should say. Vicky, Liz and Alex had lost their third dimension, become as flat and bogus as the phoney cards they'd sent. Debbie, too, had written, to say she was expecting her second baby, and had moved to a new bungalow with picture-windows and a pear-tree in the garden. Could she and Deb have actually been so close, spent so many evenings together, discussing witless subjects like boyfriends, pop groups, wonder cures for spots? Now they lived in different universes, spoke different languages.

She drifted to the window, peered out at the street. All the other houses had exploded into life; plum pudding in their stomachs, tinsel in their hair; their waste-bins overflowing with turkey bones and gift-wrap. Yet they seemed no more real than the pictures in the magazines; cut off from her not only by their hedges, but by the fact that she didn't belong; didn't know the neighbours' names or histories; couldn't call 'hello' when a car drew up, or face appeared. She had watched a boisterous family group pile out of a Ford Capri and knock at the house opposite; the door flung open to a hail of hugs and greetings – she alone excluded.

She looped the curtain back, so that she could see the scrum of little boys playing on their bikes further down the street. They too were yelping with laughter, and the sound jolted and alarmed her, like the clapping on the television. No one should be laughing or applauding – not yet, not till he came.

She trailed back to the phone, dialled the surgery once more. He might have had an accident, or have been taken ill himself, so that they'd had to change the message on the tape. No – still the same, still faithful Dr Edwards, which made everything worthwhile – the sleepless night in the coldly sterile spare room; the silent limping morning, with only a slice of staling bread for breakfast. Dave had offered to leave her food, stock the fridge and larder, but she'd told him not to bother, said she and 'Michael' were actually relieved to be spared all the palaver of Christmas dinner, and would simply buy in a few pizzas and a twelve-pack.

She switched off the television, went to fetch her books and files, which she'd brought with her in a plastic bag, in place of beer and pizzas. If she settled down to do some work, it would make the time pass quicker, distract her more effectively than elephants and clowns. She had written up her biography of Dr Michael Edwards, as far as she was able, though it was nowhere near complete. She had netted quite a shoal of facts about his present life and work, but had fished up very little about the years he'd spent in Leicester. She'd found no one there who'd worked with him – or no one who would talk to her – and she'd been met with cool suspicion when she'd rung the Leicester surgery. It had proved so baffling and frustrating she'd put the thing aside; embarked instead on a series of long letters – elaborate, formal letters, modelled on those of Heloïse.

She was more aware than ever of the parallels between them. Like Heloïse, she'd been driven from her house and home on account of one cruel man, and was living like a nun, shut away from the outside world and all its former pleasures; renouncing sex completely, and no longer bothering overmuch with clothes or food or sleep. Yet today she had the feeling that Heloïse had withdrawn from her – refused to come to Dave's place – perhaps wary of its atmosphere, or opposed to the deception. She missed their usual contact, the sense of someone listening, but if she plugged away at her letter-writing project, her soul-mate's living presence might well come stealing back.

She picked up her copy of the *Letters*, which was breaking apart at the spine from over-use – countless phrases marked and underlined.

'*My heart was not in me, but with you*,' Heloïse had written in her first letter to Abelard (and she herself had paraphrased, to Michael). '*And if it is not with you, it is nowhere. I implore you to make sure it is with you – as indeed it will be if only you treat it kindly, offering it love in return for love, crumbs in return for a banquet . . .*'

She rechecked her own version, trying to improve it; wondering if she would ever capture the frantic mix of reproach and passion,

245

bitterness and ardour, which Heloïse had poured out from the cloister, and which came over still more powerfully in her famous second letter. '*If I lose you,*' Heloïse had cried, '*what is left for me to hope for? What reason for continuing on life's pilgrimage, for which I have no support but you, and none from you save the knowledge that you are alive? For I am forbidden all other pleasures in you, and denied even the joy of your presence . . .*'

Tessa closed the book. She wouldn't copy that, wouldn't even think it. She might be banned from Dr Edwards' home, shooed out of the Health Centre every time she hung around hoping for a glimpse of him, but that didn't mean she'd be denied the joy of his presence. He was visiting tonight – Christmas night – and once they were on their own, removed from Joyce's clutches, and the whole restraining influence of his surgery or his house, they would be able to communicate, establish a true closeness. In fact, she ought to phone him now – not wait, as she had planned, and then discover to her horror that his spell of Christmas duty had ended in the early afternoon. It would be terrible to miss him, face a long dark evening all alone. The light was already failing, swallowing up the houses in the street, returning them to the ghostly gloom which had shrouded them at dawn. The sun had failed to show itself all day; seemed like Michael up in Newcastle – keeping its distance deliberately, refusing to brighten up her Christmas, or disperse the threatening shadows.

She wiped her clammy hands before picking up the receiver; braced herself against the wall, trying to summon the courage to dial Dr Edwards' home. Easy to ring the surgery, listen to a recorded message, but any second now she would hear his actual voice, have to answer when he said hello.

'Hello?' He'd said it twice, repeated both his number and his name. She couldn't stand there any longer in tense and trembling silence, or he'd simply put the phone down.

'It's . . . er . . . Tessa Reeves,' she faltered.

He made no response at all. She might as well have given strangers' names – Pat Hughes or Debbie Bailey. Did her own name mean nothing to him, or was he still enraged about the débâcle of the babysitting? She must somehow rouse his sympathy, concern.

'I've had a haemorrhage,' she blurted out. At least she knew the symptoms, could make it sound convincing. All she had to do was fill in the grim details from the emergency twelve weeks ago, when she'd collapsed bleeding on the stairs. She continued for a minute or two, then broke off to let him speak – expecting to be told that he'd be on his way immediately, once he'd grabbed his coat and car-keys.

'No!' she almost shouted, when she heard different words entirely – he would phone through for an ambulance and she must rest in bed until it came. She began to backtrack swiftly, appalled at the thought of landing up in hospital with wrecks or crocks all round her. 'The bleeding's stopped,' she insisted. 'And it wasn't all that heavy in the first place.'

'Do you think you could be pregnant again?' His tone was cool, dispassionate.

Her second 'No!' was even more emphatic. How could he imagine she was sleeping with just anyone, when her whole heart and mind and body embraced him, and him alone?

'Is there any pain?' he asked.

'No,' she said, third time. It was essential that she removed his mind from hospitals; made him see it was him she needed, not some faceless foreign doctor in a casualty department. 'It was more the shock, I think. It frightened me, you see, and I'm still feeling a bit jittery.'

Now she'd gone too far the other way. His voice was almost casual as he advised her to go to bed and rest, and to ask her mother to ring him, if there were any further problems.

'She isn't here. I'm all alone in an empty house in Croydon.' Another stupid move. She had hoped that he'd feel pity, even horror, to hear she was shut up on her own on Christmas Day, but once she had revealed she was in Croydon, a good ten miles from home, he said it was out of the question for him to drive that distance, and she must phone a local doctor.

They went back and forth, back and forth – he suggesting yellow pages and her father's friends and neighbours; she insisting she knew no one in the area, possessed no local directories, and was too weak to leave the house. Soon she was in tears; had never envisaged such a battle to persuade him to come out. She no longer needed to invent – she was genuinely ill now – ill with deprivation, the dark stirrings of despair. She remembered Heloïse's words: *'What is left for me to hope for, what reason for continuing life?'* – began to echo them again, not on paper this time, but weeping down the phone.

As she paused for breath, she realized he was wavering – his voice becoming softer, more compassionate; the way it had been when she'd seen him in his surgery. Her own voice was incoherent still, but she continued trying to speak, doggedly repeating Heloïse's reproaches.

Suddenly, abruptly, he cut through her tirade. 'All right,' he said. 'I'll come. Give me the address.'

She was so overwhelmed with gratitude, so astounded, so relieved, she could barely spell out the street-name; begged him to repeat it to make sure he'd got it right.

'Yes, that's it,' she exulted, laughing now as well as crying – the two mixed up together: her body soaring with relief, while tears streamed down her face. She started flooding him with directions – which junction to take when he came off the main road; how he should look out for the Mason's Arms, so he wouldn't miss the . . .

'I know Croydon pretty well,' he interrupted, his tone tetchy, almost rude. 'And I've got to get a move on. I was just on my way out to see another patient. I'll call round after that – okay?'

She was about to speak, stammer out her thanks, when she heard his curt 'Goodbye' and then the click of the receiver. It didn't matter. She, too, must get a move on; had to prepare herself, transform herself; do her hair and face in exactly the same way as when she had seen him in the surgery. He'd held her hand on that occasion, leaned close and spoken lovingly, whereas every time she'd seen him since, he had been much more inhibited. The only problem was, her hair and face had changed; complexion dingy-pale; hair thinner and more lank. But she had brought her make-up with her, her curling tongs and volume-spray, and would probably have the best part of an hour by the time he'd seen his other patient. She was glad she hadn't eaten; didn't want her belly full of half-digested stodge, when he ran his hands across it; had no need for food at all, now that he was coming. The whole nation would be stuffing – gorging Christmas cake and trifle, turkey and mince pies – but the more empty she remained herself, the more Michael Edwards could fill her.

She ran upstairs to Dave and Antonia's bedroom – the only one which contained a double bed – checked the whole room quickly, to make sure that it looked welcoming. It was elegant but chilly, since she hadn't turned the central heating on. It was almost second nature for her to economize on heating, but she'd been especially careful not to take advantage of her father. The house was gift enough, without wasting his electricity. But she could probably find a fan-heater, to keep Dr Edwards comfortable; thaw her own numb body, so that he wouldn't flinch away from her.

248

Fifty minutes later, she was glowing – blood pounding round her veins from sheer elation; her face enhanced with highlighter and blusher. He would expect her to look ill, of course, but she had opted for a fever, not a pale and shivery illness; wanted everything high octane and high colour. She had even lit the fire downstairs – Dr Edwards was used to a log fire – and they might relax there for a while before retiring to the bedroom. She was sitting right in front of it, to retain her warmth and flush; clad only in the nightie – bridal-white and slit from thigh to ankle. She had taken off her watch, but the clock on the mantelpiece was ticking ponderously: a nerve-wracking reminder that he'd be arriving any second; his Citroën sweeping up to the house, his footsteps on the path. She had already heard two cars, but neither had been his. She scanned the shadowy street once more, beginning to hate the patient who was taking up his time. It was probably Alicia de Courcy, or some other bitchy type, who was deliberately delaying him, using all her wiles. She stalked back to the mantelpiece, turned the clock's face to the wall. Pointless to count seconds, or curse a dawdling minute-hand. After all, it was quite a trek to Croydon, and he might have missed the junction – that tricky one she'd been trying to explain.

She stared into the fire, but she could still see other patients – all female and all naked. He must have examined countless women in his time – his skilful fingers parting moist pink labia, or plunged deep into cunts. She watched them stripping off for him, opening mouths and legs for him, flaunting perfect breasts. That was the price you paid for loving a doctor – you were forced to share him with droves of unknown women, whose wombs and tongues and nipples he had savoured. She lay back, pushed her nightie up, tried to turn her own hand into his, astonished by its fierceness. Where had these voracious feelings come from? – wild images of Michael gushing out from some invisible projector, in Technicolor and Sensurround: Michael at the picnic, or naked in his flat, thrusting on his hands and knees, or pressed against her body, mouth to cunt.

She scrambled to her feet again, slapped her feverish hand. She must wait until he came; didn't want to greet him dishevelled, out of breath. She started pacing round the room instead, pouncing on the Christmas cards which crowded every surface. So many fervent messages from so many avid females: Samanthas and Alicias, Cecilys and Sukies. She knew damn well where Michael was – not ministering to a patient, but to all these fancy creatures who'd sent him love and kisses; insinuated their way into his life. She hadn't had a card from him – had nothing from him, nothing – not even a prescription. A prescription was a sort of letter, scribbled in his handwriting and personal to her; something she could keep for ever, refuse to surrender to the chemist. She'd suffer almost any illness, just to have him write one; would risk paralysis or breakdown to receive a proper letter. She thought back to her project – the letter she'd been working on an hour or so ago, based on Heloïse's. If she hurried, she could finish it, and he could read it when he came. It shouldn't take her long – only lacked two sentences, and a brief word of introduction – and the task would help to calm her down, keep her mind on painless things like adjectives and verbs.

She returned to the cold dining-room, sat down at the table where she had left her work spread out (first removing the crisps and Coke can, to make it more a desk). She opened the *Letters* at random – always needed it beside her as a guide and inspiration – began reading the short passage she'd highlighted in red:

'The lovers' delights which you and I enjoyed together are so sweet to me that I am totally unable to erase them from my thoughts. Wherever I turn, they thrust themselves before my eyes, kindling new desires and lusts, which obsess me even in my dreams.'

Her hands were shaking so violently she could hardly hold the book. Heloïse had returned! Her voice was ringing through the room – not the usual quiet confiding tone of their sisterly discussions, but an impassioned flood of words: erotic and uncensored words, all the more extraordinary on the lips of a chaste abbess shut up in her cloister with a bodyguard of virgins – a frustrated tortured nun who was actually admitting that even during Mass, she was so preoccupied with what she called 'lewd visions', she couldn't put her mind on prayer at all.

'I should be groaning over the sins I have committed, but I can only sigh for those I have lost. Everything we did, together with the times and places where we did it, are engraved so vividly on my mind that I am continually reliving it, when awake or in my sleep.'

She no longer needed to read the lines – Heloïse was still crying them aloud – sobbing out to Abelard the very words she'd written to him all those centuries back, but now including Michael in her onslaught. A week ago, she herself had copied that same text, meticulously transferring it to her own stiff-backed college notebook, but not until this moment had she experienced its power and pain with such unbearable intensity. Yet Abelard had dismissed that pain in his sanctimonious reply, which had been not so much a letter as a sermon. He'd preachified at length about the sufferings of Christ, and urged his former mistress to devote herself to God, rather than to him, since he'd been motivated in their affair by lust and lust alone. *'I took my fill of my wretched pleasures in you, and that was the sum total of my love.'* He had already trashed those pleasures in his letter, denouncing them as 'pollution and contagion', 'filthy and obscene', and had described himself and Heloïse as 'wallowing in the mire'. He'd even said he welcomed his castration, since it had rid him of his 'vile and shameful parts', and she too must thank the Lord for it – for saving them from any risk of further 'contamination'.

Tessa jerked up from her chair, shivering with cold and fury mixed. Men always looked at everything in their own self-justifying terms; couldn't grasp the concept of all-consuming love – the sort of agonizing love which would go through fire for one soft word, and was a million miles from lust. Neither she nor Heloïse would ever dream of denigrating what once had been the high point of their lives, nor turn their torrent of desire into a cesspit and a sewer.

Dr Edwards was every bit as pitiless, equally rejecting and cold-hearted. It was already nearly six, yet he still hadn't showed his face; was probably sitting snug at home, shrugging off her own love as 'wretched' in some other sense – threatening, inconvenient. Or maybe he was dead. Christmas was a dangerous time to venture out at all – idiot drunken drivers weaving all over the road, overtaking recklessly, speeding through red lights.

She strode into the sitting-room, the *Letters* in her hand still, though she couldn't bear to read them any more. Better to watch some fatuous soap on television, to take her mind off pile-ups on the bypass. Like Heloïse before her, she would rather die herself than have to face her lover's death, since the only reason for living was that he shared existence with her. She remembered the story in the *Chronicle of Tours* of how Abelard's cold corpse had stretched out loving arms to embrace his wife's dead body when she was laid in the same tomb. But she wasn't Michael's wife. If he reached out arms to anyone, it would be to tepid Joyce, or to that loathsome girl in Newcastle.

She turned up the sound on the television, trying to blast away her thoughts – the fact that she'd had no letter postmarked Newcastle for twelve demeaning weeks. But who was she to complain? Heloïse had heard nothing for nearly fifteen years; imprisoned in her convent without a word of comfort from her lover and still-husband, not a single passing reference to their love, their plight, their child. And even when he did write, in response to her own outburst, he'd not only deeply wounded her by debasing their great love, but also insisted that she put away her bitterness, since it endangered her immortal soul, and upset his peace of mind.

His peace of mind, for God's sake! And what about Heloïse's peace? She'd been living in inner torment since he'd packed her off to the nunnery, and when at last she'd bared her soul, he'd drafted her a homily about the efficacy of prayer. No wonder her poor sister was beside herself with misery; her soft voice choked, distraught.

'*Of all wretched women, I am the most wretched, and amongst the unhappy I am the unhappiest. The higher I was exalted when you preferred me to all other women, the greater my suffering over my fall . . .*'

'Save your breath, Heloïse!' she shouted. 'He doesn't give a damn. Oh, I know he said he'd come, but he was lying, wasn't he? He deceived you from the start, when he kept telling you he loved you. It wasn't love at all. But don't you dare complain! You're not allowed to bitch at him, or even show your feelings. It upsets his precious peace of mind, puts him off his work.'

She slammed the book shut, hurled it on the fire. It smouldered for a moment, then kindled into flame; the fragile pages curling in the blaze – her words and Heloïse's totally wiped out. No point writing letters or sobbing down the phone – Abelard and Michael were deaf to all entreaties. Heloïse had used every skill she had to pour her passion on the page, yet what had been the use? She had never felt her lover's skilful hands again, stroking down her body from throat to breast to thigh, or his wild mouth fused with hers; had never seen her child again – her son and his a stranger.

She edged closer to the fire, crouching down in front of it, to watch the remnant of her love charring into brittle flakes of black. So be it. Even Heloïse had been forced to don a muzzle, and after Abelard's two sermonizing letters, had never alluded to her pain and grief again. She must do the same, seal her mouth, swallow her despair.

The stairs seemed longer, steeper, as she toiled up to the spare room. She removed the stupid nightie, scrubbed off all her make-up, tore a brush through her sticky lacquered hair. She looked hideous now, back in her old tracksuit, with dark rings beneath her eyes and her pale face undisguised. Could she really blame Dr Edwards for deciding not to come, or feel bitter towards

Dave because he didn't want her either, favoured his two pretty girls?

She crept to the window, peered out through the glass. The shadowy back garden seemed menacing, forlorn: clumps of swarthy shrubs lurking like intruders; the sky still overcast, moon and stars engulfed. It was barely ten past six, though it felt more like the early hours – nothing-time, nightmare-time – no noise except a faint and eerie rustling, where the tendrils of a creeper were nudging against the pane. She turned away, limped towards the bed. Nothing left to do now but burrow beneath the blankets and try to sleep till Christmas Day was over, itself a blackened remnant, crumbling into ash. She was about to yank the covers back when she tensed in sudden shock: the rustling sound outside was submerged in an imperious bray – the pealing of the doorbell.

'*No*,' she whispered, horrified. 'Not now! You can't come now.' She dived over to the mirror, began pinning up her hair; couldn't let him see her in this repulsive frowzy state, or watch his physical recoil – his first eager steps reversing, like a movie running backwards, as he retreated down the hall. Yet equally impossible to leave him standing on the doorstep when he'd come at last, kept his solemn word. She stripped off the grubby tracksuit, undressing at such fever-heat that she clawed a hole in her tights. She pulled the nightie over her head, grimacing at the reflection of her washed-out naked face. But perhaps it didn't matter what she looked like. Any second now they would be alone for the first time, without the interruption of receptionist or wife. He would hold her hand again, speak caressingly again, and his words would make her beautiful.

The bell shrilled a second time. 'Coming!' she called, dashing down to answer it, hearing now the Oxford bells ringing in May Morning – waves of wild triumphant sound reverberating through the house. She jumped the last three stairs, tore along the passage and unbolted the front door, Michael's name already on her lips.

Her eyes moved swiftly from the mid-brown hair to the neat and tidy brows, blue eyes and blue-grey tie; then further down to fawn cords and polished shoes. She hunched her shoulders against the blast of biting air, rubbing her bare arms. A cruel wind had sprung up, and dead leaves were blowing in – brown and withered leaves, which had once been bright, and young.

'I'm Dr Conway-Gordon,' said a clipped and well-bred voice. 'The duty-doctor from the deputizing service. Dr Edwards asked me to call round, to visit a Miss Tessa Reeves. Is this the right address?'

She shook her head, kept shaking it and shaking it as she pushed the door shut in his face, rammed the two bolts home. She trekked slowly through the house, switching every light off, plunging it in darkness before groping back to the spare room. She drew the heavy curtains, to blank out the world beyond, then slid between the stiff white sheets, their arms as cold as hers.

'No,' she whispered to herself as she lay staring into nothingness. 'No one here of that name.'

22

'THANKS,' SAID TESSA, accepting a fruit pastille from the woman on the bench beside her – a fatso in a moth-eaten grey coat, wearing fur-lined slippers over a pair of turquoise bedsocks.

'Go on, love – take two.'

Tessa scrabbled at the tube again, wishing she could offer something in return. But all she had brought with her was a Ribena bottle full of cherry brandy, which she'd been sipping surreptitiously when the woman wasn't looking, or each time she'd lumbered up to check her washing. They had exchanged names half an hour ago, and she'd gleaned something of Dot's life from the contents of her laundry bag. Surprising what you could learn from people's washing – another kind of history, in a sense. You could tell their ages, whether they had children, or still lived with a partner; what sports they played, how they passed their time; how rich they were, or poor; how neat, or downright slovenly. Dot's old man was even pudgier than she was, judging by the size of his pyjamas, and her football-playing son was also quite a hulk, unlike her skinny daughter, who went skating and liked pink. Dot herself was either extremely house-proud or obsessional, since she'd washed two dozen dusters in the same load as her daughter's shell-pink nightie and coral skating skirt.

'You got kids?' Dot asked.

'Yes,' she said. 'One son. He'll be ten months exactly on January the tenth.'

'Smashing! Who looks after him? Your Mum?'

Tessa played for time, plugged her mouth with the second pastille and started chewing with more vigour than it needed. She and April had been bickering a lot – not about the baby, but about her non-existent boyfriend. 'I'm having trouble with my mother,' she admitted finally. It would be a relief to talk to an older woman, get things off her chest. She was feeling better altogether since she'd come in from the sleety cold outside; allowed the warm fug of the launderette to thaw her frozen limbs. She especially liked the smells – invigorating, healthy smells of detergent and clean clothes, which seemed right for New Year's Eve. She had planned a bold new start, a whole host of resolutions, one of which was to iron out the problems at home. She swallowed the black pastille; blackcurrant and cherry flavours now mingled in her mouth. The cherry brandy was a Christmas present from Frank, while tightfisted Eric had settled for a calendar. Still, it helped to see the year ahead, to have all the days and weeks and months laid out systematically.

'Mum says I've changed,' she confided, turning back to Dot. 'She blames it on my boyfriend.'

'What's wrong with the poor feller?' Dot's eyes lit up at the prospect of a scandal.

'Nothing. She's never even met him. That's the trouble, really. She keeps pressuring me to bring him home, and when I don't, she gets suspicious, assumes he must be someone I'm ashamed of – you know, a druggie or a drop-out. She says I always used to work hard, and take a pride in my appearance, and all that sort of stuff, and now I just loaf around, looking like the Wreck of the Hesperus.'

'You looks all right to me, dear.'

Tessa couldn't speak. She was so unused to any sort of approval, that a few encouraging words from a fat and shabby stranger had moved her almost to tears. Everyone had been having a go at her, this last wretched week. Eric had called her snappy and unreasonable; Frank asked why his Madonna had turned into a bag lady, and April continually peppered her with questions. She knew her mother meant well, but the inquisition was beginning to wear her down. Why did she keep missing meals? Were she and 'Michael' living on fresh air, and wouldn't he like to join them for a decent home-cooked dinner? Did he really prefer his girlfriend not to wash her hair, and was he so screwed up by his father's death that he'd turned into a hermit?

'He's not a hermit,' she'd objected. 'He just prefers to see me on my own, Mum. And he likes me to look natural.'

'That's not the word I'd use.'

'And he takes me out for meals – anywhere I fancy.'

'So where does he get the lolly, pray?'

When she'd paused to work that one out, her mother had changed

256

tack. 'Michael' was a toff now, not a junkie – someone snobby and stuck up who couldn't spare the time of day for ordinary working people. 'It's sad to think you're ashamed of your own mother,' April had concluded with a shrug.

Tessa took another swig of cherry brandy, no longer even caring if Dot could smell it on her breath. She was determined to drown her guilt, which kept bobbing up to plague her, remind her what a louse she was to have left her mother on her own on New Year's Eve of all nights. Frank was out, Eric ill in bed, and she'd waltzed off without a backward glance, dolled up for a party. The toff-cum-junkie had invited her to a friend's house, where there'd be dancing, drinks, a disco – or so she'd said with feigned excitement, only stopping short at a firework display and midnight cabaret.

'So why can't he pick you up from home?' April had protested. 'I don't like you wandering the streets alone, especially in this weather.'

'I'm not wandering the streets. He's meeting me at the pub just round the corner.'

'He's a darkie, Tessa, isn't he? – a nigger with a brood of kids and a couple of spare wives. That's the reason he never shows his face here.'

She hadn't answered – couldn't – knew she had to get away; avoid more crass remarks, or, worse, the cosy heart-to-heart which her mother had been angling for since Christmas. It was impossible to communicate with April – had been for three months. Her love for Michael was always in the way. She hadn't time or room or strength for anything outside it; had to feed it like a hungry bear, spend every minute of the day poking titbits through the bars of its huge cage. She felt safer in the launderette, with oddballs and eccentrics who were too busy with their own problems to cross-examine her. One of them had tried chatting her up, soon after she'd come in – a weirdo wearing shoes which didn't match: a brown sandal on his left foot and a blue trainer on his right. Dot had saved her from his clutches, plonked down on the bench beside her, and literally squeezed him out. But if she hung around a while she might meet someone else, someone more presentable, whom she could take home to her mother and introduce as Michael – someone neither black, nor stoned, nor bigamous.

She unbuttoned her coat, smoothed her taffeta skirt. It felt strange to be dressed up, especially in a launderette, but there was quite a party atmosphere, in fact – paper-chains looped across the ceiling, and a large holly-edged placard saying 'A MERRY XMAS AND A PROSPEROUS NEW YEAR TO ALL OUR CUSTOMERS!' Even the name, 'The Sno-Wite Launderama', suggested fairy tales – an escape from poisoned apples, the promise of a Prince. She leaned back against the wall. The rhythmic drone of the machines was lulling her into a state of dreamy inertia. She watched in fascination as the washing tumbled round behind its porthole. If only those were her and Michael's clothes – clinging to each other as they heaved and thrust in all that steamy heat; suddenly juddering in a frantic spin, then resting for a while until the next wild spurt.

She shut her eyes, imagining Michael's sweat and dirt running into hers; their private smells and juices merged; their arms and legs entangled, like the clothes. It was the perfect way of spending New Year's Eve – tossed and churned with Michael. Her limbs relaxed, her head lolled forward, and she was aware of nothing further until an impatient hand shook her by the shoulder.

'Time to go. We're closing.'

'Dot . . . ?' she faltered, glancing around, but the place was empty now. Everyone had disappeared save a crabby-looking female in a balding fake-fur coat.

'And take your washing with you,' snapped the ocelot.

Tessa stumbled to her feet. 'I . . . I haven't any washing.'

'So what d'you think you're doing here? It's not a public lounge, you know.'

'I'm sorry,' Tessa muttered, still not properly awake. She sleep-walked to the door, flinching at the shock of cold as she pushed it slowly open. The sleet had changed to snow; large white woolly flakes whirling through the darkness, melting on her eyelashes and running down like tears. She turned her collar up, cursing her thin party-shoes. She couldn't walk the streets all night, yet where could she find shelter? Pubs cost money – as did cinemas and restaurants, bowling alleys, wine bars – and money was a problem. She'd given up her babysitting, and all her other jobs. If she was banned from Dr Edwards' house, it seemed completely pointless to work for anyone else, and anyway babies other than Michael made her cry. Her mother had been urging her to apply for Income Support, but she didn't feel she deserved support – not a monster who had murdered her child. The offices were probably shut, in any case. There was a 'closed' sign on the world between Christmas and New Year – everyone too busy with festivities. If you weren't involved in partying yourself, then you stayed out in the dark and cold, pressing your nose against the glass of other people's rip-roaring celebrations.

She passed a crowded café – happy couples laughing at each table; music spilling from the door, and a whiff of garlic butter which made her stomach seesaw with envy and revulsion mixed. Dr Michael Edwards would be eating. He'd been invited to a dinner-dance at Dr Reynolds' golf club. She'd discovered that from a friend of Mrs Webb; still kept up all her contacts, so that she would know what he was doing and especially where he was. She'd been terrified he'd disappear once he'd done his spell of Christmas duty – jet off on a skiing trip, or take Joyce and baby Michael to soak up the sun in a different, kinder hemisphere. But he was a mere eight miles away – no, closer – in her head now: sitting at a white-clothed table, starting his first course; his mouth busy with smoked salmon, fingers toying with a slice of thin brown bread. She longed to be the salmon and the bread; to be handled by him, swallowed; to travel down his gut, ferment inside him, until she was shunted into his bowel.

Reluctantly, she made herself trudge on, screwing up her eyes against the snow; her hands and feet beginning to lose all feeling; her flimsy shoes badly stained and squelching. If only she could turn it off – press a button or flick a switch, and stop that ceaseless flurry of white flakes. Everything had turned into a battle, even simple things like walking. It was a struggle to keep upright, to pick her precarious way between the puddles without slipping on the pavement and landing with her bottom in the slush. Now and then she'd stop awhile, to look in through lighted windows and watch people eating multi-coloured pizzas, or shaking crimson ketchup on to piles of glistening chips. She was picking up the crumbs – crumbs of conversation, discarded olive-stones, dregs of beer, of heat. She turned the corner, leapt back to Michael's dinner. It was warmer there, more comforting; the strains of the first quickstep kindling the grey silence; waitresses in black and white serving sirloin steak and tender green mangetouts. She could taste the juicy steak; feel Michael's hand on her bare back as he steered her round the dance-floor.

'More wine?' he offered, when they were breathless from the cha-cha, and returning to their seats. She nodded, fumbling in her bag to find the bottle, and choking down a gulp of cherry brandy. 'Shall we sit out for a while?' he asked, the words suggestive, teasing; his hungry eyes undressing her. She smiled, dived into the Kum-Kleen Washeteria (which was squeezed between a betting-shop

259

and a Pakistani grocer); shivering as she arranged herself on a battered plastic chair. She tried to transform the peeling paint into the stylish panelled walls of High Pines Golf Club, but Michael hadn't followed her inside. Not that she could blame him. The place was freezing, filthy dirty; greasy fish and chip papers littered round the chair-legs; dented beer-cans dribbling on the floor. It was also totally deserted, as if it had died and been abandoned – every washer empty, every dryer cold.

Still, she'd no right to complain; was extremely lucky, actually, to have found a second launderette so soon. Launderettes were free. If her luck held out, she could spend all night moving from one to another – rather like a pub-crawl, but without the expense. She might even find a warm one which stayed open twenty-four hours. They were the obvious place for her, offering purity and cleanliness, decontamination. She needed purging, putting through the longest wash until the murder-stain had been entirely bleached away. And launderettes were 'beautiful', according to the film, or romantic playgrounds where young hunks took their Levis off and sat waiting in their boxer shorts. Even in commercials, the Prince turned up eventually, though he might be wearing underpants instead of a cloak and golden crown.

She removed her sodden shoes, shook snowflakes from her coat, then passed the time reading all the tatty cards pinned up on the noticeboard; counting the word 'wanted', which appeared thirteen separate times. People wanted cleaners, or rooms to let, or flat-sharers; mothers wanted second-hand prams, stair-guards, help with ironing. Two builders wanted work; a scout troop wanted jumble. She shrugged and moved away; couldn't understand anyone wanting anything but Michael.

She walked up and down to keep her circulation going; suddenly noticed a camera mounted on the wall. The premises must be electronically surveyed, to make sure that no one broke the rules, or used the place as a brothel or a doss-house. She wished she had a camera concealed in Dr Edwards' home, so that she could observe him day and night, or could spy on him now in the golf club – watch him pouring cream on chocolate gâteau, or spooning in some sharp and tingly sorbet. Eating was so intimate, it should be done in private; the two of them alone. Yet she'd never seen him eat or drink – not one single mouthful, not the smallest sip.

She strode back to the noticeboard, began to take down all the cards, tugging at the drawing-pins; one or two so stubborn that she hurt her thumb trying to prise them out. She turned the cards over, so that she could write on their clean sides, using a Persil packet to lean on, which she'd found on a high shelf. 'MICHAEL MICHAEL', she printed in block capitals; repeating it on every card, then pinning them all up again, so that the board was shouting 'MICHAEL, MICHAEL, MICHAEL, MICHAEL, MICHAEL . . .'

She swung round as the door slammed. Someone had come in – a swarthy-looking character in dungarees and stubble, with a dirty khaki anorak draped across his head to protect him from the snow.

'We're shut,' he said. 'An hour ago.'

'But the door was open, and it says you close at eleven.' Tessa gestured to the notice on the wall.

'Not New Year's Eve, we don't.'

'You can't just change the times like that.'

'Oh, can't I? Thanks a lot.'

'But I'm . . . I'm meeting someone here, and he won't know where I am.'

'Tough shit! Now, move your arse.'

'But . . .'

He marched her to the door, made a point of locking it with exaggerated relish – jangling keys, shooting bolts, while he griped about the 'bleedin' weather' and 'fuckin' useless British Rail' – buggered up, as usual, by a few flakes of 'soddin' snow'.

British Rail, she repeated to herself. Perhaps not so fucking useless. They would have a waiting-room – free again – and maybe even warm. And there was a buffet on the station where she could get a cup of tea, and where people wouldn't object to her hogging a whole table when she was on her own and only spending a mingy 50p. The snow was whooshing down still – furry white where it coated roofs and ledges, but a dirty soupy grey beneath her feet. Well, at least it kept most people safely indoors, which meant far less chance of meeting someone she knew, who might report back to her mother that Tessa Reeves had been spotted all alone (with her coat soaked through and her hair in dripping rats' tails) just an hour away from midnight.

She struggled down the street and round the corner; snow stinging on her face, sneaking down her neck. *Some* trains must be running, whatever that rude slob had said. She could hear one rumbling past; instinctively quickened her pace to match its rhythmic chug. She liked the sound, which reminded her of the judder of the washing machines, and seemed to comfort and exhilarate at once. Stations were exciting places, like beautiful launderettes – busy travellers arriving and departing, reaching longed-for destinations. There was no sign of any ticket-collector, so she wandered on to the platform, and along further to the buffet; found it locked and barred. Well, that had saved her 50p, and the waiting-room was just as good – more appropriate, in fact, since she was studying for a new degree in Waiting – waiting for the chimes of midnight, waiting for the Prince.

The metal bench was cold; the chipped stone floor patterned with fag-ends; the ancient heater dead. Two girls were sitting opposite, giggling, prattling, dressed up to the nines. Their cheery talk increased her sense of sterile isolation, so that she was relieved when they breezed out to catch the 11.21 to Waterloo. Quite a little crowd had alighted from the train, and were surging along the platform, jostling up the stairs. They all had places to go – dinner-dances, parties, snug and welcoming homes. The last one straggled out of sight, and she settled back to wait again; the station now abandoned; even the busy snowflakes beginning to slow their hectic pace.

She realized she was starving, tipped out her handbag on the bench in the hope of finding some chewing-gum or a lone forgotten toffee. She stared at all the clutter – things she barely needed any more: lipstick, diary, notebook, keys. Why was life so snarled up with possessions – trivia which once had seemed important? Her university reader's ticket had fallen on the floor. That she *would* need, when she resumed her course at Balliol next year. She stooped to pick it up, glancing at the photo on the front. Was that really her, with those chubby cheeks and that stupid jaunty grin? She put her hand across the grin, but the eyes still smiled and shone – deceitful painted eyes. She hesitated a moment, then tore it into two – right between the eyes – chucked both halves into the litter-bin. Why go back to Oxford and continue her degree, when history was a sham?

She remained standing by the bin, riffling through its contents to find something she could drink from. If she was going to toast the New Year, then she must do it in style, not guzzle from the bottle. She pounced in triumph on a polystyrene cup, shaking out the coffee dregs which had muddied at the bottom, then filled it to the brim with cherry brandy; keeping one eye on her watch, so she could time her toast for the dot of twelve o'clock. There was a sudden rustling noise, and she shrank away in horror as a small grey rat scampered across the floor. It seemed equally alarmed by her and froze in the far corner, its tail coiled round its body, its whiskers quivering. She stood her ground, scared that if she moved at all, it might run across her feet, but it sat so still, it could have been a stone rat. She let her breath out slowly, checked the time again. Two minutes to go. Now she'd recovered from the shock, she was almost glad to see it there, to have a bit of company. Only tramps and failures were alone on New Year's Eve.

She counted seconds under her breath, then raised her glass to her small friend. 'Happy New Year,' she whispered, taking the largest gulp she could; spluttering and choking as the liquor hit her throat. The rat was looking at her, as if pleased to be included. 'Have a good year,' she urged it. 'No traps or dogs or poisons.' It flicked its tail, suddenly scuttled out of sight behind the heater, vanishing as abruptly as it had come. It had been startled by the Tannoy announcing the last train: the 12.02 to Esher, Hersham, Walton, Weybridge, and all stations to Guildford. She blundered out of the waiting-room, leaving half her belongings on the bench. High Pines was at Walton, and Michael was at High Pines – chafing with impatience, pacing up and down as he listened for her step, ready to sweep her into his arms for the last waltz.

'Steady!' warned a doddery old man, trying to climb down from the carriage as she pushed wildly on. She sank back on the seat and closed her eyes. She was feeling rather strange – groggy and half-dazed – but once she reached the golf club, the Prince would wake her from her slumber with a kiss.

'Can I help you, madam?' asked the steward.

'Yes,' said Tessa. 'I . . . I'm looking for my husband.' She glanced around the plush and tasteful lounge. Things weren't quite in focus, blurring at the edges, but this was definitely Michael's world – luxurious, exclusive – with bowls of hothouse flowers, bulky leather chairs, gleaming silver trophies in mahogany display-cases, and even the weather kept at bay behind sumptuous velvet curtains. She slipped off her wet coat. The steward appeared affronted by it; even more so by the sad state of her shoes. She had got lost on her way from the station, tried to take a short cut across a muddy field, then ended up having to clamber through a hedge. 'I'm . . . er . . . sorry I'm so late,' she said. 'I couldn't get a message to my husband.' It gave her a real thrill to say 'my husband', and she'd used the words several times already –

to a car-park attendant, a waitress going home, and two chauffeurs in peaked caps, leaning against their gleaming snooty cars.

'What's his name?' The steward seemed suspicious still, eyeing her scratched hands with disapproval.

'Dr Michael Edwards,' she announced, bending down unsteadily to remove the offending shoes – mustn't spoil their carpet.

He shook his head, his frown so deep it was shuttering his eyes. 'He's not a member, madam, so I'm afraid he won't be here. This is the members' private lounge. I suggest you try the bar – first right along the passage.'

'Thank you,' she said graciously, then zigzagged through the door, keeping as close as she could to the wall, in an attempt to regain her balance. Although it was easier to walk barefoot, the floor kept surging up to meet her.

'Good evening,' she smiled to a couple in the corridor; next greeting an old fossil with silver hair and whiskers, who'd stopped in an alcove to light his fat cigar. They might be Dr Edwards' friends, so they must be treated with respect. She was glad she'd made an effort to dress up. All the men she'd seen so far had been wearing dinner-jackets; their partners looking glamorous in formal party frocks – though most of them seemed to be leaving: kissing, hugging, calling out goodbyes.

'Don't go,' she said to no one. 'I've only just arrived.'

She paused to get her bearings, peering into a large room on her left. The dining-room, the dancing-room – though more or less deserted now. Drunken streamers straggled down the walls; a stray balloon was expiring on the floor, while its mates hung smugly above it, pink and plump and looped with silver bows. The food had all been cleared away, except a few odd wilting parsley sprigs and a waterlogged bread roll. But they'd kindly left some bottles out – claret, sparkling wine, even vintage Bollinger. Most of them were empty, or very nearly so, but if she mixed all the dregs together, she could almost fill a glass. And the glass was really elegant – not a polystyrene cup. She sipped her heady cocktail, then stuck a frond of parsley into the disintegrating roll, and bit into it greedily. She wished the rat could share her soggy sandwich, hoped it wasn't hungry, or moping on its own. 'Happy New Year,' she murmured again, to the rat, the room, the world; toasting them in bread and wine. She mustn't be too long, though – she'd come here to claim Michael, not to fill her stomach. She took one last bite before relinquishing her dinner, then tottered on towards the bar, stood uncertain at the door, bewildered by the throng of faces. She clutched at the wall, almost keeling over. *There* was Dr Edwards – or at least his broad black back – leaning down to kiss a fluffy blonde. No sign of Joyce at all – no sign of any woman, save that obnoxious little tart.

'*Michael!*' she screamed, her voice rising in a hysterical wail as the girl opened her wet lips and closed her eyes.

There was an instant damning silence as everyone wheeled round to stare at her aghast; drinks frozen in shocked hands, conversations broken off, the kiss itself aborted. The man also turned his head – he was fair, with a moustache, and years younger than Dr Edwards. She met his eyes – cold grey eyes, hostile and accusing. She staggered from the bar and lurched along the passage, half-blinded by tears, but still sobbing Michael's name. She had to find him, leave with him, keep her resolution. She had sworn to supplant Joyce Edwards, to be the new and only woman in his life. Joyce was a mere stand-in, a temporary and disposable wife, who cramped his style, made him tame and timid, stifled those fierce passions she would unleash in him herself. Midnight had struck, so it was time for her to make her solemn vows: to love, honour, cherish and obey him, till death did them part – even beyond death, and eternally.

'Michael,' she kept calling, frantic now to find him; swerving round a corner and bumping into a group of men who were roistering down the other way. 'Michael?' she repeated, as her eyes scanned every one, trying to pick his features out from the swimmy blur of faces.

'Someone wants you, Michael,' crowed a raucous jokey voice. 'A damsel in distress!'

Vulgar guffaws reverberated round her, followed by a tramp of feet as the bodies barged on past. Silence for a moment, then a softer and more kindly voice said, 'Can I help? I'm Michael.'

She stared at the new face – a pale and rather insipid face, with thinning hair cut neat and short, sandyish in colour, but greying at the sides. The eyes were hazel, and surrounded by fine laughter-lines; deeper, sadder lines etched into his forehead. He was slim and fairly short, an inch below her own height, whereas Dr Edwards was tall, broad-shouldered, younger.

She shook her head, turned wretchedly away. 'No,' she said. 'You're not Michael.' People were always deceiving her, promising they'd come, then sending someone else; slipping out of a dinner-dance just seconds before she'd got there; claiming names which weren't their

265

own. She slumped against the wall, had no more strength or spirit to go on.

'But I am,' the man insisted. 'Michael Chalmers. And I work here, in the office, so maybe I can help you find your own Michael.'

She raised her head, a tiny flame of hope flickering in the ashes of her mind. This man understood – had just referred to Michael as 'her own', must realize that she had to track him down. *Yes*, she tried to shout – yes please, I beg you, search him out, do anything to find him. But the words had made no sound, simply blown away like smoke, and her legs were sand and cobweb, could no longer hold her up. She was aware that she was falling, made one last desperate plea – 'Michael. *Find* him!' – then collapsed into his arms.

23

TESSA PEERED AT the bunny-patterned wallpaper. She'd had rabbits on her bedroom wall when she was a child of five or six; had often lain in bed counting them or christening them – once had been ticked off for colouring in three tails. She wasn't in any sort of state to try to count them now. Her brain was completely immobilized; her whole body taken over by a monster of a headache, which seemed to claw her in its talons, throb and pound and hammer through her skull. She pressed her fists against her eyes, as if to knead away the pain; glancing in surprise at the long sleeve of her nightdress. She didn't own a nightie in pink-flowered winceyette; hadn't worn long sleeves in bed since she was a podgy and unglamorous thirteen. Even more peculiar, she still had her bra and tights on, underneath the flowers. She turned over on her back, frowning in perplexity; couldn't work out where she was, or how she'd landed up there. All the solid landmarks she normally awakened to had disappeared entirely; in their place a wicker chair, a fluffy rug, and a print of Jemima Puddle-Duck quacking on the wall.

The curtains were still drawn, but enough light was filtering through them to reveal the room quite clearly – a warm and kindly room, which, despite its unfamiliarity, seemed to assure her she was safe here; that if she lay patiently and quietly, somebody would turn up with some medicine or Lucozade. She ran her tongue across her lips, longing for a drink. Her mouth was dry and scratchy; its usual moist pink lining stripped off in one piece, and replaced by offcuts of sandpaper, whose edges didn't meet. She half-sat up, to listen: someone was bustling about downstairs. She must be still a child – ill in bed and waiting for the doctor, while her mother tore round like a steam-train tidying up the mess. April had always treated doctors like visiting royalty – every speck of dust attacked before they stepped into the house, and at least the worst of the clutter bundled into cupboards or stuffed haphazardly in drawers. No time to do much now. She could already hear his footsteps on the stairs – slow and heavy footsteps, stopping just outside her room. There was a tap-tap on the door. Doctors didn't knock.

'Come in,' she called, confused.

At first she hardly recognized him. He was wearing not a dinner jacket, as he had been at the golf club, but a brown home-knitted cardigan over neat but dull grey slacks. His face looked even paler, and a strand of sandy hair had fallen over his forehead; the hazel eyes anxious and uneasy. She couldn't bring herself to meet those eyes, felt too ashamed and overwhelmed as the horror of the night before began replaying in her head – the general plot still vague, but every scene condemning her. She turned to face the wall.

She heard him clear his throat, take a wary step towards her. 'I've . . . brought you up a cup of tea.'

'Thank you,' she said stiffly, trying to focus on a bunny, a blue one with a carrot in its mouth. The 'thank you' seemed to give him courage to walk right up to the bed, set the cup down on the bedside table.

'Thanks,' she said again, knowing that her debt to him went far beyond the tea. This stranger, this Samaritan, had brought her to his home, somehow managed to undress her (considerately leaving on her underclothes), lugged her semi-conscious form upstairs and heaved it into bed. Yet he probably weighed little more than she did. Or perhaps his wife had helped. There must *be* a wife, since she was sleeping in their child's room. Wives could leave, though – walk out of a marriage, bugger off with someone else. She rolled over again to face him, to see if he wore a wedding ring. He did.

'How are you feeling?' he enquired, sounding genuinely concerned. His eyes were very sensitive, instantly reflecting his slightest change of mood. They were no longer apprehensive, simply kind.

'I . . . I'm not quite sure. My head hurts.'

'Shall I fetch some aspirin?'

She nodded, scared she'd cry. He was waiting on her, nursing her, not shunning her as a stupid drunken fool. By the time he returned with two aspirins and a glass of water, she had already drained the tea and now gulped from the tumbler he'd put into her hand. Her thirst was so intense, she could have knocked back the entire contents of the Thames.

He remained standing by the bed, like a conscientious doctor, checking that his patient had taken all her medicine. 'Look, I . . . don't know who you are – I mean, not even your name or . . .'

'Tessa.'

'Pleased to meet you, Tessa,' he said with mock formality. 'And you know I'm Michael, don't you? Michael Chalmers.'

'Yes,' she said. 'I know you're Michael.'

He took the empty glass, kept hold of it, as if relieved to have something to do with his hands. 'I do hope you don't object to my bringing you back here. I couldn't take you home, you see, since I'd no idea where you lived. My friends suggested calling the police, but I didn't like the thought of you waking up in a cell on New Year's Day.' He gave a nervous laugh, still fumbling with the glass, fingers stroking round its rim. 'But what I'm really worried about is whether you were expected back last night. I mean, is there someone I should phone? They must be in a frightful state by now – out dragging ditches, or searching for a corpse – your Michael, for example?'

She didn't answer. 'Your Michael,' he had said – in a frightful state about her, dragging ditches to find her precious corpse. She could kiss this man, worship at his feet.

'Or you could make the call yourself, if you're feeling well enough. The phone's down in the hall.'

She shook her head. It was April who'd be going spare; who wouldn't have slept a wink last night, wondering where the hell her daughter was, and why she hadn't rung. But she felt too weary and whacked out to face her mother's anger, fob off all her questions, fabricate more lies. Instead, she lay back on the pillows, pulled the duvet right up to her chin. 'If you wouldn't mind, I'd like to sleep my headache off.'

'Of course,' he smiled. 'I'll draw the curtains properly. The sun's coming through that gap. It's a marvellous day outside, you know – sun and snow together.'

She shut her eyes. Sun and snow were both too cruel. One glared and mocked; the other glared and froze.

'Goodnight, then,' he said softly, still fiddling with the curtains. 'Or should I say good morning? It's well after ten o'clock.'

'No,' she said. 'Goodnight.' It was night till she found Michael, but she was already halfway there. This other Michael had been sent to help – she knew that beyond all doubt.

*   *   *

269

'Afternoon?' groaned Tessa, sitting up in bed again, remembering where she was this time, and why she'd woken up to find a strange man in her room. 'It can't be.'

'It's five past one,' said Michael, 'which is strictly speaking afternoon. I came to see if you wanted any lunch.'

Tessa asked her stomach, astonished when it shouted 'Yes!' How could she be hungry, and no longer have a headache; all the throbbing/churning/griping calmed and quelled? She tried to concentrate. He was running through the menu, expecting her to choose – tomato soup, cheese omelettes, Welsh rarebit, toasted sandwiches. She plumped for toasted sandwiches. They'd be warm and filling, the most solid thing he had mentioned on his list.

'Would cheese and ham be all right?'

'Perfect!'

'And perhaps you'd like to put these on.' He gestured to the wicker chair, where he had draped a pale pink jersey and a pair of navy slacks. 'You're a good bit taller than my wife, so I'm afraid they may not fit. The trousers look miles too short – I can see that straight away. You could wear a pair of mine, instead, but I wasn't sure if . . .' His voice petered out, embarrassed by the mention of his trousers. 'Anyway, I'll leave you to get dressed. The bathroom's just next door. Come down when you're ready. I'll be in the kitchen.'

And where will your wife be? she was tempted to demand. He hadn't said 'my ex-wife', and if her clothes were still around, then it was unlikely she'd waltzed off with someone else. So why wasn't she at home on New Year's Day, or helping her husband with the lunch?

She shrugged, pulled back the curtains, jolted by the scene outside – everything transformed by snow: thick white powdery pristine snow, glittering in the sun, with blue shadows cast across it from bushes iced like Christmas cakes; the lawn criss-crossed with bird-prints. Every branch and smallest twig boasted its white coating; each withered brown hydrangea-head had burst into white bloom. She suddenly felt a child's delight, longed to race downstairs and play – build a snowman, make her own footmarks on the still virgin garden-path.

The garden looked familiar – the same size and shape as theirs at home; neat wooden fences either side, and a small shed at the back. This was semi-detached suburban-land – no extensive grounds nor sweeping drives, no ostentatious architecture; each small-boned house no different from its fellows; not allowed to spread, or shout 'Look at me! Look at me!' She was back where she'd been born, and surprisingly content with it. She had often criticized her mother's boring semi, aware how mean and commonplace it was, compared with Vicky's mansion, or the Harvey-Taylors' country house, or even Dr Edwards' place, but today she was almost glad of the confinement. That meagre plot below the window was all the grounds she needed; a child's bedroom plenty big enough, and it was somehow right and fitting that she'd found refuge in this undistinguished haven.

It also seemed important that the landscape was disguised – snow shrouding all the landmarks, concealing normal colours, prettifying mundane things like wheelbarrow and washing-line. Even the peg-bag wore a white tiara, and the compost-heap had turned into Mont Blanc. She, too, felt revived – her raw wounds staunched by snow; the sun lighting up her own internal landscape, so that she dared to hope again. The hope was linked to her surroundings, even to the fact that she had no idea where she was; could have fetched up anywhere – a hundred miles from the golf club, or a few short streets away. It gave her a sense of adventure, like someone in a fairy tale who had entered an enchanted forest, or set out on a journey – a new beginning, which tied in with the New Year.

She dashed to the bathroom, bursting for a pee, then washed and cleaned her teeth, feeling guilty when she realized she could well be using Mrs Chalmers' toothbrush. The wife's gear was all around – her cleansing cream and make-up on the shelf; her gingham shower-cap hanging on the door. It felt really weird putting on her clothes – the sweater far too skimpy, the trousers barely meeting round the waist, and only reaching halfway down her calves. She never wore that prissy shade of pink, or frumpy fabrics like Crimplene, which made her feel like some menopausal housewife. But there was no sign of her own clothes, so she didn't have much choice; was forced to go downstairs in her stockinged feet, and with a gap around her midriff. She had expected Michael to laugh, but instead he looked so stricken, her own shy smile died instantly, and they both stood in rigid silence in the kitchen, avoiding each other's eyes; she mystified by his reaction.

Suddenly, he swung back to the stove, alerted by a sputtering noise. 'Blast! The soup's boiled over.'

She grabbed a dishcloth, helped him mop it up. 'I thought we were having toasted sandwiches?'

'We are. They're done and keeping hot. The soup's to start with – what's left of it.'

It was tinned soup – Heinz tomato – and again she was relieved. She couldn't quite explain it, but she didn't fancy exotic food, expensive snobby meals. Everything seemed right – the cramped and humble kitchen – no microwave, no freezer; the cheerful china, with poppies splashed across it; the sunshine-yellow walls.

Michael tipped the soup into two bowls, put them on a tray with spoons and paper napkins. 'We'll eat on our laps in the other room. You can hardly swing a cat in here.'

'I like it, though. It's cosy.'

'Yes, my wife chose the colour. I wasn't all that keen at first, but I must admit it's grown on me.'

This wife, thought Tessa – everywhere and nowhere. Would she breeze in any moment? Had she gone to work? New Year's Day was a bank holiday, but some people must still work – traffic wardens, policewomen. She couldn't imagine Michael's wife as either; decided not to mention her, didn't want more complications, when things appeared to have quietened down, at last.

She followed Michael into the sitting-room, exclaiming at the shields and silver cups. 'I didn't realize you were a second Ballasteros.'

He laughed. 'I'm not. I'm afraid my handicap's a struggling seventeen. No, our dogs won those.' He placed the tray on a low coffee-table between two chintzy chairs, then picked up the largest trophy, weighing it in his hands, fingering the inscription. 'My wife used to show our three West Highland terriers, and as you can see, they all did rather well. We've got so many rosettes upstairs, we could paper a whole room with them.'

'Where are they?' Tessa asked. 'The dogs, I mean, not the rosettes.' Easier to stick to dogs – though perhaps they and Mrs Chalmers were together, at some top-notch championship show, even now posing for the cameras as they carried off yet another prize. But wouldn't there be some evidence of dogs – leads or baskets or food-dishes – or even a faint doggy smell clinging to the house? There was no trace or whiff at all.

'We . . . er . . . gave them away,' said Michael, settling her into the right-hand chair and passing her a bowl of soup. 'Fortunately, our favourite went to a friend in the next road, so I still see him at least once a week. In fact, I promised I'd take him out this afternoon, so perhaps you'd like to join me for a walk in Bushey Park?'

'I'd love to,' Tessa said, spooning in her first mouthful of soup. 'I've never had a dog.'

'Really? I've owned dogs all my life. That's how I met Eileen.'

272

'Who?'

'My . . . wife. I was out hiking in the pouring rain on the Sussex Downs one Sunday. It was early March, I remember, and the weather was appalling – not just wet, but really cold and windy. I saw this tiny figure, all wrapped up in waterproofs, with her hair blowing back behind her . . .' He paused a moment, savouring the memory, smoothing down his own hair as if he could feel the wind once more. 'Anyway, it was our dogs who introduced us. My two ounces of Yorkshire terrier attacked her two ton of Great Dane. I'm not sure who got the worst of it!' The laugh was unconvincing, and his voice had lost its vigour, become constrained, forlorn. She sensed he was making an effort to control himself, especially when he changed the subject to something safe and bland. 'I do hope the soup's all right, Tessa. It seems to have got a sort of scum on top. I don't think it's meant to boil.'

'It's fine,' she said, wishing she dared to call him Michael, as he had called her Tessa. But the name was too explosive, might blow up in her face.

'They say tinned tomato soup is full of sugar, but I've always had a sweet tooth,' he confided.

'So have I.' They smiled at one another, as if confessing to some secret heinous vice. The smiles were followed by another awkward silence, in which they were both aware of the noise they made swallowing the soup.

Michael put his spoon down, returned to wife and dogs. 'Eileen was into big dogs when I met her. Her parents had this huge great place with a jungle of a garden, so Great Danes weren't a problem. But once we married, we had to scale down. She wasn't keen on Yorkies, so we compromised with Westies.'

'I don't think I've ever seen one. What are they like?'

He abandoned his soup to rummage through the top drawer in the sideboard; came back to his chair clutching sheaves of photographs, which he sorted on his lap, passing some to Tessa with descriptions, explanations.

'That was Snowy as a pup. He's only a few weeks old there, and still a bit unsteady on his pins. And here's his mother, Sophie, who gave us quite a shock last year by producing seven puppies, instead of the usual three or four. Oh, and this will make you laugh – Jasper in the river, looking more like a drowned rat! I took it just this summer.'

'You mean you still had the dogs as recently as that?'

273

He nodded, gazing at the photo with devotion and regret, as if Jasper were a child he'd lost.

'So why did you get rid of them?'

It was the longest silence yet. Michael continued shuffling photos, but she noticed that his eyes weren't really focusing. He was looking inwards, backwards.

'Eileen . . . passed away,' he admitted finally, his voice a ghost, a tatter.

Tessa stared in horror at her navy knees. She was wearing a dead woman's clothes, a corpse's Crimplene trousers. Except that Mrs Chalmers wasn't dead. Michael hadn't used the word, nor called her his 'late wife'. She was still his wife; her things all round the house: her apron in the kitchen, her jacket in the hall, even her *Woman's Owns* on the table in the corner.

'Hell! I'm sorry. I'm so sorry.' Tessa pushed her bowl away, no longer able to eat.

'That's all right.' Michael forced a smile. 'I try not to talk about it. It only happened in the summer – the thirteenth of July – and I was the one who always said thirteen wasn't unlucky.'

'How did she . . . ? What did she . . . ?' Tessa stopped, defeated. The word 'death' was unavoidable.

'Cancer,' he mumbled, crumpling up his paper napkin, then shredding it to bits. 'And it was all so horribly quick. They only diagnosed it in February, and less than five months later, she was . . .'

Tessa had never seen a man cry; found she, too, was crying. They sat in their separate chairs, weeping silently and rigidly, as if they wanted to deny their grief, suppress it, or conceal it; not disrupt the lunch. She didn't have a Kleenex, so tears dripped slowly off her chin on to Mrs Chalmers' clothes, making tiny damp-stains. Michael's face was hidden in his large white handkerchief. She could see his shoulders heaving, but he didn't make a sound. The only noise was from outside – a car reversing in the street, a child's sudden yelp of laughter. Time seemed to fray and warp, so that instead of minutes passing, she was conscious of whole hopeless months dragging slowly by – months of loss and bitterness; not one grim death, but many.

'I'm sorry,' Michael said at length, putting away his handkerchief and straightening his shoulders; his voice so carefully controlled now, he might have been apologizing for burnt toast or tepid soup. 'I shouldn't have looked at the photos. That's what set me off.'

'I'm sorry, too,' she whispered. Sorry for his wife's traumatic death; sorry for the death of Michael; the murder of a baby; sorry for the death of Oxford; sorry for last night.

'I'll . . . er . . . bring in the toasted sandwiches.'

'Can I help?' she offered, aware her face must be blotched from tears; her eyes inflamed and puffy.

'No, you sit tight. And how about something warm to drink? Coffee? Tea? Or perhaps you'd prefer herbal tea? Camomile, I think it is. Eileen used to like it.'

'Okay,' she said. 'I'll try some.' If she was wearing the wife's clothes, sitting in her chair, then why not drink her herbal tea as well?

Once he'd gone out to the kitchen, she flicked quickly through the photographs. Eileen was in most of them – though not the ones he'd shown her. The wife looked small and shy and eager to please: a little like a dog herself – a friendly and obedient breed, ready to retrieve a stick, or lick her husband's hand. She returned the photos to the drawer, all except for one – a happy family group of Michael, Eileen, and the dogs. She could understand his grief. He'd lost them all – his entire family wiped out; his love destroyed, aborted. The picture seemed to change, and she was looking at herself – sitting next to Michael with their baby in his arms; Michael smiling and devoted, his cheek against her own.

She replaced the photo face-down in the drawer and stood leaning against the sideboard, fighting a new surge of desolation, when her attention was caught by the initials M.I.C., stamped across a leather-bound address book. She picked it up, inspected it. How odd that his initials were also the first three letters of his Christian name. She wondered what the 'I' was for; couldn't think of many names beginning with an 'I' – only Ian, or Ivan, or Irving, and the last two weren't that common. She found a pen, and began to doodle with it, scribbling his full name in various combinations: Michael Ian Chalmers, Michael Ivan Chalmers, Michael Irving Chalmers.

She wrote the Chalmers one last time, separating the letters out, rearranging their order; her idle curiosity changing to excitement as she realized that six of them were the letters which spelt Michael. Only the 'I' was missing, yet there it was in his middle name; completing a second Michael. He was Michael twice over, which must surely be significant. Wasn't it a sign that this man had not turned up by chance, but been sent to play a crucial role in her life? Even his wife's death must be part of the whole plan. However terrible and crushing for him, it meant he was freed now for his mission: to help her find her own Michael. They were already bonded by their grief – both in mourning; both suffering an irreplaceable loss – and had obviously been brought together to support and serve each other. She would do and be whatever he required – become another Eileen if necessary – as a small return for his restoring Michael Edwards to her.

She shut the drawer hurriedly as she heard his footsteps just outside, sat back in her chair, stretching out her legs towards the fire – a hideous one with imitation logs and switch-on flames in an unconvincing shade of cherry red. Michael entered with a tray, passed her a plate of sandwiches oozing melted cheese, and a steaming mug of tea. The Peter Rabbit on the mug reminded her immediately of the rabbits in the room upstairs. He hadn't said a word about his child. In fact, it struck her now as rather odd that he should have one quite so young – a tot who still liked bunnies and Jemima Puddle-Duck – when he was getting on a bit himself. She wasn't good at guessing ages, but he must be nearly fifty. She didn't want some cherished son or daughter taking up his time; diverting his attention from the task she had in mind for him.

'What about your child?' she asked, observing with surprise that she'd cut her toasted sandwiches into fingers, as if she herself were an under-five. 'I mean, who looks after him?'

'What child? We haven't got a child.'

'But I thought . . . I mean, those rabbits on the wallpaper.'

He hesitated, picking at the shreds of paper napkin still littered on the table. 'We . . . we . . . lost our baby, Tessa. She only lived three days. My wife went into labour prematurely, and at first they thought the little mite would survive, though she can't have weighed much more than a couple of pounds. They wired her up to all these frightening tubes and things, but I'm afraid she died of lung failure. We called her Amy – had her christened by the chaplain just before her breathing gave out. The name means "loved", so we felt it was appropriate. No child could have been loved more than that small scrap.' He cupped his hands together, as if cradling Amy inside them, then slowly opened his fingers; forced to let her go. 'We never had another, despite the fact that we tried for years and years; went through all those dreadful tests. And we never altered her room. I suppose it's all we've got left of her – that and a few baby-clothes.'

Tessa said nothing, though she felt strangely agitated; cramping pains juddering through her stomach, very like the contractions she'd had in hospital – her womb registering its loss. Both she and this new Michael had endured a double blow: their babies wrested from them; their partners dead or gone. It was almost unnerving, the links between their lives. Other, less perceptive people might shrug it off as one of those chance things, but she herself knew better. Their double dose of suffering had been destined from the start; a further proof that they were meant to be together, until such time as she moved on to Michael Edwards' home, with Michael Chalmers' help. She began to eat like a robot, hardly tasting anything, but speculating privately how much she dared risk telling him; how far she could rely on him.

Michael talked enough for both of them, keeping the conversation deliberately light, as if in compensation for the trauma of their first course – Jasper's exploits (the dog he still took out); his eccentric next-door neighbour, who wore a ginger toupee; a recent little triumph in a golfing competition.

Tessa saw her chance. 'Yes, you work at the golf club, don't you? What's your actual job there?'

'I'm the assistant secretary, which means checking members' records, keeping track of all the competition results, organizing the social events, answering the mail – anything and everything.'

'Do you know a Dr Reynolds?' she asked casually. 'Dr Alan Reynolds – a GP? He's a member of High Pines.'

'Oh yes,' he said. 'I know Alan pretty well. Eileen and his wife were close, so . . . Good Lord! Is that the time – twenty-five to three? We'd better get our skates on, if we're going to have that walk. Have you finished your tea?'

She nodded, annoyed that he'd digressed from Dr Reynolds. But once they were out walking, she could always steer him back again, ask a few more questions, move from Dr Reynolds to his partner, Dr Edwards. It was becoming clearer by the moment that Michael Chalmers was part of her whole destiny. It wasn't just coincidence that he knew Alan Reynolds well.

'You'll need a coat, and boots, Tessa. What size shoes d'you take?'

'Sevens,' she admitted, grimacing at her feet and wishing, as always, that they were dainty and petite.

'I take seven and a half, so with two thick pairs of socks, my wellingtons should fit you. And you can borrow my brown golfing jacket. It's got a nice thick furry lining and a hood. And how about another sweater, to cover up that gap?'

She felt warmer already, basking in his kindness. She followed him into the hall, stopping abruptly as she caught sight of the phone. 'Oh God!' she exclaimed. 'I haven't rung my mother to tell her where I am. She'll be going round the bend.'

'But I thought you said . . .'

Tessa struggled to remember what she had said; could recall nothing but a splitting headache, and legs too weak and groggy to take her to the phone. 'I wasn't feeling up to it earlier on. Do you mind if I try now?'

'No, go ahead. I'll pop upstairs and sort you out a jersey, then you can make the call in private.'

Private! Tessa winced at April's voice – a blast of rancour and reproach exploding down the phone with such volume and sheer vehemence she was certain half the street could hear.

'Where in God's name have you been, Tessa? I was about to ring the police. I've been going almost spare – didn't get a wink of sleep, pacing up and down all night, imagining you raped or murdered or cut up into bits. I kept turning on the news, listening out for accidents or bomb scares, wondering how the hell we'd cope if you'd lost your legs or something. You promised you'd be back at half past one. You must have known I'd worry. Couldn't you at least have picked up the phone or . . . ?'

Tessa tried to interrupt, but her mother was in full flood, blaming 'that bloody cretin Michael', saying if she ever met the swine, she'd tell him exactly what she thought of him – how he'd changed her lovely daughter from a hard-working and considerate girl to a selfish slob who never spared a thought for . . .

'Look, Mum, I'm really sorry – honestly I am.' She kept one eye on the stairs, watching out for Michael; shuddered at the thought of trying to explain to him who the 'bloody cretin' was who shared his name. Or perhaps she *should* explain . . .

She was so startled by this new idea, she hardly heard her mother ranting on. It had only dawned on her this minute that she actually had a ready-made solution – a man called Michael, whom she could introduce at home. Of course, she'd have to fill him in first, confess the whole dilemma, and then beg his help, connivance. He was miles too old to be accepted as her boyfriend, but, looking on the plus side, he was white, English, law-abiding, well-mannered and well-spoken, with a safe and steady job – which, compared with all the horrors bristling in her mother's mind, would make him very nearly Mr Right.

And he wasn't even married. Widowed was a different thing entirely. April might well sympathize, since she'd been widowed herself, in a sense.

'Listen, Mum . . .' She swallowed, cupped her hand round the mouthpiece to muffle any sound, though her voice had already stumbled to a halt. The idea was still a risky one, which could land her in a worse mess if she didn't think it through, and put Michael in a spot as well. Yet if he was going to be important in her life, as catalyst, intermediary, the man who led her on to Michael Edwards, then wouldn't it be easier if April got to know him? She couldn't keep on lying to her mother, dreaming up excuses as to where she was, and why.

She switched the receiver to her other hand, put a new determination in her voice. 'Mum, you've hardly let me get a word in edgeways, and there's something that I . . .' She broke off in mid-sentence, hearing Michael coming down. 'I'm sorry, but I've got to go. No, it isn't Michael – someone else. I can't explain. We're late. Yes, I'll be back this evening – promise. And Mum . . .'

'What?'

'Happy New Year.'

She was frowning as she put the phone down, distressed by April's anger and her own audacious plan. There were so many complications, so much that could go wrong.

'Everything all right?' asked Michael, noticing the frown.

She nodded, chewed her thumb.

'Your mother wasn't too upset?'

'No,' she lied. 'She understood.'

'D'you live with your parents?' He handed her a sweater – what looked like a brand new one in cosy Shetland wool.

'With my mother, yes.' She said nothing about her father, though if she did introduce Michael as her boyfriend, she would have to make things clear, acquaint him with the facts about her parents' lives, her own life.

'And what sort of work do you do?'

She was beginning to feel harried by his questions; muttered something about having been unwell the last few months.

The responsive hazel eyes instantly signalled their dismay. 'But I can't drag you out into two foot of snow if you're ill, or convalescing! We'd better stay here, in the warm.'

'No, honestly, I'm over it now. And I'm really looking forward to our walk.'

279

'Okay, but do wrap up really well.' He delved into the cupboard, produced a pair of wellingtons, a mohair scarf and some thick red woolly gloves.

'I'm all set for the North Pole!' she grinned, pulling on the heavy rubber boots.

'Well, you can't be too careful if you've been off-colour or run down. I always used to say to Eileen . . .'

The phone cut through his voice. She retreated to the kitchen, to grant him the same privacy he'd kindly given her; though he was back in just two minutes.

'That was a dear friend of mine, inviting me for tea. I told him I had company already. People are so good, you know – always ringing up to see if I'm all right, or asking me round for meals, or dropping in at weekends, to make sure I'm not too lonely. It's funny, though,' he added, almost talking to himself now, 'it seems to make it worse, in a way, as if it's rubbing in the fact that I'm alone. I don't actually think that anyone can ever understand, unless they've been through a bereavement themselves.'

'*I* understand,' she whispered, daring to meet his eyes. She watched them flood with gratitude, his face flush in confusion.

'Yes,' he murmured shyly, passing her the gloves, his hand lingering slightly longer than it needed. 'I think you really do.'

'*Sit*, Jasper!' Tessa ordered, thrilled when he obeyed; his dark eyes fixed on hers, the white ears pricked to hear her next command.

'Okay, fetch!' She hurled the stick and raced after it herself; Jasper trying to beat her, the two pouncing on it together in a flurry of legs and snow.

Michael panted to keep up, laughing as he saw them wrestling for the stick. 'He'll expect this every week now. I can see I'll have to get in training! All I usually manage is a sedate stroll round the pond, not this sort of marathon.'

'I'm surprised he can run so fast, when he's only got short legs.' Tessa flung the stick again, watched Jasper streaking after it.

'Four, though, to our two.'

'When I was a kid, I always wanted a Dalmatian – or a hundred and one Dalmatians, if we'd only had the room for them. Imagine – four hundred and four legs!'

Michael laughed again, an easy, friendly laugh. He seemed much more relaxed since he'd left the house behind, as if he'd escaped from all the memories of Eileen's tragic illness; from the cold black hand of death. 'How come you never had a dog at all – a smaller breed, at least?'

'My mother was always working, so it wouldn't really . . . Jasper, *look* at you, you tramp!' Tessa knelt down in the snow to remove a trailing bramble from his coat; put her arms round him on impulse and kissed him on the muzzle. The dog had taken to her from the moment they first met; his stubby tail wagging almost off; his eyes intrigued and trusting; no flicker of suspicion or alarm. Rare to be accepted, when she'd become so used to hostility, or out-and-out rejection. And it was equally unusual to be enjoying so much company – not just fellow dog-walkers whom Michael knew already, but even total strangers who would stop to fondle Jasper or exchange comments on the weather. They'd got chatting to a poodle-owner, and a stout arthritic woman with her stout arthritic Airedale; then cheered up an au pair girl, battling with three boisterous boys and an unruly Irish setter.

Everything conspired to make people less restrained – the sun, the snow, the holiday, the antics of the dogs, as they romped and frisked and slithered in the snow. Only now did she realize how alone she'd been – living in a sort of purdah, shunning any social life. But this afternoon she'd blossomed in her new-found family, becoming not only Jasper's mother, but also a child again herself. She had forgotten the simple pleasure of playing ball and tag, running for the sheer hell of it, scrunching through untrodden snow – snow which looked like a clean white page, inviting her to write on it. She found a pointed stick, used it as her pencil. 'TESSA', 'JASPER', 'MICHAEL', she wrote, then traced a second 'MICHAEL' underneath – a larger, more triumphant one, a symbol of new hope.

Jasper seemed tireless, was prancing round in circles now, echoing her own exhilaration. Those printed letters in the snow would melt to watery slush, but the letters in her mind would last for ever – 'MICHAEL' engraved in bronze, in beaten gold.

'Shall we feed the ducks?' she suggested, keen to prolong the childish treats. Just as they were leaving the house, Michael had gone back to the kitchen to hack off a chunk of bread, which he'd wrapped in a paper bag and stuffed in his coat pocket. All his pockets were bulging – Bonios for Jasper, a chocolate bar for her, the ball, a rubber bone. Her father Dave kept nothing in his pockets; wouldn't dream of spoiling the line of his expensive city suits.

'Yes, let's,' said Michael, patting his pocket to check the bread was there still. 'I always like to bring them something, especially at this time of year when the poor creatures are half-starved. We'll go back by the boating pond.' He pointed to the right-hand path, swinging Jasper's lead in rhythm with his step.

Tessa pounded on ahead again, Jasper in pursuit, then doubled back to Michael so he wouldn't feel left out. Once they reached the pond, they joined a motley group of humans, dogs and wildlife – the snow blazoned with their traces: footsteps, pawprints, pram-tyre marks, and the tracks of every sort of bird from swan to coot to sparrow.

'Won't Jasper chase the ducks?' she asked.

'Oh, no. He's too well-trained. He's a show-dog, remember, so he's had to learn to behave in the ring – not attack the other entrants, or bite the judge.' He walked down to the water's edge, passed the bread to Tessa. '*Leave!*' he ordered Jasper, who was already eyeing a large mallard with quivering curiosity. 'Sit! *Stay!*'

Jasper obeyed instantly, but sat there looking like a rocket ready to explode, primed to leap up from his haunches the very second he received the next command. The temptations were severe – a squawk and squall of water-birds were threshing all around him; new arrivals swooping in, landing on the pond with a cascade of spray; webbed feet splaying out as they hit the surface of the water. Coots, ducks, moorhens, gulls tussled with each other over every smallest scrap; one drake almost choking as he gulped his down too fast. Tessa threw some more, fascinated by the different shades of white – the bread, the swans, the gulls, the dog – and all the variations in the snow, from blinding white to dirty sludgy-grey, and a glistening golden white where it sparkled in the sun. It was years since she'd fed ducks. Her mother had always been too busy to fit in outings to the park; hated walking anyway – which was hardly any wonder when she usually attempted it in flimsy high-heeled shoes and skin-tight skirt.

She started chewing absent-mindedly on a crusty piece of bread, still upset about her mother. If she did bring Michael home to meet her, maybe that would help. Or make things even worse. Could April accept an age-gap of close on thirty years?

'Hungry?' Michael asked.

She shook her head, then nodded. 'Well, yes, I am a bit. It seems awful, after all that lunch, and a whole bar of Toffee Crisp.'

'Lunch was only sandwiches, and you've been going like a steam-engine since then! Let's treat ourselves to tea. There's this rather special tea-shop just round the corner from Hampton Court Bridge, which does home-made cakes and wonderful hot chocolate with frothy cream on top. We'll take the car, to save the long trudge back.'

'Oh, yes!' she said. 'I'd love tea out.' She didn't want the day to end, or dusk to fall, and darkness threaten again; wished it could be summer – eternal childhood summer with frothy cream on top. She turned back to the water, threw the last small knob of bread. 'Jasper's just amazing! He's hardly moved a muscle, yet he's itching to dive in and scare the living daylights out of a duck.'

Michael bent down to fondle the white ears, his expression one of pride and deep affection. 'They're a marvellous breed, you know, exceptionally intelligent.'

Tessa let her hand brush his, as she ran it slowly from Jasper's head, along his wiry back and up his jaunty tail. 'I feel quite ashamed that I'd never even heard of them.'

'Well, their history goes back donkeys' years. They were used on the Spanish Armada – or so Eileen's dog-book says – to catch rats on the ships.'

She recalled the rat in the waiting-room, the one she'd wished a happy new year. With any luck, her new year would be happy, too, now that she'd met Michael – Michael I. Chalmers. 'What's the "I" for?' she enquired.

Michael looked completely baffled. 'What eye? What d'you mean . . . ?'

'The "I" in your initials – M.I.C.'

'Oh, I see.' He made a face. 'It's "I" for Ivor. I loathe the name. My mother called me after Ivor Novello – one of her great heroes. I fear I proved a dreadful disappointment, though. I can't even sing in tune!'

'I suppose we're all a disappointment to our mothers.'

'Yes,' said Michael sadly, as they set off towards the Teddington gate, where they'd left the car in a quiet cul-de-sac outside the park.

All except Michael the Archangel, Tessa didn't say. She could see her lover in her mind, much clearer than he'd been for months – the burnt-almond eyes, obstreperous hair, hair damp from the May Morning rain. He was chatting to her in the car, as they hurtled

283

through the countryside, to Woodstock and their steak-and-strawberry breakfast.

'My mother named me after the conqueror of Satan, and I've always felt I couldn't let her down.'

'And have you?' she had asked.

'In my mother's eyes I can't do any wrong.'

The picture was already fading; another Michael taking over – blue eyes caged in glasses; straight hair lying flat; the voice itself quite different – less arrogant and dramatic.

'Michael . . .' she began, feeling totally bewildered. Two Michaels, but both lost now; both dissolving like a mirage; nothing in her mind except emptiness and longing.

She stumbled, almost fell. Michael Chalmers grabbed her by the jacket to stop her keeling over; linked his arm through hers so that she wouldn't trip again. She stared at him, half-dazed, hungry for some reassurance, some sense of safety, certainty. Yes, his face was real enough – not crumbling like the other two – a man of flesh and bone and blood; a Michael she could touch. Thank heavens he had come, and was actually physically supporting her. That was surely appropriate, because with him as prop and mainstay, she too would be a conqueror, rejoin her conquering archangel.

'I'm afraid I've overtired you.' He was frowning in concern, deliberately slowing his pace.

'No,' she said. 'I'm better now. I just came over dizzy for a second.'

'It's my fault, Tessa. I'm sorry. I shouldn't have dragged you out.'

'Of course you didn't drag me,' she insisted, determined to dispel the guilt now clouding his whole face. 'And I've really loved the walk. It's the first time I've enjoyed myself for weeks.' She could feel hope growing like a tiny seed embedded in dark earth, about to sprout and shoot, burst out and touch the sky.

Michael, too, was heartened, still drinking in her words; obviously delighted to be the source of her enjoyment. She allowed herself to lean on him; liked the way he held her arm with something close to tenderness, as if the arm were an injured creature which needed cosseting. Yet she was aware that he was embarrassed by the contact, even slightly shocked that it had happened in the first place. It seemed to overwhelm him, put paid to conversation, and they continued tramping through the snow in a tense, self-conscious silence, though closer than they'd been before – closer in all ways. Jasper filled the silence for them, barking into rabbit-holes, growling at a Doberman, whining in excitement when he glimpsed a squirrel or ferreted out some luscious doggy smell.

'Goodness! Look at that sunset!' Michael exclaimed, as they were turning out of the park towards the car. He shaded his eyes against the dazzling fiery red, which had dyed his drab grey anorak, flushed his pallid skin.

Tessa had been struck by it already, and now stood stock-still, feasting on the spectacle. The snow was crimson-tinged; the small mean houses in the street transfigured and ablaze, so fiercely bright she had to look away. Everything was dramatized – by snow, by fire, by flame – the dreary road spectacular; the dull lacklustre window-panes glowing like stained glass. She breathed in the whole scene, so that she could store it in her mind; knew it was symbolical – a sign to her of how Michael would transform her life; sweep her from a leaden grey to a resplendent, scorching red.

Suddenly, impulsively, she flung her arms around the other (smaller) Michael. 'Thank you,' she exulted.

'What for?' he asked, electrified and bashful both at once.

'For the walk,' she lied. 'And Jasper. And tea out in a tea-shop.' But her other voice was shouting to the sky: 'For Michael. For the conqueror.'

24

'DOES MICHAEL LIKE his beef well done, or rare?'

'I've no idea,' said Tessa, more concerned with the cluttered kitchen table. She wished they had a proper separate dining-room, so they could spread themselves a little, instead of rubbing shoulders with the oven and the sink. If they weren't forced to take in lodgers, there'd not only be more space, but she wouldn't have to introduce poor Michael to two embarrassing 'uncles', as well as to her mother.

April basted the roast beef, then turned the oven down a fraction. 'Well, you don't know much about the love of your life, that's for sure. Every question I've asked so far, it's been "dunno" or "couldn't say".'

'He's *not* the love of my life, Mum. And don't talk like that in front of him, or I'll die.'

'What? I'm not allowed to ask him how he likes his beef?'

'You're not allowed to mention love, or anything personal at all – and say nothing about me. You can just chat about your job – or his – or the weather, or . . .'

'What on earth's the matter with the man? Anyone would think you were bringing home the blooming Prince of Wales! "Don't say this, don't say that, make sure you say the other . . ." I'm not used to being told what I can do in my own house.'

'Look, you promised, Mum, you swore.'

'Okay, okay, don't shout! Anyway, I'd better go and change. He'll be here in quarter of an hour.' April removed her apron, cast an approving glance at Tessa. 'I'm glad you've made an effort to look nice, Toots. I always like you in that get-up, and you haven't worn it for an age. I was beginning to think this Michael of yours must be a rag-and-bone man, the way you've let yourself go.'

'Mum, listen . . .'

'What?'

'You do realize he's quite a bit older than me?'

'Well, if I don't, I must be deaf or daft. You've told me twenty times. The problem is, you're always so damned vague. What's "older" supposed to mean? Are we talking ten years, fifteen, or what?'

Double that, thought Tessa, preparing water for the sprouts. 'I don't know his actual age.'

'There you go again – don't know, don't know, don't know! What *do* you know, for heaven's sake? You spend enough time with the creep. Anyway, it's asking for trouble, marrying an older man. They could pop off any moment, or start piddling the bed or losing their teeth, when you're still in your prime.'

'I'm *not* marrying him – or anyone.'

'Well, I sometimes wish you would. It would be a weight off my mind to see you settle down.'

'But you're always saying you can't wait for me to get the hell back to Balliol and finish my degree.' Tessa sprinkled salt into the sprout-water. Even the word Balliol sounded rather strange now, and the place itself had become increasingly remote. She had a sudden vision of herself sitting at High Table in her scholar's gown, next to her new tutor, Robin Bowden, who was passing her the port. But both figures looked unreal; stuffed-shirt illustrations from some esoteric book.

'You can be a married student, can't you?' her mother was demanding. 'You know, like whatshisname – that dark-eyed little fellow I met your second term, when I came up with the meringues.'

'That's different. He's from Paris.'

'Oh, they make special rules for frogs, do they? Typical! Once we get into this blinking Common Market, it'll be fancy treatment for everyone but Britain.'

'We're in it, Mum, already – been in it twenty years. And, by the way, you're not to start on politics. You'll only upset Michael.'

'He's not one of these loonies, is he? – the sort who march with banners for save the lesbian whales?'

'No. He'd never march for anything. He's quiet and rather shy.'

'The quiet ones are the worst, Toots. He's probably hiding something. My Uncle Leonard used to say, "Never trust a silent man."'

'Mum, have you been drinking?'

'What d'you mean?'

'Well, you're sounding sort of manic.'

'Manic? What's manic? I wish you wouldn't use these foreign words. I've had one small glass of sherry, if you must know – well, maybe one and a half – and anyway I reckon I deserve it after cooking Sunday lunch for my ungrateful daughter's sugar-daddy.'

Tessa stalked into the sitting-room, replaced the cork in the Bristol Cream, then stared out of the window at the messy, dripping garden. It had been snowing on and off for the last two weeks or so, but a thaw had just set in and everything was slushy-grey and sodden. A few splodges of unmelted snow still carbuncled the lawn, but it was dull and dirty snow, with no sun to light it up. The sky was pale and listless, and the whole day seemed despondent, cringing like a sick and shivering dog.

She bustled around, tidying up the room – which she'd done three times already – wishing it was as easy to transform the wintry garden: hang new leaves on the trees, plant a few bright flowers. Michael's house was always neat, and he groomed and trimmed his garden as he must have once groomed and trimmed his Westies.

'Jasper, *sit!*' she whispered, picturing her companion sinking to his haunches in split-second obedience. They'd had half a dozen walks together, since that first tramp in Bushey Park. She'd begun taking him out in the mornings, while Michael was at work, and now Jasper recognized her knock, raced down the hall to meet her as if she were a doggy Father Christmas with a sack of marrow-bones.

'You've really made a hit with him,' Michael had remarked last week. 'It was love at first sight, you realize. He's never been like that with anyone, except my wife, of course. I suspect Brian and Bev are just a wee bit jealous. They've had him for five months, you see, yet now he's lost his heart to someone he's only known five days.'

She'd been secretly delighted by his words, though outwardly making light of them, mumbling something in reply about Jasper being a friendly dog who doted on all comers. But she knew that Michael was right. Her bond with Jasper was a source of pride and some surprise. Why should he have taken to her like that? Unless even a dumb animal understood instinctively that her life was meshed with Michael's. Jasper was the link between them; the natural acknowledged reason why she continued seeing Michael, the first thing they always talked about. She had spent almost every evening with him since they'd first met eleven days ago. He'd usually pick her up at six, when he had finished at the golf club, and they'd eat together at his home – uncomplicated foods like scrambled eggs or sausages, with Instant Whip for pudding, or tinned peaches with tinned cream. He never let her do the cooking, always waited on her, as if she were an invalid or child who had to be looked after. And they never did grown-up things like going out to theatres or dining in smart restaurants, but simply sat and talked.

She had told him quite a lot – about the termination (which had affected him so deeply, he'd actually broken down and cried again); about her loss of Oxford, and her parents' odd relationship – but she'd still said almost nothing about Michael. He was the father of her baby – that she had admitted – but whenever she'd attempted to describe how much he meant, how far he ruled her life, she'd become completely tongue-tied. She remembered Miss O'Brian, her English teacher at school, who always used to rave about the language – how rich it was, how expressive, how fertile its vocabulary. Yet when it came to Michael, that vocabulary seemed totally inadequate, so that she could never hope to find the words to do him proper justice.

It had been easier to explain her much more recent 'boyfriend', the one she had invented. She had merely told him the truth – well, part of it, at least – how she'd needed to be alone at Christmas, to escape April's constant questioning, and give herself a breathing-space. Now she wished to God she'd never mentioned it at all; had ditched the whole senseless plan when it was still a sickly notion in her mind. Supposing Michael got it wrong; forgot his 'mother' up in Essex, who'd been so recently bereaved; or overlooked the 'fact' that they'd spent Christmas Day together? He hated lies – he'd made that very clear – had only agreed to come today because she'd been so terribly upset when he refused.

She checked her watch – eight minutes to go – though he'd probably be early, turn up any second. He never kept her waiting, never let her down. She suddenly realized she was missing him, as much as she missed Jasper; knew her tension would evaporate once he was ensconced in their small sitting-room, giving April his full polite attention, listening with that seriousness she liked so much herself. Even if he fluffed his lines, would it really matter? Her mother would be hooked by then. She couldn't fail to warm to his sincerity, the way he made you feel important, drinking in your every word, even if you were rambling on about nothing in particular.

Ah! There was her mother now, teetering into the room, singing 'I'm gonna wash that man right out of my hair' in a loud off-key contralto. She was dolled up in her catsuit, which was shocking-pink

– and tight – with a daringly low neck, and a vulgar gold appliqué flaunting on one hip. The high-heeled shoes were also gold, and adorned with a rosette on each peep-toe; looking for all the world as if they'd been left over from the Christmas decorations.

'Mum, you can't wear that!'

'Why not?'

'Because it makes you look like a tart, that's why! And it's far too dressy for Sunday lunch.'

'Well *you*'re dressed up.'

'I'm not.'

April fumbled for her cigarettes and lighter. 'I bet I know what's eating you! You're worried that your Michael's going to take a shine to *me*, instead, especially seeing as he's probably nearer my age.' She gave an exuberant laugh, which turned into a cough as she lit up, inhaled deeply with her eyes shut. 'I was reading this story in *Woman's Realm*, where the daughter's boyfriend runs off with the mother. She dies, though, in the end. Funny – you never used to have a death in women's magazine stories, not even a few years ago. Things have changed – no more happy endings.'

'Mum, isn't there anything else you can wear?'

'It's too late now. By the time I've struggled out of this little lot, he'll be knocking at the door. Or d'you *want* me to greet him in my birthday suit?' April grabbed the sherry bottle, steered Tessa towards the sofa. 'Come on, pet, get a drop of this down you. It'll help you to relax. I've never seen you in such a state. Anyone would think your mother was an ogre.'

Tessa refused the drink, watching with disapproval as April refilled her own glass, slopping a few driblets down her cleavage. 'At least take those awful earrings off.'

'What, my sozzle-eyed pink elephants? But they *make* the outfit, Tess, and they're exactly the right colour. I spent ages choosing them. This man of yours sounds a right pain in the arse. I always say a bloke without a sense of humour is worse than one without an arm or leg. Which reminds me, love, there was a piece in the *Express* today about a poor old geezer with no arms or legs at all – you know, one of those thalido-whatsits. His mother took that awful drug in the sixties. Rosie, she was called, and he was Tom – or was it Tim? Anyway, he was nothing but a stump. They showed him in his wheelchair with his shirt-sleeves sort of flapping and a rug across his lap. And would you believe he'd married this quite pretty girl, who said he was a laugh a minute. I suppose you don't miss arms and legs if you're rolling in the aisles.'

'Well, if *I* brought a stump home, I'd never hear the end of it.'

'He may be a stump, for all I know. You're so secretive about him, I'm expecting a member of MI5 crossed with the Invisible Man. I only hope undercover agents are partial to banana loaf. He will stay for tea, as well, won't he?'

Tessa nodded. 'I don't see why not. And he has got a sweet tooth.'

'Good Lord! The child's come up with a solid fact, at last!'

'I'm not a child.'

'I know,' said April wistfully, the sudden sad expression on her face contrasting with the dangly leering elephants. She reached out for her daughter's hand, clasped it in her own. 'We used to be so close, Toots. What's gone wrong?'

'Nothing.'

'Are you sure you're not ashamed of me? I know I'm always banging on about it, but I sometimes can't help thinking . . .' She let the sentence peter out, released her daughter's hand, as if sensing that neither her words nor touch were welcome. There was silence for a moment, apart from some radio announcer's voice droning down the hall from Eric's room. April made to flick her ash in the skull-and-crossbones ashtray, missed, and blew it off the sofa. 'Now listen, pet,' she said, putting on a cheerful voice, and lolling back on the sofa, to demonstrate that problem-time was over. 'You're not to fret about today. I'll really make a fuss of Michael, I promise. Though I wonder where the heck he is.' She pushed her bangles up her arm, so that she could see her glittery watch. 'We've got to eat at half past one, whatever time he gets here. Frank's going bowling, and he has to leave by three.'

Tessa grimaced at the mention of Frank's name. 'I wish to hell he'd push off now. He's been unbearable all morning, making all these cracks about Prince Charming.'

'As bad as me, you mean?'

Tessa shrugged, pulled at the fringe on the peony-printed cushion. There were no flowers in the garden; too many in the sitting-room – flowers from every season blooming in mid-January on cushions, sofa, curtains, chairs.

'He paid for the roast beef, you know, so you can hardly grudge him his lunch. Beef's a shocking price! But I thought it would be nice for Michael. I mean, now he's lost his wife, he must miss things like home-cooked Sunday lunch. Poor soul! He's really been through it. First his wife, then his mother, and all within six months. You know what they say – deaths always come in threes, so I only hope . . .'

'Mum, whatever you do, don't talk about his wife. He's still terribly upset about her, and you're bound to put your foot in it.'

April lurched up from the sofa, tugged her jumbo earrings off, then drained her glass of sherry in one gulp. 'Okay, I've got the message. I'm not to say a single word. In fact, better if I don't exist at all. Why don't I just vanish, and leave you and bloody Michael to eat your beef alone?'

Tessa trailed over to the window, stood peering out disconsolately at the liquefying garden, feeling ashamed now of her carping. Her mother had been cooking since eight o'clock this morning, preparing lunch and tea, and though Frank had bought the topside (out of a recent win at 'Jackpot' in the *Sun*), April had paid for all the rest. She'd splashed out on cream and wine and fancy cheeses; really gone to town on the desserts – made a raspberry pavlova as well as peach and walnut pie. 'I'm sorry, Mum,' she said, at last. 'I didn't mean to upset you.'

'Well, you have – you do. You've been like this for weeks. I just can't understand you. We're like strangers to each other.'

'I'm a bit on edge, that's all.'

'You're telling me!' April forced a laugh, took a long drag at her Silk Cut. 'Come on, love, let's cool it, both try and simmer down. We don't want Michael to find us flipping our lids. And talking of lids, I'd better put the sprouts on.'

'Not yet, Mum. It's far too soon. We can't drag him to the table the minute he walks in.'

'When's nosh?' demanded Frank, suddenly appearing at the door in a primrose-yellow sweatshirt proclaiming 'WORLD'S GREATEST LOVER – DON'T ALL RUSH AT ONCE'.

'One-thirty sharp,' said April, 'though it'll be burnt nosh at this rate. I'd better turn the oven down again.'

'And where's his nibs?'

'Ask Tess.'

Frank strode over to the window, clicked his heels to Tessa, made a low and sweeping bow. 'Prince Charming let you down, darling?'

Tessa stalked out of the room, and up the stairs, bumping into

Eric who'd just emerged from the bathroom and was still zipping up his flies.

'When's lunch?' he asked. 'I'm ravenous!'

'If anyone else asks me when . . .'

'Okay, keep your hair on! It's just that I promised this poor mate of mine I'd . . .'

'I know, I know, you're rushing off! So's Frank. And Mum insists on watching Alex Higgins, so Michael will be sitting talking to himself by the time we reach the cheese.'

'Can't he talk to *you*? Any why are we havin' cheese? We never usually do. No, hold on a sec – I get it. It's VIP treatment for boyfriends. I s'pose she's laid on brandy and cigars, and them after-dinner mint things.'

Tessa ignored his sarcasm. Her thoughts were back with Michael, wondering if he'd changed his mind. He might be feeling guilty about having agreed to the deception, and so decided not to come. After all, if he'd been delayed by something unavoidable, wouldn't he have phoned? And he only lived four miles away, in Teddington, so it wasn't a question of hold-ups on the motorway. She closed her bedroom door, went over to the mirror to take another look at her swept-up hair, her glossy coral lipstick and matching silky blouse. She'd started taking trouble with her clothes again, especially since Michael had told her she was beautiful. He'd said it very shyly, and she had blushed as well, though hardly knowing why.

She sprawled across the bed, picked up the *Observer*, but found she couldn't concentrate at all. If Michael didn't show up, or – worse – broke off the relationship, she would never find the more important Michael. One led to the other – that she knew intuitively. She prowled downstairs again, rang his home, relieved when there was no reply. He must be on his way; perhaps had taken a wrong turning, or got stuck in the one-way system in Kingston. She mooched back to the sitting-room, dismayed to see her mother squeezed up on the sofa with Frank and Eric either side, all three of them knocking back the sherry.

'Mum, *please* don't drink so much.' Michael would assume they were a family of alcoholics. She'd been paralytic herself the first night that she'd met him, so it wouldn't look too brilliant if she introduced a mother in much the same condition.

'We haven't any alternative,' grinned Frank. 'If we're not allowed to eat, we've got to fill the hole with something.'

'There's some crisps and nuts and things,' she said, glancing round the room. 'I put them out in little wooden bowls. Where the hell have they all gone?'

'In here!' said Frank, slapping his primrose paunch.

'Ate the bowls, too, did you?' Eric asked sardonically.

Tessa noted his flushed face. He usually looked pasty, and this morning he had claimed to be half-dead, fighting off a stinker of a cold. At the time she'd worried about him passing on his germs to Michael, but if Michael wasn't coming . . . She seized a glass herself, splashed some sherry in it, and was about to toss it back when they were all startled by the doorbell.

'Prince Charming!' Frank exclaimed.

'Or Hurricane Higgins,' April giggled. 'Snookered!'

Eric leaned back in his seat, tilted his glass above his head, and tipped the last few drops of sherry straight on to his tongue. 'Or it could be the bloke who reads the meter.'

'Not on Sunday, you dolthead. More like some perishing god-man. Brethren, Are We Saved?'

'Yep,' cried April. 'We are! I think it must be Michael.'

Tessa was already at the door, but her welcoming smile froze in horror as she stared at the figure on the doorstep – his hair awry, black grease on his best jacket, and a rent in the right sleeve. He was clutching a large bunch of pink carnations; his eyes distraught, like Jasper's when she had to say goodbye and leave for home. He leaned against the door-frame, panting, almost hoarse, the words tumbling out in short apologetic gasps.

'So terribly sorry . . . My starter-motor jammed . . . I had to crawl under the car to free it . . . even then it didn't work . . . I did try to ring, but the phone was out of order. In the end, I left the car and walked – or rather *ran*. These are for your mother.'

Tessa stammered out her thanks, trying to play the gracious hostess, but uncomfortably aware of the official hostess hovering behind her. Her mother was studying the 'boyfriend' with highly critical eyes, her face registering its instant disapproval. Michael could never be called good-looking – he was too drab and short for that – but he was always neat and tidy, except on the one day that it mattered. His clothes were not just stained, but creased; he'd transferred a gungy smudge of oil from his hands to his right cheek, and his brow was filmed with sweat. He even smelt of sweat: a ripe, offensive smell which overlaid a last faint trace of aftershave.

'Mum, this is . . . er . . . Michael,' she said, unnecessarily, praying that they'd like each other, despite the bad beginning. 'I'm afraid his car broke down.'

'Yes, I can see it did,' said April.

'How do you do.' Michael proffered a hand, realized it was grease-stained, retracted it again, let out another flurry of apologies.

'You'd better have a wash.' April's voice was terse. 'I'd suggest a full-scale bath, if you weren't so late already.'

'*Mum!*' hissed Tessa *sotto voce.*

April ignored her. 'My daughter will take you to the bathroom,' she said grandly, making 'my daughter' sound proprietary, as if she were already warning Michael not to trespass on her rights.

'Mum, look! Michael's brought you these lovely flowers.' Tessa placed the bouquet in her mother's arms, hoping it might mollify her. She was caught between the two of them, aware of April's bitter disappointment in the man she'd been imagining as her future son-in-law; yet equally in tune with Michael's utter wretchedness. Each was seeing the other at their worst – Michael shaken, stuttering, devoid of all his usual friendly charm; her mother hostile and aloof, nothing like her normal bouncy self. Tension seemed to be choking through the hall like a cloud of acrid smoke, so she ushered Michael up the stairs, away from April's scrutiny.

'Help yourself to anything you want,' she urged as she left him in the bathroom, hoping to God that he'd borrow her deodorant, as well as soap and flannel. She waited for him in her room, knowing how alarmed he'd feel having to walk into the sitting-room alone. She was so keyed up herself, she began prowling backwards and forwards in the tiny space between the wardrobe and the door. She wondered what her mother was doing – drowning her sorrows in Harvey's Bristol Cream, or regaling Frank and Eric with her first appalled impressions of the dumb dishevelled tramp who had dared to take an interest in her daughter?

She avoided looking at the clock, though every minute that passed seemed like half an hour. Michael would be even more unpopular if he didn't come down soon. Perhaps he was so shaken by her mother's cool reception that he couldn't find the courage for an encore. She crept out of her room and stood listening outside the bathroom door; heard a tap running and then a nervous cough.

'Almost ready, Michael?' she called out.

'Yes, coming!'

He sounded very flustered, and when he appeared a moment later, his hair was neatly combed, but there was a red mark on his cheek, where he'd been scrubbing at the oil. He smelt of Dabitoff, not sweat; must have found the bottle in the bathroom cabinet, but found it too late, when he'd already sloshed the stains with water. His jacket was a mess. Curdled grease and water had made damp grey blotches all across one side. His eyes were still a hurt dog's eyes – a dog starved, abandoned, beaten.

'That's better,' she said encouragingly, leading him downstairs like a small shy child reluctant to brave the party. She'd already warned him about the lodgers, but they were usually relatively sober, not exhaling sherry fumes.

'Eric, this is Michael. Michael, Frank.'

'Hi-de-hi!' boomed Frank. 'Hear you had a spot of bother with your old banger?'

'Well, actually, it's not that old. It's . . .'

'I've never had a car myself,' Eric remarked morosely. 'What is it they say? "If God intended us to drive, He'd have created us with wheels."'

'That's not a bad idea, chum.' Frank punched his fellow lodger on the arm. 'When I was having all that trouble with my verrucas, I'd have gladly traded my poor old trotters for a decent set of wheels.'

'Where's Mum?' asked Tessa, motioning Michael to a chair.

'Dishing up the lunch.'

'But Michael hasn't had a drink yet. Would you like a glass of sherry, Michael?'

'I'd say no if I was you, chum,' Frank chipped in. 'There isn't any left.' His uproarious laugh hit Michael like a brick.

Tessa offered him a tomato juice instead, then took up a position which would block Eric from his view. The bunged-up lodger was busy blowing his nose, and she knew from past experience that the process would be followed by a meticulous examination of the contents of his handkerchief.

Frank pulled his chair up closer and leaned across companionably to Michael. 'I hear you run a golf club, Mike.'

'Well, no. I only . . .'

'Marvellous game, innit? Are you teaching Tess to play?'

'I haven't really . . .'

'She's a clever girl, is Tess. I've got my money on her. She'll either be another Maggie Thatcher, or Richard Branson Mark Two.'

'Dinner is served,' announced April, flouncing into the room. 'Would you do the honours, Frank, and carve?'

'Right you are. Though if the knife's as blunt as it was last week . . . I couldn't even kill my ex-wife with it, and she's so fat and floppy, a butter-knife would do her in.'

He offered Tessa his arm, escorted her into the kitchen, as if in deliberate challenge to Michael, who was left with Eric and his handkerchief.

'You sit next to me, Michael,' April ordered. She made it sound a threat, though neither of them sat, in fact, since she was busy transferring dishes from the oven to the table, while Michael waited politely till she'd finished.

'And Tessa, you sit there and keep an eye on Frank. I don't want him ruining the beef – though it's already burnt to a cinder. We were meant to eat an hour ago.'

'Don't be silly, Mum. We said lunch at half past one, and it's only five to two.' Tessa tried to catch Michael's eye, to let him know she was on his side, and that he mustn't worry about her idiotic mother, who merely needed humouring. But he stood staring at the floor, shoulders hunched, hands clamped to the back of the chair. She had never known her mother behave as shrewishly as this – it simply wasn't in character – nor had she seen Michael quite so cowed.

'Do sit down,' she coaxed him, though he seemed still more uneasy once he was squashed up at the table between Eric's snuffles and her mother's plunging cleavage. She must make some conversation, choose a subject which was safe and painless, or would at least stop Frank from embarking on some risqué joke, or Eric discussing the condition of his internal organs, one by morbid one. 'How's Jasper?' she asked brightly, though she'd seen him only yesterday.

The hazel eyes softened and relaxed. 'He's absolutely fine.'

'Is Jasper your kid?' Frank quizzed him, chopping off a lump of fat, then cutting chunky slices from the joint. 'Funny how kids today get landed with these fancy names. My boss's son's called Ferdinand. I ask you! Though of course he *is* a dago, so what can you expect? Got just the one boy, have you?'

'No, I . . .'

'Jasper's Michael's *dog*, Frank.'

'Dogs is better than kids,' Eric put in darkly, 'if you ask me.'

'No one did,' said Frank. 'What sort of dog you got then, Mike? Pit bull terrier?'

Tessa frowned at Frank's derisive snort of laughter. Michael was so sensitive, he'd imagine Frank was getting at him, implying that he looked the type to own a miniature poodle.

'Jasper's a West Highland White,' she explained, wondering why she was answering for Michael, though painfully aware that he hadn't yet completed one full sentence. Her mother would be judging him as dumb in every sense.

'Never heard of 'em,' said Frank. 'The only dog I ever had was a fucking pedigree mongrel.'

'Watch your language, Frank.' April passed the vegetables to Michael, though she did it almost grudgingly, as if she would prefer him to get up and leave before he'd touched a mouthful.

'You're a fine one to talk!' Frank hacked into the bone; juices from the joint spurting on to his sweatshirt. 'I learnt half the swear-words I know from you.'

'That's a blooming lie! I never swear, do I, Toots?'

'No,' lied Tessa in her turn, in an attempt to keep the peace.

'And I suppose you never drink?' mocked Frank. 'Which is a crying shame, when I'm just about to open this Château Tesco's, 1992. Drop of wine for you, Mike, when I'm through with all the carving?'

'Yes, please. I'd . . .'

'Count me out,' said Eric. 'That flippin' sherry's still giving me gyp. The doctor said I've got a dicy liver, so I shouldn't really touch the stuff.'

'If you gave up doctors instead of drink, you might be less of a misery-guts.' Frank speared a slice of beef, dangled it in front of Eric's face. 'D'you want this, pal? Or is red meat on the no-no list as well? They say it's . . .'

'Talking of doctors,' April interrupted, turning back to Michael. 'My daughter used to go out with a surgeon – an Oxford man, quite brilliant, and still only in his twenties.'

Tessa dropped the serving-spoon, spattering peas across the table-cloth. She began to scoop them up, so livid with her mother that she couldn't seem to control her hand, and was spilling more than she retrieved. If she'd been near enough, she would have kicked her under the table, but April was still prattling on to Michael.

'Unfortunately, I never met him. Tessa's always very cagey about her boyfriends, never bothers to tell me the important things, like how old they are, or . . .' April's final words were drowned as she gulped a draught of wine. She put her glass down not exactly with a bang, but with just enough vehemence to startle the whole table.

The silence which followed seemed to last for ever. Only Frank was eating, his energetic chewing sounding louder in the hush. 'Nice beef,' he observed, at length, 'though I wouldn't say no to a spot of horseradish. Mike, it's down your end.'

Michael sprang to life, reminded of his duties as a polite considerate guest. He passed the horseradish to Frank, the mustard to Tessa, and the cruet set to April – a pair of plastic figures dressed as bride and groom. 'Salt and pepper for you, Mrs Reeves?'

'Do call me April, please. I know we're not quite the same generation, but no need to stand on ceremony.'

Tessa picked her knife up, put it down again. So it was the age thing which was really bugging April. Michael was in fact very nearly old enough to be her mother's father, though she hadn't worked that out before today. She'd been lying when she claimed that she didn't know his actual age – he'd be fifty-four next month – but it had never seemed important. Only now did she realize how much it bothered April; appeared to make her mean and spiteful, drive her almost mad. And Michael was looking older by the minute; shrivelling as he sat there; his pale complexion and quiet-toned clothes fading even further in contrast with her mother's screaming pink. If only she hadn't dragged him here, away from his own home, where his age was immaterial, everything was safe and quiet, and meals were calm oases. They had hardly started the lunch yet; had still to work through pudding, cheese and coffee. How would she survive, or Michael, for that matter?

'Are you in work?' Eric was just asking him. He must have missed the bit about him running the golf club; always tended to assume that people were either unemployed (as he'd been himself, last year), or else in imminent danger of the sack. But at least he was being polite, making an effort to include Michael in the conversation.

'Yes, I'm the assistant secretary at High Pines Golf Club in Walton.'

'Men aren't usually secretaries,' April objected, stabbing a potato on her fork.

'Well, actually, they often are at golf clubs.'

'When do you get promoted?' April continued, ignoring his remark. 'To secretary, I mean, rather than assistant?'

'Oh, I'd never be made the secretary! They're VIPs. The one at

High Pines is an ex-wing-commander and used to be a big wheel in the City.'

'So what do you do – the typing?' April blotted her mouth, leaving a fuchsia-coloured lip-print on her paper serviette.

'Well, no, I . . .'

'Mum! You're completely out of touch. Of course Michael's not a typist – he's in charge of the computer. It's all technology these days – complicated databases and spreadsheets and what-have-you.'

'I never trust them computers,' Eric interjected. 'They're spyin' on us, I reckon – got all our private details on their files.'

'What are you so scared of, mate? You a terrorist or something? Or one of them serial killers that's always in the headlines?' Frank removed a piece of gristle from his mouth, then shovelled in more sprouts. 'And if you're planning another blood-bath, do me a favour, will you, and bump off my ex-wife while you're about it?'

Tessa squashed a pea to nothing with her fork. Couldn't Frank avoid the subject of ex-wives, especially their gory deaths? 'I'm just going to get a hankie,' she informed the company. She had to leave the table, at least for a few minutes; couldn't bear to hear her mother continue her hatchet-job on Michael. She'd already demolished his job, and was now watching him surreptitiously, about to pounce on something else – his height, his hair, his tie. And his beautiful carnations were still lying in their paper on the draining-board, not young enough nor bright enough to have merited a vase.

'You haven't caught Eric's cold, have you?' April's eyes swivelled from Michael to her daughter, their hostility undimmed.

'You can't catch colds,' Frank pronounced. 'They proved it at that research place. If you're run down, you get 'em anyway, and if you're not, you don't.'

'What about germs?' barked Eric. 'Or them viruses and things?'

'What about 'em?' countered Frank. 'We all know they make a beeline for *you*. Pity no one else is quite so keen.'

Tessa edged out of the room and sloped upstairs. Her 'family' had never seemed so crass. If only she and Michael could slip away, boil a couple of eggs and eat them on their laps in the peace of Elsham Close, then go and pick up Jasper and . . .

'Tess!' hissed a voice outside her door – Frank's baritone, though slightly slurred from wine.

'What d'you want?'

'I just came up for a wee. But now we're on our own, I wondered if you were free tomorrow night? If I'd known you went for the older man, I'd have asked you months ago. To tell the truth, what always made me hold my horses was basically the hair department' – he patted his bald dome – 'but I see your dear Prince Charming is going the same way. It'll be toupee-time for him before you can say Kojak. Or perhaps baldies turn you on?'

She slammed the bedroom door, rummaged for a handkerchief – April's eagle eyes would notice if she returned downstairs without one. She found a lacy hankie in the bottom of her bag – a flimsy, rather useless thing with a small blue E embroidered in the corner. Michael had lent it to her last time she'd been round there; then insisted that she kept it, saying it was high time he made an effort to part with Eileen's bits and pieces. She'd been afraid he might start offering her a whole load of other things, all stamped and branded 'E'; was extremely apprehensive about coming that close to death. She noticed, when he'd given her the handkerchief, that he had used the phrase 'late wife' – the first time she'd ever heard it on his lips.

Angrily, she scrubbed her eyes. Why in God's name was she blubbing again? For a dead wife she'd never met, or because she knew now in her bones that her search for his namesake was going to be both cruel and hard, and that she might even have to choose between her mother and a poor balding assistant secretary?

'Don't cry.'

Michael's voice was so harrowed and distracted, he sounded on the verge of tears himself. He and Tessa were sitting in his conked-out car, awaiting the AA. They'd been discussing the disastrous lunch (which had been followed by a mortifying tea), and Tessa's fury with her mother had suddenly run down, changed to hopeless tears.

'She was so *rude*,' she sobbed. 'I've never known her like it. I feel terribly ashamed.'

'Well, I can see her point of view.' Michael took her hand tentatively, as if scared of seeming presumptuous. 'You're her only daughter, and a precious lovely daughter, so she's obviously upset at the thought of your going out with someone almost old enough to be your grandfather.'

'Yes, but she needn't have been so horrid.'

'She's worried, don't you see? It's only because she loves you, and wants you to be happy. She's probably terrified you're making a big mistake, which could mess up your whole life. I can understand that, Tessa. She reacted like a mother lion, baring her teeth and unsheathing her claws, to drive off the intruder.' He gave a hollow laugh, then fumbled in the glove-compartment for his box of paper hankies. 'I did try to warn you it might not work, but . . .'

Tessa completed the sentence in her mind: But I overruled you, didn't I, insisted on having my own stupid selfish way. She wiped her eyes, crumpling up the Kleenex he'd passed her into a damp and soggy ball. 'Look, it doesn't really matter,' she told herself as much as him. 'Since you're *not* my boyfriend, Mum's no need to get on her high horse. I'd like us to go on meeting – just as friends, I mean – so long as you don't mind. I'll simply tell her I'm seeing someone else.'

'I don't think you should lie to her.'

'Well, what else can I do?'

Michael didn't answer. He had let go of her hand and was staring through the windscreen, his eyes troubled and despondent. She felt a stab of panic. She mustn't lose this man. He was the path to Michael, the key to her whole future. 'Are you trying to tell me you don't want to see me anyway, don't want us to be friends?'

'No, of course I'm not. But . . .'

'But what?'

They sat in edgy silence, suddenly aware of the sounds outside the car – an old van rattling past; two cyclists shouting directions to each other; the tramp of someone's footsteps on the pavement.

'I'd love to go on seeing you,' Michael said at last. 'But I think it's probably wiser if I don't.'

'Because of Mum, you mean? That's stupid! We shouldn't let her . . .'

'No,' he interrupted, speaking so softly she could hardly make out the words. 'Because of me.'

'I'm sorry, I don't follow.'

'Look, it's . . . er . . . getting late, and your mother will be worrying. I think I'd better phone her from a call-box, tell her we're still . . .'

'It isn't late. It's only six o'clock, and she said herself the AA might be hours.'

'Yes, but she wasn't very keen on our going off together in the first place – she made that pretty clear.'

Tessa jerked back in her seat. 'Why the hell did you suggest it, then, if you're so keen to get rid of me?'

'I'm not! How can you think that?'

'Well, it's obvious, isn't it? I've been boring you to death each night, and you've had enough – you're sick of me.' Her voice was cracking up. She was losing Michael once again. There must be some inescapable law that he would always disappear, or ban her from his house. She could see Michael Edwards roaring up to Newcastle; Dr Edwards slamming his front door; their forms and faces dwindling, fading into nothing; she herself as cold and insubstantial as the thin mist coming down across the rooftops. She peered out at the scene: a dismal suburban waste lit by ugly street-lamps, their unhealthy glow showing up torn posters on the billboards, a broken pram dumped outside a newsagent's. The shops were closed and shuttered, the rooms above them cramped – mean homes in a mean street. Everything looked stagnant and deserted, as if even tomorrow this place would never spring to life and cast off Sunday's shroud. It wasn't just the car which had broken down. She, too, was kaput, waiting for a rescue-service which would probably never come.

Michael's voice erupted through her thoughts – a heated voice repeating her own words. 'Boring me to death? You must be crazy! You're the least boring girl I've ever met. I love your visits, look forward to you coming more than anything else in my day. But . . . but I think now's the time to go our separate ways.'

Her next words were lost, distorted, as she fought to hold her tears back.

'I can't bear to see you cry.' Michael was shifting in his seat, chewing on his knuckles, then he snatched up his driving gloves and started pulling at their limp and empty fingers.

'I suppose you were just being kind – taking pity on me.' Tessa's voice was muffled still, but accusatory and harsh. 'You led me up the garden path, pretending that you'd help, but really . . .'

'I wasn't pretending anything. I . . . I . . . *love* you, for Christ's sake! Don't you understand that?'

'*What?*'

He let out a stifled groan, his face hidden in his hands. 'I didn't want to tell you. It isn't fair – not to you, or Eileen. I'm still missing her and mourning her, totally bound up with her, and yet . . . I mean, I never thought I'd ever feel the slightest interest in another woman – it would be betrayal if I did – but here I am, unable to stop thinking about you, even dreaming about you at night; resenting every minute of my work because it prevents me being with you; treasuring my golfing jacket because it touched your lovely body . . .' He broke off, as if he'd gone too far; gave a sudden bitter laugh. 'I'm as bad as Jasper, aren't I? Love at first sight for both of us. Except it's more excusable in him. He's only a youngster, not an old dog of fifty-three, and he hasn't recently lost a very dear and faithful wife. I can't forgive myself. It seems so disloyal to Eileen, so embarrassing for you. And yet it's Jasper's fault, in one sense. I mean, the way he took to you like that, as if you were Eileen in another skin, and the fact that you're so involved with him, so good with him – a natural. But it's not just that. You're . . . you're perfect in yourself – the most stunning-looking girl I've ever met, and so clever and unspoiled and . . . I feel quite humbled when I'm with you, imagine everyone must be looking at us, envying me my incredible good luck, wondering why you bother.' He touched her hand, his voice the merest whisper. 'Why *do* you bother, Tessa?'

She shook her head, too overwhelmed to speak.

'Look, I'm sorry. I've upset you. I was terrified of that – which is why I vowed I'd never say a word. I don't know what came over me, but I promise that's the end of it. Forget everything I said.' He rammed the box of Kleenex back, crossed his arms in front of him, as if trying to hold in his emotions. 'We can't meet any more. Your mother disapproves, and can you blame her? I *am* too old – that's the plain unvarnished truth, though I'd give anything on earth to be twenty-five again, if it meant that I could stick around.'

'You can,' said Tessa softly.

'What?' Michael swivelled back to her, the expressive hazel eyes now caught between despair and hope, anguish and sheer longing.

She let her hand rest on his knee, the agitation in her mind beginning to subside. She was no longer anxious and appalled that Michael Chalmers loved her; only grateful to the power which had yoked their lives together, roused this passion in him. She had been made to see in the last few startling moments that his love was an essential part of the predestined bond between them, part of the whole scheme. Because he felt so strongly, he would do anything she asked; would never vanish, as she'd feared, never let her down. There was a symmetry about the situation, a perfect sort of logic. Michael loved her; she loved Michael. The fact that it was another Michael meant

304

that he would suffer, but suffering was unavoidable – for them both. It was up to her to try to ease his pain, make it less unbearable, give him any comfort that she could.

'I'm in love as well,' she murmured. She could say it in all truth.

'Oh, Tessa, you can't mean it!'

'Yes,' she said. 'I do.'

Suddenly, he kissed her, a kiss so urgent, she was back with Michael in Foxlow Woods, responding to his frenzied greedy mouth.

He drew back just as abruptly, immediately apologizing; alarmed that he'd disgusted her, or taken her by surprise. 'I've never known myself like this, but when you said you loved me . . . I mean, not even in my wildest dreams could I have ever thought . . . I want you to understand, Tessa, I haven't allowed myself the slightest shred of hope, especially when you told me about . . .' He swallowed, cleared his throat. 'About the . . . father of your child. You see, I knew how much he meant to you. You were shouting for him, for heaven's sake, the first night I bumped into you. And yet . . .' He ran his finger round his lips, reverently and slowly, gathering up the traces of the kiss. 'Look what happened to *me*! I was so involved with Eileen, even after she passed away, that no other girls existed as far as I was concerned. But you changed all that – and changed it almost overnight. I think I knew I loved you when we went on that first walk. Was it special for you too, Tessa?'

'Yes,' she whispered. 'It was.'

'I kept wanting to ask you more about your Michael, yet dreading what you'd say, knowing he could . . .' His voice rose almost threateningly. He controlled it with an effort, continuing more soberly. 'Even now, I'm not too sure whether you'd rather talk about it, or . . .'

'No,' she said. 'Not yet.'

'Oh, thank God! Forgive me – that sounds selfish – but I don't want anyone or anything to come between us at this moment – this amazing marvellous moment! I can still hardly believe it's happening. I'm so worried I'll wake up and find it's just a dream, like the dreams I've been having recently, where I reach out to take you in my arms and find I'm holding nothing – only air. Oh, Tessa . . .'

'What?'

'Say you love me again. Say it exactly like you did before, with all that sort of fierceness, so I know you really mean it.'

She wiped the steamed-up window, so that she could look out

beyond the dreary street, beyond Surrey, London, and right up to the north. 'I love you!' she affirmed, with such force and fire and passion she could hear her words resounding through every street in Newcastle, until at last they reached her true beloved Michael.

25

TESSA STOOD SELF-CONSCIOUSLY, watching Michael sign the register, wishing his pen seemed a little more assertive. Mr and Mrs Kerry, he had written, in a wavering script, above his (real) address. Kerry was the name of one of Eileen's dogs – the first Westie that she'd ever owned. They couldn't seem to get away from Eileen, though the only reason they had come to a hotel at all was to do exactly that.

'Would you like early morning tea, sir?' the receptionist was asking.

'No, thank you,' Michael muttered. She could feel his tension beginning to affect her as he fiddled with his fingers, fiddled with the pen, made unnecessary adjustments to his tie.

'And how about a newspaper?'

He appeared unable to decide whether he wanted one or not, turned to her with something close to anguish. 'Tessa, would you like a paper?' He made it sound a life-and-death decision, which she alone could settle.

She shook her head, couldn't imagine trying to concentrate on terrorist attacks in Northern Ireland or bombs in Sarajevo, when she was away with Michael, in bed with Michael; naked, nervous, maybe even panicking.

The receptionist switched on her scarlet smile, to indicate that the registration was over. 'I'll get someone to show you to your room.'

They trotted after the porter, whose lovat-green uniform toned in with the wallpaper and the matching thick-pile carpet. The foyer, perfectly tasteful yet impersonal, reminded Tessa suddenly of their local crematorium (where she'd been last year for her Uncle Ronald's funeral) – the same elaborate flower arrangements, the same pleated Dralon curtains, the same air of hushed solemnity; furnishings and furniture as stiff and artificial as the primped deodorized corpse. She kept seeing corpses in her mind – tiny ones, not embellished by an undertaker, but chucked out with the waste. Today was 1 February – the weekend her baby would have been due – her and Michael's baby. She stopped a moment, disoriented. No. She'd had the baby, hadn't she? – held it in her arms, given it its bottle, soothed it back to sleep. It hadn't been thrown out, but spirited away, like so much else; taken from her, lost to her.

Mechanically she walked on towards the lift, where Michael and the porter were waiting with the luggage. She glanced up at the gilt-framed pictures of ancient sailing ships, the fussy wall-lights with their brass fittings and pink shades. One night at a hotel like this probably cost more than April earned in a whole week. And she doubted whether Michael could afford it. But he was obviously trying to compensate for the fiasco of two weeks ago, when he'd attempted to make love to her, first in his (and Eileen's) bedroom, then downstairs in his (and Eileen's) sitting-room. The late wife had never seemed so conspicuous, intrusive, clearly disapproving of everything they did – or rather didn't do, since Michael had eventually given up the struggle, explaining shamefacedly that he was totally unnerved by the feeling that his wife was watching the proceedings from some realm beyond the grave. She herself had experienced only fear – fear of getting pregnant, fear that they were going too fast; yet she knew she must agree to anything he wanted, for the sake of finding the father of her baby.

She forced a smile as the porter unlocked the door of a low-ceilinged, rather oppressive room with a double bed, and a smaller bed in the corner, evidently for a child. The room was fuggy-hot, yet somehow chilling – everything too formal; nothing shabby, homely, kindly – except Michael. She fought the sense of being trapped, shut up here for twenty-four hours, expected to perform, to be worthy of the decor, the expense. Michael also looked uneasy. He had unbuttoned his thick coat and was fumbling through his pockets for some coins to tip the porter. He was so jittery he dropped them, and a couple rolled under the bed, so he had to crawl round on his hands and knees to gather them all up again. He was crimson with embarrassment, though the porter's face remained a mask of suave aloofness. Finally, when coins and porter were united, Michael bustled to the door to see him out, as if reluctant to be left alone with the girl he said he loved. Except of course they weren't alone – Eileen was bound to have scuttled in

308

with them, and had doubtless arranged that second bed so that she could spend the night as chaperone. And what about a third bed – for April?

Tessa drifted to the window, stared out at the floodlit garden. April completed the foursome; had been with them in the car for most of the long journey, not disapproving, just sad. Her mother was as acutely aware as she was that 2 February was B-day – or should have been, if things had gone to plan. She was mourning her lost grandchild; had been depressed and tearful yesterday, even proposed that they went away themselves – took a little break together, braved the wind and sea, stayed in a bed-and-breakfast place somewhere on the coast. Instead, she'd come to Somerset with Michael. She had chosen the location, feeling an urgent need to be in Michael country. *Her* Michael had been born and bred in the Quantocks, and his parents still had a house there – not that she'd ever seen it, or was ever likely to. Pretty crazy to flog so far for just one night away, but Michael Chalmers had seemed happy to indulge her, perhaps secretly relieved to put as many miles as possible between him and Eileen – who'd been born and bred in Suffolk.

'Tessa, darling, are you all right?'

He was hovering behind her, solicitous, as always, about her spirits and her health. Perhaps he'd got so used to nursing Eileen that it was second nature for him now to mollycoddle any woman, especially one who'd recently been ill. She had to make an effort not to shake his arm off: his constant fussing was beginning to get her down.

'What would you like to do, darling? Go and have some tea in the lounge, or take a little walk, or . . . ?'

A walk, she thought, but on my own, or just with Jasper, whose love was less of a burden. Michael's dog might gaze at her adoringly, try to stay as close to her as possible, pursue her everywhere, but at least he'd never try to mount her, or keep lamenting the huge difference in their ages, wishing he could have his life again, so as to share his puppy-youth with her.

She stood there at the window, screwing up her eyes against the floodlights' silver swathes; seeing not the dapper garden, but the barren hills beyond. The moon was out already, but thin and frail – an invalid.

Michael gave a mock shiver as he rubbed the clammy pane. 'It's a bit cold and dark for a walk, and probably too late for tea, so . . .'

She knew he wouldn't admit that, for all his apprehension, he was dying to go to bed with her, so she'd better do the decent thing and put him out of his misery by suggesting it herself. As far as April was concerned, she was away with a new and younger man, called Ivor. The name Ivor meant 'Lord' – she'd looked it up in her book of babies' names – and a Lord was someone you obeyed. If Michael wanted sex, she must submit. No. Submit was the wrong word. It was her resigned and fatalistic state which had put him off the first time, when she'd lain passive like a sack of bones, freezing at his touch. She must feign some passionate response, even play the courtesan, forget herself in him. If one of them didn't overcome their nerves, they'd land up watching television, goggle-eyed till closedown. It should be easier this time round. At least they weren't in Michael's home, with the omnipresent Eileen, and she wouldn't have to worry about pregnancy, since she'd gone back on the pill.

'Why don't we try out this enormous bed?' She tossed her coat and jacket on a chair, sprawled across the counterpane, reaching up her arms to him. Strange how small he felt, once he was lying right against her – no broad and powerful shoulders, no opera singer's chest; even his hands modest in their size and strength – modest like their owner, too timid to unbutton her blouse. She began to do it for him, touched by his reaction when he saw she wasn't wearing a bra. He was Jasper offered sirloin steak; Jasper allowed to chase the ducks; Jasper worshipping.

'Oh, Tessa, you're so beautiful!' He put out a hand to stroke her nipple – timorously, as if frightened it might break. 'May I . . . er . . . take your blouse off?'

It seemed odd that he should ask, especially with such diffidence. Michaels stripped you bare, grabbed anything they wanted. She slipped it off herself, suspecting he would find it so daunting to undress her that she'd still be sitting in her skirt and shoes by breakfast-time next morning. She wouldn't have been surprised to learn that he and Eileen had made love with half their clothes on, to save them the huge challenge of removing them. She sat up on the bed, pulled off her skirt and tights as well, as if determined to show Eileen that there was a different and more flagrant way to turn her husband on. Though Michael appeared mesmerized by the sight of her bare body, and was gazing at it with something close to awe. He was still armoured in his clothes – jacket, shirt, trousers, tie, and a hand-knitted Fair Isle pullover – the last Eileen's own handiwork, she guessed. No, she must banish Eileen from the room, concentrate on Michael – Michael Chalmers.

'Darling, you're just . . . just . . .' He was lost for words. If only Jasper were there to help him out. The dog could practically talk – made low gargling rumbling noises when he was excited or worked up, and had a whole impressive repertoire of whines and barks and yelps. All Michael had managed was a stifled exclamation as he ran his fingers through her hair. She shook it free provocatively, knew he liked to see it loose around her shoulders. The Eileen of the photographs had a short and rather sparse crop, tightly permed and flecked with grey.

'You've got marvellous hair, so thick and . . . Oh, Tessa, I don't deserve you. You're too good for me, you know.'

'Ssh,' she said. 'Don't say that.' It alarmed her that he saw her as all-good – beautiful inside and out, innocent and virtuous – when soon she would have to leave him, betray his hopeless love. He had proved that love already in so many small endearing ways, continually buying her presents – things her Oxford friends would trash – a china dog which looked identical to Jasper, a pair of woolly gloves, some boring lavender scent more suited to a grandma. And even now, he was stuttering out his compliments, absorbed still by her hair.

'It's so dark it's almost black, darling.' He glanced down at the pubic hair escaping from her pants, as if comparing the two thatches, though his hand had strayed no further than her neck.

'I'm going to award you a gold medal for your fuzz-pie! It's the greediest damn snatch in the whole of Oxfordshire, and probably in the world. And it tastes fantastic, darling – a touch of the old caviar!'

Michael Edwards' taunting voice exploded through the room. She could hear his sensual laugh, feel his hungry mouth lapping up the caviar. She pushed the other Michael off, blundered out of bed, startled by a sudden intuition that her lover was close by – staying with his parents for the weekend. For the last half-year, he'd been so far away – in a foreign northern country with a high wall all around it – but now he was a stone's throw down the road. She could reach his house in minutes, demand to be let in, dash up to his bedroom, naked, as she was.

'What's wrong?' asked Michael Chalmers, sitting up in alarm.

'Er . . . nothing. I . . . I just need the loo. And I'd better have a wash while I'm about it.' She grabbed her toilet things from the suitcase, locked the bathroom door. She was torn all ways – torn between the Michaels, torn between her duty and her memories of Oxford; recalling other tastes and smells – strawberries, mangoes, runny Brie, the taste of sweat and sperm. She unzipped her sponge-bag, her eye lighting on her pack of pills. It was the same batch she'd been prescribed in May – six months' supply, most of which she had never used. When she'd dug them out two weeks ago, she'd been so overwhelmed with misery, she had found it quite impossible to force one down until much later in the day. The half-used packet seemed symbolical of the broken-off relationship, the underdeveloped foetus; of things begun, but not completed – thwarted, unfulfilled.

She tossed the packet aside, drew out the tube of spermicide, which she'd decided to use as well as pill and condom. Three-way contraception was probably excessive, but she couldn't be too careful; had no intention of conceiving again – not with the wrong Michael. She ran some water in the basin, unwrapped the floral soap. There were several other guest-soaps in a tiny wicker basket on the shelf, along with miniature shampoos, conditioner, and bath foam. She was tempted to take them home for April, buy her a whole shower of gifts, to make up to her for the lies and the deception, for the fact that she earned nothing, let her mother keep her, contributing only grouses in return. But she could hardly admit she'd been staying in a swish hotel, when she was meant to be at Ivor's house, meeting his large family.

'And when do I meet *him*?' April had demanded, the day before she left.

'You don't, Mum – not after the way you behaved with Michael.' She had said it semi-teasingly, softened her words with a laugh, but the ensuing silence had been fraught with guilt – guilt on both their parts. She had informed her mother that Michael had vanished from her life after that fateful Sunday lunch, so the bust-up was all April's fault. It was only sheer good luck, she'd said, that she'd met another guy so soon, and she'd no intention of jeopardizing this important new relationship by bringing Ivor home.

'But he *is* younger, isn't he, Tess?' The worry in her mother's voice had amplified the guilt.

'Oh, yes – he's twenty-three.'

Ivor wasn't simply an alibi, but another kind of present for her mother. She had made him everything April could desire – dynamic, handsome, wealthy, and only four years older than herself. She longed to please her mother – as she longed to please this Michael – yet each case involved deceit and complication.

She washed, and cleaned her teeth, applied the slimy spermicide, sprayed her breasts with scent – all as a duty, an offering to Michael. When she emerged, she found him sitting on the bed in just his underpants, peeling off his navy nylon socks. She stood rigid by the wardrobe, feeling the same distaste for his body as she had experienced the first time. Although he couldn't be described as fat, his flesh was slack and flabby, the consistency of uncooked dough. He had very little body-hair, apart from a few grizzled hairs untidying his chest. Even his underpants were saggy – plain white ones drooping down his thighs. *Her* Michael's were low-cut and tight – black satin or bright scarlet – and he'd never keep them on when she was standing facing him stark naked; still less back away from her with such obvious agitation.

'I . . . er . . . think I'll have a wash myself.'

Don't go! she almost shouted, suddenly yearning to cling on to him, forget about good hygiene, ditch façades and duty, and simply pour out all her jumbled tangled feelings. If only she could tell him what the date meant: not the first of a new month, but the end of hope, of motherhood. But he had already closed the bathroom door, leaving her imprisoned in the labour ward – her baby fighting to be born, butting at her body, screaming its way out and down, only to discover that life meant death.

She lay down on the child's bed, pulled the covers right up to her chin. She was a kid again, on holiday with Daddy; nothing more expected of her than to enjoy the treats he provided: ice-cream in a silver dish, a donkey-ride, a visit to the zoo. Or perhaps he'd tell her a story. Once upon a time, there was a tall and handsome doctor. His name was Michael and he met a girl called Tessa, and they fell in love and had a son (whom he loved as much as life itself), and the three of them lived happily ever . . .

She sprang out of bed, stood trembling by the window. Why was she so shivery when the room was boiling hot? She jammed the window open, cold air slapping at her face, noises rushing in: a foreign voice rising from the kitchens, a woman's tinkling laugh, a discordant snatch of jazz. She gazed up at the rows and rows of lighted curtained squares – all these people interned in the hotel with her – foreigners and strangers, couples sharing rooms, but little else. She turned her back, surveyed their own stern room. It looked unfriendly, even menacing; the television blank and dead; the flower-print on the wall opening its devouring mouth, its stem engorged, distended.

The bathroom door was opening. She shut the window quickly, stuffed her fears and horrors into the cellar of her mind. She could no longer be a frightened child – or even a carefree one on holiday – but must now become an adult, a sophisticated woman who could rouse him, take the lead. Michael needed help as much as she did, was standing marooned between the bathroom and the bed, as if awaiting her permission to come closer. He still had the white pants on, and his hair was neatly combed. She knew he would have combed his face, groomed his ears, polished up his eyeballs, if he'd felt that it would make him more acceptable – younger, taller, handsome, like the doctor in the story.

Impulsively, she ran to him, put her arms around him, pressed his body close. She must give, not take – give him everything she could: all the love she had stored up in her childhood for her absent distant father, who'd rejected it; all the love she'd saved for Michael; bruised and hopeless love. Yet every time she thought of Michael she was paralysed again, missing him, desiring him, resentfully aware that Michael Chalmers couldn't measure up – not even literally. He was shorter still without his shoes, and she had to bend her head to kiss him. His mouth tasted of Listerine – a sterile kiss in all ways, and nothing like that wild first kiss which had knocked her off her guard. He seemed unable to relax here, his lips tentative and stiff. She tried to slip her tongue inside his mouth, but he pulled away, glancing nervously over his shoulder, as if afraid of being watched.

'Shall we switch the lights off?' he murmured, already edging to the door.

'If you like, but let's keep this bedside lamp on. It makes a nice soft glow.' It also made strange shadows, left pools of gaping darkness, where things could lurk which she didn't want to see – tiny crippled embryos; deceitful smiling doctors looming at the door on Christmas Day. She removed the heavy counterpane, deliberately narrowed down her focus to Michael Chalmers, blocking out the other faces, trying to convince herself that they were safe and snug in a nice warm cosy room. She lay back on the pillows, reached out her hand, inviting him to join her.

He crouched above her, uncomfortable and huddled, but his hazel eyes enthralled. 'Oh, Tessa, I could look at you for ever! I don't think I'll sleep a wink tonight because I can't bear the thought of closing my eyes with you lying there beside me. It seems such a dreadful waste.'

'Touch my breasts,' she whispered.

He obeyed, like Jasper – instantly – his hand clammy-damp with nerves; began talking almost too much now, as if compelled to fill the silence. 'You've got this darling little mole on your left shoulder. Would you let me kiss it? There – I have! And I love those tiny golden hairs on your arms. Everything about you's so amazing, Tessa. I mean, your breasts, they're . . .'

She drew him down on top of them, to distract him while she eased the dreadful pants off; the prick beneath them as self-effacing as himself: timid, small, and sheepish, and shrinking coyly back between the safety of his legs. She knew he'd be distraught because he didn't have an erection – again – but she must pretend it didn't matter, help him to relax. She shifted slightly, so that she could use both hands to try to stroke him stiff; also kissed him on the mouth, nibbling at his lips, inserting her deft tongue. She kept her eyes open, to study his reaction, check on any progress. He appeared lost in the kiss, savouring each sensation, his lips and tongue gradually responding, becoming more and more alive. But he remained dead further down, despite all that she was doing with her hands. He was wounded, incapacitated, his drooping prick a casualty. The hotel had become a hospital again, and now both of them were patients. But she must also play the part of nurse, restore his strength, coax him back to health.

She rolled out from underneath him, so that they were lying side by side, then knelt above his body; sensed his shock, surprise, as she took the paraplegic in her mouth. It tasted of carnation soap, and felt pappy and inert, like a piece of tepid asparagus. She must treat it very gently, not use her teeth, as her Michael had adored, but sneak her tongue lightly round and round it, while her hand moved up and down. It was Michael who had taught her, so right that she should use her skills on the man who'd bring him back. He seemed embarrassed, wary, astounded, all at once, so she suspected it was a completely new experience for him, not part of Eileen's repertoire. He was stiffening only slowly, making not the slightest sound; his silence quite unnerving, since she'd no idea whether he was enjoying it or not. The only noise was outside the door – footsteps shambling to a halt, a man's deep throaty guffaw. Her hand and mouth both faltered, and she lay transfixed, frightened they'd burst in, despite the fact she knew the door was locked. She could hear keys jangling on a

315

ring; held her breath in horror as one was inserted in the door. There was a fruitless fumbling rattle, another bray of laughter, followed by a muttered curse, then finally the footsteps lurched away, the maddening laugh fading into nothing.

Michael, too, had faded into nothing. She was right back to square one – or worse – since her mouth was getting tired, and she had cramp in her left leg, where it was doubled up uncomfortably beneath her. Well, she'd simply have to start again. She'd been called a whore, a courtesan, and whores did what they had to, regardless of their own feelings.

Michael was struggling to sit up, stuttering out apologies, suggesting that they stop, leave it till after dinner, or maybe even till the morning, when . . .

'No, just relax,' she soothed him. 'You'll be fine again in a sec. It was only the interruption which put you off your stroke.' She was the mother now, the parent, explaining, reassuring.

'But it isn't fair to you. I'm getting all the attention and the pleasure, and you're getting nothing back.'

'Well, I only hope it *is* pleasure. Maybe I'm not doing it quite right. Would you rather I . . . ?'

'Tessa, it's . . . it's heaven!'

His voice was husky with emotion, and his rapturous expression confirmed his words, gave them still more force. So why was he still limp? Was there something physically wrong with him? That might be the reason why he'd never had more children – he was incapable of the act. Or could he sense the fact that she wasn't genuinely involved; that her feelings, body, passion, were committed to another man, which meant she was short-changing him? She would never find her real Michael if she didn't serve his namesake – that was the unwritten law.

He continued to protest that he was doing all the taking, and she the giving, but she wanted it that way; felt no flicker of desire herself, only a relief that he couldn't enter her.

'I'm loving it, don't worry. It's great for me as well. But let's try something different. You sit in that armchair and I'll kneel between your legs.'

'Oh, Tessa . . .' He seemed overwhelmed, bemused, moving almost in a dream towards the pink plush chair. 'Do you realize what it means to me when you do all this for me? I've never met a girl like you before. Well, I haven't met that many girls at all. But you're

316

unique, incredible – so . . . so giving and so clever. And when you say it's great for you, I just can't tell you how that makes me feel. And even if I could find the words, I'm not sure you'd understand. You see, I've always been . . .'

The sentence died away. She could see that he was close to tears; felt choked herself by the fervour in his voice, by his sense of humble gratitude. She suspected he was hinting at some sort of sexual problem in his past. Perhaps beloved Eileen hadn't loved him physically – been prudish, even frigid; or perhaps he'd never satisfied her, or the two of them had been somehow incompatible. Whatever the frustrations, she mustn't let him dwell on them, but keep him in the here and now; be the clever giving girl he'd just described.

She knelt back on her heels, spread his legs apart, started gently kissing the insides of his thighs, then moved her lips towards his balls; also changed location from Somerset to the Cotswolds; moved her mind to another hotel room. The last weekend she'd been away with Michael, she had sucked his balls again; driven him half-wild, been almost too impassioned and voracious. He'd had to warn her to be careful; explained how vulnerable they were – much more so than his cock. 'Look, if you hold them in your mouth with almost no pressure at all, then you can use your tongue quite firmly, draw it up from the base and gently lick the undersides, sort of pushing them against my prick, okay?'

Okay, she told herself as she followed his instructions, encouraged by the other Michael's sudden gasp of pleasure – spontaneous, near-passionate. She made her tongue as loving as she could – gentle yet insistent, licking a slow path from their lumpy base to the tautening root of the prick. She tried to blank out the aversion she was feeling, the unpleasant texture of puckered flabby flesh; take comfort from the fact he was responding – his excited cries gradually crescendoing.

He was stiff, at last – really stiff – a triumph for them both. She changed position, sucked his small but swollen prick right into her mouth, kept her lips braced around it, tongue flicking back and forth. She could feel him thrusting, pumping, as if he'd suddenly been galvanized, transformed from a shy spaniel to a wolf. She relaxed her throat, to try to make more room for him, and also stop herself from gagging; was rewarded by an exultant strangled shout.

'Oh, darling, it's so wonderful! Oh precious, precious, precious . . .'

Semen spurted on to her tongue – warm and salty, the consistency of blood. Michael gave a jarring cry, then slumped back silent in the chair, his deflating prick sliding slowly out. She dropped down to the carpet, hands across her ears. She couldn't suppress that cry – a baby's cry, anguished and accusing, screaming on and on. She was tasting blood, swallowing blood, the blood of her murdered baby. She spat it out on the carpet, kept spitting, retching, spitting, in an attempt to purge her mouth.

She could hear a voice somewhere far above her, an appalled and anxious voice, but trying to offer help. It must be Michael, come at last, realizing the date.

She lunged towards him, started pounding on his chest with her clenched fists. 'I killed him, Michael, don't you see? I killed our child, our son! If I hadn't murdered him in that hospital, you'd have held him in your arms today.'

26

'TELL ME ABOUT Oxford,' Michael said, sipping his schooner of sherry, which had come free with the meal – a special St Valentine's Day promotion.

Tessa broke a piece off her bread roll and stuffed it in her mouth, to give herself time to think up a reply. There was only one thing she could tell him about Oxford – and that was Michael – but the moment wasn't right. It seemed never to be right, and she was becoming increasingly impatient at devoting so much time to Michael Chalmers with so little in return.

'Don't you miss it?' he was prompting. 'I mean, all your friends and the social whirl and the lectures and . . .'

'No,' she said. 'I don't.' She could barely remember her friends now, and since she'd ignored their Christmas cards and letters, they had stopped writing altogether. And 'social whirl' was hardly an apt description of her leisure-time at Oxford.

'What periods of history did you study? Or did you start at the beginning and . . . ?'

She arranged the crumbling flakes of roll into a pattern on her plate. It was a sign that things were strained between them that Michael was reduced to this polite interrogation. She had snapped at him ten minutes ago, when he told her he adored her; refused to drink the toast he'd proposed to Saint Valentine and love. Now he was trying to make amends, sticking to safe subjects, showing a pathetic interest in a life that was dead and gone.

She answered dutifully but flatly, still fiddling with the crumbs. 'Well, we were meant to cover a good chunk of British history – to give us a basic grounding, I suppose – and if I'd stayed, I'd have ploughed through a fair bit of that. But we also did special subjects which we studied in more detail. I chose Early Gothic France the last term I was there.'

It obviously didn't mean much, so she reeled off a few twelfth-century names – Abbots Suger and Guibert, Galbert of Bruges, Orderic Vitalis, Abelard, Saint Bernard – but he looked still more perplexed.

'Have you never heard of any of them?'

'No, I'm afraid I haven't.'

'Not even Abelard and Heloïse?'

He shook his head in embarrassment. 'You must think me dreadfully ignorant.'

'Not at all. They're only very marginal.' She could see now how she had wasted time and effort studying esoteric subjects which meant nothing to most people. All that arid stuff about Abelard's dialectic was all very well in the ivory tower of Oxford, but what relevance did it have to normal life? Abelard had championed logic, regarded it as an instrument of order, applied it to all fields of thought, including matters mystical, used it to elucidate his faith. Saint Bernard had opposed him, been equally pig-headed; the two twelfth-century giants entangled in abstractions and irrelevances, and fighting tooth and nail. And to top it all, Bernard had been made a saint, when he was actually an intolerant fanatic who bungled most of what he touched.

'I have to admit I was never any good at history,' Michael confessed, unfolding his paper napkin, which was embellished with a red heart in the corner. 'I just scraped through my O-level, but I found it a bit musty – you know, all those dates and battles. Though I wouldn't go as far as Henry Ford.'

'Oh, you mean history being bunk?'

'Yes. Except I don't suppose he meant that. I'm sure it's tremendously important, but I simply wasn't bright enough to do it proper justice.'

'Abelard saw history as the Truth,' she told him, suddenly envying the philosopher his certainty. 'Truth with a capital T. In his time, most people took it for granted that history had to mean something, because it was part of God's plan, and the product of His will. So all the musty dates and battles, as you call them, make ultimate sense. But if you don't believe in God,' she shrugged, 'then Truth and history go out of the window as well. But maybe you're religious?'

Michael appeared as awkward as if she'd asked him about his

bowel-habits. 'Well,' he answered hesitantly, 'Eileen and I always used to go to church on Sunday. And I like to think there's Someone up there. I mean, it helps with death, doesn't it? – to know you'll be reunited with your loved ones, and even with your pets. Eileen used to believe in a sort of doggy heaven – green fields with lots of lamp-posts, and no leads, or baths, or horrid spoilsport notices saying "Keep off the grass!"'

Tessa didn't laugh. A phrase from the *Historia Calamitatum* was suddenly twingeing in her mind – Heloïse's chilling words to Abelard: *'Now only one thing remains; that we shall be destroyed, and that there will follow no less pain than there was love before.'* She could already feel the pain – the bitterness of failure in her hopeless search for Michael. Yet she mustn't let her suffering show. Michael Chalmers was quite anxious enough about her state of mind; had been so distressed in Somerset when she'd screamed and sobbed over the corpse of her dead baby, it had wrecked the whole weekend. This weekend was an attempt to set things right, to have a second mini-holiday without the trauma of the first. He'd chosen a much cheaper hotel, only fifteen miles from home; was trying to keep things casual and relaxed; save her from the strain of a long drive. If only she could explain to him that it wasn't the motoring which tired her, but the never-ceasing conflict in her head: the pull between the Michaels; the images of babies – dead, alive, deformed.

'Was it you who ordered the soup?'

A beanpole of a waitress had sauntered up to their table, carrying two bowls of murky liquid with tiny globules of yellow fat floating on the surface.

'That's right,' said Michael. 'Oxtail.'

Tessa peered at the pallid khaki-brown, wondering if the girl had brought mushroom by mistake. The menu described it as 'home-made' and 'heartwarming', but was mistaken on both counts, since it was clearly from a packet and only just lukewarm. They had booked dinner in the hotel restaurant because it was offering 'a lovers' feast', with the lure of a free aperitif and ten per cent off every couple's bill. It was really a glorified Berni Inn, but the basic steak and chicken had been romanticized with pretentious names. She had ordered Chicken Cleopatra, while Michael had chosen Rump Steak Madame Pompadour. The restaurant itself was called The Far Pavilions, for no other reason she could fathom than the presence of a few panoramic photographs of Thomas Cook's Far East. There was a plastic rose in a plastic vase on every red-clothed table, and schmaltzy muzak was playing in the background, all in honour of Saint Valentine. Michael had made an effort, too, and was sporting a new ambitious tie in a swirl of vivid blues, which was entirely out of place with his stolid tweedy jacket. He had also grown his hair, presumably because she'd mentioned several weeks ago that she liked long hair on men. She hadn't meant on older men, and poor Michael's just looked messy, straggling over his collar and slightly curling at the ends.

His eyes were on her – as always – and she sensed that he was about to ask another question. If he couldn't keep the conversation circling endlessly around their love, then he liked to quiz her about her health, her past, her future; storing up each answer like a new jewel in his treasure-trove. If only she'd been as zealous in enquiring about her own lover. Yet she hadn't even managed to bring the subject up, despite the fact that she was constantly on the alert for some convincingly casual lead-in, some context which would make it seem appropriate. The occasion hadn't arisen so far, but why not now – tonight? Wasn't it the perfect date? – the one day in the year dedicated to lovers, when the birds were said to choose their mates, start to build their nests.

She decided to take the plunge, leaned forward in her chair. 'Nice soup,' she said, to please him, then made her voice sound chatty and low-key. 'You know Dr Alan Reynolds?'

Michael put his spoon down. 'Yes.'

'I wondered if you could tell me a bit about him. I want to change my doctor, you see, but I'm not sure where to start. I mean, would you recommend him, or maybe one of the other GPs in his practice?'

'Well, I don't know him as a doctor, of course, but he's extremely nice as a person – an easy-going sort of chap; always got the time of day for everyone. I've played golf with him on a few occasions, and he's a very decent sportsman, not one of these prima donnas who sulk if they don't win, or go storming off the course.'

'And how about his partner, Dr Edwards?'

'I hardly know him at all. But Eileen met him several times. You see, she was very close to Paula Reynolds – they went to the same dog-training class, every Tuesday night – and as Paula and the Edwardses were good friends, they sometimes found themselves together at various social gatherings and what-have-you.'

Tessa smeared butter on the remnants of her roll, silently blessing his late wife, who, though unconscious of the fact, had been pre-ordained to play her part, lead her closer to Michael. 'And what did Eileen think of them?' she asked.

'To be honest, she preferred the wife.'

'Joyce, you mean?'

He nodded. 'She's his second wife, you know.'

Her spoon was halfway to her mouth. It fell back in her bowl, soup splashing on her dress. 'His . . . his second wife?'

'Yes. Apparently he married very young, just a month after he qualified. Hey, careful, Tessa darling! You don't want to spoil that lovely frock.'

She let him mop up the spills, glad of the distraction; only wishing he could wipe away as easily the dark and threatening pictures in her mind. She could see Dr Edwards' first wife – ravishing, provocative, a figure she knew well, since she was more or less identical to Michael Edwards' fiancée. She pressed both hands against her forehead. Why were there so many dangerous rivals – all those nurses at the hospital, Joyce herself, and now this bolt from the blue? How could she compete? She was a nothing, a non-starter. 'Get out!' she shouted soundlessly, trying to drive them all away; focus only on that first wife – the most recent threat, contender. Did Dr Edwards see her still? Were there any children – other Michaels, Jon-Jons – whom he loved and fed and cherished?

Michael gently prised her hands away, his own hands cosseting, like his voice. Did she have a headache; should he go and buy some aspirin; was the room too hot? She answered no to everything, doing all she could to appear calm and in control, swilling down her panic with a determined draught of sherry. She mustn't frighten him again, spoil another evening. She wiped her mouth, feigning an air of nonchalance; resumed the conversation, as if she were simply making small talk. 'So what happened?' she enquired. 'Did the first wife die, or . . . ?'

Michael cleared his throat. 'No,' he muttered. 'It ended in divorce.'

'Oh, I see. D'you happen to know why? And when exactly? And did *he* leave her, or the other way round?'

Michael drummed his fingers on the table, infected with her own unease. 'Look, it's a rather tricky subject. D'you mind if we don't go into it?'

'Yes,' she said, 'I do mind.'

The fingers stopped their drumming, started worrying at a loose thread in his jacket. 'It was all years and years ago, Tessa. And I was only told in confidence. Eileen made me promise never to say a word to anyone. I couldn't break that trust.'

'It must be something pretty horrendous if it has to be swept under the carpet.'

'Not at all. It was just an unhappy chapter in his past, and according to Joyce, he prefers to leave it in his past, and get on with the present.'

Tessa pushed her soup away, all appetite lost for anything save news of Dr Edwards. 'It sounds more and more mysterious.'

'Not really. I suppose he's scared of gossip, especially in his line of work. Doctors are so much in the public eye, they don't want people tittle-tattling.'

'Well, it's because he is a doctor I feel I have a right to know. After all, I don't want to change to a GP who's hiding something scandalous.'

'I can absolutely assure you, darling, that it isn't scandalous – nothing of that sort. More rotten luck, I'd say – the sort of awful tragedy which strikes without any warning.'

Tessa picked up her fork and jabbed the prongs viciously into her palm. The physical pain was nothing compared with the wound and shock of Dr Edwards' tragedy. How could she have researched his life, spent so long hunting down the details, yet missed a major disaster? 'You've got to tell me, Michael. It's not fair for you to hint at things, then leave me in the dark.'

'I'm sorry, darling, honestly. I'd no idea it would matter to you a jot. I mean, you don't even know the fellow.'

'Yes, but he may be my GP.'

'But I thought you were going to change to Dr Reynolds.'

She frowned, played for time by re-buttering her roll. 'I . . . I was, but someone told me Dr Edwards is better.'

'Well, I couldn't give an opinion on that, but from what I've heard, they're both extremely sound. And it's not their private lives which matter, surely, but their expertise and training and . . .'

'Didn't you like the soup?'

The waitress had frisked up again, and was gazing reproachfully from bowl to bowl; both scarcely touched and now congealing with a scum on top.

'Yes, it's . . . er . . . very tasty.' Michael grabbed his spoon and took an eager mouthful, as if he couldn't bear to upset another female.

'We're just saving a bit of room for the main course,' Tessa put in tactfully.

'Well, it's ready when you are. Want me to fetch it now?'

She removed the bowls, returned in minutes with two thick brown oval platters. 'One Chicken Cleopatra with French fries and onion rings, and one Steak Madame Pompadour with baked potato and sour-cream dressing. Now who was having what?'

'The Cleopatra for me,' said Tessa, shrinking in dismay from the daunting pile of chips, the greasy onion rings in their thick overcoats of batter. Both the chicken and the steak were decorated with little paper flags, again bearing a red heart. She checked the other tables – red hearts in profusion. If only love were as simple as that – a word, a colour, a symbol – mass-produced, renewable.

'And you get a free trip to our salad bar, remember. But one trip only, I'm afraid. You can't go back for seconds.'

Tessa glanced across at the array of oblong dishes – sweetcorn, coleslaw, hard-boiled eggs, and at least a dozen other salads, all slurped with gluey mayonnaise. She couldn't cope with that lot, as well as what was on her plate. Yet if she didn't eat, Michael would start fretting, and they'd waste time on the problems of her appetite and health, rather than getting back to Dr Edwards. She cut a chip in two, forced down the smaller piece.

'Just tell me who his first wife was – I mean, her name and what she did.'

'Tessa, darling, let's leave that subject, shall we? Don't you see how difficult you're making it? I feel torn between you and Eileen, and, anyway, it's a complicated story – not so much the wife, but . . .' He broke off, as if he'd said too much already; pulled the flag out of his steak and began fiddling with it nervously, poking its sharp end into the tablecloth.

Tessa put her fork down, her whole attention riveted on those last few cryptic words: 'not so much the wife, but . . .' What on earth could Michael mean, and if it was so complicated, then why hadn't she discovered it when she'd been working on her thesis? Dr Edwards must have hushed it up. That would account for the big hole in her biography; that worryingly blank stretch, which she had never understood. Didn't it point to some disaster which had to be concealed, some trauma he'd kept under wraps? She chewed the lemon slice which had garnished her braised chicken, to kid Michael she was eating still, then slipped in a few more questions. 'You say there was a tragedy, but what sort of thing do you mean? Tragedy's a frightening word, so I can't just shrug it off. And did it happen to the wife, or to Dr Edwards himself? And why was . . . ?'

'Look, please don't ask me, Tessa. There's nothing I can say. I promised Eileen faithfully I wouldn't tell a soul.'

'Yes, but I'm not just anybody. She probably meant odd friends, people she couldn't trust to keep a confidence. You know you can trust me. You *love* me, Michael – or so you keep on saying – and yet you dig in your heels when I ask you about one really vital thing.'

'But that's the point – I can't make out why it should matter quite so much. All right, I can see you want to feel secure with whoever you choose as your GP, but there are half a dozen doctors in that practice, so if you're worried about Edwards, why not go for one of the other five?'

She detected a note of irritation in his voice – the first time he'd ever been anything but totally indulgent. She was wasting her breath, pushing him too far – worse, endangering her whole plan. He would never betray Eileen in cold blood, but if she waited till he was wild, on heat and reckless – as he had been when he climaxed in her mouth – he would do anything she asked. She was being made to realize by some unseen force or power that she hadn't played her part; that apart from that one session, she had cheated him and rationed him, as he was rationing her now. She had kept her distance sexually since that Saturday in the Quantocks; actually spent the night in the child's bed, so he wouldn't touch her in his sleep. How grudging she had been, how stubbornly shortsighted. The fact that he was resisting in his turn was the clue to her own failure, her lack of any progress. But she was being shown the way; told how she should act – not only in the bedroom, but here at table, too. No good picking at her food, making him worry needlessly that she was sickening for some illness. She must eat with greed and gusto, as she had always done with Michael; savour every mouthful, relish taste and smell.

She crammed in a chunk of chicken breast, then half a dozen chips, only pausing for a second to gulp down her Blue Nun.

'Fantastic wine!' she said. 'And the chicken's really great – so tender I can cut it with my fork.'

Michael cut into his own steak, like a happy prisoner granted a reprieve, allowed at last to relax and enjoy his meal. He swallowed his first mouthful, then cocked his head, listening to the music. They were playing 'Endless Love', and he began to mouth the words, repeating

326

them with such intense emotion she had a sudden crazy fantasy he'd written them himself, then ordered his private love-song to be relayed on the loudspeakers.

> 'My love, there's only you in my life,
> The only thing that's right . . .
> And I want to share all my love
> With you – no one else will do –
> Yes, you will always be my endless love.'

The second verse was drowned by a burst of clapping. An enormous ice-cream sundae was being carried in triumphantly and set down on the table next to theirs. Three celebratory sparklers were spluttering on the summit, like beacons on the Mount Everest of cream. It looked enough for an army – bananas, cherries, pineapple, heaped up in the dish, and at least half a dozen different coloured ice-creams. The lower foothills were sprinkled lavishly with flaked and toasted nuts, curls of chocolate, shreds of candied peel. Tessa watched the four couples at the table all dig in with their spoons, wolfing cream and ice-cream, crunching nuts, guzzling juicy cherries. That sundae was important, a sign to her how she must be herself – unstinting, inexhaustible, and wildly hugely sensuous. She must allow Michael to devour her, suck out her cream and syrup, enjoy all her luscious fruits. She must sparkle for him, overflow; froth and flame and glisten.

'Hey, Michael, shall we order one the same?'

'Not quite as big, I hope!'

'Yes, just as big! I'm starving. I don't know what's come over me, but I feel I could really pig myself today.'

He gazed at her with such undisguised relief, she felt tears start to her eyes. He'd been agonizing recently about how little she was eating. Eileen had died of stomach cancer, which had started with a loss of weight, so he was probably secretly terrified that history would repeat itself. It was part of his obsessive love to watch her every mouthful; tempt her with choice titbits, like a scraggy puppy who needed fattening up. She must respect that love, encourage it, despite her guilt at being unable to return it. She picked her wine-glass up again. 'So how about that toast you were proposing? Shall we drink it now?'

He raised his glass, delighted, chinked it against her own, but left the words to her this time.

'To St Valentine's Day,' she whispered. 'And to true and endless love. And to a perfect meal with a marvellous man. And especially to our last course – the one we'll have upstairs!'

'Dry me!' Tessa ordered, as she emerged dripping from the bath. She snuggled against Michael, enveloped in two towels. He began to dab her gingerly, but she didn't want things tentative; knew she had to play the hussy, the abandoned panting whore – and this time bring some conviction to the role. She tossed her hair back, thrust her naked breasts towards his face. He hadn't finished undressing, so she unzipped his neat grey trousers; discovered he'd bought new underpants – white boxer shorts patterned with tiny aeroplanes. She fumbled at the waistband, touched, despite herself. He had tried so hard, and even though he'd got it wrong – looking comic rather than sexy, with Tiger Moths swooping across his groin – there was no way she could laugh at his earnest wish to please her.

She was still feeling rather thrown by the fact he had her photo in his wallet. She'd noticed it in the restaurant when he was settling up with the waitress, and had realized only then why he'd asked her very casually, a week or so ago, if she happened to have a snapshot of herself. She'd dug out a rather ancient one taken in the garden, with a background of a rubbish heap and a yard or two of washing-line. He had snipped off line and rubbish, keeping only her head and smile, which were now treasured in his wallet and carried with him everywhere. It had startled her so much because what she'd craved two months ago (when she'd first seen Joyce's photograph in Dr Edwards' wallet) had happened with the wrong Michael. Apart from that cruel irony, it was also a reminder of how far she was from the goal of finding the real one; of sitting in his pocket, nestling close against him every day.

Well, all the more reason for changing course this evening; using every trick in the book to satisfy this Michael, so he'd divulge what he knew about Dr Michael Edwards. She eased his pants off sensuously, hands lingering on his buttocks, stroking down his calves, then returned her slow soft fingers to the insides of his thighs. He wasn't stiff at all yet, but that was her own fault, for behaving so hysterically their first weekend away. She would have to win his trust again, prove that sex needn't end in trauma.

She kissed him on the mouth, tasting fierce mint toothpaste, which had killed the subtle flavour of their rum-and-raisin ice-cream. His expression was ecstatic; his eyes were tightly shut – the closed lids like a barrier partitioning them in separate worlds. She had deserted him, pushed off, left this cheap and garish room, and returned to Michael Edwards – to his arms, his smell, his skills, his bed, his bulk. The kiss grew wilder, involving teeth and tongues; Michael Chalmers learning – her obedient eager pupil, while she was back in Oxford, as Michael Edwards' acolyte.

At last, she pulled away. Michael slowly opened his eyes again, gazed at her, entranced. 'God bless you,' he said softly, his voice unsteady and intense. 'I thank Him every night, you know, for sending you. I know I don't deserve you, and when I think of what you give me – all your love and . . .'

His reverent, almost prayerful tone roused shame in her, and pity. She was tempted to ditch her role of whore and play the part of mother – make up to him for the fact that the love he prized so much was nothing but a sham. But that would ruin everything, turn him into a little boy, when he was limp enough already. She must try a different tack.

She took his hand, led him to the mean-sized bed with its hideous purple coverlet in some shiny cheapo fabric. The only other things in the room were a wooden chair, a tatty built-in cupboard, and what was labelled a hospitality tray, consisting of cups, kettle, tea-bags and a mini-pack of custard creams, with a notice propped against it, saying 'Beware of overfilling kettle'.

She stretched out on the bed, settled him beside her, trying not to recoil from his small and pasty body, the almost hairless legs, the red mark round his waist where the elastic from his boxer shorts had impressed its knobbly pattern on his skin. She cupped her left hand round his prick, while her right hand dawdled down her own body and began to stroke her pubic hair. He watched her with a mixture of guilt and fascination, like a schoolboy sneaking his first look at a pornographic video. She opened her legs wider, let her fingers brush her labia, languorously caressing them, spreading them apart. She was doing it for Michael, could hear his gloating voice: 'You've got these quite amazing labia, which stick out like little wings.'

She tweaked the little wings, recalling all his other words – excited and admiring words, which had turned her from a novice into Jezebel, Delilah. He'd loved to see her masturbate; had encouraged her to go quite wild their last weekend away together – that fatal worrying weekend, when she'd realized she was pregnant still, but had let her body scorch and slam, while her shocked mind slunk away. He'd known nothing of her fears; had simply egged her on; told her she looked sensational with her fist stuck up her snatch, and her nipples stiff like tent-pegs. She'd come five times in a row, spurred by his involvement, the way he seemed to share each come; crying out when she did, gliding his hands across her breasts, then teasingly down her thighs; slipping a finger into her mouth so she could bite it at the height of each explosion. His namesake was less blatant; still the paralysed voyeur, watching furtively but greedily as she licked her finger, slid it slowly in. She moved her hips in time with it, circling, gently rocking; eyes now closed, so she could transport herself to Foxlow Woods, feel the warm sun smooching her, the tall voluptuous grasses tickling her bare skin.

Her hand faltered, fingers tensing, her whole body taut, uptight. Something had gone wrong. It was hurting, really hurting; what had once been pleasure now experienced as pain. She must have been damaged in the hospital – maybe even deliberately, as a punishment for murdering her child. Punishment like that was only natural. Abelard had suffered it himself, accepting his castration as perfectly appropriate. *'They attacked that part of my body which had sinned.'* The same applied to her. How could she arouse herself by fondling her baby's passage to the world? That baby had been dead, deformed; must have somehow tainted her as it struggled out and down; left her insides botched. And if one small finger hurt so much, then how in God's name would she bear it when Michael started ramming in? If only they could go to bed to sleep. She was so tired she ached all over; her body like a dragging weight with nothing to support it; her mind so full of chaos it needed emptying into a litter-bin. She longed to transform Michael from a lover to a nurse, so that instead of trying to screw her, he would wrap her in a blanket, dose her with a happy-pill, and sit and watch beside her while she slept. Or if only she could call for April; hear her mother charging up the stairs – a Band-Aid for her damaged cunt; some sweeties for the invalid.

She was tempted to escape, to dash back home and tell her mother everything – that there wasn't any Ivor, no blossoming romance, no wealthy cultured parents who already accepted her as one of the family; that there was only Michael Chalmers, his thirty-four-years-older body damp against her own. But she couldn't let him down, especially not tonight, when she'd committed herself to serve him, focus solely on his pleasure. She'd simply have to accept the pain, or try to disregard it; continue to play Jezebel, as her atonement for his own pain. He was already looking anxious, probably wondering why she'd stopped; snuffed the sparklers on his sundae, axed the best treat of his life. She spread her legs again, used two fingers this time, thrusting them right up, and smiling when they hurt – for Michael Edwards' sake. She began to rub herself quite fiercely, determined to keep her mind on Foxlow Woods and the Cotswolds; remembering how she'd come then, duplicating the movements – the screwed-up face, splayed legs. She added Michael's feverish voice to help her bear the pain; his sudden rasping shout resounding through the countryside: 'You randy little bitch – you great brazen shameless hussy!'

Her eyes blinked slowly open. She could hear a different voice – sheepish, inarticulate, as it stammered out her name.

'Oh, Tessa, you're . . . you're . . .'

She must be doing right. Michael Chalmers was in paradise, judging by his face; his small prick stirring slightly as she cradled it with her other hand. She wouldn't stint him this time. If she'd come five times with Michael Edwards, then he should have no less.

'Does it turn you on to watch me?' she asked tauntingly.

'Christ, yes!'

She had never heard him swear before, realized he was so carried away, that his usual tepid language must now seem quite inadequate. She could feel his eyes devouring her as she changed position on the bed, kneeling up and leaning back against the wall, with her pelvis pushed right forward and her hair streaming down behind her. Michael Edwards had taught her that, and had joined in with his hand and mouth; lying underneath her with his head between her knees. She craved to see him there now; to be the brazen hussy screaming out 'Go *on!*' instead of the cringeing booby struggling not to cry. At least it didn't matter that her voice was choked, since he could interpret that as passion.

'Oh, it's wonderful!' she sobbed. 'I just can't tell you how it feels!'

He squeezed her hand, the damp and sticky hand she was using to torment herself – and enthral him in the process. Her other hand was busy with his fast-reviving prick. That was all that mattered – Michael was responding – his eyes burning with excitement, his cheeks a hectic pink, a dribble of saliva seeping from his lips. His words were incoherent – a babble of superlatives, mixed with astonished exclamations that any girl would actually let him watch her, and could still be so worked up when she'd come several times already.

She dropped down to the bed, so that she was crouching on all fours, gently took Michael's hand and guided it between her legs, using his finger as a dildo. His hand hurt more than hers did; the dildo clumsy, jabbing at her, sending waves of scarlet pain juddering through her groin.

'It's fantastic!' she cried out. 'Don't stop. Go on, go on!'

His prick was pluming in response; his face flushed with bursting pride. She didn't begrudge him his delight. Every climax she feigned – however much it cost her – was a milestone on the way to Michael Edwards. Later on this evening, she would be rewarded in her turn.

'Oh, Tessa, *please*, I . . .' The sentence petered out. He was attempting to show her with his body what he wanted; nudging his stiff prick against her thighs, begging to come into her.

She stroked the swollen tip, then ran a tantalizing finger right down to the hilt and back. 'Would you like it if I came like that when *you* come – at exactly the same time?'

He nodded, too hyped up to form any words at all now. His hair was damp, dishevelled, one strand falling in his eyes; a film of sweat glistening on his forehead.

'And come so loudly I wake the entire hotel?'

He laughed, a whooping belly-laugh, nothing like his usual modest chuckle.

'And shall we do it like dogs? You be Jasper, I'll be Snowy.' She pulled him to the floor, knelt down on the carpet, explained the way she wanted him to mount her. She kept working on his prick, kneading it and boosting it, to make sure it didn't slacken while she spelt out the conditions. It was vital that he understood.

'Listen, Michael, darling, there's something I want *you* to do – for me.'

'Of course,' he panted, desperate to ram in; his body braced and quivering like a greyhound's at the starting-gate.

'You promise that you'll do it – I mean, promise really solemnly?'

He didn't answer, but his prick was shouting 'yes!'; no longer able to hold back, but butting roughly in.

She kept her own hips still. 'Say "I promise",' she commanded.

'I promise.'

'I promise faithfully to do whatever Tessa asks me.'

'I promise faithfully to do whatever . . .' He was coming – straight away – slamming from behind; his laboured gasps and whimperings swelling to a full-throated Jasper yelp. She kept her own part of the bargain, yammering and heaving; trying to blank out the sensation of being torn apart. How could such a small man grind and stab like that, and why was there no room for him, when she'd always opened avidly for Michael? But Michael was the reason she was doing it at all. Once she was restored to him, the ordeal would be over, and any moment now she would be closer to that goal; shown the way by what Eileen Chalmers knew. She gave a last wild shout of triumph, arching her whole body up, shimmying with her hips, and paying Chalmers in advance by her final breathless words.

'Michael, you're amazing! That was the best come of my life.'

27

TESSA STOOD OUTSIDE the Oxfam shop, gazing at the wedding dress on the dummy in the window. It was perfect – simply perfect, with its nipped-in waist and full dramatic skirt, the embroidery on the bodice, the long tight buttoned sleeves. And it was obviously significant that it was being sold by Oxfam, and not by the Cancer shop or the Spastics Society, or some mere market stall. Oxfam had been born in Oxford – as had her love itself. The only problem was the price. There was no ticket on it – always a bad sign – and she had precisely £4.22 in her purse. She'd still not found a job, and although she'd now applied for Income Support, it hadn't yet come through. Even when it did, she would have to give the bulk of it to April. That was only fair, when she'd been living at home for the last six months and contributing almost nothing.

She pushed the door of the shop, which shared its smells (and customers) with the adjoining Indian takeaway. She grimaced at the waft of spice and curry; waited at the counter behind a thin bald-headed man haggling over a job-lot of old crockery.

'I'm sorry,' said the woman in charge, a horsy-looking matron with over-white false teeth (not unlike the china she was handling). 'We can't reduce our prices. It's one of Oxfam's rules.'

Tessa was familiar with the rule, had regretted it a score of times in the past, though never more so than today. Who would sell a wedding dress for £4.22?

The old gaffer shuffled out with a curse, but not his cups. The woman cleared them from the counter, then smiled at Tessa with a kindly 'Can I help?'

'Yes,' said Tessa. 'I was just wondering what you were asking for the wedding dress.' She pointed to the window, hoping that her offhand tone would conceal her burning interest.

'It's £19.99 – a real bargain, I'd say! It's a designer dress, you know, and looks as if it would fit you to a T. The girl who brought it in was very tall and slim.'

'Could I try it on?'

'Yes, 'course you can – if you don't mind waiting while I get it off the model. It's quite a job, what with that train, and all the buttons.'

Tessa wondered how on earth she could find the extra money. She had to have the dress. It was meant for her – she knew that – a style she loved, and exactly the right size. And £20 was peanuts, when it must have cost a thousand, new. It had also turned up when she needed it, just six weeks before the wedding. The whole thing was intended – the fact she'd happened to walk this way, for no particular reason and no plans to buy a thing, as if guided by some power.

The dress felt weighty, sumptuous, when the woman eventually laid it in her arms; the satin slippery-cool; the embroidery encrusted with tiny gleaming pearls. The only blemish was a slight yellowy patch under each arm – a perspiration stain. Its owner must have sweated at the ceremony – nervous yet elated, as she would be herself.

She slipped into the tiny cell-like fitting-room, with its skimpy floral curtain and scratchy square of carpet – hardly an appropriate place to try on so grand a gown. She pulled off her old tracksuit, noticing how creased it was, bundled it into the corner like a piece of dirty washing. She held her breath as she stepped into the dress, deliberately refusing to look in the mirror until she was certain that it fitted her and she'd done up all the fastenings. It wasn't easy on her own – the long back zip kept sticking, and the buttons on the sleeves had maddeningly small buttonholes which called for skill and patience. She wished she had a bridesmaid – no, half a dozen bridesmaids – in stunning midnight-blue, to wait on her and serve her, make the last adjustments, arrange the stiffened petticoats, smooth the flouncy skirt. The saleswoman had asked if she could help, but she didn't want those veined arthritic hands pawing at the satin. Everything connected with her wedding must be beautiful and fresh.

At last, she was ready to check on her reflection. Tentatively, she raised her head, astonished at the transformation. She was no longer a scruffy dropout, but a triumphant radiant bride – the shimmering white contrasting with the darkness of her hair; the low scoop-neck revealing just a hint of teasing cleavage; the sleeves balling out at the top, then narrowing down the forearm, clinging at the wrist. There was no room to unfurl the train in the confined space of the cubicle, so she walked out through the curtain and let it flow behind her, enchanted by its swishing sound, the feeling of sheer weight. She practised gliding to and fro, as if she were processing up the aisle, self-consciously at first, but gradually gaining confidence. Every eye had turned towards her; all the other customers admiring and exclaiming.

The woman who had served her was fairly goggling at the change. 'It's sensational!' she exclaimed. 'It looks as if it was made for you.'

Tessa shut her eyes. The people in the shop had become the congregation, awed to solemn silence as she repeated her vows; watching as the bridegroom slipped the gold ring on her finger, then sealed the marriage contract with a kiss. She yearned to prolong that kiss, to linger in the church amidst the fragrant smell of orange-blossom, instead of returning to the reek of Chicken Madras and the pressing problem of how to raise £15.77, and raise it double quick.

'Could you reserve the dress for me?' she asked. 'I'm definitely going to buy it, but I haven't brought my chequebook, and I'm a bit short of ready cash. I'll have to go and fetch some.'

The woman scooped a strand of greying hair back into her bun, secured it with two hairpins. 'I'm afraid we're not allowed to put things by. It's against the company rules.'

Damn the rules, thought Tessa, embarrassed when she realized that several people in the shop were listening in, with undisguised curiosity. 'I could leave you £4.20 as deposit,' she offered *sotto voce*, fumbling for her purse.

'I'm sorry, dear, it really is forbidden. They're very strict about how we run the shop.' She edged a little closer, lowered her voice to a confidential whisper. 'But look, I'll tell you what I'll do. If you promise me you'll come straight back with the money, I'll pop the dress on this shelf here. It's so high up, I doubt anyone else will see it. You'd better give me your name, though, in case I've gone for tea. Then I can tell the others you're coming in, so there won't be any mix-up.'

Tessa hesitated, invariably confused when she had to give her name. Was she Edwards? Chalmers? Reeves?

'Hughes,' she said uncertainly. 'Pat Hughes.' Her friend from school was also getting married. She hadn't seen Pat in an age, had fobbed off all her overtures and phone-calls, pretending she was still unwell, or too washed-out to fix a meeting. Pat had finally got the message and stopped ringing altogether. But April had met Mrs Hughes a month or so ago, and been regaled with all the details of the wedding. April was so impressed – not to mention downright envious – that she still talked of little else: the reception for a hundred guests, the four bridesmaids and two pageboys, the honeymoon in Marbella at the Hotel Emperador, which had a jacuzzi in every bathroom and a real fountain in the foyer.

'You must get back in touch, Tess. You and Pat were once as thick as thieves. I can't think why you've dropped all your old girlfriends. My Aunt Adie used to say one female friend's worth two blokes, any day. Though, when I come to think of it, she was a bit of an old hypocrite. She always had a string of men in tow, and God help any girlfriend who as much as fluttered her eyelashes at even the less hunky ones. Anyway, if you go and call on Pat, she'll invite you to the wedding, won't she? The reception's at the Manor Park, so we're probably talking thirty quid a head, and so much blooming champagne you could wash your hands and face in it. I threw out a big hint to Mrs Hughes, told her how you'd missed Pat and would definitely be popping round to say congratulations.'

'Well, I wish you hadn't, Mum. I'm too busy at the moment.'

'Busy! That's a good one! You don't know the meaning of the word.'

She'd been working every hour, in fact, having returned to her Dr Edwards thesis, filling in the early part with the help of Dr Reynolds' wife. Even her introduction to Paula Reynolds had demanded time and guile: a week of planning, a plethora of lies. A month ago, she couldn't have cared less about either Pat Hughes or her wedding, but now things were very different. Since she was leaving to get married herself, she needed someone to confide in, someone her own age who could advise her, boost her courage, and especially help with April, who'd be frantic once she realized that her daughter had done a bunk. Pat might even bail her out right now, if she called there straight away and begged a loan. £16 sounded quite a hefty sum, but she had never stinted Pat during their seven years at school together: all that help with homework, all those loans of books, the hours of patient listening when Pat's first callous boyfriend waltzed off with someone else.

'I'll be back as soon as possible,' she told the woman in the shop. 'Please don't sell the dress. It's desperately important.'

She struggled out of it as quickly as she could; feeling oddly insubstantial once she was standing in her underclothes, as if she'd lost her bones and purpose. The tracksuit seemed so grotty in comparison, she could hardly bear to put it on again; wished she hadn't shed her winter coat. Yet it was no weather for a coat – the sun surprisingly strong as she hurried from the shop and up the High Street. There was still a week of March left, but spring had hatched already: trees bursting into bud; the recently bare flower-beds bejewelled with crocuses; the sky a confident blue. She shared the season's optimism, felt better altogether – decisions made, her future assured, the jangling conflicts solved.

She pounded past the Midland Bank, and round the corner to the Post Office, envying those smug customers who had deposit accounts, or savings books, or money in a building society. Had she really got the nerve to turn up on Pat's doorstep, after so long and rude an absence, say 'hello', and ask for money almost in the same breath? Yet if she wasted time in idle chit-chat before she broached the subject, the dress might well have gone. Spring was the busiest time for weddings, and second-hand designer dresses were extremely rare and likely to be snapped up. She slowed her steps, reflecting. Was there no other way she could get the money quicker? She was tempted to squat down on the pavement with a placard saying 'Homeless and hungry. Can you spare some change?'

It wouldn't be a lie. She supposed she must be hungry (despite the fact she never felt it physically), because she rarely bothered much with meals; managing to convince her mother that she was either out with Ivor, or eating with his family. And she was homeless, too, in the sense that there was nowhere she belonged. Michael Chalmers' house was still jointly owned by Eileen. He'd got rid of half her things now, but her presence lingered on, her iron grip on the fabric – the very bricks and mortar of the place. And as for her mother's semi, she felt less and less at home there, oppressed by April's constant fretting questions: Why did she always look like death warmed up? Couldn't she make an appointment with the doctor, or at least get more fresh air? Or if there was nothing seriously wrong with her, then wouldn't she feel better if she went out and found a job? And as for Mr Mystery Man, that sodding stuck-up Ivor, was he really so unnatural that he hadn't the slightest desire to meet his girlfriend's mother? And April seemed obsessed with marriage, bringing up the subject several times each day: her eldest niece's engagement; the

338

recent wedding in 'Neighbours'; what a fantastic catch Pat's Tony was – head of a computer firm, with a degree in economics – and if a dunce like that could land him, then what was Tessa doing?

She realized that her own wedding would solve a lot of hassles. April was obviously finding it a strain, both financially and emotionally, to cope with a daughter she no longer understood. Marriage made for happiness – and not just for the couple. Everybody loved a bride. Look at how those biddies in the Oxfam shop had all cooed and beamed and clucked. Which brought her back to the problem of the money. She wasn't very likely to light on £16 while she wandered round in circles, with her mind in second gear.

Reluctantly, she retraced her steps to the High Street. No good approaching Pat. She must keep her friend lined up for something much more vital – to support and calm her mother once she herself had fled – so she dared not risk alienating her by asking her for money. But how else could she raise it? She had no other friends left. Michael was at work, and couldn't be disturbed; Frank had gone to Kempton Park to put 'a bob or two' on Jack the Lad, and Eric was out shopping. Half the world was shopping, judging by the crowds. A woman passed her with a basket on wheels, laden to the brim with groceries and fruit. On top was a red purse – almost asking to be nicked. Stealing was an option she hadn't yet considered, though the old girl could probably spare three mingy five-pound notes, when she'd clearly spent a fortune on her food and her smart coat. Tessa followed at her heels, the red purse like a beacon, luring her in pursuit. The woman turned to glance at her, as if she'd read her mind and was labelling her a thief. Tessa froze, dodged into an alleyway. The face was Eileen's – the Eileen of the photographs – an open, trusting, honest face, though pale and rather drawn. Even the hair was similar: short and permed and neat.

She slumped against the alley wall, scraped her hand deliberately across its rough unplastered surface, welcoming the pain, which at least proved that she was real. Life and death kept merging – Eileen resurrecting; all the Michaels dying, their cold grey corpses stinking out her dreams. Her morals must be dying, too. How could she have even contemplated using stolen money to buy her wedding dress?

She waited a few moments, till both Eileens had disappeared – the live one in the High Street, and the defunct one in her head – then mooched on down the road. Her attention was suddenly riveted by a notice in a jeweller's shop: GOLD AND SILVER BOUGHT FOR CASH.

BEST PRICES IN THE AREA! NO ITEM TOO SMALL. She clasped her wrist, cursing her stupidity. All the time she'd been searching for the money, she actually had it on her person, in the shape of her charm-bracelet. Well, she could hardly call it that when it held only two small charms as yet, but both were solid gold. Both had also come from Michael Chalmers, who had promised to buy her a new charm every month. He'd chosen the first with tender loving care – a tiny dog like Jasper, complete with studded collar and tongue lolling from its mouth. The second was a horseshoe – for good luck. She was loath to surrender her luck, would prefer to sell the dog – though selling either would make things awfully difficult with Michael. Could she pretend the dog charm had dropped off? Unlikely, when he'd fixed it on himself, secured it with such finicky precision. Well, she'd tackle that dilemma once she'd got the money; couldn't afford to waste more time hanging round outside.

The man behind the counter was heavy-jowled and swarthy, with dark suspicious eyes. He examined each charm closely through his spy-glass, then weighed them on a scale; his expression one of snooty contempt, as if they were only gimcrack trifles. She felt outraged for Michael's sake, guessing he'd spent a lot on them, since she knew he'd buy the best he could afford.

'I'll give you £5 each.' The voice was couldn't-care-less.

'But they're worth far more than that.'

'Not second-hand, they're not.'

'But they're new, as near as dammit. I've only had the horseshoe a few days.'

'Okay – £15 the two, but that's my limit.'

Tessa tried to control her anger. Right under her nose was a display-case of new gold charms, with their price-tags pinned beside them – £20, £53, £85.50 – the last for a poodle not that different from her own dog. 'Could you make it £15.77?' she wheedled. 'I need the extra 77p.'

'Sorry. Nothing doing.'

'Then I'll have to sell the bracelet too.'

He picked it up with a show of weary patience, repeated the performance with the spy-glass and the scales. 'It only weighs just under fifteen grammes,' he shrugged, 'so I can't give you more than twenty quid.'

Tessa paused, deliberating. Should she sell the bracelet and keep the charms, or flog the whole damn lot and have some extra money for flowers and veil, white shoes? The charms had been detached now, and she was tempted to keep the horseshoe; needed luck even more than money. Yet there'd be so many other expenses, it would be foolish to turn down an extra fiver. She pushed both charms and bracelet across the counter, watched the man count out the notes, which were old and stained and crumpled like his jacket.

'Thanks,' she muttered, glaring at the trays of trinkets as she stalked out through the door – all goods bought cheap, sold dear. She checked her watch. Only nineteen minutes had passed since she'd left the Oxfam shop, and she was back there in another four, panting, out of breath; her gaze immediately directed to the high shelf above the counter. The shelf was bare – no sign of the dress, or of the woman who had served her. The only person who seemed to be on duty was a young and pretty salesgirl she hadn't seen before, and who already had half a dozen customers. She pushed through them to the counter, tears starting to her eyes. 'My dress,' she pleaded. 'My wedding dress.'

'Oh, are you Miss Hughes?' the girl asked.

Tessa clutched the counter, felt weak and strangely dizzy. When people asked her who she was, it was so difficult to know. She shook her head, then nodded.

'The one who went to fetch the money?'

'Yes,' she said. 'That's right.' It helped when people prompted her, reminded her of what she'd just been doing. Her memory kept playing tricks, or sleeping. Weird that, when she slept so little herself.

'Peggy said to tell you she had to put the dress back on the rail. It's right there, in the corner. If you wait a sec, I'll serve you, but you'll have to take your turn.'

Tessa rushed to fetch the gown, whispered to it, stroked it; exulting once again in its perfection, its sheer style. Everything would be all right – she simply had to trust. And suddenly, to prove it, the older woman emerged from the back room, and greeted her like a friend.

'Ah! You're back!' she beamed. 'I was beginning to get worried. You looked so striking in that dress, I just knew you had to have it.'

Tessa pressed her cheek against the satin. How extraordinary it was that even strangers realized it was meant for her. Were they also aware, at some unspoken level, of how destiny had played its part, and was even now leading her to a denouement?

The woman ushered her to a vacant till, like a distinguished special customer, who was allowed to jump the queue. She handed over £20, received a penny change – a shiny-bright new-minted coin, which somehow caught her fancy. She stowed it in her pocket, rather than her purse, kept one hand curled around it. The saleswoman was hunting for a bag. The Oxfam ones were far too small, and all she had come up with was a large but rather tatty plastic carrier.

'That doesn't seem quite right,' she muttered, still rooting under the counter.

'It's fine,' said Tessa, seizing it, before it could vanish into the litter-bin. With 'TESCO' printed on the front, she could disguise her glamorous dress as just a bag of bits and pieces from the supermarket.

The woman touched her arm – a fleeting awkward gesture which still conveyed great warmth. 'Good luck,' she murmured. 'Take care.'

'Yes, best of luck!' the other girl called out, as Tessa walked towards the door. 'Have a lovely wedding.'

'I will,' said Tessa, breaking into a delighted smile. Both of them had wished her luck, restored her lucky horseshoe with their words.

'Hello, Mrs Hughes. I was wondering if . . .'

'Good gracious! Tessa Reeves! I was beginning to think you were avoiding us on purpose. We haven't seen your face in months and months.' Mrs Hughes' own small bewhiskered mouse-face expressed a whole range of emotions in succession – surprise, resentment, relish, indignation.

Tessa shuffled her feet on the doorstep, stared down at the mat. She knew she was in the wrong – ignoring an old friend, cutting off all contact with unconvincing excuses.

'Well, come on in, and mind that wretched step. You were always tripping over it when you were knee-high to a grasshopper and used to come dashing in with Pat. She'll be really pleased to see you. She told me just the other day that she thought she must have offended you, though she didn't have the foggiest notion why. "Pat," I said, "if we're talking about offence, I reckon the boot's on the other foot," if you understand my meaning, dear.'

'I'm sorry,' Tessa faltered, as she closed the door behind her. 'I've been . . . ill again.'

'Yes, so Pat kept on telling me. And your mother said you haven't been yourself. I suppose I shouldn't let this out, but she's worried sick about you. She rang again last week, asked me for the number

342

of this funny bloke my husband knows who's into nature cure, but I don't trust quacks, do you? And anyway, I can't see any point in stuffing yourself with rabbit food, when you look half-starved already. You're almost as skinny as our Pat now, and if you'll forgive me speaking plainly, it suits her better than you. Are you still under the doctor?'

'No,' said Tessa, nervous at the mention of doctors. 'I'm . . . better now, much better.'

'You're very pale and peaky, though – lost all your lovely colour. I'm sure Pat will notice the difference.'

'How is she?' Tessa asked, hoping to divert the conversation from herself.

'Never better! We're all thrilled about the wedding, and Tony's such a love. Did April tell you he's been made a director?'

Yes, ten times at least, Tessa didn't say.

'You'd never believe the perks! Trips abroad, at the drop of a hat. International conferences, big trade exhibitions – you name it, he'll be there. Last month it was Switzerland, and he's off to New York at the beginning of November – taking our Pat, too, of course! And he's got this swish new car – a Vauxhall Cavalier in a really tasteful blue – what they call Dawn Mist. He's teaching Pat to drive it, and she's doing ever so well. You're lucky to find her in. They're usually out together on a Saturday, either going for a spin, or buying things for their house. We need a bigger place ourselves, just to hold the gear!'

Tessa followed Mrs Hughes along the dark and poky hall, which hadn't changed in all the years she'd known it – sombre patterned wallpaper, thin brown haircord carpet. It even smelt the same – a faintly doggy smell, overlaid with Airwick. Pat had heard her voice and came charging down the stairs. They had never been best friends, in fact, but they embraced now as if they were – the long absence, and the wedding, and even her own illness, somehow lending real emotion to their meeting.

'God! You've changed!' Pat exclaimed. 'You must have lost two stone. Have you been on some crash diet?'

'No,' said Tessa, forcing a laugh. 'Just shed my puppy fat.'

'Tea?' asked Mrs Hughes, waddling into the kitchen and filling up the kettle.

'Yes, please,' said both the girls.

They took their mugs of tea upstairs; waited to talk privately until they were ensconced in Pat's bedroom with the door shut; a packet of Jammie Dodgers between them on the floor, to remind them of their schooldays. Tessa had already endured wedding-talk for a boring half-hour, trotting after Mrs Hughes as she was shown several dozen photographs of the future son-in-law, plus the wedding invitations, a copy of the menu, a photo of the cake they'd chosen, and finally the wedding dress itself. But now she and Pat were alone at last, so she shook out the Tesco's carrier and revealed her own creation.

Pat was almost speechless, consumed with curiosity, though clearly fighting jealousy as well. Her own dress was much plainer, less impressive altogether. 'What on earth . . . ?'

'I'm getting married too, Pat, but you mustn't breathe a word. My mother doesn't know.'

'Christ! You're a dark horse, aren't you? Who to, for heaven's sake?'

'His name's . . . Michael.'

'Michael? I thought your Mum told mine you were seeing some bloke called Ivor.'

'Oh, Ivor's just a casual friend. I only pretend I'm going out with him because I daren't tell her about Michael. I know she'd disapprove.'

Pat prised apart a biscuit, tongued out the gungy jam. 'What's wrong with him?' she asked.

Tessa hesitated. 'Well, the main thing is his age. But there are other problems, too – his looks, his lack of prospects – oh, everything, in fact.'

'So why the heck are you marrying him? Don't tell me you're pregnant again!'

'No,' snapped Tessa. 'And I don't really want to talk about it.'

'Oh, come on, don't be mean. You can't leave me dangling like that! At least let me know his age. I won't be shocked, I promise. Sharon Brown's just married this guy of forty, and she's a whole year younger than us.'

Tessa refused to be drawn, crammed her mouth with a biscuit, so she wouldn't have to talk.

'Well, tell me what he's like, then.'

'Nice.'

'I should bloody well hope so, if you plan to spend your life with him.' Pat laughed, a shade uncomfortably. 'What else?'

'Kind and sort of . . . gentle. Wouldn't hurt a fly. Loves animals, and . . .'

'Fair or dark?'

'In between, with hazel eyes.'

'Tall or short?'

'Middling.'

'And when's the big day? Or I suppose it won't be big, if your mother's not invited, and it's all so cloak and dagger.'

'Yes, that's another worry. I must admit I'm more concerned about Mum than almost anything else.' Tessa frowned, licked a smear of jam from her hand, while carefully choosing her words. 'Listen, Pat, you may think this a cheek, but I wondered if I could ask you a big favour? I mean, you've known my mother all these years, and she's always . . .'

Pat slammed down her empty cup. 'You're not expecting *me* to tell her, are you? I draw the line at that.'

'No. I plan to leave a note, explaining what I've done, but it'll be an awful shock for her, and she'll probably start going up the wall, so if you could sort of . . . calm her down, or try to make her see that . . .' The sentence petered out.

Pat was looking more and more uneasy. 'I probably won't be here,' she said, edging into the corner, as if trying to absent herself, at least symbolically. 'The wedding's in two weeks, and we've booked a fortnight's honeymoon, and after that we're spending a few days in the country, in Tony's parents' house.'

'No, you'll be back in time. Mum knew all your plans, so I've worked it out already.'

'So when's your wedding going to be?' Pat asked, reaching for the Oxfam dress, so that she could examine it more closely.

Tessa eased up to her feet, stood leaning on the window-sill, glancing out at the small sun-gilded garden – a froth of rosy blossom on the apple-tree, a green haze on the willow, even a peacock-butterfly soaring past the daffodils. It was already kindly weather – things budding and relenting – and in another month or so, nature would have reached its prime. She turned back to Pat, who was still scrutinizing the dress, picking at the little pearls as if she'd like to wrench them off.

'Or perhaps you haven't fixed the date,' Pat added. 'I know how tricky it can be. We wanted April the eleventh, which is Tony's birthday and the date we first went out last year, but the vicar already had three weddings on that Saturday, so then we tried to . . .'

Tessa interrupted. 'I know the date all right,' she said, grabbing at her dress, so that she could return it to the safety of its bag. 'There was only one day it could be – one important to me personally.'

'April Fool's Day, I suppose,' quipped Pat, with just a touch of malice in her laugh.

'No,' said Tessa softly. 'The first of May – May Morning.'

28

'THANKS FOR THE lift!' Tessa jumped down from the lorry, stretched her stiff cold legs.

'Good luck!' the driver shouted as he accelerated away. She gave a cheery wave, stored his 'good luck' in her pocket along with the new penny she had received as change in the Oxfam shop. She treasured it as her replacement charm, and if she hadn't sold the bracelet it would be weighted down with horseshoes now. Wherever she went people wished her luck, as if they knew about her wedding, even though she hadn't breathed a word. The sole person she'd confided in was Big Bill, the lorry driver. It seemed only fair when he'd driven her all the way to Leicester, without trying any funny business. Hitchhiking had always been forbidden, especially on her own, and she'd been regaled with gruesome stories about drivers who molested you, then flung your battered body into a ditch. But the journey with Bill had been quiet and uneventful. All he'd done was offer her a Polo every half an hour and complain about the roadworks on the motorway. At least there hadn't been much traffic. She'd deliberately travelled in the early hours, to arrive first thing on May Morning, just as dawn was breaking. There was no sign of the sun yet, but the light had changed from pewter to pearl-grey, and what had once been blurry shapes were now coming into focus; the scene unfolding from dark shadowland to a large and solid town.

Bill had set her down by the bus station, which looked totally deserted. She had originally planned to take the coach, but why waste £15? Her mother would have answered 'to keep you out of the clutches of those murderers and rapists', but she knew that she was safe – somehow unassailable – even if she'd hitched a lift from the most dangerous thug imaginable, instead of dozy Bill. Her luck was solid gold, and encased her from top to toe like a suit of shining armour.

She consulted her map, though more as a formality, since she'd studied it so many times already; walking her fingers in Dr Edwards' footsteps. He'd spent eight years in this town; had arrived at Leicester Royal Infirmary as a pre-registration houseman, after his initial training at Birmingham; stayed on at the hospital for another couple of years before moving to his first post as a GP. The surgery and his private house were both in Stoneygate, a pleasant leafy suburb just a mile or two from the centre. He had lived there with his first wife, who'd been moody and artistic, and had once run a little crafts shop near the marketplace. Tessa located the street on her map, realized she would skirt it on her way to the Royal Infirmary. She had planned to wander slowly through the town, finishing up at the hospital; assimilating Dr Edwards' traces, breathing the same air he'd breathed, imprinting on her mind all the sights and landmarks he must have known so well.

She only wished the place looked slightly smarter. The street she was standing in seemed dreary, almost stagnant, with flyblown shops cowering beneath ugly faceless office blocks. 'For Sale' boards sprouted everywhere – shops and businesses for sale, office space to let – as if each enterprise had foundered and was stranded in limbo, begging for a new owner, the chance of a reprieve. The weather didn't help. The day was cold and overcast; a light but sullen drizzle beginning to spatter on her face. But then it had rained on May Morning last year – a vicious, lashing downpour, which had soaked her clothes, turned her hair to rats' tails. And the sun had been equally reluctant to break through. She'd understood, much later, that it had been simply biding its time, waiting till she was in the car with Michael, before sailing out to bless their union. The same would happen again. She had to wait, that's all; was already much more patient than she had been a year ago; had gained her honours degree in Waiting.

She rearranged her clutch of plastic bags – two in one hand, three in the other, so they balanced more or less – then set off down the street. She turned left into Church Gate – a more salubrious area – the shops less cramped and squalid, the pavements free of litter. Had Dr Edwards shopped here – perhaps bought his *Daily Telegraph* from the newsagent on the corner; or taken his smart brogues to that snazzy-looking shoe-repairer's with the stuffed crocodile in the

348

window? Church Gate led her to the clock tower and the centre of the city, though it still seemed like a ghost town – the shops all shut and barred, no buses on the roads yet, no other living soul around, save a tramp sprawled in a doorway and a bearded Asian hobbling on two sticks. She wished him a good morning, though he only muttered in reply. But she didn't need companionship with Dr Edwards as her guide. She was sure he would have patronized the familiar shops now jostling on all sides – Marks & Spencer, Burton's, Tie Rack, Hallmark Cards. She hoped he'd shopped without his wife; didn't want that heartless bitch tagging along beside them – Alison, the cruel first wife, whom he'd married when he was only twenty-three, and who now lived with an architect in Rhodes.

She dawdled on down Gallowtree Gate, shuddering at the name. Images of death still kept drifting through her mind, but she knew that they would dissipate before the day was over. She was reminded of the scrapyard they had passed whilst driving up – a rusting heap of battered cars, which might look superficially like wreckage, but was about to be reforged, transformed to a new life.

She continued into Granby Street and branched right past the Grand Hotel. She could imagine Dr Edwards there, downing a quick sherry in the lounge or lunching with a colleague in the carvery. Again, she banished the wife. Alison had no right to slap-up meals when she'd behaved so callously, proved herself a quite unnatural mother. It had been difficult to ferret out the facts about Dr Edwards' first (elusive) wife. Michael Chalmers had told her everything he knew – reluctantly, shamefacedly, aware that he was betraying Eileen's trust, yet honour bound not to break the promise he'd made so recklessly in bed. He'd also introduced her to Dr Reynolds' wife, but Paula Reynolds was a reserved and uncommunicative type, and had eventually put her on to someone else: an old schoolfriend of Alison's, who'd proved much more forthcoming. She was a widow with no job or kids and nothing much to do, and therefore seemed to welcome the chance of a good natter, though it had taken ingenuity (and a whole new web of lies) to extract the crucial details and even wheedle a few photographs. She had brought the snapshots with her, in the carrier bags, with addresses, other maps, her Dr Edwards thesis, and of course her wedding gear. She stopped a moment to make sure the dress was safe; well-wrapped in its polythene, protected from the rain. The drizzle was now heavier, a more persistent shower, but she didn't let it bother her. It was only another form of tears, and all tears and grief would pass.

The daylight was still grudging, as if night and morning were sleeping in each other's arms, and had merged their breaths and bodies. The streets were silent; the sky murky, overcast; a lone white gull soaring into the greyness and being swallowed up and lost. She started as a dustcart clattered down the road; its whirring circling brushes scouring debris from the gutter. She was now in Welford Road, a wide but charmless thoroughfare with graffiti-scrawled buildings, some boarded up or propped and braced by scaffolding, like cripples with their zimmer frames. An old man with a mongrel was weaving his way towards her, and as he shambled past, she caught his whiff of whisky and stale sweat. She increased her pace, breaking into a run, the carrier bags bouncing at her sides. She was almost at the Infirmary, where Dr Edwards' traces would be so thick they'd coat the walls. But another wall was rearing up – the grim façade of Leicester gaol, menacing and merciless with its crenellated towers in lowering dark grey stone; the vast brick wall sweeping to the right, with searchlights glaring on the top – a barrier so high and solid it dwarfed mere human scale. She paused to read the notice by the heavy wooden door: 'It is an offence for any person to help a prisoner to escape.' She was smiling as she crossed the road, turned her back on prison bars. She herself had already escaped, slipped her chains, and was on her way to freedom.

She had reached Infirmary Road; gazed up at Dr Edwards' famous hospital with a mixture of reverence and elation. This was the older part of the complex: a nineteenth-century building in mellow weathered brick, which combined solidity and grace. She hurried round to the old main entrance, which she knew from her researches was no longer used, though when she tried the doors she found they were unlocked. 'This reception area is closed', said a placard on the desk, but she ignored it, walked straight past. Nothing could be closed to her if it had links with Dr Edwards. She glanced around the foyer, impressed by its quiet elegance – the dark red-patterned carpet and tall-case antique clock – so different from most modern arid hospitals, which were sternly, plainly functional. Even the indicator-board looked venerable – probably Victorian, with its highly polished wood and hand-painted gold lettering. The names of all the doctors working in the hospital were printed on that board, so Dr Michael Edwards would once have been included, outshining all the rest.

She sauntered down the corridor, stopping to scrutinize a notice-board on which were listed details of conferences, committees, study-groups and ward-rounds – countless meetings and engagements for all the various medical staff. Dr Edwards would have stood in this same spot, reading items more or less identical. He had probably touched the board, left his fingerprints behind. She put her carrier bags down to run her hands across it, hoover up all vestiges, then wandered on, surprised that there was nobody around. She hadn't seen a single nurse or doctor; no cleaner coming off a shift, no tired and harassed houseman clocking up his hundredth hour that week. The hospital seemed abandoned, as if it had lost all heart since Dr Edwards' departure, closed its wards, dismissed the other staff.

She was flagging, too; exhausted by her walk, and feeling rather faint. She retraced her steps to the nearest seat: a red upholstered bench in an attractive waiting-area, which was like a sort of crossroads – one passage leading back to the main entrance and the street; another signposted 'WARDS'. If she positioned herself here, then she couldn't miss anyone coming either way; might even meet a medic who remembered Dr Edwards, or had worked with him, or taught him. She piled her bags beside her on the bench, massaging her hand where one broken plastic handle had cut into her palm. Her ring was hurting, too, and had left a red weal on her finger – it was obviously too tight. She was still not used to wearing it, though Michael Chalmers had presented it to her as far back as Easter Sunday. After days of guilt and agonizing, she had decided not to return it, but keep it as her wedding ring. She couldn't afford another one, and in any case, it would have been cruel to give it back. It had meant so much to Michael that she wore it every day, and he'd chosen an eternity ring, as a token of his undying love – a narrow silver band, set with tiny glittering stones.

She touched the stones, secretly rejoicing in the small red mark emblazoned on the third finger of her left hand. In medieval times they believed a vein ran directly from that finger to the heart, which was why it had been earmarked as the wedding finger. She found the notion appealing, since it implied her heart was still linked to Michael Chalmers, and that was very apt when he was the one who'd made her marriage possible, helped her trace Michael Edwards' son.

Yet it also fuelled her guilt, especially when she thought back to their last sad day together – not sad for him, of course, as he'd no idea that they'd never meet again, but unbearable for her. He'd been his usual loving self; cooking for her, spoiling her, hanging on her every word. She'd kept wanting to apologize, aware how he would suffer when he discovered she had vanished; how deeply she'd be hurting him, maybe destroying his whole life. But once it got to midnight, she had merely said a brief goodbye, as if she'd see him the next evening, resume their conversation and their kiss. The kisses were still wrong – the sex wrong, and the presents wrong – but that didn't make the parting any easier. She had felt so weighted down with grief, with shame at her own cruelty, she could scarcely hold back her tears. But it had been dark by then, as they lingered outside her house in the ill-lit murky street, so he couldn't see her face, and before driving off he'd simply whispered fervently, 'See you tomorrow at six.'

She glanced up at the stately tall-case clock. It was twenty past six – in the morning – and Michael would be sleepless, probably beside himself with worry. She sagged back in her seat, recalling all the other cruel goodbyes – the farewell to her home, where she'd lived nearly her whole life; the last meal with Frank and Eric, who'd been baiting her as usual, bickering and teasing, just like any other evening; her last long walk with Jasper, who had tried to lick her tears away when she'd pressed her streaming eyes against his coat.

She was almost crying now, yet furious with herself for such self-pity. That life was over, finished, and she was about to start a new one; had no business to be wasting time mooning over shadows when she'd come to the Infirmary in search of Dr Edwards so that she could put the past behind her – his past as well as hers. Today, she'd meet his son: the new young Michael Edwards, who had been named after his father, and his grandfather before him – every eldest Edwards son christened with the family name of Michael. That name had such a charge, she could hear it always resounding in her head; knew it was etched into her skin like a tattoo.

She gathered up her bags, marched along the corridor and out into the street, banishing all thoughts of home; returning to her quest. She must investigate the new wing of the hospital, where there were bound to be more signs of life, more data for her Dr Edwards thesis. She wondered how he'd found his way about in such an amorphous, sprawling place. New structures seemed to have been built on quite haphazardly, with no apparent regard for the overall effect, and resulting in a hotchpotch of conflicting styles and vistas – concrete glowering at red brick; stark and brutish tower-blocks dwarfing eighteenth-century harmony. But perhaps he'd been too busy even to notice his surroundings; had spent his time, like Michael at the Radcliffe, dashing from one crisis to the next. It was easier for her. She could proceed at a more leisurely pace; stop and look if something caught her eye – like that stone sculpture she was passing now, mounted on the wall in Infirmary Close. The work was really powerful: two huge healing hands cradled a sick woman, who lay slumped and pale across them; her eyes half-shut, her body swathed in a hooded cloak. Tessa moved a little closer, struck by the resemblance between the woman and the morning – both listless invalids. The light was still anaemic, the sky wishy-washy, sallow, with no gleam of colour or glint of sun; the rain reduced to an apathetic dribble.

She shivered in her lightweight suit, wished she'd brought a mac or a thick coat. But she would soon be in the warm again; was only a few yards away from the main entrance of the modern wing. Its stained and dingy concrete was made still more unsightly by a hideous sort of canopy erected in the front, with garish steel excrescences sprouting underneath it. But the building didn't matter – the important thing was that Dr Edwards had swept through this same door, gone striding down that corridor, left his footprints on the two-tone vinyl floor. She followed in his tracks. Again she found the place deserted: no one at the reception desk; the shop and florist closed; the tea-bar shuttered; chairs and tables empty and forlorn. Where were all the nurses, and Dr Edwards' successors in their white coats or green gowns, and why was there no sound at all – no porter with his trolley clanging round the corner, no shrilling phone, or clack of busy heels?

She drifted back to the tea-bar, attracted by the tariff tacked up on the wall: cheese and chutney sandwiches, ham rolls, buttered scones. Only now did she realize how ravenous she was; nothing in her stomach save excitement and six Polos. That must be the reason she felt so tired and dizzy; had to keep on stopping, to rest or put her bags down. She subsided on a chair again, checked each bag in turn, relieved to see that the rain had done no damage to her bridal wreath or veil. The veil was tatty anyway – discovered in a junk shop after weeks of patient searching. The wreath she'd made herself from artificial flowers – second-hand like all the rest, and amassed from various market stalls. She'd also bought a packet of rice and a large box of confetti, both symbols of fertility, which would ensure she had her child. She would conceive tonight, her wedding night – produce another baby in nine months, another fateful Michael.

353

She was tempted to open the rice and guzzle it straight from the packet – hard, uncooked and dry – or pretend the confetti was a box of scented cachous, and let the pastel-coloured shapes melt slowly in her mouth. She took out two paper horseshoes, placed them on her tongue, could almost taste their peach and lilac sweetness. She was about to eat a paper heart when she heard footsteps in the corridor – perhaps a nurse or doctor, at last, restoring the Infirmary to life.

No. Two Asian women were coming into view, their features so alike they must be mother and daughter, though their style of dress was so utterly at variance they might have sprung from different cultures and completely different centuries. The mother wore a gold and purple sari, with her hair in a long braid, while the daughter sported skin-tight denim jeans and a mask of tarty make-up, her bleached and tousled hair tumbling loose around her shoulders. Yet the two were laughing and joking together, obviously good friends. They sat down at a table, unconcerned apparently that the cafeteria was closed. They'd brought their own provisions, and appeared to be using the place as their private breakfast bar – swigging from a thermos flask and sharing three samosas. Tessa licked her fingers, as if scooping up the greasy crumbs, her own hunger swelling like fresh yeast in a bread-mix as she smelt hot spicy pastry. Perhaps the mother worked here and was snatching a quick bite before signing on for duty, or maybe the daughter had an appointment with a doctor. She considered going up to them, to ask what time the staff came on, but they probably wouldn't welcome an intrusion. They were speaking their own language, whose very strangeness made her feel excluded. She was cut off from them twice over: first by race and tongue, but also – far more painful – because that precious mother-daughter bond was now lost to her entirely. Once, she and April had been every bit as close – shopping together, giggling in the mirror as they tried on silly hats, or relaxing over a coffee in the Wimpy Bar, ordering one portion of cheesecake and two forks.

She poured a shower of confetti on the table, trying to distract herself by spelling out Michael's name in coloured paper shapes. It was sheer torment to remember how she'd taken leave of her mother – sloping out of the house with five carrier bags of cast-offs, pretending she was delivering them to the scout-hut for a jumble sale.

'But why the dickens are you going at this unearthly hour?' April had objected. 'They'll have shut up shop by now. Can't you leave it till the morning?'

'No. Mrs Brown's expecting me. I won't be very long.' She'd been almost at the door when she suddenly dashed back, hugged her mother so hard that April yelped with pain and pushed her off.

'Careful, Tessa! That's my dicky arm.'

'Mum, I . . . I love you.'

'Well, it's a funny way to show it. I've had no end of trouble with that flipping arm today, and now you've gone and made it ten times worse.'

'I'm sorry,' she'd exclaimed, and had continued saying sorry, over and over again, as a futile reparation for the suffering she would cause her mother in the coming weeks and months – the loneliness and bafflement, the feeling of betrayal.

She shifted her chair a fraction, so that she could observe the Asian pair again without being noticed herself. The woman was pushing back her daughter's hair with that exasperated resignation all mothers seemed to show, obviously complaining how untidy it looked. Instinctively, her hand moved to her own hair, as she imagined April's voice asking if she'd lost her comb, or been sleeping in a hedge. How extraordinary to miss her mother's nagging; actually ache to hear her sounding off about messy clothes or chores undone. But no, she mustn't weaken. Things were best left as they were. And she really had done all she could to ensure that April wouldn't be left alone. Pat Hughes had finally promised to help out, and they'd arranged that she should call round there last night; stay all night, if necessary, if April got too frantic or distressed. Pat wouldn't – couldn't – betray her, since she didn't know the truth; believed her friend had gone to Plymouth, not to Leicester. If the odd word did leak out, then April would go chasing off to the West Country instead of the East Midlands.

Tessa kicked her chair back, collected up her things. It was time to ditch her fears, stifle all remorse about her mother. Once she'd recovered from the initial shock, April would be better off without her; without the constant worry and expense; without an ungrateful daughter who no longer belonged at home.

The Asian couple were also getting up – the daughter making for the lifts, while the mother scurried back towards the exit. Tessa followed at a distance, feeling a strange affinity with this small figure in her sari. Both of them were aliens who'd come to a foreign land, and would have to adapt and turn it into home; both would need to learn a different language, struggle to communicate in a new, frustrating way. She caught the woman up outside the door, and was about to murmur a greeting when she was suddenly transfixed by a notice she had missed before – 'ACCIDENT & EMERGENCY' – in large imposing letters, white on red.

She plunged towards it, the Asian woman instantly forgotten, her whole mind somersaulting with memories and flashbacks. Michael worked there, didn't he? – in what he called A and E – saving lives, patching up the victims of crashes and disasters. He had written to her about it, way back in the summer of last year, though it seemed another lifetime, so dim it was and shadowy. And yet she'd kept his postcards (had them in her bag), knew every line by heart – brief and blotchy scribbles dashed off in a hurry because he was busy, pressured, committed to his patients. All she had to do was step through the glass doors, and she would lay eyes on those patients – injured bleeding wrecks – *lucky* to be injured, because soon they'd feel the blessing of his hands; could look into his blazing eyes, as she so longed to do.

Even now, she wasn't sure exactly how she'd reached him, except she'd travelled north – a fair distance, she remembered – rattling up the same motorway he always used himself. Long ago – aeons ago – he had invited her to join him, and she'd spent blissful evenings poring over the map, counting miles, counting days, wishing she had wings, to soar above the traffic jams, overtake the fastest of the cars. She was flying in one sense already – so excited and so overwrought, she had taken off, taken wing; her dazed and shaken body somehow left behind, and jumbling all its functions, so that she was breathing with her liver, digesting via her lungs. She had better rest a while, until she could control her legs; calm her racing heartbeat, return to earth from the dizzy stratosphere.

Her steps were still uncertain when she finally ventured into casualty, stood keyed-up at the door. Yes, there were all his patients, slumped passive in their chairs, waiting for his touch to revive them, resurrect them. One man sat with his arm in a sling; another had a blood-soaked rag swathed around his wrist; a mother with three fractious kids was glaring at a punk lad, who looked drunk, or drugged, or both. And here were all the other staff – a plump blonde nurse emerging from an office; two ambulance-men conferring with the receptionist; a policewoman supporting a young girl.

Michael powered this hospital – she could see that clearly now. He alone had transformed it from an empty hulk to a dynamic humming Healing Centre. Everything was functioning as it should, even incidentals like telephones and drinks-machines – a woman with a bandaged eye ringing for a cab; a gawky boy inserting coins to get a can of Pepsi. And above the stir and hubbub, the huge wall-mounted television pumped out its own bright life – a romantic glowing film; the lovers locked in a celluloid embrace. She slipped into a seat right at the back, hoping nobody had noticed her come in. She wanted to sit there anonymously and study all the patients, acquaint herself with the injuries which Michael would be treating, so she could admire his expertise.

She focused on the old man on her left, imagining the dramatic change as Michael stood above him: the huddled body beginning to relax; that drink-flushed face, with its bloodshot eyes, sobering in a smile. And how about the woman sitting next to him? Her leg was badly swollen, her expression sour and crabby, but when Michael laid his hands on her, she'd . . .

A cry ripped through the room – the furious full-throated yell of a newborn baby, startled by the world. Tessa stumbled to her feet, jolted in her turn. She was looking at her own baby – her and Michael's child – a dark-eyed, dark-haired infant, being cradled by a nurse. They must have brought him to be fed, so she could cuddle him and hold him, show him to his father. She blundered towards the nurse, calling out his name; desperate not to lose him again. But her voice was just a fading sigh, and her legs had lost their bones. She clutched at the wall, her fingers grasping air; the solid, four-square, brightly-lit room contracting to one dark and spinning pinpoint. She tried to shout for help, but the shout stayed trapped inside her throat; the whole of her imprisoned now in a coldly private world. That world was switching off, losing power, running down, dwindling into silence. She staggered, lost her balance, started falling in slow motion; sinking deeper, deeper, into black and hungry nothingness.

She opened her eyes, saw Michael bending over her as she lay shaken in the road. It was a wet and grey May Morning, and she'd tripped on a champagne bottle; been very nearly killed by a breakneck driver hurtling round the corner of a narrow Oxford lane. Instead of trying to help, he'd sworn at her and shouted, but now Michael had appeared, left all his other patients to attend to her. He was lifting her to her feet, his powerful arm supporting her, his voice supremely comforting. She knew she was too weak to walk, but he was lending her his strength, leading her to safety; had somehow steered her to a small quiet room and laid her on a couch.

He spread a blanket over her, then took her hand, felt her pulse. She gazed at the dark eyes, the wayward hair and unruly brows she'd thought she would never see again – Michael's lustrous Latin eyes, Michael's ardent face. She could hardly believe that they were actually in contact – physically, emotionally. He was asking her intimate questions, clearly anxious to catch up with her news, insisting that she told him her address. His hand was on her forehead now, his warm breath on her face; the familiar prick of stubble shadowing his chin. She remembered how those bristles had aroused her and excited her; left her sore but worshipping. She yearned to run her hand across them, feel their rasp and strop; aware that she was burning not with fever, but desire.

'Don't talk,' she longed to say. 'Use your lips to kiss me; your tongue to suck my breasts.' They had no need of words, and she couldn't concentrate her thoughts with him so close, attentive. It was wonderful to hear his voice, to have him show such interest in the details of her life, but all the same, his questions were distracting.

'Why did you come to casualty in the first place?'

She smiled at his mock naivety. As if he didn't know! 'To find you, of course,' she whispered, exulting in the fact that she'd succeeded; that her months and months of waiting had been so dazzlingly rewarded.

'Are you in any sort of pain?'

She shook her head in surprise. How could she be feeling pain with Michael leaning over her?

'The doctor won't be long,' he said, suddenly edging away and making for the door.

She struggled to sit up, reaching out her hands as if to haul him back. But he had already disappeared, leaving her alone, distraught, and baffled by his words. What doctor could he mean? Michael *was* the doctor – the only one that mattered – and she couldn't understand why he had eluded her again. She lay staring at the door, praying for it to open; every sense straining as she listened for his step. She heard other noises, other doctors; lighter feet than his bustling to and fro; a coarser, less attractive voice barking out instructions to a nurse. She could even hear time passing – a mournful, leaden sound which seemed to toll right through her skull, and was only silenced by the bellow of a panicked child in pain. She, too, wanted to scream – bawl out her loss and fury with no restraint or shame. But she willed herself to lie there like a marble effigy, trying to accept the fact that Michael must have been called to an emergency, and she must simply wait – have faith.

Finally, triumphantly (when she was almost losing hope), the door swung open, and two men in white stepped towards the couch; two faces looming over her: Michael's and an older one. She was too overwhelmed to speak. She recognized that second face – the blue eyes behind their glasses, the fine-textured mid-brown hair: Dr Edwards returned to his old hospital. He began to ask more questions, but she couldn't take them in; could hardly grasp the miraculous fact that she had found both Michael Edwardses, and that here they were, standing either side of her.

She gazed from face to face; closed her eyes as they seemed to merge, combine. Even when she looked again, the two were strangely blurred; the once distinct and separate features now filmed and hazed together – light hair darkening; blue eyes becoming brown. She experienced a stab of shock at the dawning recognition: there was only one Michael – had always only been the one – though she'd been seeing him divided. All this time, she'd confused reality with namesakes; regarded the mirror and the reflection as two divergent forms; split the voice off from its echo, the copy from its carbon. But if she went by touch and feeling, then she knew the truth instinctively: one pair of hands now stroking down her body – Michael's gifted surgeon's hands, back where they belonged. Michael's voice, as well – that forceful cultured claret voice, impatient and caressing, both at once. Time had turned full circle and they were lovers once again – she his favoured courtesan, his beloved greedy whore. She could tell he still desired her. Why else would he be slipping off her jacket, unbuttoning her blouse? She shut her eyes in submission, offering him her body, everything she had. He was seeking out her most vulnerable secret places, touching her bare flesh, listening to her heart – knowing that it beat at such a reckless pace because he had returned to take command of it. If only she could respond as she had done in the past. He would expect her to be tigerish, as unrestrained and impetuous as he always was himself, but she felt drained of all her energy.

'How are you feeling now?' he asked.

She didn't answer – couldn't – didn't have words fierce enough to express her brimming happiness.

'I think you only fainted. I can't find anything wrong. Everything appears to be working as it should be.'

She nodded, still too dazed to speak. Michael had pronounced her healed, confirmed what she already knew. Her illness had been turmoil and confusion, seeing things distorted and in duplicate. But all those dangerous mirages had been swept away, dispersed, so of course her body was working. She might feel physically weak, but that meant nothing much. What counted was her re-awakening, her reunion with Michael.

'I suggest you have a cup of tea, then if you want to get off home, that's fine by me.'

Again, she nodded dumbly, unable to express how deeply she was touched. Michael knew where she was going, understood that she must be on her way, and had just given her his blessing, sanctioned her new home.

'Nurse, perhaps you'd arrange some transport – see if someone can pick her up, or call a cab or something. And she'd better have a biscuit with her tea. She doesn't appear to have eaten for some time.'

Tessa stammered out her thanks. She had never known him so indulgent, so concerned about her health. He must have changed, as she had, during their many months apart; learned compassion through despair.

She sat waiting for the taxi, sipping the tea and nibbling a sweet biscuit – Michael's strong reviving tea; Michael's sustaining food. Somewhere in the distance, the newborn baby was crying, but she felt no more involvement. Of course it wasn't hers: her baby wasn't born yet – that joy was still to come – and now with Michael's knowledge and approval.

He had even got the cab right – an immaculate white saloon, perfect for her wedding – its handsome driver standing to attention as he opened the rear door. He settled her in the back, then purred away, swinging round the corner past the sculpture on the wall.

'Stop!' she told him suddenly. 'Right here.'

Only now did she understand that sculpture, and felt compelled to re-examine it in light of her new certainties. The invalid was her – passive and irresolute, as she had been since the summer; cloaked in her delusions, and depicted with her eyes shut because she was blinded to the truth. And the huge healing hands were Michael's, since it was Michael who had cured her, opened her eyes, brought her to fulfilment. She was off the danger-list, with no risk of a relapse.

He had also revived the morning, kindled the grey silence. The first blue was streaking the sky, and eager birds were fluting all around her; the noise of headstrong traffic rising from the road beyond. She kept her eyes fixed on the sculpture, admiring the strong fingers, the cupped and tireless palms. Those hands were still supporting her; would be there always – a prop and comfort through the silent years ahead.

'Michael,' she said softly, spinning out the name. Only one Michael, but Michael Prince of Light, perpetually breaking through and banishing the darkness.

She turned away, content; sank back on her seat, watching the gradual lightening of the sky – a quilt of shimmering damask laid across the soiled and lumpy mattress of the clouds.

'Drive on,' she ordered. 'Fast, please. It's my wedding day today and I can't keep the bridegroom waiting any longer.'

29

'CAN YOU SET ME down just here, please. I'll walk the last little bit.'

Tessa paid the driver, ashamed of her meagre tip. She hadn't budgeted for taxis, but at least the cab had saved her half an hour, not to mention the discomfort of a stop-start bumpy bus-ride. It was only 8.15, which was why she had decided to approach the house on foot. Michael might be still asleep, and she'd no wish to disturb him with the noise of tyres scrunching on the gravel. She also needed to calm herself, prepare for the encounter, and a brief stroll through the countryside would provide the perfect chance. They had left the shabby town behind, and the surrounding fields were so tranquil and unruffled they could have been a painting – an idyllic pastoral landscape enclosed in a gold frame. The day was very still, as if holding its breath, keeping itself tidy for a long-awaited visitor; no puff of wind stirring leaves or rippling through the grasses.

But when she turned into the narrow lane which led to Kelcott Grange, the hedgerows either side of her seemed to be exploding with new life – coarse and thrusting hogweed unfurling green umbrellas; young hot-headed nettles running riot in the ditch. Birds were busy nesting, constantly surprising her as they flapped up from the hedge or shrilled their raucous greetings to a mate. Some trees looked bare from a distance, but once she got up closer, she could see their tight-curled buds encased in rosy scales, almost ready to erupt. Others had broken out already – crinkly sprigs, like parsley, on the hawthorns; a horse-chestnut fully clothed and spiked with embryo flowers. The recent rain had washed and freshened everything; the muddy puddles in the ruts only waiting for the sun to make them glitter. She used one as a mirror, peering down to check that her hair was neat. She didn't want to prove a disappointment.

She picked her way between the ruts, gulping draughts of air and sky, wishing she could soar like the lively darting swallows crisscrossing the hazy blue above her. The clouds had paled and thinned; mere gauzy wisps and shreds now, and changing as she watched.

The lane curved sharply to the left, and her exhilaration mounted as she caught her first sight of the house; its sturdy red-brick walls guarded by a security force of three pines and two gnarled cedars. She stopped to admire the garden – the beds laid out with tulips in rows of stippled gold, and an ornamental lily-pond glinting in the foreground. She had guessed that Michael Edwards' son would live in style and luxury; wasn't surprised to find a gardener already hard at work, nor fazed by the imposing drive which swept up to the entrance.

Yet her steps began to falter as she approached the stout oak door. It was still only half past eight, and there wasn't a single soul around except that old man with his spade. She moved a tentative finger to the bell-push; withdrew it straight away. Supposing some officious type appeared? They might treat her not as Michael's bride, but as a suspicious-looking stranger; even send her packing like a tramp. No, that was hardly likely, when she had taken such pains to make herself presentable – put on a smart suit and just the right amount of make-up, remembered to bring her one good leather handbag, to counteract the tatty plastic carriers. Her finger hovered over the bell once more, still not making contact. Then suddenly, on impulse, she pushed the door instead, sending up a prayer of thanks when it opened, let her in. Why did she keep forgetting that she only had to trust, and the power protecting her would open any door?

She found herself in a spacious hall with panelled walls, a claret-coloured carpet, and an ancient carved stone hearth. The fireplace was no longer used, contained a flower arrangement in place of logs or coals. But the house was warm and welcoming, seemed to exude an atmosphere of acceptance and goodwill. Friendly family noises were coming from overhead – a murmured conversation, a burst of laughter, water running for a bath.

'Can I help you?'

A petite but graceful woman was emerging from a small room on the right, her severe grey hair contrasting with a fresh and youthful face.

'Yes,' said Tessa. 'I've come to see Michael Edwards.' She spoke in her best voice – the one she'd used for all her Oxford interviews.

'We don't usually have visitors this early. Is Michael expecting you? I wasn't told anything about it.'

'I did write two days ago.' Tessa put her bags down – an indication that she intended staying put. 'I'm a friend of Michael's father, Dr Edwards. Perhaps the letter hasn't arrived yet. I know the post is . . .' The sentence petered out. *Had* she actually written? She couldn't quite remember. The last few days had been so confused, so fraught.

'Are you a relative?' the woman asked, her lake-blue eyes darkening with tiny currents of unease.

I will be, Tessa thought – the closest person in his life, his next-of-kin, his wife. 'Er . . . not exactly, but very close. I've known the family for years.' That was true in one sense. She knew them through her researches; had culled the facts in such rich obsessive detail, she had surely earned the right to call herself if not a blood relation, then at least an intimate. She let spill some of those facts – enough to reassure the woman that she was a bona fide friend of Dr Edwards – lived just round the corner from him, was welcome in his home, familiar with his job, sometimes helped with Jonathan, and knew the whole sad story of his first son.

'Well, there shouldn't be a problem, then – except it's still so early. We don't really like our visitors to arrive before mid-morning, and it's particularly inconvenient just now. You see, Michael's being washed and dressed, and then he has to . . .'

'I'll wait,' said Tessa. 'Don't worry.' She could tell the woman was still a shade distrustful; knew it must seem odd to her that someone should swan in at such an hour. 'I came up with a friend,' she added, by way of explanation. 'She prefers driving overnight – you know, to avoid the traffic. We got here at the crack of dawn, and I've already waited ages so I wouldn't be a nuisance and disturb you any earlier.'

Sympathy and wariness were conflicting on the woman's face. 'Look, I'll have a word with the senior nursing officer. She's the one who has the final say. Would you take a seat a moment while I phone her?'

'Certainly,' said Tessa, perching on a chair.

'Oh, and I'd better have your name.'

'Tessa Reeves.' It came out pat, without the slightest hesitation. She knew now who she was – and who she would be. This was her

364

one remaining chance of becoming Mrs Edwards, being accepted as a member of his family; bearing Michael Edwards' son, carrying on his name. And she knew that they belonged together – both handicapped, both rejects, displaced from home and family, living in a different world from the unreal one she'd just left. She had never told a soul – not even her mother – what the gynaecologist had said when she'd killed her unborn baby: that there was a one-in-twenty chance that she might produce another 'affected' child – 'affected' meaning crippled, stunted, monstrous (though fastidious Mr Lawson-Scott had avoided such expressions). He had advised genetic counselling, but she'd sat silent in her chair; stunned by the horrific fact that she was a carrier of deformity. No normal man would accept her as a wife – indeed, how could she accept herself? – branded as an outcast, a threat to her own children. But once she married Michael, the whole situation would change. If she and her new husband produced a disabled child, no one would recoil from it – or them. It would be loved here and accepted, regarded as the norm, not hacked out of her body like some malignant cancerous growth.

'Right,' said the woman, reappearing in the hall. 'Miss Cookson says it's fine for you to stay, but you'll have to wait till Michael's finished breakfast and had his medication, and she'd like to have a word with you first. She's tied up just at present, seeing someone else, so I'll take you to the sitting-room. It's more comfortable in there. I'm Beryl, by the way – Beryl Hedges.'

Tessa murmured an acknowledgment, then followed Beryl down a wide high-ceilinged corridor; hearing banging doors and muffled shouts coming from upstairs; the high-pitched wail of a vacuum cleaner; the sudden solemn chime of an old clock striking the quarter.

'It should be a bit quieter in here,' Beryl laughed, ushering her into a light and airy room which looked elegant yet lived-in. 'Most of our residents are either having breakfast or still getting washed and dressed. Do sit down – make yourself at home.'

'Thanks,' said Tessa, smiling. She *was* at home, at last.

She chose the largest of the easy-chairs, taking in her surroundings as she settled snugly into it. The room was well-proportioned, with picture windows and a view across the garden. Books and records were piled up on the shelves, and flowering plants clustered in one corner, a few of them in exotic purple bloom. There was a noticeboard on the wall above her head, covered with a collage of colour photographs – the residents at a garden fête, or away on various holidays: some sitting on the promenade; others lined up in their wheelchairs watching a brass band. She examined all the faces, trying to pick out Michael's – the hazel eyes and light brown hair she'd seen in the blurred snapshots Alison's friend had sent, which for some reason were all slightly out of focus. They were also pretty ancient, dating from his childhood, so she had very little notion of what he looked like now, though she'd told Pat Hughes everything she knew – that her fiancé was of middling height and colouring; a gentle type who was very fond of animals. She scanned the board for someone who would fit that vague description, paying particular attention to any of the photos featuring dogs and cats – one man on a stick, leaning down to stroke a tabby cat; another with a puppy on his lap. But neither could be Michael – the first too old; the second dark and fat.

Only a handful of the patients seemed able to walk unaided – some on zimmer frames, but most confined to wheelchairs; a few so torpid and inert, it was difficult to tell whether they were actually still alive when the photographs were taken. Scarcely anyone was engaged in an activity. Two brave souls were swimming in a pool, and a middle-aged woman, with pathetic stumps for arms, was being led around a paddock on a pony – but the majority were immobile, their eyes and faces blank.

The contrast was the crueller when she compared the one child on the board – clearly not a resident, but a bright-eyed little tearaway careering past a sideshow at the garden fête. He looked four or five years old, roughly the same age as Michael would have been when he was admitted to his first residential home. It was Alison who'd insisted that her son be sent away, despite her husband's protests; Alison who couldn't cope, couldn't accept a defective child, and had finally had a breakdown and landed up in hospital, forcing Dr Edwards to give in. Once she had recovered (and the cause of her collapse been shunted safely out of sight into a children's home for the handicapped), she had repaid her husband for his months of grief and worry by running off with a wealthy foreign architect. After that, she never saw her son again, refused to visit even once, leaving the whole burden to a shattered Dr Edwards.

Tessa reached up to the noticeboard, touched the boy's tanned face. 'If Michael had been more like you – a normal kid who could play and race around – his mother would have loved him, but I'm afraid no one wants the rejects.'

'Miss Reeves?'

She swung round at the sound of her name. A dumpy fair-haired woman stood beaming in the doorway, well-upholstered like the chairs; her floral dress even bearing some resemblance to their chintzy blues and mauves. 'Hello. I'm Olive Cookson. No, don't get up – I'll take a pew beside you. Beryl tells me you're a great friend of Dr Edwards.'

'Yes,' said Tessa. 'That's right.' More than just his closest friend, she added to herself – soon to be his daughter-in-law.

'How is he?'

'Very well.'

'I'm glad to hear it, Tessa. You don't mind if I use your first name, do you? Surnames always sound so stiff and starchy.'

'Not at all. I prefer it, actually.'

'And please do call me Olive. It's our policy here to try to be informal, create a family atmosphere. Now, where was I?'

'You were asking about . . .'

'Dr Edwards. Of course I was! Yes, to tell the truth, I've been getting a bit anxious about him. You see, it's quite some time since he last came up, so I was beginning to wonder if he might be ill or something.'

Tessa didn't answer. Was Dr Edwards getting fed up with the visits? She knew he'd made a deliberate break with Leicester and his past; moved south to avoid the gossip – and the pity – started a new chapter in his life. At first, he'd lived alone, probably wary of entanglements, but eventually he'd met and married Joyce, and the birth of a normal healthy child must have proved a huge relief. Yet he'd never neglected his elder son; had driven here each month – though the journeys were discreet, and he'd been careful to keep the whole business of his previous marriage a secret from his new friends in the south. But perhaps he reckoned that Michael was now old enough to do without visits from his father. Which meant that she'd arrived herself at exactly the right time – to save him from abandonment, neglect.

Olive was still chatting, plying her with questions, all of which she answered as politely as she could, though she was relieved to hear the clock strike nine – a welcome interruption to the interview.

'Goodness! Is that the time already? I don't know where the morning goes! I've been on since seven, yet I hardly seem to have done a thing.' Olive bounced up to her feet, moved towards the door. 'Anyway, I'll go and see what Michael's up to. He should have finished breakfast by now.' She paused, looked back at Tessa, lowering her voice. 'It's just occurred to me, my dear, that perhaps I ought to warn you. I mean, I've no idea how long it is since you've seen him, but I'm afraid he won't be able to recognize you, and he *is* a very shy young man. Don't rush up to him, will you? He's easily alarmed by unexpected movements and might even have a seizure.'

'I understand,' said Tessa, as Olive closed the door. She stood smiling by her chair, twisting the eternity ring round and round her finger. She hoped she'd learn to love Michael, however shy or ill he was, and she'd certainly also promise to obey. In the Middle Ages – the period she'd been studying in her shadowy former life – the first of all the marriage vows had been to obey one's husband; repeated at the altar before the vow to love.

She glanced out of the window, saw a girl about her own age, though dressed more like a child and clutching a rag doll. She was shambling along the path with an uneven seesaw gait, muttering to herself and occasionally bending down to pick imaginary flowers, which she then offered to her 'baby'. A nurse hovered close behind, doing her brisk best to supervise a woman in her seventies, who suddenly lifted up her skirt, revealing bare and veiny legs, and a stained disposable nappy bulging from its plastic pouch. Tessa turned away, distressed that Michael Edwards' son should have to live with such companions. Now, more than ever, she knew she had been right to come.

The sound of footsteps in the corridor brought her attention back inside. She stood holding her breath as Olive manoeuvred a wheelchair through the door. She was determined not to move a muscle or do anything to frighten Michael or undermine his confidence. But inwardly she was staggered by how extremely young he looked. She knew already he was only seventeen, but was still unprepared for the frail and narrow shoulders, the baby face, soft skin, the fact that he didn't shave. All his limbs were bent, the spastic hands locked stiffly into position, the fingers useless claws. His face was also twisted, and a drool of slow saliva made a tremulous silver loop from his surprisingly full and sensuous lips to his scrawny concave chest. His eyes were not quite focused – troubled hazel eyes, staring into nothingness; his toffee-coloured hair very fine and silky like a child's. He had calipers on his legs – ugly clumsy things, clamped into surgical boots, which looked far too big and brutish for his body. He was wearing a child's tee-shirt, with Garfield on the front; the cat's wily grin only seeming to emphasize his own expressionless face. His faded denim jeans couldn't disguise the thinness of his legs; their baggy folds enclosing skin and bone.

Olive was reassuring him, talking kindly and protectively, as if he were indeed a child. 'This is the lady who's come all the way to see you, Michael. She knows your father very well. Are you going to give her a smile?'

He showed no reaction whatsoever, but Olive continued unperturbed. 'She's coming towards you, Michael. See that pretty blouse she's wearing? Isn't it a lovely colour? Yellow, like a sunflower. Don't worry, she won't hurt you. She's stopping now. She's smiling at you. She's very pleased to see you.'

'Hello, Michael.' Tessa tried to make two words contain all the intense emotion she was feeling – the sympathy, affection, the desire to please and serve.

Still no response at all, no flicker of expression on the pale and listless face. But it didn't matter – she mustn't be upset by it. It was only natural that he'd need a while to get used to her, and she had all the time in the world – a whole uninterrupted lifetime to devote to him.

'Why don't you hold his hand, Tessa? Touch is tremendously important for people who can't speak or understand. They like to feel in contact.'

Tessa took two careful steps till she was standing by the wheelchair, then touched the boy's right hand. It was nothing like a normal hand – not supple or responsive, with a sense of warmth and life – but so cold and stiff and rigid it was difficult to hold at all. But she stroked the skin, let her own warm fingers run along the delicate blue veins, building up a steady soothing rhythm.

'That's right,' said Olive, smiling her approval.

Tessa raised the hand to her cheek, let it lie against the contours of her face. 'My name's Tessa,' she told him, hoping he would get to know her through his fingertips, his nerve-endings. 'And I'll be seeing you each day now. Perhaps you'll let me take you out, once you feel okay with me. I could wheel you round the garden and show you all the different flowers, tell you what their names are. And I know you're fond of animals, so maybe we could go and feed the horses. I saw some in that field just down the lane.'

'You'd enjoy that, Michael, wouldn't you?' Olive repositioned the wheelchair so that Michael was facing the window. 'He loves the open air,' she observed, peering up at the sky. 'And the weather looks as if it's brightening up a bit, so there's a good chance he can sit out on the patio today.'

Tessa took his hand again, edging in so close that when she bent to smile at him, the ends of her long hair flicked across his shoulder. He made a violent twitching movement, like a nervous colt starting at a gunshot. She was startled in her turn, terrified he'd have a fit, but he quickly quietened down again, and – what really thrilled her – he hadn't withdrawn his hand. She was aware that the first frail bonds of trust were being forged between them, as she gently touched his neck, even smoothed his hair. It felt downy like a kitten's fur; smelt faintly of shampoo. She longed to bury her face in it, but knew she must be patient, proceed with infinite care. It was enough for the time being that he enjoyed this sensual stroking and appeared to have accepted her – in fact, more than she had dared to hope. There was so much they could say through touch, without the need for words.

She glanced out at the garden. The first timid gleam of sunlight was dappling the wan sky; strengthening as she watched it, making the whole landscape come alive. All the colours were glowing and intensified; long shadows flung across the lawn, like fingers pointing to her bridegroom; accentuating the fact that she and Michael Edwards were finally together, finally at one. The sun had chosen this moment to break through – a sign to her that the time for consummation had arrived. Green and brown had been alchemized to gold: gold flickering on the tree trunks, spangling the spring leaves – gold for wealth and fruitfulness, the radiance of her wedding day.

She turned to look at Michael. His pallid face was transfigured; a bloom of rosy health flushing his sick cheeks. She noticed tiny details she had missed before – his fair fine brows, pale lashes, the faintest childish down on his cheeks and upper lip. And there was so much more she'd yet to see – all the parts still hidden under clothes – his naked feet, for instance, which she pictured thin and tapering; his secret navel and the soft hair under his arms; all his private crevices. Those were hers, to discover and explore, once the ceremony was over.

She had left the carrier bags beside the sofa, but her bridesmaid was unpacking them, shaking out the creases in the magnificent white gown, untangling its long train, in readiness for the bride. As the girl approached with the dress held reverently in her arms, Tessa stared at her in surprise. Wasn't there something familiar about that tall imposing figure with her clear grey eyes, her braided auburn hair? She looked into the eyes, suddenly recognized the voice – that gentle reassuring voice she'd heard so often previously.

'Heloïse!' she whispered, overwhelmed with gratitude that her sister should have come today, especially after so many weeks of absence. But of course Heloïse would understand, more than anyone, the importance of the day – how critical it was and how demanding. Her own wedding had been similar: a secret marriage, held early in the morning after an exhausting night-long vigil – with no parents there, no joyful congregation, and her child left far away with someone else. And both marriages had come about only after a period of turmoil; both doomed to bring more suffering in their wake. Yet she and Michael, like Heloïse and Abelard, would live on beyond their death, famed for ever as great lovers who transcended pain, and whose love would be immortalized.

She stood beside her sister, as if trying to absorb from her the devotion she had shown in that great love. Heloïse, her dearest friend, her soul-mate, must now become her model for the future – the woman who gave everything and asked nothing in return. Even in her role as bridesmaid she was displaying her sweet nature, carrying out her duties with the greatest care and tenderness – not just helping the bride to dress, but arraying her with courage; twining confidence and selflessness into her orange-blossom wreath. The heavy gown felt light as mist because Heloïse was there to ease it on for her, to arrange the stiffened petticoats, smooth the majestic skirt. And the veil was frothy cumulus, billowing around her face as Heloïse secured it with the wreath. Next, she brought the bride's bouquet, placed it in her hands; her fingers closing over Tessa's on the heavy lace-swathed stems, and remaining there in contact, to encourage her. Bride and bridesmaid stood together in one aureole of light, united by their lives, and loss; united by the wedding flowers: lilies for fertility, white roses for perfection, a sprig of rue for sorrow. Tessa gripped her sister's fingers, tempted never to let go, to slip back into history with her and let the shrouding centuries close behind them. But Heloïse was prompting her, gesturing to Michael, to remind her that he was waiting, that it was time now to dismiss her fears and cleave only unto him.

Solemnly and slowly, Tessa turned to face the groom, leaning down towards him, so that her dress and veil cocooned them both in a bridal bed of white. 'Michael, look!' she urged him. 'See how beautiful I am.'

371

His eyes began to focus – the first time since she'd been there – and they, too, assumed a beauty of their own: unclouded trusting hazel eyes, shining with anticipation. She backed away a pace or two, to show him her full glory; the sun casting a gold lustre on the yards of swirling satin, highlighting the horseshoes on her bracelet. She watched with mounting pleasure as a crooked almost-smile contorted his thin features, and he groped out a stiff hand.

'He loves to feel the light on his face,' Olive murmured, moving from the glare herself.

Tessa jerked her train impatiently, resenting the intrusive remark, the facile explanation. The groom was smiling because his bride had come at last, and come to end his racking isolation. She took his outstretched hand, pressing it against her gown, so he could delight in its rich sheen, feel the sumptuous fabric cool against his skin. He was obviously enthralled, taking in each detail – the tiny rosebuds in her wreath, repeated in the embroidery on the dress; her exposed and naked throat, sloping down to the slow curve of her breast; the thrust of her warm thigh beneath his fingers.

She waited a few seconds more till the window-pane was suffused with dazzling light – golden streamers banding the beige carpet, dancing on the sill – a row of slender poplars in the garden blazing like the candles in the church. Olive remained in shadow, a witness, a mere guest; only the bridal couple bathed in sun and splendour as they knelt to make their vows. The bridegroom had no power of speech, so it was the bride's task to repeat them; to speak the words twice over, once for him and once for her. Michael's part would be to seal them with a kiss – his mute consent, his wordless affirmation – and once she had received that kiss, no man could put the two of them asunder.

She whispered the groom's vows, trying to reach him with her eyes, as well as with her voice, to convey to him the depth of her commitment. Then, speaking slower, louder, to make each word distinct, she began a second time:

'I take thee Michael, Michael,
to my wedded husband,
to have and to hold,
from this day forward,
for better, for worse,
for richer, for poorer,
in sickness . . .'

He was still gazing at her, smiling, ready to confirm the vows in the only way he could, once she had pronounced the final line.

'And thereto I plight thee my troth.'

Silence rushed towards them, a silence bright with wedding hymns, carillons of bells. Reverently, she bent her head, stooped down by the wheelchair until her face was almost touching his, then kissed him on his open, drooling, chastely loving lips.

HSH